GHOSTBUSTERS

A NOVEL BY **RICHARD MUELLER**

BASED ON A MOTION PICTURE WRITTEN BY
DAN AYKROYD & HAROLD RAMIS

BASED ON THE CHARACTERS CREATED BY
DAN AYKROYD & HAROLD RAMIS

AN IVAN REITMAN FILM STARRING
BILL MURRAY, DAN AYKROYD,
SIGOURNEY WEAVER, HAROLD RAMIS,
RICK MORANIS

For Mom and Dad

1

How much there is in books that one
does not want to know...

- JOHN BURROUGHS

It was a bright sunny day in early autumn, one of those days New Yorkers dote on, take pictures of, and point out to their country cousins as an example of the city at its best. The city after summer, after the pavements stop frying. The city not yet locked into the icy streets and frozen dog-wastes of winter. A picture-postcard day, a day to write home to Cincinnati or Scranton or Tullahoma about, and every New Yorker with an excuse was out of doors, clogging the sidewalks, slowing traffic, frightening the pigeons. Tour buses, hot dog vendors, street musicians, flower sellers; all had noticed an increase in trade. People were more cheerful. There was an excess of happy normalcy in the air.

The sun had risen that morning—as it did every morning—by bubbling up out of Long Island Sound, climbing over the Chrysler Building, and casting its warmth down on midtown Manhattan. By dusk it would be finished and sliding quickly toward the Jersey marshes.

If it sent down its warmth anywhere else, New Yorkers were not aware of it, and cared less. It was here, and it felt good. That was enough.

Two men who particularly reveled in the sunlight that September day were Harlan Bojay and Robert Learned Coombs. Bojay had once been a jockey, until, at the age of twenty-four, he had inexplicably gained forty-five pounds and four inches in height, which finished forever his dreams of winning the Triple Crown. This had been some thirty-five years ago, and Bojay had been unemployed since. His partner, Coombs, a taciturn Oklahoma Indian, had come to New York to make his fortune as a singer. He had drive, ambition, daring, pizzazz; everything in fact but a voice. And so, Harlan Bojay and Robert Learned Coombs were now partners in leisure, philosophy, and life.

They sat beneath the great jaws of a stone lion guarding the Fifth Avenue entrance to the New York Public Library, passing a bottle of Chateau Plain-Wrap back and forth and discussing the nature of existence.

"Robert, my lad. Have you ever been in there?"

"In there? In the library? Sure, I guess so. Coupla times."

"Wonderful things, books..."

"Right."

"But dangerous, exceedingly dangerous. Lots of dangerous things in books..."

Coombs was nonplussed. Once again Bojay had run off with the thread of the conversation. "Dangerous? You mean like guys who cut the centers out and hide guns an' dope an' stuff inside?"

Bojay snorted in exasperation. "I'm speaking of ideas, you melonhead. Dangerous ideas, ideas and philosophies." He took a long draw on the wine. "Dangerous ideas..."

* * *

Coincidentally, less than a hundred feet away, Alice Melvin was thinking exactly the same thing, for an entirely different reason. Like Bojay and Coombs, she, too, had had big dreams, and like them she had come to New York to make them come true, but fate had once again taken down the roadsigns and painted out the center line. Instead of becoming a fashion designer, she was, at the age of 29, working in the New York Public Library. Stout and plain, any sort of meaningful social life had eluded her, and she'd become an exile in her own mind and a prisoner of her fantasies. The last man who had gone home with her had left in the morning with her VCR, and she'd given up trying, grimly resigned to a life in the stacks, moving books about, gaining wisdom and greatness through osmosis, hoping to return in the next life as Lonnie Anderson. That is, until she had discovered the incunabula.

There were many locked and private collections of books at the main branch, and she'd had keys for some of them, but one day at the main desk she'd picked up the wrong set of keys by accident. At least she told herself it was an accident. She had then proceeded to try a few doors that had been closed to her. Behind one of them, in a collection of European popular incunabula, she had discovered a book of woodcuts depicting sexual positions and concepts she'd not dreamed existed. They were crude in comparison to better works of both the period and the subject, but they touched a chord deep in Alice Melvin.

On that sunny September day, deep in the stacks where no sunlight ever reaches, Alice Melvin was reshelving books, working her cart slowly along the aisles near the card catalogue. As she turned over each title, checking the numbers on the spine, she failed to notice the vaguest hint of an odor on the air, a sickly sweetness that seemed to waft at right angles to her path, drifting toward the endless rows of card files.

Alice's mind was only half on her job. Part of her attention was fixed on the books themselves, their titles, the esthetic effect on her imagination. When the first of the card catalogue drawers began to slide soundlessly open, her mind was miles away, traveling hopefully through a series of renderings on Hellenic pottery themes.

Alice had just discovered a truly provocative illustration, when something landed in front of her on the cart. It was a catalogue card. Had it fallen from an upper shelf, or was it the work of some prankster? She turned angrily, then froze.

Dozens of drawers had opened in the long line of cabinets, and millions of carefully indexed cards were shooting into the air, caroming off the stacks, and settling and swirling in great blizzards to the floor. As she watched in horror, more drawers began to open, more cards exploded into the air.

Alice Melvin's jaw worked convulsively; she turned, and ran. Not pranksters, her mind supplied. Definitely not pranksters.

At the end of the row she halted to catch her breath. Report, she realized. I must report this to someone. Carefully, tensely, she tiptoed down a parallel aisle, heading for the stairwell to the floor above, yet keeping as far from the card catalogue as possible. Through the ranked books she could still hear cards spewing into the air. Little piles had even drifted into the intersections, and she hurried past them, lest one of them reach out and grab her by the ankle. As she made her way along the last group of stacks, something crashed to the floor behind her and she leapt into the air.

No, I'm too young to have a heart attack, she thought. She turned, and saw a large book lying in the aisle. Another was wobbling on a shelf to her right. And as she watched, a third launched itself into the air and drifted across the space, neatly reshelving itself on the other stack. Then another, and another, and suddenly dozens of books were in motion, crossing back and forth across the aisle like rush-hour pedestrians. It was too much for her.

"No!" she cried. "I won't do it again, I promise. I'll never look at another dirty picture..."

And at that instant she turned the final corner and came face to face with the thing. They heard her scream all over the building.

2

There are worse occupations in this world than feeling a woman's pulse.

- LAURENCE STERNE

Dr. Peter Venkman loved his work. He often said it to himself in precisely those words. "I love my work. I'm not always quite sure what it is, but I do love it. I love getting up in the morning. I love coming down to my lab in the basement of Weaver Hall. And I love getting paid by Columbia University for doing whatever it is that I do." In fact, he often considered that a large part of what he did, perhaps the major part, consisted of just that: the search for identity, for purpose, for the meaning of just what it was that he did do. God, I love psychology. It's so wonderfully... formless. You can get away with anything.

He smiled warmly at his two subjects. "Scott, Jennifer, are we ready?"

Jennifer favored him with a coy look and a quick anxious breath that made her breast rise and fall. She was convinced that Peter Venkman was a genius, or she soon would be. God, I love teaching, Venkman decided. He turned to Scott.

"Okay, partner?"

Scott Dickinson nodded nervously, his mouth pumping away on a quid of gum. He smiled crookedly at Jennifer, who froze him right out. Venkman pulled a card out of the Zener deck and held it up.

"All right, what is it?"

Scott set his jaw and concentrated, but Venkman could tell that part of his attention was on the copper cuff strapped to his wrist, its wires running to the control box on Venkman's side of the table.

"A square?"

"Good guess," Venkman replied, "but no." He turned the card over. It was a star. "Nice try." He pushed a button, sending a mild shock through the boy. Dickinson twitched, but smiled gamely.

The next card was a circle. "Okay, Jennifer. Just clear your mind and tell me what you see." She did, chewing on one adorable finger.

"Is it a star?"

"It is a star! That's great. You're very good," Venkman said enthusiastically, burying the card in the deck and extracting another. A diamond.

"Scott?"

Scott rubbed his wrist nervously. "Circle?"

"Close, but definitely wrong."

This time Scott gave a little whimper. Venkman ran through a few more cards, letting Scott get only one right, watching the boy's growing impatience, his fear of the electric punishment. He even inched the current up a little. The monkeys had been able to take it, it shouldn't have any effect on a sophomore business major. And if it did, who would notice? Besides, it was time to wind up this phase anyway.

"Ready? What is it?"

Jennifer licked her lips excitedly. "Ummm, figure eight?"

Venkman buried the triangle. "Incredible! That's five for five. You're not cheating on me, are you?"

"No, Doctor. They're just coming to me."

"Well, you're doing just great. Keep it up. I have faith in you." He considered stroking her leg under the table with his foot, see how she'd react, then rejected it. Might get Scott's leg by mistake. He smiled thinly at the young man.

Scott Dickinson's own smile had slipped a few notches since they'd started. He let out a noisy breath, his tongue flapping on his uppers, and sniffed loudly.

"Nervous?"

"Yes. I don't like this."

"Hey, you'll be fine. Only seventy-five more to go. What's this one?" Wavy lines.

"Uh... two wavy lines?"

No, you don't. Venkman buried the card. "Sorry. This just isn't your day."

This time the kid's knees came up against the table and his gum popped out and skittered across the floor. "Hey! I'm getting real tired of this."

"You volunteered, didn't you? Aren't we paying you for this?"

"Yeah, but I didn't know you were going to be giving me electric shocks. What are you trying to prove?"

Venkman shrugged softly. "I'm studying the effects of negative reinforcement on ESP ability."

Dickinson leaned across the table and pulled off the electric cuff. "I'll tell you the effect. It bugs me.

"Then my theory is correct."

"Your theory is garbage. Keep the five bucks. I've had it!" He slammed the door hard enough to rattle the glass, leaving Venkman and Jennifer alone in the lab. Venkman shook his head sadly.

"That's the kind of ignorant reaction you're going to

have to expect, Jennifer, from people jealous of your ability."

Jennifer smiled bravely. "Do you think I have it, Dr. Venkman?"

Venkman jumped as something touched his ankle. Her foot. He favored her with his shyest, most boyish smile.

"Please, Peter."

"Okay... Peter."

He leaned forward across the table and took her hands in his. "Definitely. I think you may be a very gifted telepath."

At that moment his arm came down on the button, sending a soft jolt through both of them. Jennifer jumped back, her sharp breath once again lifting her breasts. Ah, the wonders of modem science.

Suddenly the door to the lab flew open and Ray Stantz hurried in. He didn't bother to close the door behind him, just ran to the storage bins and began pulling out equipment. Venkman noticed that someone had once again defaced the door. Written in red—in what was supposed to pass for blood, no doubt—were the words VENKMANN BURN IN HELL. His name had been misspelled.

He waited a moment, then sighed.

"Ray. Excuse me, Ray?"

"Yeah, Peter..."

"Ray, I'm trying to have a session here."

Stantz pulled his head out of the parts bin, his eyes wide and wild with excitement. "Sorry, you'll have to drop everything. We got one."

Jennifer was looking at Stantz as if he had just fallen off the surface of the moon. Good thing he didn't bring Egon, Venkman thought. He touched her hand.

"Excuse me for a minute."

Stantz was plugging battery grid analyzers together when Venkman grabbed him by the arm. "Ray, I'm right in the middle of something here. Can you come back in an hour?"

Stantz put a finger to his lips, then dragged him back behind the bins.

"Ray, I've never seen you like this."

"Peter, at one-forty this afternoon at the main branch of the New York Public Library on Fifth Avenue, ten people witnessed a free-roaming, vaporous, full-torso apparition. It blew books off shelves at twenty feet away, and scared the socks off some poor librarian."

Venkman thought of beautiful Jennifer, and weighed the thought of her against the clear call of scientific exploration. "That's great, Ray. I think you should get right down there and check it out. Let me know what happens."

Stantz handed him a valence meter and slipped the strap of a heavy duty tape recorder over his head. "No, Peter. This is for real. Spengler went down there and took some PKE readings. Right off the scale. Buried the needle. We're close this time, I can feel it."

So can I, Venkman sighed, but it looks like I'm not going to feel it now. "Okay, just give me a second here. And take this stuff..."

He slipped up behind the girl, placed a hand on each shoulder, and smiled sadly. She looked up at him as if... as if... Oh, the things I do for science.

"I have to leave now, but if you've got the time I'd like you to come back this evening and do some more work with me, say..."

"Eight o'clock?"

Venkman laughed delightedly. "I was just going to say eight. You're fantastic."

"Until then..."

Fantastic.

* * *

The cab let them off in front of the library. Venkman made sure that Stantz paid the driver, then helped him bundle his equipment out onto the sidewalk.

"Help me carry this."

"Sure, Ray." Venkman picked up a plasmatometer about the size of an electric razor. "You got the rest of that?"

"There's something happening, Peter, I'm sure of it," Stantz said, struggling to his feet with a double armful of gear. The tape recorder around his neck made him look like a pack animal. "Spengler and I have charted every psychic occurrence in the tri-state area for the past two years. The graph we came up with definitely points to something big."

"Ray, as your friend, I have to tell you that I think you've really gone around the bend on this ghost stuff. You've been running your butt off for two years, checking out every waterhead in the five boroughs who thinks he's had an experience. And what have you seen?"

"What do you mean by seen?"

"As in 'seen.' You know, 'looked at with your eyes.'"

"Well, I was. once at an unexplained multiple high-altitude rockfall."

"Uh-huh. I've heard about the rockfall, Ray. I think you've been spending too much time with Egon."

Peter Venkman was not the first person to have uttered those words. Throughout his childhood, in the quiet suburbs of Cleveland, Egon Spengler had provoked that reaction more than once. "I think you've been spending too much time with Egon." While his friends were indulging in the delights of childhood—cutting school, shoplifting, minor vandalism—Egon Spengler was making a nuisance of himself at the public library, ordering books that the librarians had neither heard of, nor liked the sound of. *The Mysteries of Latent Abnormality. Electrical Applications of the Psycho-sexual Drive. Your Friend the Fungus. Astral Projections as an Untapped Power Source. The Necronomicon.*

While his friends were playing pranks and throwing firecrackers, Egon was developing a compact new explosive made of guncotton and chicken dung. He wrapped a fist-sized lump of the stuff in aluminum foil, set it atop a waist-high Erector set tower in a vacant lot, and surrounded it with three concentric rings of Plasticville houses stolen from his brother's Lionel train layout. Then he ran wires to a handcrank generator and, retiring to a makeshift bunker he'd built, set the thing off. He'd been intending only to knock down the houses, but both houses and tower were vaporized, and he'd broken every window in a three-block radius. "I think you've been spending too much time with Egon."

While his friends were going out on dates and fumbling around in each other's underwear, Egon was observing their mating rituals through binoculars and taking notes. Then—based on a complex formula he had worked out involving ambient temperature, phases of the moon, tidal cycles for Lake Erie, and a dozen other factors—he calculated the exact number of cases of venereal disease that would be reported over the next three months, and posted his findings on the high school bulletin board. "If I catch you around that Spengler kid, you've had it."

Somehow Egon survived to enter college, then grad school, then the real world, but it never quite affected him. He was always happier in the company of other mavericks like Stantz and Venkman than with the educators and businessmen with whom he was eventually forced to deal. He was always more at home with the arcane, the bizarre, the scientifically disreputable. Today he was at home with a table.

Venkman and Stantz found him sitting beneath a heavy oak reading table in the library's Astor Hall, listening to the wooden underside with stereo headphones connected to a stethoscope. As usual, there was a large area around Egon totally devoid of people, and several patrons were peering warily at him from behind their books and newspapers. Even in New York, few people listened to tables.

Venkman motioned to Stantz to hand him the heavy copy of *Tobin's Spirit Guide,* then rapped softly on the table. Egon froze, instantly alert, his wild eyes swinging from side to side. Oh boy, Venkman thought, this is wonderful. Any credibility we might have established with these people was officially shot down. He rapped his knuckles on the table again.

"Egon?"

Egon adjusted the control on his headset and peered closely at the table bottom, the rims of his glasses scraping the wood. Venkman slammed the spirit guide down on the top.

"Gnnaaauuuhhhh!"

"Egon, come out of there."

Egon Spengler adjusted his glasses and goggled up at Venkman. "Oh! You're here."

"What have you got, Egon?"

Spengler clambered to his feet. "This is big, Peter. This is *very* big. There's definitely something here."

Venkman rubbed his temples. The day had started so well. "Egon, somehow this reminds me of the time you tried to drill a hole in your head. Do you remember that?"

"That would have worked…"

Spengler's explanation was cut short by the arrival of an unhappy-looking man in a rumpled suit. Venkman shook his offered hand.

"Hello, I'm Roger Delacourte, head librarian. Are you the men from the University?"

"Yes," Venkman replied, all business. "I'm Dr. Venkman and this is Dr. Stantz. You've met Dr. Spengler..."

Delacourte nodded. "Thank you so much for coming. I'd appreciate it if we could take care of this quickly and quietly. You know..."

"I understand," Venkman said soothingly. "Now, if we could see the woman who first witnessed the apparition..."

"Certainly."

"You stay here and keep tabs on it, Egon," Venkman suggested. No sense in shocking this poor woman twice in one day.

Alice Melvin had been made comfortable, which is to say that she had been stretched full-length on the couch in Delacourte's office and was being tended by several of her colleagues. However, she seemed far from relaxed. Her body was stiff and severe, and little tremors passed through her limbs. Delacourte shooed the other women away and made introductions. While the woman related her experience with the card catalogue and the books, Stantz grew increasingly excited, until Venkman made him sit down, shut up, and take readings. Ray Stantz subsided behind the peeps and clicks of his apparatus. While he directed probes and counters at the librarian, Delacourte, and various inanimate objects in the office, Venkman tried to make some sense of the woman's story, but it all boiled down to the fact that they would have to go into the stacks and look for the blasted thing. The woman didn't look like a loony, but appearances can be deceiving. Spengler hadn't seemed that crazy on first meeting either, and Stantz usually fooled most people, but nowadays you couldn't tell. He decided to steer the questions around to credibility.

"Did the thing have two arms and legs, or what?"

Alice Melvin remained staring at the ceiling. "I don't remember seeing any legs, but it definitely had arms because it reached for me."

"Arms! Great! I can't wait to get a look at this thing."

"Cool it, Ray." Venkman set down his pad and pencil. He smiled reassuringly. "All right, Miss... Melvin. Have you, or has any member of your family, ever been diagnosed as schizophrenic or mentally incompetent?"

"Well, my uncle thought he was St. Jerome."

Stantz and Delacourte looked at each other. Venkman smiled again. "I'd call that a big 'yes.' Do you yourself habitually use drugs, stimulants, or alcohol?"

"No," Alice Melvin replied shakily.

"I thought not. And one last thing. Are you currently menstruating?"

Delacourte turned several shades of red. "What's that got to do with it, Dr. Venkman?"

"Back off, man! I'm a scientist!"

Delacourte, outraged, turned to Stantz for support, but he only nodded sagely and ran an ionization meter up and down the man's tie. Alice Melvin did not seem offended.

"It's all right, Mr. Delacourte. He *is* a doctor..."

"Well, I never..."

"Just answer the question, Miss."

But Venkman got no answer, for at that moment the door flew open and Spengler raced in. "Hurry. It's moving!"

The two followed Spengler down the darkened corridors leading into the stacks, as only Spengler could make sense of his complicated, primitive equipment. Every so often he would stop, observe the pattern of blinking lights on the plasmatometer, then indicate a new direction. Stantz was as excited as a kid with an armful of new toys, but for Venkman the thrill was rapidly wearing thin.

"You sure you know where you're going, Egon?"

"Shhhhhh."

They reached a spiral iron staircase and tiptoed down into the dimly lit basement. Corridors stretched away in all directions, flanked by steel shelving covered with books. In the distance some piece of machinery—a water pump most likely—was softly humming. Spengler stopped short.

"My God, look!"

The floor was covered with books and catalogue cards, tumbled and strewn in all directions. An overturned cart blocked one aisle. Venkman experienced a sudden chill. Loonies I can ignore, but there *are* books all over the floor. Those are real. Spengler pocketed the plasmatometer and held up a black teardrop-shaped device with wings. He called in an aurascope. Venkman thought it looked like it had come from one of those sex places on Forty-second Street, but the lights on the thing's upper surface immediately began to blink. Spengler let out a thrilled squeal.

"Through here. Careful."

They worked their way slowly toward the catalogue cabinets, the piles of Dewey cards getting thicker on the floor. Venkman tried not to think about the possibility that they'd actually found one this time. That they were way in over their heads. Stantz passed him a plastic Petri dish.

"What's that for?"

"Specimens."

Specimens? He considered trying to fold a file card into it, then gave up and slipped the dish into his pocket. Spengler halted and raised one hand.

"Will you look at that?"

"What?" The three crowded together and peered at the card files.

The file drawers were in all manner of disarray; some in, some out, some on the floor, which was knee-deep in file cards and… paste? No, some sort of gluelike substance. It was everywhere; bubbling and oozing in streams from the drawers, speckling the books, dropping in stringy blobs from the ceiling. Venkman fumbled the Petri dish from his pocket, then stopped, not sure how to go about it. Stantz and Spengler were huddled together, whispering.

"… incredible, a plasma flow of this magnitude…"

"… hasn't been anything like it since the Watertown Pus Eruption in 1910. This is making me very excited…"

This is making me very sick, Venkman said to himself. He turned the Petri dish sideways and managed to capture a quantity of the discharge, then snapped the top on it. It still got all over his hands. Just what I need, cosmic boogers.

"Come on, Peter…"

Venkman tried to wipe his hands off on the cabinet, then on the remaining books, finally settling for the tail of Ray's sport coat. He caught up with Spengler at the end of the corridor and passed him the specimen.

"Here, Egon. Your mucus."

But Egon was staring at an eight-foot pile of books standing against one wall. They teetered gently but did not topple. Again Stantz and Spengler went into a huddle.

"What do you make of that?"

"Classic. Symmetrical book-stacking. Like the Library of Alexandria Incident…"

"Sure," Venkman added. "It's obvious. No human being stacks books like that." He grabbed Spengler by the arm. "The ghost, Egon. Where is it?"

"Right." He held up the aurascope. "This way."

Halfway down the passageway a book jumped off the shelf and flew at Venkman. He caught it neatly. It was a copy of *The Shining*. Real nice.

A few steps later the hair went up on the back of his neck. Spengler turned and held up the little detector, its bat wings now extended outward, their miniature bulbs blinking rapidly. The device was emitting a low hum. Spengler pointed wordlessly. Stantz and Venkman nodded and pointed back. Their meaning was clear. You go first. Swallowing a lump the size of his fist, Spengler leaned out and peeked around the corner. A second later he slipped back and nodded.

"It's here."

"What is it?" Stantz asked.

"What do you think it is? It's a ghost. See for yourself."

The three tiptoed quietly into the hallway and looked on in amazement. There, floating about four feet off the floor between the stacks, was a glowing ethereal presence, a swirl of colored lights bobbing among the books. Stantz attempted to raise yet another instrument, but Venkman slapped it down. "No sudden moves," he whispered, not knowing if the ghost even registered their presence, but unwilling to take chances. Spengler slowly closed his gaping mouth.

"Look. It's forming."

The light swirled in tighter and began to take on a definite shape, that of a somewhat portly torso, the essence still vaporous where the arms, legs, and head should be. The lines of two large, sagging breasts began to emerge.

"What is it?" whispered Stantz.

Venkman shrugged. Whatever it was was hardly threatening in this state. "It looks like a pair of breasts and a pot belly."

Stantz very slowly raised his camera and began to take infrared photos. Spengler toyed with the aurascope. A head and arms began to take shape.

"It's a woman," Spengler gasped.

It was. The apparition had taken on the form of a matronly, somewhat elderly woman, complete with a bun of silver-green hair and a dress of the style popular around the turn of the century. She was reading a book. Venkman noticed that there were still no legs connecting the phantasm to the floor, but he wasn't in the mood to quibble about it. This was pretty amazing.

"Nice goin', Egon," he whispered.

Stantz snapped another picture, then moved to switch cameras. Their subject had still taken no notice of them. "I told you it was real."

"Yes, you did, Ray. So, what do we do now?"

Stantz shrugged. "I don't know. Talk to it."

Venkman nodded. Why not? He took a step forward, the other two moving in behind him. The phantom still hovered silently in the air. "What do I say?"

"Anything. Just make contact," Stantz replied, snapping pictures as fast as he could work the camera. Venkman squared his shoulders, took a deep breath, and cleared his throat.

Nothing.

"Uh… hello. I'm Peter."

This time she turned in his general direction and seemed to look right through him. "Where are you from? Originally?"

The apparition put a finger to its lips and mimed a shushing sound, then went back to its spectral book.

"Ray, the usual thing isn't working. Think of something else."

"Okay, okay," Stantz whispered. "I got it. I know what to do. Stay close to me. I have a plan."

Stantz edged forward, shifting from foot to foot, the others keeping close behind him. Venkman's mouth was dry. He realized that he hadn't been so frightened since he was a kid. Spengler's Adam's apple bobbed up and down.

Stantz paused when they were barely three feet from the woman. "Okay, now everybody do exactly as I say. Ready?"

Venkman and Spengler nodded.

Stantz tensed to spring. "Okay… *get her!*"

He flew forward, his arms reaching around the ghost. She was, of course, not there, and Ray Stantz hit the bookcase, bounded back, and went down on top of Venkman and Spengler, who had run into each other. The ghost reformed a few feet away and exploded upward and outward in a rush of air into the form of a hideous demon, claws outstretched, coming toward them. They stumbled back, smelling the horrible breath of the thing, feeling the heat as it screamed forth a single word.

"QUIET!"

On the steps out front, Harlan Bojay and Robert Learned Coombs were getting ready to move along. The day was waning and they had lost the sun, the drop in temperature portending the approach of winter's chill. Bojay shook himself loose from his perch and staggered up, a day of inactivity and half a bottle of wine having taken their toll, when the front doors of the library flew open and three men came tearing out, pursued by the chief librarian, Delacourte. Bojay knew who he was because the man had hassled him more than once, but something had kept him busy this day because Bojay and Coombs had remained unmolested. Bojay drew back behind the stone lion to listen as Delacourte caught one of the men by an arm. "Did you see? What was it?" he cried, but the other man broke free, shook his head, and ran, calling over his shoulder, "We'll get back to you." After a moment Delacourte headed back into the library, looking very much like a man summoned to witness an execution. Perhaps his own. Bojay shook his head. Curious town, he thought, and getting curiouser by the moment.

Then something caught his eye and he moved out to see what it was. A small curved and rounded black object on which lights flashed. He picked it up carefully. It had obviously been dropped by one of the running men. He listened, for it made a humming sound, but he could find no button, switch, or trigger. Very strange. Coombs moved up to his shoulder to look at the artifact.

"Whatcha got there, Harlan?"

"I honestly do not know, my friend. A cunning device of some kind. A mechanism, an artifact, a construction."

"Do you think we can get anything for it?"

Bojay smiled. "At least a bottle of wine."

3

Some people are so fond of ill luck that they run halfway to meet it.

- DOUGLAS JERROLD

It is over seventy blocks from the New York Public Library's main branch to Columbia University, and it seemed to Venkman that it took him at least half that distance to get Stantz and Spengler stopped and settled down. They bundled into a taxi and rode uptown in silence, none of them feeling like speaking. The taxi driver frowned, knowing that three sourpusses like that wouldn't be much good for a tip, but Stantz had regained his usual cheery composure by the time they arrived and the cabbie did better than he had figured. As he headed off for his next fare, the three trudged back across campus, falling into their old ways. Stantz babbled happily. Spengler worked calculations on his pocket computer. Venkman wondered how difficult it would be to get them both committed, ghosts or not.

"It really wasn't a wasted experience," Stantz said doggedly. "I mean, you can't expect results from every experiment, can you?"

Venkman was having none of it. "I can expect to survive them, can't I? I mean, that thing almost killed us."

Stantz shrugged, plainly embarrassed. "Hey, Peter. It was only a ghost. Come on, you know there's an element of risk in the scientific method."

"Yeah? Yeah? 'Get her'? That was your whole plan? You call that science?"

"Hey, I guess I got a little overexcited. Wasn't it incredible? I'm telling you, this is a first. You know what this could mean to the university?"

But Venkman wouldn't buy it. "Sure, this is bigger than the microchip. They'll probably throw out the entire engineering department and turn the building over to us. We're probably the first serious scientists to ever molest a dead old lady."

Spengler stepped between the two, adjusting his pace to theirs. "I wouldn't say that the experience was completely wasted. Based on these new readings, I think we have an excellent chance of actually catching a ghost and holding it indefinitely."

"Then we were right," Stantz said enthusiastically. "This is great. And if the ionization rate is constant for all ectoplasmic entities, I think we could really clean up—in the spiritual sense."

But Venkman had stopped, his mind reeling. The beginnings of an idea were forming in his agile mind. Why, there could be opportunities in this; for advancement, for scientific discovery and recognition… For money. But could they get the university to go along with it? He hurried to catch up to the two.

"Spengler, are you serious about actually catching a ghost?"

Spengler turned a stony expression toward his friend. "I'm always serious."

"Wow!" Venkman said softly. He glanced at Stantz, who grinned. Spengler just nodded solemnly.

"It can be done."

Venkman reached into his pocket. "Egon, I take back every bad thing I ever said about you. Here." He held up a candy bar. Egon smiled delightedly and reached for it, but Venkman pulled it back. They looked at each other for a moment, then Venkman pressed it into his hands. "You earned it… "

"Baby Ruth," Spengler said reverently, ripping off the paper and cramming it into his face. "Gooomph!"

They passed into the familiar dark confines of Weaver Hall, talking excitedly, making their way past knots of students and an antlike stream of men carrying equipment.

"If you guys are right, if we can actually trap a ghost and hold it somehow, I think I could win the Nobel Prize."

"C'mon, Peter. If anyone deserves it, it's Spengler and me. We're doing all the hard research and designing the equipment."

"Yeah, but I introduced you guys. If it wasn't for me, you never would have met each other. That's got to count for something."

"Uh, Ray. Those guys are coming out of our lab. That's our equipment!"

Dean Yaeger was standing in the doorway, watching with great satisfaction as a workman scraped the names of Venkman, Spengler, and Stantz off the door. Venkman hurried up to him.

"I trust you are moving us to a better space somewhere on campus."

Yaeger, an overfed career hack with a ratty Joseph Goebbels smile, stared coldly at him. "No. We're moving you *off campus*. The Board of Regents has wisely decided to terminate your grant. You are to vacate these premises immediately."

"This is preposterous! I demand an explanation."

"Fine." Yaeger smiled again, favoring Venkman with all the warmth of a state executioner. "This university will no longer continue any funding of any kind for your group's... activities."

"But why? The kids love us."

The workmen and janitors had stopped looting the lab long enough to watch the little drama, their arms full of rheostats, vacuum chambers, and oscilloscopes. Stantz and Spengler stood close behind Venkman, less in support than in the gut feeling that the mob might turn and rend them on the spot. But Yaeger was just warming up.

"Dr. Venkman, we believe that the purpose of science is to serve mankind. You, however, seem to regard science as some kind of 'dodge' or 'hustle.' Your theories are the worst kind of popular tripe, your methods are sloppy, and your conclusions are highly questionable. You're a poor scientist. Dr. Venkman, and you have no place in this department or in this university."

"I see."

Stantz poked Venkman in the ribs. "You said you floored 'em at the Regents meeting."

Venkman put a hand on Stantz's shoulder and shook his head sadly. "Ray, I apologize. I guess my confidence in the Regents was misplaced. They did this to Galileo too."

Yaeger's rodent smile broadened. "It could be worse, Dr. Venkman. They took the astronomer Phileas and nailed his head to the town gate."

That makes me feel so much better, Venkman decided.

The sun was setting on the campus and, so it seemed, on their careers. Spengler had gone off to find a phone to break the news to his mother. Stantz and Venkman, having no living parents, lounged on a sidewalk bench, marking time. Stantz shook his head sadly. He had given up being angry at Venkman, at Yaeger, at the university, and now despair was setting in.

"This is a major disgrace. Forget M.I.T. or Stanford now. They wouldn't touch us with a three-meter cattle prod."

"You're always so worried about your reputation. We don't need the university, Ray. Einstein did his best stuff while he was working as a patent clerk. They can't stop progress."

Stantz somehow did not find that reassuring. "Do you know what a patent clerk makes? I *liked* the university. They gave us money and facilities, and we didn't have to produce anything! I've worked in the private sector. They expect results or bingo, you're out on your keester. You've never been out of college. You don't know what it's like out there."

But Venkman did know what it was like. So, it's tough. So, they don't know us. Yet. Which means there's room—for vision, for experimentation, for three guys with genius and a dream. And an idea no one has ever had before. Yes, yes, yes. He turned and grabbed Stantz by the arm.

"Let me tell you, Ray, everything in life happens for a reason. Call it fate, call it luck, karma, whatever, but I think that this is our moment. I think we were destined to be kicked out of there."

"Huh? Why?"

"To go into business for ourselves!"

Stantz's jaw dropped, then he closed it, tilted it to one side, and let loose a low hum. Venkman grinned.

"You're thinking. That's a thinking sound you're making. I know that sound. What do you think?"

"I don't know. That costs money. And the ectocontainment system we have in mind will require a load of bread to capitalize. Where would we get the money?"

"Ray, trust me."

4

The usual trade and commerce is cheating all round by consent.

- THOMAS FULLER

Ray Stantz was very distressed. Of the three, he was the product of the most normal childhood, having been raised on Long Island by his doctor father and housewife mother. He had an older brother (Air Force officer in the Middle East) and a younger sister (journalist in California). Brother Carl was married, sister Jean was divorced. Carl was a Republican, Jean a Democrat. Carl had two sons in the Boy Scouts, Jean a daughter in ballet school. Carl drank heavily and was a Sustaining Member of the National Rifle Association, Jean was a feminist with two lovers, one of each sex. Carl and Jean did not speak to each other. And neither spoke to Ray.

This state of affairs had begun some three years ago during a family reunion at the ancestral home in Islip. Carl's family had flown in from his base station in South Carolina, and Jean and her daughter from San Francisco. Everyone had arrived on time except Ray, who had been late driving the thirty miles in from New York because

Peter Venkman had borrowed his car to romance a graduate assistant and had gotten it stuck in a mud flat near Greenwich, Connecticut. By the time Venkman had extricated the old station wagon (now covered in drying, salt-flat slime) and returned it to Ray, Stantz had already missed dinner with the family and was chafing to leave. He was on the point of calling a cab when his car sputtered up in front and Peter jumped out into the street, braying, "Ray! Get your butt down here. You'll be late." He was on the way out of town, with Venkman at the wheel, before he thought to ask:

"Peter, why are you driving? This is my car."

Venkman shrugged. "I'm a better driver, I know the roads, and I can get you there on time…"

"Dinner was two hours ago."

"… and I need to borrow your car again."

Stantz pondered that for a moment, then decided that—as much as he hated to let Venkman use the car again after he had covered it in mud the first time—Peter's presence would be a good excuse for his own lateness. Venkman agreed to have the station wagon washed and return it with a full tank. Stantz decided that he was pretty clever, turning the reason for his lateness into its own alibi. It had a scientific neatness that appealed to him, like a Mobius loop. He had not reckoned on two things: that his parents would offer the hospitality of the house to Peter Venkman, or that his sidekick would come down with a case of instant hots for his sister Jean. Peter then proceeded to destroy the weekend.

The senior Dr. Stantz plied Peter with alcohol while encouraging him to talk about their work in parapsychology, a subject that brother Carl held in equal repute with Communism and homosexuality. Doc Stantz asked, Peter talked, Carl sneered, and Jean—unbelievably—seemed attracted to the disreputable and energetic Peter Venkman. This didn't worry Ray. He had met Jean's first husband, a classics scholar and part-time beet farmer—a combination considered perfectly acceptable in California—and figured that she could take care of herself. When he'd gone up to bed, Peter was still holding forth. Carl had caught up with him in the hall.

"Where did you dig up that character?"

"He's a colleague of mine from the university."

"Your 'colleague' is a dipstick and a raving lunatic," Carl said bluntly. "And you're still a jerk."

Ray and Carl had never gotten along, but Ray had never realized how badly things had deteriorated. No wonder Carl never sent a card at Christmas. He thought about saying something conciliatory but he just wasn't up to it.

"Well, at least neither of *us* has to play with guns or fighter planes to prove he's a man."

Before Carl could react, Ray had locked himself in his room and gone to sleep. He reasoned that the worst thing that could happen would be that Carl would climb in through the window and kill him. He hadn't reckoned on Peter's persuasiveness or his ingenuity. When he came down to breakfast, Peter, Jean, and Carl's rental car were missing. Taking stock of the situation, Ray Stantz tiptoed out to his own car and raced back to the city, spending the rest of the weekend hiding at Egon's apartment, watching Spengler rotate the crops on his rooftop fungus farm. He didn't go home until he was sure that Carl had returned to South Carolina, and then it took him two hours to get up the courage to listen to his answering machine tape. There were screaming insults from every member of his family, including Jean, whom Peter Venkman had stranded in a motel in Secaucus, New Jersey, after showing her New York by night and God only knew what else.

He had tried to talk to Peter about it, but his friend denied any wrongdoing, saying that Jean had seemed to enjoy herself and that Carl was a Fascist meathead, a judgment call that Ray had to agree with. He let the matter drop, but never again loaned Peter anything more valuable than bus fare. Eighteen months later came the shock.

The 727 carrying Ray's parents had gone down in the sea on a flight to Puerto Rico. Ray took it well. Dead was dead (even though Egon insisted that there was a good chance that his parents were alive in the Bermuda triangle, and persisted until Ray punched him in the nose), and death was an idea that held few terrors for Ray Stantz. In a way it was a blessing. His parents had been getting on, and he knew that their greatest fear had been of growing old and sickly, succumbing to cancer, Alzheimer's, or senility. It was the way of nature, and until science found out how to reverse or halt the process, people would go on dying. The shock was the letter from his father, passed on by the executor of the estate.

Ray,
There'll be a distasteful reading of the will, with the three of you glaring and sniffing at each other, but I wanted to tell you in advance that I'm leaving you the house. You should know and prepare, in case Jean or Carl decides to contest the will. It's not that I think you're worthier than either of them. It's because of that Peter Venkman character you brought to the house. I figure that as long as you've got friends like him, you're going to need all the help you can get, so I want you to have some property to fall back on…

To fall back on.

Stantz had a terrible feeling in the pit of his stomach as Venkman carefully guided him out of the headquarters of Irving Trust.

"You'll never regret this, Ray."

Stantz stared at Venkman, unable to keep the deep sense of guilt off his face. "My parents left me that house. I was born there."

"You're not going to lose the house. Everybody has three mortgages these days."

"But at nineteen percent interest! You didn't even bargain with the guy."

Spengler stuck his head between them. They were all wearing suits, and Spengler looked like an undertaker. "Just for your information, Ray, the interest payments alone for the first five years come to over ninety-five thousand."

"Thanks, Egon. I feel so much better."

"Will you guys *relax*?" Venkman cried, grabbing Egon's calculator away from him. "We are on the threshold of establishing the *indispensable defense science* of the next decade—professional paranormal investigations and eliminations. The franchise rights alone will make us wealthy beyond your wildest dreams."

Stantz considered. "But most people are afraid to even report these things."

Venkman smiled slyly. "Maybe. But no one ever advertised before."

"Advertised?"

"A name?"

"Trust me, Egon. Peter's right on this one. We need a catchy name, something that people will remember and trust."

"Okay. How about Ectophenomenological Exterminators?"

"I don't know..."

"Ray, Egon. *I'll* come up with a name..."

The firehouse was in an alley near Mott and Pell, in that area where Chinatown butts up against the city, state, and federal court buildings around Foley Square. Good, thought Stantz. If they arrest us, we won't have far to go. Venkman was scanning the old structure from several angles, doing the geometry of entrances and exits, escape routes and strongpoints. He glanced at Mrs. Scott, the real estate rep who'd brought him out to see it, figuring ways to get her to knock down the price.

"Shall we go in?"

"Assuredly," Venkman replied. "Lead the way."

A sign hung precariously from the brick front: engine company 93. Stantz gave it a dubious look, then nudged Spengler, who was again tapping buttons on his calculator.

"You know, we may not have all that far to look for ghosts."

"Good," Egon mumbled.

The garage bay was knee-deep in dust and discarded equipment. The windows were broken, and here and there tiny red rat eyes peeped from behind a missing board or from a darkened corner. Stantz and Spengler had disappeared into the building's upper reaches and could be heard stumbling around, kicking over the leavings of a century of firemen. Venkman did a mental estimate on the garage. The engine bay was long enough for an emergency vehicle of some sort and an outer office and reception area, provided no one got excited and drove through it. The basement would serve for equipment storage and Stantz's containment grid, and they could live upstairs. Venkman took a deep breath and sneezed.

"Gesundheit, Mr. Venkman."

"Thank you. Dust. And that's *Doctor* Venkman."

The dust didn't seem to bother her. She probably spent so much time in abandoned buildings that she'd learned to thrive on it.

"Besides this, you've got the basement, a substantial work area in the rear, sleeping quarters and showers on the next floor, and a full kitchen and laundry on the top level. And closets? Has it got closets? It's ten thousand square feet total."

Spengler appeared specterlike in the cellar stairwell, holding up his calculator like a sacramental offering. "Nine thousand six hundred forty-two point five five square feet, to be precise."

Mrs. Scott frowned at Spengler. "What is he, your accountant?"

"May I present the eminent doctor of physics, Egon Spengler? Mrs. Scott."

"I never shake hands," Spengler said quickly. "Osmotic transference of bacteria. Parasitic corruption. Nasty."

"Charmed. I'm sure." She turned back to Venkman. "So, now then. What do you think?"

Venkman thought it was perfect, but he had no intention of tipping his hand too soon. "This *might* do... I don't know. It just seems kind of pricey for a unique fixer-upper opportunity, don't you think? We're trying to keep our costs down. You know how it is when you're starting a new company."

"Yes, I know. What are you calling your business?"

"Ghostbusters," Venkman said coolly. The name had come to him in the middle of the night, a flash of inspiration, and he was rather proud of it.

"Oh, well, this place is perfect for it."

"Perfect?" Spengler echoed sarcastically. "It needs a new floor, rats have been gnawing the wiring, the plumbing's shot, it looks like hell, probably in violation of at least a dozen building codes, and the neighborhood's a demilitarized zone. I think..."

"Geronimo!" rang a scream from above, the fire pole gave a terrible shudder, and Stantz came sliding into view, hitting the floor with an impact that must have given half the rats in the building cardiac arrest. "Wow, this place is great! I love this pole. Can we move in tonight?"

Mrs. Scott gave Venkman and Spengler a toothy smile. "I think..."

"I think we'll take it," Venkman sighed. "Stantz, you dingbat, this had better work."

Janine Melnitz picked her way around the scaffolding and peered into the garage bay. A line of makeshift work lights were strung from the ceiling so that the carpenters who were laying the new floorboards could see to work. She gingerly stepped up to a hairy young man who was wrestling with an immense power cable.

"Excuse me. Do you work here?"

He pushed back his hard hat. His eyes were rimmed with grime. "Lady, does this look like relaxation?"

Janine decided that she didn't like him at all. "Don't get smart, fella. I mean, do you work for Ghostbusters?"

"Nah, I work for Con Ed. You want those nuts in the back."

"Thanks, I think."

Peter Venkman was standing in a cleared area, giving instructions to a team of painters. He was amazed that there had turned out to be so much to do, and even more amazed that it looked like it was actually getting done. He himself had not worked so hard in years. Private industry. At least in the university system you could get the grad students to do everything, but here the work was your own. Of course the profits were too. He still had a few misgivings but they were rapidly fading. There wasn't room for them. All available space was becoming filled with electrical equipment, protective clothing, sensors, storage batteries, bins, boxes, cartons, crates, containments. Used to be I didn't worry because I didn't care. Now I don't have time to worry. A shower of blue sparks rained down from above, and the men ducked protectively.

"Egon!"

"Sorry."

Venkman brushed himself off, and then noticed a young woman crouching fearfully against the wall, looking up at the ceiling.

"Miss, are you all right?"

She looked at him; big eyes, red hair, thick glasses and, when she spoke, a Queens accent. "I'm not sure. Is that going to happen again?"

"Probably, but it's harmless. Can I help you?"

"I hope so. The agency sent me over. Janine Melnitz."

"Dr. Peter Venkman. How soon can you start?"

She looked around at the chaos. Somewhere in the building a circuit breaker blew with a deafening snap, and all of the lights went out. "The question is, how soon can *you*?"

Venkman watched them hang the sign over the garage doorway: GHOSTBUSTERS, with their new logo, a cartoon ghost encircled by the red international sign for prohibition. Pretty good. The logo had been Janine's idea. So far the woman was working out. She hadn't yet asked to be paid.

"Hey, Peter!"

Venkman turned to see a long, battered 1959 Cadillac ambulance pull up into the garage bay, Ray Stantz at the wheel. He hit the emergency lights, gave a blast on the siren, and killed the ignition. The big battle cruiser backfired noisily, emitting a puff of black soot, then rolled to a stop. God, Venkman thought, listening to it settle on its springs. Is that ours? Stantz hopped out and patted the fender proudly.

"Everybody can relax. I found the car. How do you like it?"

Venkman listened to the dripping sound coming from beneath the hood. "Do you think it's wide enough? How much?"

"Only fourteen hundred."

Spengler and Janine had come out of the office to stare in awe at the monster. Venkman stepped experimentally onto the front bumper and rocked it. The Cadillac wallowed badly. Stantz shrugged.

"Just needs a little suspension work… and a muffler… and brake pads, new brake pads… universal… water pump… thermostat… timing belt… clutch cable…"

Venkman turned and walked rapidly away before things got any worse.

5

God may still be in his heaven, but there is more than sufficient evidence that all is not right with the world.

- IRWIN EDMAN

Dana Barrett was not aware that she was being watched as she stepped out of the cab, shouldered her groceries, got a good grip on her cello case, and walked toward the building. Across the street in Central Park, Robert Learned Coombs made an off-color remark about her legs, for which he was sternly admonished by Harlan Bojay. Two fair-haired young men, strolling hand in hand toward the baths, exchanged comments on her simple but tasteful wardrobe. An old duffer out walking his schnauzer gazed at Dana and remembered how long it had been since it had been long. The doorman gauged her speed so as to open the door with precision for one of his favorite tenants. And, high above on a ledge overlooking the street, Louis Tully was awarded with the completion of his vigil. Dana was home.

Louis hopped down into his apartment, scattered a few towels and exercise books strategically about, and slipped an exercise tape into the VCR. Then he ran in place, trying desperately to work up a sweat in the short time he had left. I'm active, he thought. Athletic. She'll like me if I show signs of self-improvement, pride in my appearance, ambition. Those were the keys, according to *I'm a New Me—Be a New You,* the latest hip awareness book that Louis Tully had been suckered into buying. I'll be a self-improving, proud, ambitious, yet sensitive and caring guy. I'll be a man for the Eighties.

He heard her fumble for her keys, raced to his door, and peered out.

"Oh, Dana. It's you..."

"Uh, hi, Louis..."

Louis sniffed, alert for smells, wondering if he'd overdone the exercise binge. "I thought it was the drugstore man," he said casually.

"Are you sick, Louis?"

She's concerned, he decided. Good. He trotted down to her door, not noticing his own swing shut behind him. "Oh, no, I feel great. I just ordered some more vitamins." He pointed at her velour sweatshirt. "I see you were exercising. So was I. I taped 'Twenty-Minute Workout' and played it back at high speed so it only took ten minutes, and I got a really good workout. You wanna have a mineral water with me?"

Dana smiled kindly. "No thanks. Louis. I'm really tired. I've been rehearsing all morning."

Louis took it with aplomb. "Okay, I'll take a raincheck. I always have plenty of mineral water and nutritious health foods, but—heh heh—you know that. Listen, that reminds me. I'm gonna have a party for all my clients. It's gonna be my fourth anniversary as an accountant. I know you fill out your own tax returns, but I'd like you to come, being that we're neighbors and all..."

Dana touched his shoulder. Gee, Louis thought, she really is taller than me but she does seem to like me. "Oh, that's nice, Louis. I'll stop by if I'm around."

"You know you shouldn't leave your TV on so loud when you go out. That creep down the hall phoned the manager."

Dana listened at the door. There were sounds coming from her apartment. "I thought I turned it off. I guess I forgot."

Louis got ready to spring his big gun. "So, you know what I did? I climbed out on the window ledge to see if I could disconnect the cable but I couldn't reach it so I turned up the sound on my TV real loud so they'd think there was something wrong with everyone's TV. You know, Dana, you and I should have keys to each other's apartments so—"

"Later, Louis," she said, and closed the door.

"So… so… we can get in… in case of emergencies…"

Well, he thought, I'll do better next time. He turned back to his door. It was locked. Emergencies. Emergencies like this one.

Poor Louis, Dana thought as she slipped the cello into its niche in the entry hall. He's like a puppy. I don't want to hurt him, but he's as far from my idea of the perfect man as I can imagine. My mother would probably love him.

She started for the kitchen to put away her groceries, and then remembered the television. Strange. I'm sure I turned it off this morning. In fact, I don't think I ever turned it on. Could a defective switch do that? She reached for it, then stopped, fascinated by what she was seeing.

What was it, an old movie? No, it's shot like a commercial. She settled down to watch the picture—two adorable children asleep in their beds, modern house, nicely furnished room. Suddenly there was a deep humming sound, and then a low disturbing moan, rising, getting louder. The children woke, looked up, then screamed. When All-American Father and Perfect Mother entered they found the children cowering in the corner.

Typical slick advertising, Dana thought, and again reached for the switch. Again she stopped.

"What is it? What's wrong?" All-American Father was saying. The children pointed toward the camera. "Look," they cried. Perfect Mother slipped a comforting arm about them. "Oh, dear. It's that darned ghost again. Can't you do something about it?" Father shrugged manfully. "I've tried everything, honey. I guess we'll just have to move."

What?

"Gee, there must be a better way," Mother sighed. Suddenly a tall man in a field-gray coverall stepped into the picture. A large red patch on his pocket read STANTZ. "Are you troubled by strange noises in the night? Do you experience feelings of dread in your basement or attic? Have you or your family actually seen a spook, specter, or ghost? If the answer is yes, then don't wait another minute. Just pick up the phone and call the professionals—Ghostbusters."

Dana's jaw dropped. It was too early for Monty Python, but this had to be a parody. She watched as the scene shifted to three of the coverall-clad men standing in front of what appeared to be an old firehouse. A wild-looking Ghostbuster with thick glasses stepped forward, hit his mark, and said, "Our courteous, efficient staff is on call twenty-four hours a day to serve all your supernatural elimination needs." The scene shifted again to a receptionist answering the phone with a big, cheery smile. "Ghostbusters. We'll be right there." And again to the children's bedroom, which was now swarming with Ghostbusters. The first one jumped up and exclaimed, "Got him. I don't think you'll have any more trouble with that ghost." He handed All-American Father the bill, who looked up, beaming. "And it's economical too."

"How can we ever thank you?" Mother asked. The third Ghostbuster leaned into the camera, boyish good looks and the smile of a con man. "All in a day's work, ma'am. After all, we're Ghostbusters."

You must be, Dana decided. *No actors could do that badly.*

The family, now clustered together like a moral-majority ad, was singing, "If you have a ghost, but you don't want to play host, you can't sleep at all, so who do you call? Ghostbusters—Ghostbusters." A phone number flashed on the screen—1-212-NOGHOST—as the three Ghostbusters leaned in on the camera. "We're ready to believe you!"

Dana snapped off the TV. *That was, without a doubt, the strangest thing I have ever seen on television. Where do they get these people? Best get the groceries put away.*

She turned on the radio, got a Boccherini concerto, and started unloading the bag. *Eggs, milk, bread—everything was getting so expensive. Forgot the yogurt again. Guess I must really not like the taste.* She opened the cabinets and was putting away the few canned goods she'd picked up, humming along with the Boccherini, when she noticed a hissing sound. *Interference? No, more like… eggs frying,* her nose informed her. *But I'm not cooking anything.* She turned around, saw what was happening, and backed fearfully away from the counter.

On the Formica countertop eggs were frying. They were still in their box, but the top had flown open and egg white was bubbling out. As drops of it hit the counter, they sizzled. *But the milk and the bread,* she thought. *They seemed to be unaffected. What the hell's going on here?*

She stepped forward gingerly, like a man walking the plank, and extended her fingers. The eggs were hot. She approached and then touched the countertop, but it was cool. Could the eggs have been bad? Could bacteria do that? That's crazy. Suddenly the hair went up on the back of her neck. There was a low humming sound coming from behind her. Without looking she reached out and switched off the radio. There, she could hear it, a deep throbbing sound like chanting. Like natives worshiping in some temple. She turned and looked but there was nothing out of place.

Louis, if this is some creepy trick to get my attention, I am not in the least amused. Then she realized that the sound was coming from her refrigerator. She picked up the carton of milk—half deciding to put it away, half planning to use it as a weapon—and moved closer. There it was, a rhythmic chant like… like the temple scene in *Gunga Din,* she decided. Not the sort of thing I want in my refrigerator. Could that little dingaling have gotten in here and put a tape recorder in my fridge? That's it, she decided, and opened the door.

Hot air rushed out, strange malignant smells, and the atmosphere of another place entirely, for the interior of the refrigerator was gone. Inside was a pathway of stone steps, flanked by leaping fires and leading to a stone platform before a great steel door. On either side of the door stood the statue of a mythological beast—bizarre, yet somehow familiar—its claws poised. The chanting rolled over Dana in waves.

She wanted to run, to scream, anything, but she was paralyzed by the insanity of what she was seeing. A temple, in my refrigerator. And then, ever so slowly, the doors began to open.

Dana was struck by a terrible impression of what she could think of only as living evil, nothing definite, but the worst, most frightening feeling she had ever known. I'm going mad, she thought. It's that commercial, it's Louis. I've been working too hard. The temple doors clanged back.

The steps somehow continued to rise beyond into the sky or a mass of blue vapor, and there was something on them that she could not see. It was too far away and somehow indistinct, as if it were not mortal. A superior being, a god. Now, why would I think that, Dana thought with one part of her being while the rest of her concentrated on breathing, on not passing out. And it sees me. It's coming for me.

The chanting stopped. There was an instant of fearful silence, and then a voice so deep, so shocking, that it could only have come from the thing on the stair.

"ZUUL!"

Dana lunged forward, slamming the door, cutting off the evil orange light, the rising chant. She turned, stumbled toward the phone, trying to remember the mnemonic number, and then decided that she'd just as soon not be here anyway. Grabbing her purse, she ran for the elevator.

6

Ghosts remind me of men's smart crock about women, you can't live with them and you can't live without them.

- EUGENE O'NEILL

Janine Melnitz was beginning to have serious doubts about her job. In fourteen days no one had come in, no one had called, nothing had happened. Zip. She'd read *Vogue, Cosmo,* and *Playgirl,* made and consumed endless coffee, browsed through the various spirit guides, done her nails at least six times a day, and attempted to have conversations with the three men she was working for. It wasn't easy. Stantz seemed to spend all of his time under the hood of their disreputable ambulance, converting it into something he called an Ectomobile. Venkman hustled in and out, made phone calls, and smooth-talked their creditors. And Spengler was always buried in a mess of wiring and constructing devices he would not explain and which Janine could not even pronounce. Today, at least, he was doing something comprehensible, crawling around beneath her desk, connecting up an alarm system. Occasionally he would poke his head up, look around to get his bearings, and disappear below once more, his hands full of tools, a wire clamped in his mouth. Janine sighed luxuriously. He *was* cute, in an intellectual sort of way. Janine had always had a thing for brainy guys. They were all so absentminded. They needed guidance, and Janine liked to guide. Maybe I can draw Egon out, get to know him, find out what he's really like. At that moment, as if on cue, Egon Spengler popped up from under the desk, adjusted his glasses, and groped around for his coffee mug. Janine favored him with a warm smile.

"You're very handy, I can tell," she said, passing him the cup. "I bet you like to read a lot."

"Print is dead," Spengler snorted derisively.

Janine was undeterred. "That's very fascinating to me. I read a lot myself. Some people think I'm too intellectual. But I think reading is a *fabulous* way to spend your spare time."

Spengler looked at her, shrugged, sipped his coffee. "I also play racquetball. Do you ever play?"

"Is that a game?"

"It's a *great* game," Janine said brightly, warming to the chase. "You should play sometime. I bet you'd be good. Do you have any hobbies?"

Spengler nodded. "I collect spores, molds, and fungus."

Janine's jaw dropped, and she eased her chair backward a few inches. "Oh. That's a very unusual."

Spengler shook his head confidently. "I think it's the food of the future."

"Remind me not to have lunch with you."

Dana was still confused and upset when the cabbie let her off. At first she could not believe he could have gotten the right address. The neighborhood looked so seedy. It was obvious that nothing had happened in this corner of town in a long time, at least nothing pleasant. Some long-haired

Chinese hoods watched her from a warehouse loading dock, debating whether to approach her. There must have been some mistake, she thought, and then she spotted the old firehouse with its red and white "no ghosts" logo. There really was such a place. She hurried to the door and went in.

In the garage bay a man was hanging over the fender of a battered Cadillac ambulance, cigarette in mouth, attempting to dismantle what appeared to be the carburetor.

"Excuse me," she ventured. He looked up. It was Stantz, the tall one from the commercial, but she still asked, "Ghostbusters?" He pointed toward the rear. There was a redheaded woman at a desk, filing her nails and looking disconsolately at a bank of phones.

"Excuse me?"

"Yes, may I help you?" the redhead asked pleasantly.

"I—I uh, wanted to see a Ghostbuster."

"Hello!"

She looked up. Another of the men from the commercial—the cute one—was standing in the doorway to an office. He dashed forward, leapt the low rail between the office and the garage bay, and stepped up to her, a bit too close for her tastes, but she didn't pull away. He's not nearly as threatening as that thing in my refrigerator, and I do need help.

"I'm Peter Venkman. What can I do for you?"

"Well… yes… I'm not sure. What I have to say may sound a little… unusual."

Venkman slipped his arm around her, kicked open the gate in the railing, and ushered her toward the office. "We're all professionals here. Miss…"

"Barrett. Dana Barrett."

"You just sit down and we'll talk about it." He leaned back out of the office. "Janine, hold all my calls."

"What calls?"

The office was not what she had expected, but then neither had she expected to find a cult living in her refrigerator. It was a cross between a doctor's office and a TV repair shop. Diplomas hung on the walls, but the books on the shelves competed for spaces with oscilloscopes, dials, gauges, meters, nests of colored wire, and' a series of strange instruments. She recognized a video camera and recorder, what appeared to be a polygraph, several tuning forks, a computer terminal, a crystal ball, a mine detector, and some old television sets. The tall one, Stantz, appeared in the doorway, wiping his hands on a rag, and smiled.

"Customer, Peter?"

"Yes. This is Dana Barrett. Dana, Ray Stantz. Ray, you want to get Egon in here?"

She told her story, then allowed the one with glasses, Spengler, to hook her up to the polygraph and fit a headset device that he called a visual imaging tracker. She told the story again, Peter nodding pleasantly, and the other two monitoring their instruments and making little guttural sounds to each other as they compared results.

"And you slammed the door and ran? You didn't open it again for a second look?"

Dana laughed nervously. "After seeing what I saw? Would you have opened that thing again, Doctor?"

Venkman's smile was engaging. "Yes, I would have. But then. I'm a scientist. So, what do you think it was?"

She paused, listening to the tick-tick of the polygraph. The colored map of her head on the imaging scope flickered and shimmered, Stantz watching it intently. She turned back to Venkman, who cocked his head to one side.

"Well."

"I think something in my refrigerator is trying to get me."

Venkman's expression seemed to flatten uncertainly, then he gave a little bob of his chin, as if he were trying to swallow this new theory. He didn't look entirely convinced.

"Generally, you don't see that sort of behavior in a major appliance. What do you think, Egon?" Spengler looked up from the graph. "She's telling the truth—or at least she thinks she is."

"Of course I am. Why would anyone make up a story like that?"

"Some people want attention," Venkman said. "Some are just crazy."

Stantz tapped the video screen. "You know, Peter, this could be a past-life experience intruding upon the present."

"Or a race memory stored in the collective unconscious," Spengler said excitedly. "And I wouldn't rule out clairvoyance or telepathic contact either."

It was too much for Dana. "I'm sorry I'm laughing. It's just that I don't believe in any of those things. I don't even know my sign."

Spengler tapped on his calculator, then looked up. "You're a Scorpio with your moon in Leo and Aquarius rising."

"Is that good?"

Venkman winked. "It means you're bright, ambitious, outgoing, and very, very sexy."

"Is that your professional opinion?"

"It's in the stars."

She smiled at him, then thought, no, Dana. Not another nut. First a science fiction writer, then that filmmaker last year. You've got enough trouble with a monster in the cold cuts without a dingbat in the bedroom. Carefully she asked, "What would you suggest I do?"

"Why don't I check out the building?" Stantz said. "It may have a history of psychic turbulence."

"Good idea, Ray." Venkman looked at Dana, his eyes merry but unreadable. "Were any other words spoken, any that you remember?"

"No, just the one word, 'Zuul,' but I have no idea what it means."

"Spengler, why don't you check out the literature, see if you can find Zuul in any of the standard reference works. I'll take Miss Barrett home and check her out."

"I beg your pardon."

"Your apartment," Venkman corrected himself smoothly, slipping on his sport coat, and hefting a device that looked like an electronic watering can with a squeeze-bulb arrangement. He held it out like a golf club, took a few practice swings, then slung the thing over his shoulder. "Got to find out what's really bothering you."

Oh fine.

On the taxi ride over, Venkman tried to put her at ease with small talk, noncontroversial chitchat, but she was having none of it. Still too upset from her earlier experience, he decided. Not the best thing for a chick to find a temple of devil worshipers in among the meat loaf. I know it'd put me off my feed.

Deep down, Peter Venkman was still skeptical that what they were doing would work. Even after the incident at the library he wasn't convinced that there was a way to capitalize on this thing. Oh sure, Egon said they could catch and hold ghosts, and he and Ray were certain that the equipment they had built would do the job, but it was a job that no one had ever done before. And staking your life's work and your life savings—or at least Ray's life savings—on Egon's word could reasonably be considered self-destructive behavior. Egon was unconventional, even by Venkman's standards.

Egon was the one who had attempted to nullify gravity by wrapping a high tension power cable around a playground jungle gym, certain that reversing the polarity of that much steel would propel the object into space. He had succeeded merely in browning out the northern third of Ohio for six hours until someone had discovered his immense electromagnet and cut the line. Granted, Spengler had accomplished a few firsts. He had been the first scientist to hypnotize a hamster by subjecting to it low-frequency radio waves. Peter tried it later and found that it also worked on coeds. Egon, in an attempt to build a death ray, had come up with a sonic gun that had little effect on people but set off soft-drink cans at a hundred yards. After the night that Peter had gotten drunk and taken it down to the local Coca-Cola warehouse, Egon had insisted on dismantling it.

On the plus side, the detectors that had registered the presence of the ghost in the library had been Spengler-designed and Stantz-built, and Ray vouched for the soundness of Egon's theories regarding the traps and containments they had designed for the firehouse basement. "They'll catch 'em and hold 'em," Ray had assured him. "I'll stake my life on that."

"We all will, Ray," Venkman had replied, wondering how dangerous a ghost could be. Well, if it can throw books around, I don't think we're talking about *Sesame Street* here.

Peter Venkman sometimes wondered how he'd ever gotten mixed up with Stantz and Spengler. He had never believed in most of the things those two took for granted—ghosts, Bigfoot, UFOs, the Bermuda triangle—what Venkman referred to as "the implied sciences"; and Venkman had only entered the study of parapsychology because grant money had been readily available and because the study of ESP was in its infant stages and therefore formless, malleable. There was no map, no structure, and if a thing has no structure, who's to say that the one you put up is wrong? In fact, until Dean Yaeger had thrown in the monkey wrench, Venkman had had a pretty successful career studying just about whatever he wanted. I'm not a dilettante, he decided. I'm just surveying new ground. And as long as a surveyor keeps moving, keeps out there ahead of the builders, he's got a job.

Dana Barrett's building was a 1920s high rise on Seventy-eighth and Central Park West, a towering ziggurat of red stone. From the street he couldn't see the top but sensed that there was some sort of ornate cap. Well, if it was built in the twenties, maybe someone had planned to moor dirigibles to it. The doorman gave him a funny look as he carried the analyzer into the lobby but spoke pleasantly enough to Dana. Good-looking woman, he decided. Intelligent, attractive, sensible, the kind that never falls for me. He stood behind her in the elevator, gazing at the soft wisps of hair curling down over her neck, wondering what she'd be like. Probably thinks I'm not good enough for her. Still in all…

The apartment was dark, but he noticed that she had no fear of walking in, switching on the lights, and hanging up her coat. The disturbance had been in the kitchen and she was satisfied that it had stayed in the kitchen. Maybe, but after that fiasco at the library I'm not so sure.

"Have you thought of moving out—at least until this disturbance blows over."

"No," she said firmly. "If I moved out now, I'd be acknowledging that what happened was real. I'm not ready to do that."

"Gutsy, that's good," Venkman muttered, looking around the living room for dark corners, hidden secrets, spotting her cello instead.

"You play the cello! It's my favorite instrument."

"Really? Do you have a favorite piece?"

He picked up the instrument. Lighter than I thought. "I'd have to say Prokofiev's Third Concerto."

"That's a violin concerto," she said, carefully untangling his fingers from the strings and putting the instrument away.

"Yeah, but it's got a great cello break."

She turned back to find him peering at the embroidered pillow on her couch. "Souvenir of Fort Hood, Texas?"

"My uncle was in the army. Look, you really don't act like a scientist."

Venkman smiled broadly. "No? What do I act like?"

"Like a game show host."

"Thanks," he said wryly, unslinging the analyzer. He began to circuit the room, poofting on the squeeze-bulb, and watching the dial for any hint of ectoplasmic energy. Ray had never explained the device, but it seemed simple enough.

"Are you sure you're using that thing correctly?"

"I think so." He peered into the nozzle, wondering whether it was turned on. "I mean, it looks right. What's in there?"

"That's the bedroom, but nothing ever happened in there."

"That's too bad," he said, noticing for the first time that she had shed her heavy coat. He had to stop himself from staring.

"What?"

"Nothing. Is that the kitchen?"

"Yes." Was that a touch of apprehension in her voice? He motioned her forward.

"Well, let's check it out."

"I'll wait here if you don't mind."

"Sure." He gripped the analyzer at high port, like a rifle, and stepped boldly through the swinging door into the kitchen. It was a mess. He detoured around a nest of mixing bowls that had fallen to the floor and peered at the cold, hard, fried eggs on the countertop. There was a spilled carton of milk on the floor, a loaf of bread, six-pack of Coke, package of Stay-Puft marshmallows on the drainboard, bunch of celery near the eggs, head of lettuce in the sink. Excepting the fact that all of the little decorator magnets had fallen on the floor, the refrigerator looked normal. He picked up a yellow metal banana and placed it on the door, but instead of sticking it slid back down on the tile. Strange. Magnets don't work.

"You're a hell of a housekeeper."

"I told you," she called.

"I know, it happened by itself." He checked the analyzer again. Well, if this thing's working, the ghosts aren't. "You can come in. There's nothing here."

She poked her head through the door, looking chagrined at the mess. "You're sure?" He nodded. "You checked the refrigerator?"

"No, not yet."

"Well, aren't you going to?"

Well, he thought, this is where I start earning my money. "Sure. Why don't you stand over there?"

He approached the refrigerator from the side, easing up to it, then moving his body around to shield from any possible reaction. Well, here goes nothing. The things I do for a beautiful woman. He pulled slowly on the handle and the door swung back. Venkman let out a cry of terrified surprise.

"What is it?"

"Bologna," he said, letting the door open fully. "And processed cheese food. Twinkies. You eat this stuff?"

"Blast it," she cried in exasperation. "That wasn't there before."

"I know, it was a temple with flames coming out. Well, there's nothing there now, and I get no significant readings."

"This is terrible. Either there's a monster in my kitchen or I'm completely crazy."

Could be, he thought, except for those eggs on the counter. He followed her back into the living room. "If it's any comfort to you, *I* don't think you're crazy."

She laughed incredulously. "Thanks. Coming from you that really means a lot to me."

"I'm a qualified psychologist. I've got a degree and everything. I believe that something happened here and I want to do something about it."

She crossed her arms protectively and stared back at him. "All right. What do you want to do?"

He shrugged disarmingly. "I think I should spend the night here."

"That's it. Get out."

"On a purely scientific basis."

"Out!"

He looked at her sadly. Well, that's it. I tried to help, I said the wrong thing, now she thinks I'm a geek. A crazy. And maybe she's right. I don't know... He started toward the door.

Dana was confused. "You are the strangest man..."

"Then I can stay?"

"No!"

"I want to help."

"I'll scream."

"Don't scream." He hurried to the door, hesitated, then turned back.

"Leave."

"Okay, okay. But if anything else happens, you have to promise you'll call me."

She held the door open for him. "All right, but I want to be alone now."

"Okay, I'll go."

"Good-bye."

He leaned forward for a last try. "No kiss?"

The door neatly met his nose. Peter Venkman stepped back and smiled. Wow, he thought. I think she likes me. He trotted off toward the elevators, not seeing the two suspicious eyes watching him, the furtive shape enter the hall and move toward Dana Barrett's apartment. A door slammed, but Peter Venkman—in a world of his own—stepped into the elevator and rode down.

Oh no, thought Peter Venkman. In love again.

Oh no, thought Louis Tully, pounding futilely on his door. Locked out again.

7

It is one of the blessings of old friends that you can afford to be stupid with them.

- EMERSON

Spengler was leaning across the kitchen table, an eggroll in each hand, his face a mask of intense concentration. "Imagine, if you will, that this eggroll is equivalent to the total amount of extrasensory energy available to the average man. We will call it one… one…"

"ER," Stantz suggested.

"ER?"

"Eggroll. E-R. ER."

Spengler lifted one eyebrow. "We can't call it ER. An eggroll is a thing, therefore a conceptual entity, but it is not a unit of measurement. Eggroll length? Eggroll width? Eggroll what?"

"Call it ERM. Eggroll mass. One ERM."

Spengler was satisfied with that. "Okay, one ERM is the equivalent measurement for the amount of ESP available to the average man. Now," he said, bringing the eggrolls together, "I believe that if you double the amount, to, say, two ERMs, you'd have enough energy to blow the lid off a city the size of New York."

"What lid?"

"The psychic lid. The inbred controls that make even one ERM unavailable to most people." Spengler smiled smugly, popping one of the eggrolls into his mouth.

"Sort of like critical mass at a nuclear reactor, huh?" Stantz asked. Spengler nodded. "But how would you join two ERMs? What kind of psychic link would you need?"

Spengler whipped out his calculator, made a few notes on the side of an overturned carton from Hong Fat's Noodlerama, and announced, "It could be done. A modification of the visual image tracking headset, filtered through an archetype unscrambler, locked into a psychic potentiometer on a feedback circuit would do it."

Stantz was dubious. "Do we really want something like that?"

"Not unless you've got a powerful grudge against the City of New York. An unbridled psychic link between even two people would pull out the stops. It would be like unleashing all the ghosts that have ever lived in New York." He stopped, thought about it for a moment, then shook his head. "Nah, that scares even me."

Venkman came clattering up the stairs, hung his analyzer on the coatrack, and yawned.

"How was your date? We saved you some Chinese."

"It wasn't a date, it was an investigation. I think something's possible there, but I'm going to have to draw a little petty cash, take her to dinner. Don't want to lose this one."

"Did you see anything?" Spengler asked.

"On the first date?"

"Ghosts. Did you see any ghosts?"

Venkman shook his head, then proceeded to rummage through the ravaged Chinese dinner, picking garlic shrimp out of the rubble. "Didn't see anything. Didn't get anything. Nice girl—no ghost. I don't think she was lying though. Nobody cooks eggs on their countertop."

Stantz and Spengler looked at each other. This wasn't like Venkman. Something was affecting him. He picked up Spengler's remaining ERM and popped it into his mouth.

"Anything happen here?"

They shook their heads.

"Nothing, huh? How's the cash holding out? In English, Egon. Forget the calculator."

Egon nodded. "Sure, in English. If you want to take Miss Barrett to dinner, I'd suggest you make it a Big Mac. This Oriental feast took the last of our money, and until we get a job, we're flying without motors."

"Ray, you said that all the indications were pointing to something big happening soon. You told me that things were going to start popping."

"They will."

"When?"

Stantz looked to Spengler for support. Spengler considered telling Venkman about their ERM theory but he didn't look ready for it. He glanced out the window. It was a clear, red sunset, the darkness coming fast and hard, implicit in a front of heavy clouds hanging low over North Jersey. An omen? A portent? More like an analogy to the coming demise of their bank accounts. That eggroll must be getting pretty full. Something would have to break. It was only a matter of time.

"Soon, Peter. Soon."

Though he would have rejected the concept on scientific grounds, Egon Spengler had just made a good guess. The crack in the cosmic eggroll that had manifested itself at the New York Public Library, and in Dana Barrett's refrigerator, was about to widen at a first-class old hotel called the Sedgewick. Built in the thirties on the edge of the garment district, the Sedgewick was home to businessmen, trade shows, conventions, and vacationers. It was also the home of something else.

In the bridal suite on the twelfth floor, a time-honored ritual had just taken place and two people were whispering in the dark.

"Oh, Roy, aren't you glad we waited?"

"I don't know. It probably would have been the same."

"Well, thanks a lot!"

High in one corner of the room, a light film of dust on the air vent was dislodged by something floating through it; a nebulous, persistent yellow vapor.

"What are you doing? Are you just going to roll over now and go to sleep?"

"Uh-huh."

"I don't believe this."

"C'mon, honey. It was a long day, with the wedding, and the drive from New Jersey, and… you know."

"Yeah, I know."

The vapor spread to the four corners of the room, hovering just below the ceiling, then began to intensify. A few curious tendrils reached out in the dark, looking for something interesting to examine. One of them discovered a small travel alarm on the bedside table and curled around it. This was fun. This thing had energy. Perhaps it could be induced to play. With a sharp snap the plastic clock face split, turning a sickly, fire-scorched brown. Confused, the tendril withdrew.

"Roy, your clock broke."

"Nice going, honey. It was brand new."

"I didn't break your precious clock, Roy! Now where are you going?"

"To the bathroom, where do you think?"

My God, she thought. Have I made a serious mistake?

The light went on in the bathroom and the door closed. This was noticed by the vapor, which immediately flowed down and through the cracks of the door. Here, perhaps, would be something to play with.

"Brauuuuugh."

"Roy, are you all right?"

"Brauuugh! Brauuugh! Brauuuuugh!"

"Sweetheart, that's disgusting. Cut it out." She slipped out of bed, wrapping the sheet around her, and started for the door.

"BRAUUUUUGH!"

Roy came charging out of the bathroom, both hands clamped over his mouth, stumbling for the other side of the room. That does it, she thought. If that's the effect I have on him, he can just sleep alone. She stalked into the bathroom and slammed the door. My God, that smell…

"What did you do in here? It's like something died…"

The room itself was discolored, the sickly yellow-brown of old damp newspapers, and smoke seemed to hang in the air, smelling of vomit and rot and old meat. As she watched, gagging, it coalesced and flowed into the mirror. That's impossible, she thought. Smoke can't go into a mirror. But it did, swirling in a whirlpool, forming, becoming solid, with features and movement…

It was a face.

The thing smiled, wagged a foot-long tongue at her, and belched. The mirror cracked.

Roy caught his wife as she ran by, screaming, and clamped a hand over her mouth so he could shout into the phone.

"Right… it's smelling up the whole suite… I don't know, it's in the bathroom…I've never seen anything like it… twelve ten, the bridal suite, for godsake… Hurry!"

* * *

Janine Melnitz was fed up. She'd never been so bored in her life. When she'd first taken the job with Ghostbusters she'd assumed that it would be exciting. She'd been in a TV commercial with three men who were supposedly going to be catching real live ghosts. She'd seen the money pour into their building, their equipment, the bizarre ambulance that Ray Stantz insisted on calling an Ectomobile. And then they'd waited. And nothing had happened. She wasn't even getting anywhere with that cute Dr. Spengler. Face it, kiddo, she thought. You've waltzed into another dead end. Best to cut your losses and move on, pick up some takeout, go home, watch *Dynasty,* read the want-ads.

She snapped off the light and grabbed her purse. The phone rang. Probably the man from Telectronics wanting his money again. She hesitated, then picked it up. After all, I am a receptionist. It's not my money they want.

"Ghostbusters..."

The voice at the other end sounded nervous. "Is this really Ghostbusters?"

"Yes it is."

"And they're... they're serious about this?"

"Of course they're serious," Janine said impatiently. Crazy, but serious.

"Oh, good. My name is J. M. Shupp. I'm the manager of the Sedgewick Hotel, and I wish to contract for their services..."

"You do?"

"I... we... have this ghost..."

"You have?"

She took down the information with a trembling hand. It's real, she thought. It's not a con; they're really going to catch ghosts. Oh, Egon, you're not crazy.

"Don't worry, they'll be totally discreet."

She set down the phone, took a deep breath, and laughed. We really got one. We got one. "We got one!"

The alarm bell blasted Venkman out of bed just as he was falling asleep. He stumbled up, pulling on his socks, and ran for the lockers in the kitchen, where Stantz and Spengler were trying to put on the same pair of coveralls. A real call? Please, don't let this be a false alarm.

"Ray, are the accelerators charged?"

"Certainly. Have you seen my boots?"

"In your hand. The traps?"

"The traps are fine. It's the ERM, Ray. The crack is widening."

"Yes, and so soon. My calculations were correct."

"What are you guys talking about?"

"The crack in the cosmic eggroll, Peter. We're going to have more business than we know what to do with."

"I certainly hope so," Venkman replied. He launched himself at the pole, hit, and plummeted into the garage.

"Where's my trinocular visor?"

"It's in the car, Ray."

"It's not a car, it's an Ectomobile."

"Whatever you say, Ray," Spengler cried, grabbing the pole and descending. Stantz looked about him and realized that he was ready. He took a run at the brass pole.

"Geronimo!" he cried, but his legs were too far apart and the impact was cushioned by precisely that part of his anatomy he'd been trying to protect. With a surprised whimper he fell through the hole.

Venkman grabbed him and dragged him toward the passenger seat as Spengler, his arms full of traps and detectors, loaded the rear compartment. Janine handed him a clipboard with directions on how to get to the Sedgewick and the nature of the complaint, and then, on impulse, kissed him on the cheek. Egon, surprised, gave her a thumbs-up and grinned.

"Will you get a move on here, Egon?" Venkman cried from the passenger side. "You're driving."

"What's wrong with Ray?"

"He dented his bumper. Let's go."

With a blaze of lights the old Cadillac's motor roared to life, the banks of rooftop sensors, antennae, and microwave transmitters swinging to alertness. Janine triggered the door opener, Venkman hit the siren, and they were off.

The doorman of the Sedgewick had seen a lot of strange vehicles in his thirty years on the job, had heard a lot of strange sounds, but the moaning, ululating siren of the Ectomobile brought back childhood memories of Eastern Europe that he had taken great pains to forget, and he instinctively crossed himself. When it screeched to a halt at the curb, his jaw dropped. A radar dish and a microwave tracker swiveled about to point at him, and the old doorman probably would have run had not Shupp, the manager, appeared in the doorway.

Well, they look professional enough, Shupp thought as three men in coveralls alighted from the converted ambulance and began strapping on large electronic backpacks and belts bristling with metal implements. They wore brushed-metal, flip-down visors, boots, and knee and elbow pads over their gray coveralls. The face of one was obscured by a cyclopean headset. Another strode forward, his hand out to shake.

"I'm Dr. Venkman. You are…?"

"Mr. Shupp, the manager. Thank you for coming so quickly. The guests are starting to ask questions and I'm running out of answers."

They moved into the lobby, people turning to stare at the three outlandishly dressed men. A group of Japanese tourists immediately began snapping pictures.

"Has this ever happened before?" Stantz asked, now fully recovered from his mishap with the pole.

"Well, most of the original staff knows about the twelfth floor—the disturbances, I mean—but it's been quiet for years. Then, two weeks ago, it started again, but nothing like this."

"Did you ever report it to anyone?"

"Heavens no! The owners didn't like us even to talk about it. I hoped we could take care of this quietly tonight."

Egon shook his head. "Like social disease," he exclaimed loudly. "You think it'll go away if you ignore it, and then, eventually, your—"

"Egon, the job, remember?"

Ray Stantz was walking the manager toward the elevators, cleverly distracting him from Spengler's outburst. "Don't worry, we handle this sort of thing all the time."

"You gotta be cool with these people, Egon," Venkman said.

"I was appalled at his unprofessional attitude."

"Well, we're the professionals. That's why they called us."

Ray shook the manager's hand and the man withdrew, leaving them alone in front of the elevators.

"Twelfth floor, huh?" Venkman pushed the button. Something tugged on his sleeve. It was an old man in an overcoat and alpine hat, carrying a newspaper. He poked Venkman in the chest.

"What are you supposed to be?"

"Me? We're exterminators. Somebody saw a cockroach on the twelfth floor."

Stantz and Spengler smiled. The old man whistled. "That's gotta be some cockroach."

"Well, you can't be too careful with these babies," Venkman said. "Going up?"

"That's all right. You go ahead. I'll wait for another car."

They had the elevator to themselves.

"I just realized something," Stantz said. "We've never had a completely successful test with any of the equipment."

Spengler raised a hand. "I blame myself."

"So do I," Venkman agreed.

Stantz shrugged. "No sense in worrying about it now, right, Peter?"

"Sure. Each of us is wearing an unlicensed nuclear accelerator oh his back. No problem."

"Relax," Egon said. "I'm going to switch on."

Before Venkman could protest, the warning light on Spengler's proton pack flared red and the accelerator kicked in with a deep, disturbing hum. Stantz and Venkman edged away as the whole car began to vibrate, dust motes kicking into motion in the suddenly polarized air. The hair went up on Venkman's neck and he felt a crawling sensation on his scalp, as if a thousand lice had begun a breakdown competition among the roots of his hair. He swallowed uncomfortably, noticing that Stantz had curled his lips back and away from his teeth.

"Ray, you okay?"

Stantz shook his head. "Egon, the fillings in my mouth are beginning to heat up."

"That'll stop when you cut in your own accelerator," Spengler announced. Stantz nodded and switched on. Venkman's eyes were starting to hurt. Here goes nothing, he thought, and kicked in his own unit. Immediately the symptoms subsided as he was surrounded by the proton generator's field. Maybe these things will work. The door opened and they stepped out on the twelfth floor, instantly alert for any sign of trouble, but the floor was brightly lit, tastefully appointed, and quiet.

"What do you think?"

Spengler consulted the aurascope on his belt. "Definitely something here."

"Stay on your toes. Don't let it surprise you."

Suddenly a squeak and a clank from behind them. They froze, and then Stantz and Spengler whirled and fired, mutlicolored streams of supercharged particles ripping out of the induction nozzles. They struck the walls, shearing great ribbons of flaming wallpaper into the air, blowing holes in the carpet, exploding a light fixture. A doorknob spun through the air, striking and then going cleanly through a solid wall. The streams struck a maid's cart, twisting the metal, rebounding in flashes of uncontrolled energy. A box of soap burst into flames and a dozen rolls of toilet paper dispersed, hitting the walls and the terrified maid who crouched screaming on the floor. "Cease fire!" Venkman cried.

"What the devil you doin'?" called the maid in the sudden silence, slapping at bits of burning paper that were drifting down around her. "You crazy?"

"Sorry, ma'am."

"We'd better adjust the streams," Spengler suggested.

"Yeah," Venkman added disgustedly. "And let's split up. We can do more damage that way." He turned and stalked off down the hall. Spengler and Stantz set off in the other direction.

"I'm getting high readings near the air vents. It must be using the duct system to get around. I told you we'd find something. You head that way and I'll go north. And keep your radio on."

Why not? Spengler thought as he shouldered the

induction nozzle and reached for his trusty plasmatometer. Valences, that's the key. Ghosts leave an ethereal spore, but I can track them. He edged along the wall, tapping gently, watching the lights flashing on the little detector. He came to a door, tapped his way across it, then examined the crack at the top, sides, along the floor. The easiest way for them to get in, he figured: cracks, vents, keyholes. The door opened. He looked up to see a tall, beautiful woman in a bathrobe, her hair wrapped in a turban of wet toweling. Careful, Egon, he thought. They can be devious, like the one in the library. Still, she seemed pretty solid and she certainly had legs.

"Yes?"

He stood up. "Were you recently in the bathroom?" he asked, running the plasmatometer across her front. No response there.

"What on earth gave you that idea?"

"The wet towels, the residual moisture on your lower limbs and hair, the redness in your cheeks indicating—"

"You're a regular Sherlock Holmes. Now, what do you want? And get that thing out of my face." Spengler withdrew the detector. "When you were in the bathroom, did you notice anything that was yellow and unusually smelly?"

The woman stepped back and slammed the door in his face. Spengler shrugged and moved on.

On a lower floor, Venkman, induction gun held protectively before him, was moving cautiously down the hall, feeling stupid. Dressed up like Buck Rogers, hunting ghosts. Is this any life for a grown man? He stopped beside an unattended room-service cart and consoled himself with an order of shrimp cocktail, not noticing the trail of yellowish stains along the wainscoting.

* * *

Ray Stantz was standing very quietly in the center of an intersection, staring at his PKE meter. He had tracked the ghost down to the fifth floor and suddenly the needle was going crazy. Stantz tapped the mike on his headset.

"Egon, I've got something. I'm moving in."

He headed cautiously down the hallway toward another T-intersection at the end, around which came the sounds of clinking plates and the faint smell of something old and ugly. He pulled down his induction gun, but held it pointed toward the floor. No sense in blowing away another maid, or some Puerto Rican busboy. Still, the readings and that smell. He turned the corner at the end.

"Yaaah!"

Twenty feet away, hovering over a room-service cart, was the object of his search: a free vapor, apparently composed of a series of compacted noxious gases, with a face like a misshapen potato and a pair of spindly arms. Stantz watched fascinated as it rummaged through the dishes, tossing some of them on the floor, and cramming leftover scraps into its mouth. It had to be the one. It matched perfectly with the manager's description.

"Ray. Where are you? Are you all right?" came Spengler's voice over the radio.

"Egon, you should see this thing. It's so ugly."

The vapor raised a half-empty bottle of wine and chugged the remaining contents, the wine pouring through it and out onto the carpet. Satisfied with that trick, it tossed the bottle back over its head and began rooting around in the plates like a hog after truffles.

"Where are you, Ray?"

"Five south, I think. I'm moving in. I don't think it's seen me yet."

This time it downed a mass of half-eaten salad, which was obviously too spicy, for the thing sneezed, spattering the wall with greasy residue. It belched loudly and patted its rudimentary stomach. Stantz was disgusted.

"Ugh, what a slob. I'm going to take him." He snapped the visor down over his eyes and raised the induction rifle. "Freeze, Potatoface!"

It turned toward him and let out a piercing scream as Stantz fired, tearing a flaming crater in the wallpaper. The vapor did a wingover and sped off down the hall, dragging the cart behind it. Stantz took off in pursuit, calling for Egon and Peter to watch for it, but when the ghost reached the end of the hallway, instead of turning, it passed right through the wall. The cart hit directly behind it and overturned, trashing the carpet as Stantz arrived. He peered at the wall, which had turned an ugly yellow. There were drops of ectoplasm oozing in thick, stringy trails from the spot. Well, at least I hit it. But where did it go?

Venkman was steamed. He had wandered down to three and was leaning against a wall, pulling disconsolately on a cigarette and staring at the ceiling. This bites the big one, he thought. I actually work for a company called Ghostbusters. Not even I thought it would come to this. Beep, beep, beep. Beep?

Venkman looked down at his PKE meter. The red light was burning and the thing was signaling wildly. Quickly Venkman keyed his headset. "Ray, something's here."

"Where are you, Pete?"

"Third floor. Get down here." He unshipped the long induction rifle, and braced himself as the accelerator cut in with a whine.

"Sit tight. I'm on my way."

"Well, hurry. It's real close."

Suddenly, with a rattle of dishes, a room-service cart sailed past the end of the corridor, followed closely by a yellow-green floater trailing a haze of smog. Venkman goggled at it. The ghost stopped, turned, and goggled back. Venkman felt the blood drain out of his face.

"It's here, Ray," he whispered. "It's looking at me."

"Don't move. It won't hurt you."

"How do you know?" The vapor had begun to undulate from side to side, its attention still fixed on Venkman.

"I don't know. I'm just guessing."

With a bob the vapor started toward him.

"Well, I think you guessed wrong. Here he comes!"

"On my way."

"What do I do?"

"Shoot it!"

"Gaaaah!"

Stantz came barreling out of the stairwell, checked his detector, and sprinted down the hallway, screaming, "Peter, hang on," but when he got to the site Venkman was flat on his back, his arms and legs flailing frantically, his body covered from head to belt in thick yellow ectoplasm.

"Gross."

"Aaaagh, aaagh!" Venkman cried, spitting a glob of the disgusting stuff from his mouth. "It slimed me. The little mother slimed me!"

"You all right?"

Venkman spat again, his face screwed into an expression of extreme disgust. Stantz had never seen him look so angry. "I'm going to get that little grub if it's the last thing I do. Nobody slimes Dr. Peter Venkman! Nobody!"

"Where'd it go?"

"That way."

They hurried back toward the elevators and found

Spengler peering through the doorway of a banquet room. A sign announced: reception welcoming the tokyo trade council: 8:00 p.m. He slammed the door and put his back to it.

"It's in there. What happened to you?"

"He got slimed. Did you bring the trap?"

Spengler indicated a metal box the size of a toaster fixed to his belt and connected to a long coaxial cable. "We ready for this?"

"I am," Venkman growled. "Let's get it."

"Right," Ray agreed. "Visors down, full stream. Geronimo."

They tumbled into the room, closing the door behind them. It was an ornate formal banquet hall, high-ceilinged and ostentatious, hewn beams converging in the center at an immense crystal chandelier. A long line of buffet tables fronted one wall, piled high with food and a carved ice punch bowl. There was a fully stocked bar. Stantz looked at his watch. Seven forty-five. Only fifteen minutes to do the job before the room fills up with Japanese businessmen. "Do you see it?"

"The food," Venkman said grimly. "It'll head for the food. Spread out."

The liquid in the punch bowl boiled and erupted a stream of yellow gas. The vapor surfaced, glaring at them.

"Fire."

The searing energy bolts smashed the table, blowing food and broken bottles across the room, sending the vapor tumbling behind the bar. Stantz swung and fired.

"No, not the mirror!" Spengler screamed, throwing himself flat as the energy stream diffracted into a thousand tiny fragments, speckling the walls like shrapnel. One of them tore away Venkman's tool belt, making him dive under a table.

"Ray!"

"Sorry. Where'd it go?" They scanned the room, trying to ignore the burning buffet tables. In war there were casualties. Venkman heard a muffled pounding on the door.

"Battle area, go away," he shouted. Spengler touched his shoulder.

"Peter, there's something I—"

"There, on the ceiling!" Stantz pointed toward the chandelier where the vapor was circling, using the glass and metal fixture for cover. He dropped to one knee and fired, tracking on the ghost, setting fire to the supporting beams. The sprinkler system kicked in. Venkman tried to cut off the thing's escape but succeeded only in blowing half the chandelier to fragments. Stantz fired again and completed the job, the great lighting fixture plummeting down, breaking the back of a large dinner table. Silverware flew through the air.

"My fault," Stantz called. "I'll pay for it."

"It's probably insured. Where'd it go?"

As if it had heard, the vapor peeked out from between the great support structure. Venkman raised his induction gun.

"Wait, wait!" Spengler cried out urgently. "There's something I forgot to tell you."

"What?"

"Don't cross the streams!"

"Why not?" Venkman asked suspiciously.

"Trust me. It would be bad."

Venkman pushed back his visor and rubbed the ectoplasmic residue off his face. "Egon, I'm not your kind of scientist. Precisely what do you mean by *bad!*"

"It's hard to explain. Try to imagine all life as you know it stopping instantaneously and finding yourself confined forever in another dimension."

"That's bad," Stantz agreed, his eyes still on the lurking vapor.

"No," Venkman replied, "that's it. I'm taking charge. You guys are dangerous." They nodded sheepishly. "Now, nobody does anything unless I say 'Got it.' "

"Got it."

"Let's do it. It's not going to hang around all day waiting for us. Ray, take the right. I'll take the left. Now!"

The energy streams shot out, penning the vapor between them. It moved to slip between but Venkman and Stantz brought the streams closer together and it retreated. As long as they kept them tight, it couldn't get by.

"Good, good, ' Venkman called. "Nice and wide... move with it... steady..."

Spengler watched, fascinated, as the two streams slowly came together, the vapor caught between them.

"Now, very slowly, Ray, let's tighten it up. Hold it there, I'll come down. Egon..."

"Right here."

"Get ready to cap it."

Egon kicked in his accelerator. "Okay, but shorten your stream. I don't want my face burned off. And don't cross them..."

The vapor began to whirl, darting at the stream, and suddenly Stantz was out of control. A cascade of energy began to leap from his stream to Venkman's. "Back off!" Venkman screamed.

"I'm losing it! I'm losing it!"

The vapor slipped free and streaked for the back wall.

"It's heading for the vent. Cut it off!" Large sections of the rear wall exploded, flaming rubble showering down, turning to mush as the sprinklers hit it. Egon's stream raked across the air vent, driving the ghost back. The pounding on the outer door was beginning to grow violent and Venkman considered blowing the doors off. Let the turkeys see what *we're* up against. No, they'd just take it wrong if I fried the manager by mistake. He fired, driving the ghost back toward the ceiling as Stantz's beam went wide, exploding the liquor cabinet.

"Ray, on the ball. You gotta catch it."

This time Stantz's markmanship was accurate and they held it where the chandelier had been, tightly boxed in a grid of flowing energy. "Make it quick," Stantz cried. "Almost out of charge on these packs."

"Ready, Egon?"

Spengler hit his belt release and the trap fell to the floor. "Alternately shorten your streams. Force it down."

As they edged the vapor toward the waiting trap, it seemed to realize what was happening and erupted forth with a startling array of belches and gas, each worse than the last. The men recoiled in disgust but held their ground as clouds of the gas contacted the streams and erupted into flares of burning color. Egon poised his foot over the pedal control. "Lock it in, now!"

The streams suddenly separated and shortened, forming a cap over the vapor. Stantz was yelling hysterically, like a kid on a roller coaster. Venkman was not so sure. His charge indicator warning light was winking. "Better get it, Egon. I'm outta juice here."

Egon stamped down on the pedal, opening the trapdoors on the top. An inverted pyramid of glowing charged particles leapt toward the ceiling, cold light that streamed back toward itself even as it exploded outward, pulling the vapor down and in with a thunderous roar like a thousand locomotives. The spring-loaded doors snapped shut and everything was silent, excepting the last poots of energy on Ray's pack as the charge gave out. He switched it off and they stared in awe at the trap, sitting silently in the middle of the floor, a curl of smoke rising from it. Egon tiptoed forward and checked the valence indicator.

"It's in there," he confirmed reverently. "My God, we did it. We trapped a ghost."

Venkman picked up a severely damaged champagne bottle. "That calls for a drink," he said, pouring the remaining bubbly over his head. He looked around at the ballroom, wondering if the hotel's insurance company would consider it an act of God. Come to think of it, the very basis of insurance coverage would probably be changed by what they had done tonight.

"Well, that wasn't so bad, was it?" Stantz said happily, pulling off his visor. Venkman turned on him.

"Are you kidding? Look at this mess. We almost got killed. It was about as easy as trying to push smoke into a bottle with a baseball bat, but—"

He looked at Stantz, then at Spengler. They were staring at him, waiting for his next word, his instructions, and he realized that, like it or not, he was in charge. For better or worse, he now commanded the Ghostbusters. He looked about him, watching the water puddling on the floor from the sprinklers, the burning tables, the ectoplasm-smeared chandelier imbedded in the oak flooring. Venkman's Wrecking Crew. Well, it *was* their first time and they *did* catch the ghost.

"This was a bit rough, and we had a few technical surprises," he said, with a sharp look at Egon, who blanched and shrugged, "but it'll get easier. We just have to work out our tactics. Wanna grab that trap, Ray?"

The manager, the assistant manager, the maintainance man, the locksmith, and a flock of Japanese tourists fell back in panic as Venkman pushed open the doors. He raised his hands and announced, "We came, we saw, we kicked its butt!"

Shupp tore his eyes away from the destroyed banquet hall. "What was it? What did you do?"

"We got it," Stantz called proudly, holding up the smoking trap. The vapor, in irritation, threw itself against the walls of its polarized prison, sending little displays of static lightning over the surface of the box. The tourists backed off, cameras clicking wildly.

"What was it? Will there be any more of them?"

"Sir, what you had there was what we refer to as a focused, nonterminal, repeating phantasm, or a class-five full-roaming vapor… a real nasty one too."

Venkman tore the customer copy of the bill from his clipboard and handed it to the manager. "That'll be four thousand for the entrapment, plus one thousand for proton recharge and storage."

Shupp seemed more terrified of the bill than he had been of the original ghost. "Five thousand dollars! I had no idea it would be so much. I won't pay it."

Vankman shrugged. "Fine. We'll let it go again. Ray…"

"No, no. All right. Anything, just leave."

Well, Venkman thought. Gratitude, so to speak.

On the street there was a new surprise. Someone had tipped off New York's tireless press corps and a horde of people had converged on the scene. Uniformed police were struggling to keep them back from the Ectomobile. As the Ghostbusters emerged, covered in strange clothing, weapons, ectoplasm, and soot, the crowd broke into applause. Spengler nudged Venkman. "You're in charge. You deal with them."

"Okay, Egon, but watch how I do this because we're all gonna have to know how." The reporters surged forward.

"Nate Cohen, with the *Post*. What happened in there?"

"Dave McNary, *INS*. Did you really see a ghost?"

"Did you catch it?"

"Beverly Rose, *Omni*. Is this some sort of publicity stunt?"

Before Venkman could answer, Stantz pushed his way through and held up the smoking trap. Weak static charges played over the surface. The vapor was tiring out.

"We got one," Stantz cried jubilantly. Flashbulbs and strobes went off, and a minicam crew fought its way forward.

"Can we see it?"

"No, I'm afraid not."

Venkman leaned forward and raised his hands, and a brace of microphones was shoved into his face. "This is not a sideshow. We are serious scientists."

"What proof do you have that what you saw was real?" the woman from *Omni* called.

"Proof? Well, the manager of the Sedgewick just paid us five big ones to get *something* out of there." He wiggled the trap. "Is that proof enough for you?"

"Are you saying that ghosts really exist?"

"Not only do they exist," Venkman replied, "but they're all over the place! And that's why we're offering this vitally important service to people in the entire tristate area. We're available twenty-four hours a day, seven days a week. We have the tools and we have the talent. No job is too small, no fee too big. We're ready for anything..."

Spengler, confused by all the noise, had slipped away and was hanging back at the edge, eating a Baby Ruth he had shagged off the hotel newsstand. Let Venkman handle the reporters. I've got to figure out a way to safety-interlock that problem of stream length before someone gets hurt.

"Mister. Hey, Mister! Come here, over here, Mister!"

Spengler peered into the darkness. Hanging over a police sawhorse was a young man dressed in a black canvas jumpsuit and chains, a red bandana tying back his chartreuse hair.

"Me?"

"That's right. Come here."

Spengler had never seen anything quite like him, and wandered over to study the apparition. "Who are you?"

"They call me Mister Dave, man. You a Ghostbuster? Wha's your name?"

Egon pointed to his name, embroidered large on his chest, unaware that part of it had been obscured by flying ectoplasm.

"Okay, Spen'le. Lemme see that gun, man."

"They're not guns. They're charged particle throwers."

"Yeah, yeah," Mister Dave whispered. "I know. I just wanna see 'em."

"I couldn't do that. You might hurt someone."

Spengler turned to go, but the youth lunged across the barricade and caught his sleeve. "Wait, wait! Let me ask you something. If you like shot Superman with one of those guns, would he feel it or what?"

Spengler considered. "On Earth, no—but on Krypton we could slice him up like Oscar Mayer bologna."

"Wow! Hey, thanks, Spen'le. You okay."

"Egon, get back here."

Spengler wandered back to where Stantz and Venkman had just finished singing the theme song from their commercial. The reporters were eating it up. "Get over here, Egon, they want a group picture." Spengler stepped between the two; they closed ranks tightly around him, and the flashguns went off. We did it, he thought as his vision faded into a white blur. We got one.

8

Put a rogue in the limelight and he will
act like an honest man.

- NAPOLEON I

The pictures hit the morning editions of every paper in New York, and by evening had spread halfway around the world. The three of them standing proudly in front of the Sedgewick, captioned "GHOSTBUSTERS!" or "GHOSTBUSTERS?" depending on the editorial slant. Ray Stantz holding the smoking trap aloft. "WE GOT ONE!" The Ectomobile. GHOSTBUSTERS!! screamed the Rupert Murdoch papers. BOFFO BIZ FOR SPOOK KOOKS, cried *Variety.* A STRANGE OCCURRENCE IN THE GARMENT DISTRICT, indicated a cautious *Wall Street Journal*, but *The Village Voice* kicked out the jams and ran a Feiffer caricature on the front page. Within six hours no one was talking about anything else.

"Ghostbusters. May I help you…?"

"Hello, America. This is Ronald Gwynne reporting from United Press International in New York. Throughout my entire career as a journalist I have never covered anything as exciting and incredible as the trapping of an actual supernatural entity by a team of men based in this city who call themselves the Ghostbusters. Now, most of us have never heard of the floating, slimelike substance called ectoplasm, but these gentlemen claim we will be seeing more of it than ever before…"

"Lydia, there's something moving around in the storeroom. I told Joan it was rats, but she insists that she saw something else."

"What?"

"The figure of a headless woman."

"Oh. Okay, better not take any chances…"

"Ghostbusters, would you hold please…?"

"Car fifteen, this is Manhattan Central. Proceed to the Museum of Natural History and help twenty-one keep the crowds away from that Ectomobile. And ticket them if they park in the red zone again…"

SOHO CHAMBER OF COMMERCE HONORS GHOSTBUSTERS.

"Look, Central, I tried to ticket it. It's got some kinda detection system, radar an' microwave an' stuff. It zapped the ticket. Disintegrated, burned up, nothin' but black ashes left. I ain't goin' near it. You want 'em ticketed, you do it."

"Good morning. Today the Eastern Seaboard is alive with talk of hundreds of reported incidents involving multiple sightings in what can only be described as extreme events of paranormal extraphenomenological proportions. It seems that everybody is willing to bring their old ghosts and skeletons out of the closet. Roy Brady reports from New York."

"Thank you, Roger. Everybody's heard ghost stories around the campfire. Heck, my grandma used to spin yarns about a spectral locomotive that would rocket past the farm where she grew up. Now, as if some unseen authority had suddenly given permission, thousands of people here are talking about encounters they claim to have had with ghosts..."

"I thought it was a nun, Monsignor, until it walked through a wall..."

PHANTOM POSTULANT REMOVED FROM ST. PATRICK'S.

"So, Dr. Venkman, what's the most frightening thing you've come up against since you started Ghostbusters?"

"Well, David, I think it was running into Larry Bud Melman in the dressing room before the show."

"C'mon, now, seriously..."

GHOST RUNS AMUCK ON SUBWAY PLATFORM. SCARES 20.

"Ghostbusters. All our lines are busy right now, but if you'd like to leave your number, one of our operators will get back to you..."

"How's it going, Janine?"

"Don't ask. The cases are on the status board."

"Hello, this is Mr. Cover at Marvel Comics..."

"Hello, this is Janet Gluckstern at Revell Models..."

"Hi, this is Andy Newbry at TSR..."

GHOSTBUSTERS ANNOUNCES MAJOR MERCHANDISING EFFORT.
FIRST FRANCHISES TO OPEN SOON IN PHILADELPHIA, D.C.

Janine grabbed Venkman by the arm as he stumbled past her desk. "You said I was going to get some help on the phones. I've been at this for almost three days without a break."

"Hey," he said, suppressing a yawn. "We're all stretched here. I thought you were bored, with nothing to do..."

"Very funny."

Spengler appeared out of the storeroom. "Tough job. Want to share my Baby Ruth?"

"Aw, thanks Egon..."

GHOST TERRORIZES METS GAME.

"Ray, every time I hear about your company, I can't help thinking about that old Bob Hope movie."

Stantz smiled and nodded. "Actually, Joe, the title of that film was *Ghostbreakers.* Olsen and Johnson did *Ghostcatchers,* and the Bowery Boys did *Ghost Chasers, Hold That Ghost, Spooks Run Wild, Spook Busters,* and *Spook Chasers.*"

Joe Franklin laughed, pleased with his guest's wit. The man might be certifiable, but he was also a certifiable success and terrific copy. He leaned in conspiratorially. "Well, in any case, I guess there's one big question on everyone's mind and you're certainly in a position to answer it for us: Have you seen Elvis, and how is he?"

Venkman was sorting the mail into business, pleasure, and cranks. He looked over an envelope with the printed initials I.L.M. in the corner and a colophon he did not recognize. "Ray, who do we know in Marin County?"

GHOSTBUSTERS CLEAR EMPIRE SPOOK BUILDING.

"Tonight Johnny's guests will be Charo, Arnold Schwarzenegger, eighty-two-year-old hooker Nancy Winkie, and Ghostbuster Egon Spengler, so don't go away..."

"Guess what?" Ray said, poking his head down from the attic. Spengler and Venkman looked up from their meal of take-out chicken and light beer as Stantz lowered a small valence trap by its cord. "I just caught a ghost, a little one, right in our own attic."

"Aw, Ray. Not while we're eating."

"Mr. Director, those files you requested."

"Hmmm, yes... Really...? Well, they don't look dangerous, but perhaps we'd best keep an eye on them. Never know what they might turn up. Do you suppose there are Communist ghosts?"

PRESIDENT COMMENDS GHOSTBUSTERS.
ACLU CALLS FOR RIGHTS FOR THE DEAD.

"Peter, Isaac Asimov on two..."

"Our phone-in topic today: Ghosts and ghostbusting. The controversy builds as more sightings are reported and some maintain that these professional paranormal eliminators in New York are the cause of it all. Why did everything start just when these guys went into business? Should they be allowed to carry around unlicensed proton mass drivers? And what's wrong with ghosts anyway? Call us… all our lines are open. Hello, Larry King."

"Hello, Larry? I think what Dr. Spengler said in his interview last night was true. The world *is* in for a psychic shock, 'cause my aunt reads coffee grounds and she says…"

Lucille Zeddemore threw the newspaper in her son's face. "Okay, boy. You been back from the service a month now. Time you got a job. Get to it."

"Aw, Mom. There's never anything in the want-ads that's any good." Heck, I've got good qualifications. Hey, I've got a degree. Maybe I should move out of this city, go to Atlanta, or Silicon Valley, or Pittsburgh. He riffled through the listings for fry cooks and maintenance men, telephone sales and insurance trainees. Garbage, nothing but… A small, bordered box caught his eye.

Are you trained in computers, heavy weapons, electronic surveillance or radar maintenance, hand-to-hand combat or related activities? Are you fit and athletic, able to work odd hours for good pay, with no questions asked? This might be the job for you.

Right. Looks like somebody's getting ready to invade Cuba again. Just what I need, get my butt shot off, no questions asked. He glanced at his mother, preparing dinner in the kitchen. Hand-to-hand combat or related activities? Hoo-boy. Sounds crazy. But it might be a good deal and it sure beats being a janitor. Winston Zeddemore copied down the address.

* * *

Dana Barrett had that pleasantly weary lightness that comes with having put in a good rehearsal, and was only half-listening as Andre Wallance walked her out to the plaza. Wallance, a world-renowned violinist, was doing a series of guest performances with the orchestra and had taken an interest in her career, though Dana suspected that his interest was not entirely musical. She did not entirely object. Though thin and ascetic, Wallance was a brilliant musician, and if he wished to take her to dinner and to try in his shy, otherworldly way to get her into bed, she had every intention of letting him make the attempt. She might even let him succeed. He was not precisely her type, but then no one was, and the experience might be refreshing. Woman cannot live by cello alone.

"Your city is so dirty," Wallance sniffed, his nose buried deep in a handkerchief. "Nothing like Paris." Dana had been to Paris and knew that it could be every bit as dirty as New York, but she smiled and let the matter pass. Wallance changed his tack and began angling for a shot at a late supper.

"I'd love to, Andre, but I promised my mother I would call her tonight," she lied, keeping him off balance to make the game interesting.

"Ah, the mother, yes."

"How about tomorrow?"

"Unfortunately I am occupied. A dinner with the French consul and his family. Terribly boring. I would get out of it if I could, but alas. Perhaps Thursday..."

"Thursday. Let me check my book."

He opened the door and they stepped out onto the plaza before the Metropolitan Opera House. It was a blustery late October day, cold and sunny, with a hint of coming winter, and the concourse held only a fragment of its usual collection of peddlers, breakdancers, and itinerant hustlers. And there, in front of the fountain, hopping along in a strange little Curly Howard dance step, was a familiar figure in gray coveralls and an orange jacket. She turned to Wallance, who had paused to put in drops against the smog. "Andre, excuse me for a minute. I've just seen someone I know."

"*Certainment*," Wallance mumbled to his eyedropper. Dana strode across the plaza to where Venkman stood smiling at her.

"This is a surprise."

"Great rehearsal."

"You heard it?"

Venkman nodded enthusiastically. "You're the best one in your row."

Dana favored him with a skeptical smile. "You're good. Most people can't hear me with the whole orchestra playing."

Venkman shook his head. "I don't have to take abuse from you. I have other people dying to give it to me."

"I know. You're quite a celebrity these days. Are you here because you have info about my case?"

"You certainly know the technical terms." He indicated Wallance, who was looking impatiently in their direction. "Who's the stiff?"

"That stiff happens to be one of the finest musicians in the world and a wonderful man." Wallance looked uncomfortable; with New York, the weather, and certainly with the presence of Peter Venkman. He resorted to a bottle of nasal spray.

"Is he dying or something?"

Dana ignored the remark, preferring to study Peter Venkman's cockeyed smile. I don't know what it is about you. They never had anyone like you back home.

"He's a very close friend," she said at last. "Now, do you have some explanation of what happened in my apartment?"

"Yes, but I have to tell you in private at a fine restaurant…"

"Do you? Can't you tell me now?"

Venkman shrugged. "I'll cancel the reservation. I found the name Zuul in…" He paused to pull a crumpled piece of paper out of his pocket and pat it flat. "…the *Roylance Guide to Sacred Sects*."

"Sacred sex?"

"That too. I don't suppose you've read it."

Dana shook her head. "You must have gotten the last copy."

"Well, the name Zuul refers to a demigod worshiped around six thousand B.C. by the… what's that say?"

She huddled in close to his shoulder. "Hittites. 'By the Hittites, Mesopotamians, and the Sumerians. Zuul was the minion of Gozer.' Who's Gozer?"

Venkman tucked the paper back into his pocket. "Gozer was very big in the Sumerian religion. One of their gods. A real big guy."

"What's he doing in my refrigerator?"

"I'm checking on that. I think we should meet Thursday night at nine to talk about it."

She looked Venkman up and down. He was almost the exact opposite of Andre Wallance, of the classy, self-assured men who usually went after her, and her first reaction was to laugh at him, but somehow she couldn't. He was right. She had thought him a geek and a charlatan, but now he was one of the most famous men in the city. Not that that was important, but he and his colleagues had proven their case. There were ghosts, and Peter Venkman was out there every day, dealing with them, catching them. And that made him every bit as successful on his own terms as any man she knew. Still, he was so strange…

"I don't think so. I'm busy Thursday night."

Venkman looked reprovingly and leaned in close to her. "You think I enjoy giving up my evenings to spend time with my clients? I'm making an exception because I respect you as an artist and a dresser."

"You're too much." Dana laughed. "All right, since you put it that way."

"I'll pick you up at your place. I'll bring the *Roylance Guide,* and we can read after we eat."

"I've got to go now," she said, not adding what she was thinking: my "stiff" is waiting. There was something refreshing about dealing in Peter Venkman's terminology.

"Remember," Venkman called. "I'm the only one standing between you and a heavy Hittite." Then he turned and hopped away.

9

Beware of the man of one book.

- THOMAS AQUINAS

Janine was keeping ahead of the stream of phone calls only by dint of sheer perseverance. The lines were all lit, and each time she would clear one—case, crank, or curiosity—it would light again. She was, however, gaining an instinctive sense of what was profitable and what was not, what was dangerous and what was not, what could be contracted for and what not to touch with a ten-foot induction rifle. You would think that this would make me indispensable, she thought. You would think that this would make me a valuable asset. You would think I could at least get some help, but no…

"Ghostbusters—please hold… Good afternoon, Ghostbusters—please hold… Yes, may I help you?"

Winston Zeddemore looked up from the chair where he was filling out the Ghostbusters' job application, wondering just what kind of lunacy these people were tapped into. The little red-haired chick hadn't stopped answering calls since he'd walked in. The place was nothing but an old firehouse, but Zeddemore, with his electronics countermeasures training, could see that their equipment meant business. If it was a front, it was an awfully complex one. Surely these people couldn't really be after ghosts.

"Yes," Janine was saying. "Is it a mist, or does it have arms and legs...?" She checked the multicolored wall chart that Stantz had drawn up. "That sounds like a class-two anchored-proximity phantasm, serious, but not necessarily harmful... Would I kid you?... Well, the soonest we could possibly get back to you would be a week from Friday... I'm sorry, but we're completely booked until then... Uh-huh... All I can suggest is that you stay out of your house until we can get to you... Well, in that case. I'd be careful not to provoke it... You're welcome."

She put down the phone wearily and eyed the blinking lights without enthusiasm. Just what I always wanted to be—Jewish mother to the spiritual population of New York. Zeddemore looked up at her. "You got a question, sir?"

"Well, yeah. The ad in the paper just said what they wanted. But what's the job?"

"I don't really know, Mr. Zeddemore. They just told me to take applications and to ask you these questions: Do you believe in UFOs, astral projection, mental telepathy, ESP, clairvoyance, spirit photography, full-trance mediums, psychokinetic or telekinetic movement, cartomancy, phrenology, black and/or white magic, divination, scrying, necromancy, the theory of Atlantis, the Loch Ness monster, Bigfoot, the Bermuda triangle, or in general in spooks, specters, wraiths, geists, and ghosts?"

"Not really. However, if there's a semi-regular paycheck in it I'll believe anything you say."

* * *

Venkman wheeled the Ectomobile around a tight corner, waved wearily to the crowd of autograph hounds and tourists clustered around the front of the firehouse, and slid the old Cadillac into the garage bay. "Open your eyes, Ray. We're home."

Stantz sat up, mumbled to himself, and climbed out. The Ectomobile looked like it had been through the Battle of Stalingrad, streaked with smoke and slime. Not often we have to chase the rotten things down on the road and zap them from the car, Venkman thought. *Hatari* with ghosts. He helped Stantz to unload the smoking traps from the back, his hands sticky with ectoplasmic residue. That's the only part of this job I really hate, he had decided. The slime. Why can't ghosts be as clean as they look? No, they have to leave trails of this ecto-snot whenever they get excited. If that's what being dead is like, I ain't going.

Stantz shook the Mark II trap experimentally, watching the static charges play over its surface. "Boy, that was a rough one."

"I can't take much more of this. The pace is killing me."

Janine looked up impatiently as they entered the reception area. Venkman threw a paid invoice down on her desk. "Here's the paper on the Brooklyn job. She paid with a Visa card."

"And here are tonight's calls," she replied, passing them a bundle of work orders. Stantz shuffled through them, sorting them by way of distance and difficulty.

"Rats, Peter. We've got two more free-roaming repeaters here."

"And this is Winston Zeddemore. He came about the job."

"You're black!" Stantz said delightedly.

"Yes, I know."

"No, you see that certain forms of vapors, particularly the later types of cyclical roamers, respond better to black people." He stuck out his hand. "Ray Stantz, and this is Peter Venkman."

"Hi."

"Come on back into the equipment area, Winston, and I'll show you just what it is that we do here."

Ah, Zeddemore thought. At last I'm going to find out the real skinny. Stantz was leafing through his résumé.

"Very impressive. Strategic Air Command ECM school... black belt in karate... small-arms expert... as far as I'm concerned, Mr. Zeddemore, you're hired. Now, as you may have heard, we locate ghosts and spirits, trap them with streams of concentrated quantum energy, and remove them from people's homes, offices, and places of worship."

"Yeah, I heard that," Zeddemore replied, following Stantz down into the basement. "Now tell me what you really do."

Venkman was still standing by the desk, reading through the work orders. He calculated the rising demand for their services against the projections Spengler had made regarding approaching PKE peaks. Yeah, we'll definitely need help. Better hire the Zeddemore guy, and see about digging up another ambulance; He looked up. Janine was staring at him impatiently. "You say something?"

"I said that someone from the EPA is here to see you."

What now? "The EPA? What's he want?"

"I didn't ask him. All I know is that I haven't had a break in two weeks and you promised that you'd hire more help."

"Janine, I'm sure a woman with your qualifications would have no trouble finding a topflight job in the housekeeping or food service industries." He wandered back toward his office.

"Oh, really? I've quit better jobs than this one, believe me."

* * *

Standing in his office was the tallest, thinnest man Venkman had ever seen. He sported a fashionably trimmed red-blond beard and was dressed in a beautifully tailored three-piece suit. Venkman disliked him on sight. Another nasal-spray type.

"Can I help you?"

The man tore himself away from the collection of news clippings that Stantz had been tacking to the wall since they had started, and smiled. Venkman didn't like his smile either. Something of the predator in it, like a ferret or weasel.

"I'm Walter Peck. I represent the Environmental Protection Agency, third district."

"Great! How's it going?"

Venkman grabbed his hand and shook it warmly, managing to leave a large smear of ectoplasm on the man's suit. Peck looked at the slime with barely disguised disgust. Venkman shook his head sadly.

"Sorry about that. Holy water takes that right out."

"Holy water?"

"Right. What can I do for you?"

Peck looked him in the eyes and Venkman realized that the man wasn't especially tall, just thin. "Are you Peter Venkman?"

"Yes, I'm *Doctor* Venkman."

Peck stared at Venkman's soiled jumpsuit. "Exactly what are you a doctor of, Mr. Venkman?"

Venkman indicated the rank of framed diplomas behind the desk. Admittedly most of them belonged to Egon and Ray. "I have Ph.D.s in psychology and parapsychology."

"I see," Peck replied snidely. "And now you catch ghosts."

"You could say that," Venkman said, plopping himself down into his stuffed chair. Peck took a seat across the desk from him.

"And how many ghosts have you caught, Mr. Venkman?"

"I'm not at liberty to say."

"And where do you keep those ghosts once you catch them?"

"In a storage facility."

"And would this storage facility be located on these premises?"

"Yes, it would."

"And may I see this storage facility?"

"No, you may not."

Peck's smile dissolved instantly. "And why not, Mr. Venkman?"

Venkman's smile was all boyish innocence. "Because you didn't say the magic word."

"And what *is* the magic word, Mr. Venkman?"

"The magic word is *please*," Venkman said softly. Peck laughed nervously, totally at the end of his patience. "May I *please* see the storage facility?"

"*Why* do you want to see it?" Venkman asked sweetly.

"Well, because I'm curious. I want to know more about what you do here. Frankly, there have been a lot of wild stories in the media, and we want to assess any possible environmental impact from your operation. For instance, the storage of noxious, possibly hazardous waste materials in your basement. We want to know exactly what sort of scam you people are running here, Mr. Venkman. Now, either you show me what's down there, or I come back with a court order."

Venkman felt his blood pressure boil over. That does it. After a day like I've had, I don't have to come home and listen to this. He stood up and leaned across his desk, nose to nose with the skinny bureaucrat.

"Go ahead! Get a court order, and I'll sue you for wrongful prosecution."

Peck stood stiffly, his briefcase held in front of him like a shield. "Have it your way, Mr. Venkman."

He turned and strode quickly out of the office. Venkman followed him to the doorway. "Hey! Make yourself useful. Go save a tree! And that's *Doctor* Venkman!"

Winston Zeddemore was absolutely fascinated as he stood peering through the view slit. It's a damned prison, he thought. A prison for ghosts. Inside, the various multicolored spirits, wisps of color and light, swirled about aimlessly or slouched in despair against the walls. Occasionally one would drift up to the viewport and stare back, like a grouper in an aquarium. It was depressing, but at the same time Winston couldn't think of any other solution to letting them run loose. But this had never happened before. There had always been a few ghosts. Why so many now? Weird.

And these guys actually catch ghosts.

And I'm going to be a Ghostbuster.

Mama Zeddemore, I hope you're satisfied.

Spengler worked at the bench, repairing a damaged proton pack, muttering to himself about "hyperspatial toruses" and "magnetic monopoles," stuff even Stantz didn't understand; but at this point Stantz wasn't interested. He was worried about the grid. "Winston."

"Yes?"

"I'll show you how to unload the traps." He slid the smoking box into a slot on the wall of the storage facility. There were three, like airlocks of different sizes, for the custom traps Ray had put together. This one was a Mark II. "You set the entry grid, push this button, wait for it to cycle yellow." The slot lit up. Stantz pulled down on a heavy knife switch, and the slot emitted a loud cycled humming, like the sound a Xerox machine makes, Winston realized, as the trap was cleaned. The sound ended with a loud snap, the humming stopped, the indicator flashed.

"The light is green, the trap is clean." He tossed the little box into a bin marked for recharge. "Got it?"

"Got it. Seems simple enough."

Stantz smiled. "A lot simpler to run than to build, I can tell you."

Spengler put his head down on the bench with a low moan. "I've got to get some sleep. I'm starting to make mistakes. You okay, Ray?"

Stantz shrugged. He didn't seem to tire as fast as the others. And the job continued to be fascinating. He often came downstairs in the middle of the night to watch the ghosts through the viewing port, though lately he'd begun to have the same feelings that Zeddemore had experienced, that penning the spirits up like that was somehow wrong. But if there was an alternative to an endless matinee of *Spooks Run Wild,* he didn't know what it was. The facility was too small—this was true—but even Egon had never planned on the volume of business they were getting. Something very unsettling, very dangerous was about to break, and they had to find out what.

"Egon, I'm going to need two new purge valves. How's the grid around the storage facility holding up?"

Egon adjusted his glasses and blinked back the fatigue. "I'm worried, Ray. It's getting crowded in there. And all my recent data points to something very big on the bottom."

"How do you mean 'big'?" Zeddemore asked.

Spengler rummaged among the bits of wire, plastic, and lunch on the workbench until he located an intact Hostess Twinkie. He held it up by way of illustration.

"Well, let's say this Twinkie represents the normal

amount of psychokinetic energy in the New York area. According to this morning's PKE sample, the current level would be a Twinkie thirty-five-feet long and weighing approximately six hundred pounds."

Zeddemore whistled. "That's a big Twinkie."

Stantz nodded. "We could be on the verge of a fourfold crossover… or worse. If what we're seeing indicates a massive PKE surge, we could experience an actual rip."

The three were looking very depressed when Venkman came down the stairs. "How's the grid around the storage facility holding up?"

"It's not good, Pete."

"Tell him about the Twinkie," Winston said glumly. Venkman looked curiously at Zeddemore, then at Stantz, who shrugged.

"We had a visit from the EPA."

"What'd they want?"

"A whole lot of doodly-squat."

10

If a sane dog fights a mad dog, it's the sane dog's ear that is bitten off.

- BURMESE PROVERB

Night had come swiftly to Manhattan, the end of October bringing lengthening darkness and sunsets that crashed down like collapsing buildings. The skyscrapers glowed briefly red, then switched to their own feeble illumination, the Great White Way making a vain attempt to hold back the dusk, the billowed clouds and snapping lightning, the storms of autumn rolling in off the wind-tossed Atlantic. Approaching Halloween, the holiday of oblivion, shorn by the church from its hopeful pagan roots. Witches and spooks painted on store windows, and little Ghostbusters' no-ghost stickers, like offerings of blood to warn away the destroying angel. Or to attract something else.

A strange year, Harlan Bojay thought as he shuffled along the sidewalk. Suddenly New York is awash in superstition, and the technology of scientific spirit removal. The pockets of his greatcoat held a folded copy of *Omni* that he had found in the subway station at Times Square. He had read several articles on the new phenomenon before being asked to move on, and was pondering the question on many minds, from Walter Peck's to Peter Venkman's. Why now? Where are they all coming from, and why New York?

Lightning forked down from the roiling thunderhead, striking the cap of a nearby building. Bojay instinctively opened his mouth against the accompanying clap of sound and ducked, though it could not possibly hit him here in the street with so many tall buildings about. But something did, glancing off his shoulder and bouncing along the sidewalk. The blow stung, and Harlan looked about for some sign of trouble—a recalcitrant youth or perhaps a piece of improperly shielded machinery. There was none. He was alone on the street. He reached down and picked up the offending object.

At first it appeared to be stone, but it was not. It was a lighter substance, like terra-cotta or a given grade of ornamental concrete, and Bojay realized that it must have fallen or been blown from the rooftop by a bolt of lightning. An odd shape, like a horn or claw, he thought, peering into the hollow interior, and was startled to see a residual wash of blue static play across the inside. He dropped it on the sidewalk and peered up at the top of the building, watching flashes of light reflect from the gargoyles on the height. Yes, if it had been stone falling from up there, it would have taken my arm off. He looked again at the little claw, now lying harmless on the pavement like a cement croissant. Then he flipped his collar up and headed swiftly for the park.

High atop that building, before a templelike structure on the roof, two immense statues stood. It was a curious place to build statues, as no human ordinarily ever stood there and the building was just tall enough that they were not clearly visible from any of its neighbors, but great care seemed to have been taken in detailing them. Each depicted a doglike animal, fully the size of a man, with a flat, triangular, almost serpentine head, and four large, clawed feet. Lightning played over the huge terror-dogs, over the steep staircase, and the tall ornate metal doors that crowned them, over the ceremonial inscriptions and architectural oddities. And though they were stone, or a light grade of ornamental concrete, the eyes of the terror-dogs seemed to reflect back the energy of the storm. It crashed and cracked again, and a section of the pebbled surface fell away, freeing a glowing red eye beneath. And the claw again flexed, cracking more of itself loose.

As Dana Barrett stepped from the elevator, loud rock music suddenly competed with the fury outside. Louis's party. She had, of course, forgotten, and with Peter Venkman dropping by later any thought of attendance was out of the question. Thank God. She tiptoed toward her apartment, but Louis Tully had ears like radar.

"Oh, Dana, it's you," he said, stepping into the hall. He hurried up to her. She did her best to smile.

"Hi, Louis."

"Hey, it's crazy in there. You're missing a classic party."

"Well, actually, Louis, I have a friend coming by."

Louis was undeterred. "Great! Bring her, too, but you better hurry. I made nachos with nonfat cheese and they're almost gone. I'll make some more though."

I have to give it to him for persistence, she thought, and then had a sudden idea. Introduce Louis to Venkman. Maybe it'll scare him off once and for all. Fine, Louis. We'll stop by for a drink."

"Hey, it'll be great. You can meet all my friends, get to

know the real me..." She shut her door, leaving him talking to the number plate. He sighed and took a last shot. "I got a Twister game for later..."

Wow, she's gonna come, he thought, walking back to his apartment. She'll love the party. It'll really impress her. Maybe tonight's the night. I'll have to get rid of her girlfriend though. After all, I got great food, the latest with-it music, party games, door locked... Oh, no.

"Hey, lemme in..."

Dana tossed her coat in the closet, took off her leg warmers, and stretched out briefly in her favorite chair. It's seven. That gives me an hour before Peter gets here. I can afford to relax for a minute, then grab a shower, be all fresh when he arrives. She laughed to herself, watching the storm move off to the west over the river, the last flickering edges of lightning playing above the city. In the distance Louis's party boomed raucously. Louis Tully, Andre Wallance, Peter Venkman. I certainly can meet 'em, she thought, psyching herself up for the evening. Be ready to laugh off Venkman's childish passes, keep him off balance. But, she realized, I'm the one off balance. A month ago he was a nut, a pest. Tonight I'm having dinner with him. I have to admit, there's something in that loony approach of his that I like. Now, if I can just figure out what it is...

The phone rang, startling her out of her reverie.

"Hello... Oh, hi, Mom..."

Every Thursday, like clockwork, her mother called. No, not like clockwork, like magic. She always called when Dana was home, her voice having never appeared on the answering machine. No matter when Dana went in or out, Mother Barrett would catch her, usually, like tonight, when she didn't have time to talk. And her mother liked to talk.

Talk had been the major recreation in the Barrett household. Her father had been a railroad worker for the Boston and Maine, invalided off on a pension, which had to make do for his wife and three children. But somehow they always got by, and she and her two brothers always had whatever they needed, if not necessarily everything they wanted. There was seldom money for the movies, but Dana had new clothes each fall—not flashy but well made—and when she had expressed an interest in music, from somewhere her father had come up with a cello. Each of the children had worked after school, and her mother was always running a dozen cottage industries, so there was money for her lessons, for Doug's books, for Davey's uniforms. Now Doug was a reporter on *The Boston Globe* and little Davey was playing center field for the San Diego Padres. Mother Barrett no longer had to scrimp, proud of her three children, collecting their clippings, and looking after them as best she could via long distance. But since the boys had married, that meant mothering Dana. Mother Barrett was not yet satisfied. She wanted a son-in-law.

"Yes, everything's fine. No... nothing to speak of... Mother, I don't have time to just go out and 'meet' men... Mother! I will *not* try a dating service..."

She thought of Peter. That would scandalize the folks at home, at least give them something to talk about. Why not?

"I can't stay on the phone too long, Mom. I've got a date and I've got to get... Yes, I said a date... He's very nice, Mom. He's a Ghostbuster... Yes, the ones on television... I'll tell you all about it the next time you call... Okay, you can call tomorrow... I promise, 'bye."

Yes, Mom. A scientist. A loony, little-kid scientist. She closed her eyes and put her head back, not noticing that the storm had returned, the clouds pressing in against her windows, the ominous rumble of ripple lightning echoing over the bump-a-doop of Louis's party. And then, suddenly, a low, eerie moan. A drawn-out sigh. As if something very large and very old was awakening.

Her eyes opened immediately and she looked toward the kitchen. Intensely bright light was coming from under the door. As she watched, mesmerized, the door buckled, then drew in, like a great rhythmic pulse. Like a heartbeat. No…

"Oh, no!" she exclaimed, and started to rise, but a pair of dark, scaly hands ripped upward out of the chair and locked around her waist, pinning her to the cushions. She had time for half a scream before the second pair took her by the chest and across the mouth. The chair began to turn slowly toward the kitchen.

This isn't happening, she thought, struggling against the awful embrace. I'll wake up in a minute. The door was pulsing now, like a giant membrane; and then the chair began to move toward it, gathering speed. With a roar the door swung back, revealing a fiery chamber where her kitchen had been and, standing to receive her, the looming presence of a terror-dog. There was no way to struggle, no way to scream, and mercifully she passed out as the chair slid into the flames, the door closing behind it.

Coincidentally, in a cab heading uptown on Central Park West, Peter Venkman was also thinking of his childhood. Earlier that month one of the supermarket tabloids had run a profile on Venkman, charging that he had been a carnival con man during his summers away from college. Venkman had been furious. But you *were* a carny barker, Stantz had said, not understanding Peter's anger. What's the problem? Peter had refused to talk about it. It wasn't just a carny, he thought, it was my home. And I wasn't just a barker, I was the best. But there was no way to explain that to a reporter who was looking for an angle to titillate an audience that had trouble with the *TV Guide* crossword puzzle, to whom investigative journalism was a report on Lady Di's latest snit. He had held his tongue and planned his revenge, the next day giving Janine a card with written instructions on exactly what to do if the offices of the newspaper called. Then he waited for a combination of the right circumstances. It took ten days.

"Dr. Venkman, this is Bill Hibbler at the *National Reporter.* We did a story on you?"

"Several stories, as I remember. On each of us, and on the firm."

"Well… yes… but I'm calling on a different matter."

I'll bet you are. "And what might that be?"

"We seem to have a ghost."

The phantasm, a large and voracious creature, had terrorized the editorial offices of the *Reporter,* jamming typewriters, exposing film, setting fires in the wastebaskets. The toilets had overflowed, lightbulbs exploded, the phones sang obscene ditties. The operation of the scandal sheet had come to a standstill. The presses were full of ectoslime.

"That sounds like a class-nine autonomous roaming disrupter," Venkman had said sagely. "But I got the impression from your articles that you didn't believe in ghosts."

"Of course we believe in ghosts," Hibbler said defensively. "We never said that."

"No, what you said was that we were a bunch of fakes, charlatans, bunco artists."

"I…"

"Interesting word. Haven't heard anyone say *bunco* since the days when I was with the carnival. But you know about that too."

There was a long silence. "What do you want?"

"Oh, I'd say a retraction, an apology to Ghostbusters,

all of our employees and our families, and the admission that you libeled us. That should do it."

"We never retract!"

"Good policy. Enjoy your ghost."

Venkman hung up the phone and looked at his watch. I give them forty-five minutes, tops. It took forty-two. Venkman made the arrangements, quoted an outrageous figure, and took Hibbler's MasterCard number. Then he went looking for Zeddemore.

"Winston."

"Yo."

"Remember that class nine we dropped off last night. Well, it seems they didn't want it after all."

"Some people just can't make up their minds." Zeddemore laughed.

Right. I'm a pretty easy-going guy, Venkman thought, but nobody dumps on my dad. Peter Venkman had been born on the lot of King City Attractions, in a tent, on a field, in Sedalia, Missouri. It was the last night of the week-long run and his birth had been exceptionally easy. His mother had been taking tickets. When the show had started she'd closed the booth, gone back to the dressing tent, and had Peter. His birth had been unattended, but his baptism had been a cause for celebration by everyone from his impresario father to the lowliest rigger.

The carny wintered in Iowa City, and Peter had attended the schools there, touring summers with the show throughout the Com Belt states. He worked as a candy butcher, as a roustabout, as a painter and carpenter, but it was at the games of chance that he really excelled. Whatever game Peter was running always pulled in the nightly top take and he became adept at judging people, knowing who would bite and who wouldn't, knowing who wouldn't squawk at a good-natured skinning and who came, with dreams in their eyes, expecting to lose but hoping to win. And somewhere along the way he learned the lesson that his father had been teaching him. You can take a sucker but don't break a dream. He watched nightly as the people played his games, and he saw those dreams. And when he could, he rewarded them. And one day he realized what the dreams were that had been growing in him.

"Dad, I wanna go to college."

His father had smiled. "Why, Peter? What do you want to do?"

And he confessed that he didn't know. His father had smiled again, then laughed softly. "You'll tell me when you find out? If you find out?"

It was a strange question, but Peter Venkman was used to strange questions on the carny. "I guess you'll be the first to know."

He watched the upper Sixties slide by outside the cab window. Well, I just may finally be finding out. I wish the old man had lived to see it. The cab pulled up at a light on Central Park West at Seventy-third and the cabbie turned around.

"Excuse me, but aren't you one of those Ghostbusters?"

Venkman smiled. "Yes, I'm Dr. Venkman."

"Whaddaya make a that, Doc?"

Venkman leaned forward and looked to where the man was pointing. A spectacular lightning display was hovering over Dana Barrett's building.

Louis Tully was doing his best to keep his "classic" party going. He had set out the plates of expensive delicacies the man at the import store had recommended and made sure that the music was loud, at least loud enough to be a continual reminder in Dana's apartment. But where was she? Maybe her girlfriend hadn't arrived yet. He surreptitiously smelled his breath and assured himself that he was at his best. I look good, he decided. I look very New York, very hip. She can't help but notice. He opened a Perrier and struck a casual pose.

"Louis, do you have any Excedrin or Extra-Strength Tylenol?" a tall, chunky woman asked him. Her name was Phyllis Puffet, she ran an answering service, and, like everyone else there, Louis did her taxes.

"I have acetylsalicylic acid but I get the generic from Walgreen's cause I can get six hundred tablets for thirty-five percent less than the cost of three hundred of the name brand. Do you have a headache?"

Phyllis Puffet frowned. "I'll ask someone else," she said, and moved off toward the bathroom. Louis spotted two men pondering the lox platter.

"How's it going, Bob? Irving? That's Nova Scotia salmon. The real thing. It costs twenty-four ninety-five a pound, but really twelve forty-eight a pound after tax. I'm writing this whole party off as a promotional expense. That's why I invited clients instead of friends. Try that Brie. It's dynamite at room temperature. Maybe I should turn up the heat a bit..."

They looked at each other, wondering whether one of them should answer, but Louis had already moved off. He was being accosted by a tall pouting blonde in a dance leotard.

"Louis, this party is boring," she whined. "I'm going home."

"Aw, don't do that, Andrea. C'mon, if we dance, maybe some of the others will start dancing."

"Okay."

Andrea immediately launched into a wild frug, Louis struggling to keep up until the doorbell rang. At last, he thought. Dana. But it was only a short, pudgy couple. He helped them out of their coats.

"Everybody, this is Ted and Annette Fleming. Ted has a small carpet cleaning business in receivership, but Annette is drawing a salary from a deferred bonus from two years ago and the house has fifteen thousand left at eight percent..." Louis babbled cheerfully as he detoured around the wildly dancing Andrea and took their coats to the bedroom.

The terror-dog had made its way down the side of the building and stepped through the bedroom window, shedding glass and broken mullions like flies off armor plate. The quarry was close, the one with whom the great transformational joining would be resolved. It was here, within this very area, but not within this chamber itself. It sniffed a few coats on the bed, then sprang to alertness as Louis Tully opened the door. It is him, the guardian thought, but before it could act, Louis tossed the coats over it and left, slamming the door behind him. It is nearsighted, decided the guardian, shaking off the coats. It is ugly, too, but I have my duty. It let loose a terrible roar.

The guests had frozen at the sound. Louis looked up in annoyance. "Okay, who brought the dog?"

With an explosion of wooden fragments the guardian landed in a crouch in the center of the room, and the guests scattered in panic. Louis dropped his Perrier and scrambled for the door, yelling incoherently. Something told him not to argue as it roared and started after him. He dashed into the hall, slamming the door to his apartment, then sprinted toward the elevators. Behind him he heard the thing break into the corridor. "Hold the elevator!" he screamed, squeezing in among a group of couples obviously going out to the theater. The doors closed, then bowed inward as the beast hit them, but held. The car started to descend. Louis looked at the couples, who were staring at him in amazement. "I think there's a bear in the hall," he wheezed. They moved as far away from Tully as the car would let them.

The doorman was announcing two elegantly dressed visitors when Louis Tully bounded through the revolving door, screaming, "Help, there's a bear in my apartment!"

The visitors looked at one another, and the doorman, never a fan of Tully's, frowned. Now he's got animals up there. At that moment the revolving door spun violently and the terror-dog bounded through, running down the doorman and chasing the terrified Tully toward Central Park.

In the park, strolling along a quiet lane toward the Sheep Meadow and sharing a bottle of New York State red, Harlan Bojay and Robert Learned Coombs were discussing the world situation. Bojay, as usual, was waxing loquacious.

"I must agree with you about Central America, but on the other point we remain in contention. I think a good heavyweight can take a karate black belt every time."

"Run, run, run," screamed Louis Tully, streaking between them, almost knocking the precious bottle from Harlan Bojay's grasp. He looked sadly after the man.

"Those joggers have no sense of common politeness," he said stiffly. At that moment the terror-dog bounded by, scattering gravel. Bojay's jaw dropped.

"That is one speedy mutt!"

Coombs nodded. "He's a big one. You don't want to mess with that breed."

"Some sort of fighting spaniel I would guess." Bojay shook his head. "This city gets weirder all the time."

Louis Tully pounded through a tunnel and caught sight of the Tavem-on-the-Green restaurant ahead. He could see the well-dressed patrons inside, sitting at their elegant meals, perfect waiters gliding between the tables. He could see everything but a door. He ran along the windows, desperately searching for an entrance. There had to be one, he told himself. Then he was paralyzed by the sound of a low growl off in the bushes. No, let me in. He turned and pounded in terror on the glass. The people inside looked up. Oh, they see me, he thought. Save me, please. I'll do your taxes for nothing. The dog growled again.

Then, as if all their heads were connected to a common swivel, they turned back to their dinners. Something moved in the bushes behind Louis Tully.

He turned. It was standing there, drooling from its open mouth, four-inch fangs glittering like crystal in the light from the restaurant. It slowly started toward him. No, this isn't happening to me.

"Nice doggie. Nice," he whimpered.

Jerry Linz was having a bad night, first with the wind and then with the damned lightning. Nobody wanted a romantic ride through Central Park in this weather. Cold too. He pulled a flask from his hip pocket and nipped on it. Medicinal purposes, he thought, watching a strange, disheveled little man in horn rims come loping down the sidewalk. The creature veered from its course and bounced straight up to his horse. Great, Linz thought. This nut wants a ride.

The little man took the horse's bridle and leaned in conspiratorially. "I am Vinz Clortho, Key master of Gozer, Volguus Zildrohar, Lord of the Sebouillia. Are you the Gatekeeper?"

"Hey! That's enough of that. He pulls the wagon, I make the deals. You wanna ride?"

The little man stared up at him. Linz swore that, just for a second, his eyes looked red. Bright red. "Are you the Gatekeeper?"

"No, I'm the governor of New Jersey. Now, get outta here."

The little man growled horribly, sending Jerry Linz scuttling back on his seat. A gun, he thought. Why won't the cops let us carry guns? "You will perish in flames, subcreature!" the man declared. "Gozer will destroy you and your kind."

He leaned back into the horse. "Wait for the sign. All prisoners will be released." Then he turned and scampered away. Like a monkey, Linz thought. Some kinda religious monkey nut.

"What a jerk!" he muttered.

11

The course of true love never did run smooth.

- WILLIAM SHAKESPEARE

Venkman stopped to buy a bouquet of flowers from a sidewalk vendor, straightened his tie, and trotted up to the front of Dana's building. The lobby was filled with chattering guests, a few of them on the verge of hysteria. The doorman was nowhere to be seen, but two maintenance men were struggling to right a large magazine rack that had come loose from a wall and fallen over. Several of New York's finest were taking statements and conferring with one another, and Venkman had a sudden premonition that the night might turn out differently from what he had planned. One of the policemen noticed his curiosity and walked over.

"You got business here?" he asked pleasantly.

Venkman indicated the flowers. "Just taking my girl to dinner. What's going on?"

The policeman had not recognized him and seemed satisfied with his explanation. "Some moron brought a cougar to a party and it went berserk."

"Hey, that's New York."

"Yeah, I guess so."

Venkman headed for the elevators. The premonition had turned to apprehension. Could trouble be far behind?

On Dana's floor there were more cops. They clustered about a splintered door, interviewing a group of shaken-looking people. The party with the cougar, he wondered, or something else? He stepped quietly around them and went on to her apartment, rang the bell, and waited. Well, it seems quiet. Too quiet. This time he knocked.

"Dana?"

The door opened and Venkman dropped the flowers in surprise. Dana had been transformed. She stood before him in a loose-flowing gown, hanging low off the shoulder. Her hair was billowed outward, as if caught in a photograph, yet windblown and alive; her lips were slightly parted and wet, her skin glistening softly. And her eyes. They were wide, luminous, boring into him with the intensity of a single thought. Peter Venkman knew what that thought was. He knew that expression, but he had not expected to see it on Dana. At least not at the door.

"This is a new look for you, isn't it?" He smiled lecherously, but it didn't take. Something was going on that he was unaware of, as though he had come in in the middle of a movie and had been asked to make a decision on the action. What the heck?

"What happened to *you!* The cop downstairs said an animal got loose up here. What's the story? Are you all right?"

Okay, I said it, but it isn't registering. It's like someone hit her over the head, or put something in her drink, or... She leaned closer, and the sheer sexual power of her almost flattened him. When she spoke her voice was husky and animal.

"Are you the Keymaster?"

For a moment he wondered if this was some sort of bizarre sexual game being played for his benefit.

"Not that I know of."

She closed the door. Well, that was the wrong thing to say. He knocked again. When in Babylon…

"Are you the Keymaster?" she asked again, as if she had never seen him before. He nodded vigorously.

"I'm the Keymaster, right."

She took his hand and pulled him in, the door swinging closed behind him. Lord, what a mess. "Dana, what is it? What happened?"

"I am Zuul," she replied. "I am the Gatekeeper."

Sure you are. And I'm the Lone Ranger. Kid's got it bad, a four-alarm case of possession. Keep your sense of proportion here, Venkman. Might be more of them around, looking for souls to eat.

He stepped over a rotted gray lump that he recognized as the remains of her piano bench. The piano itself looked like it had been dredged up from a shipwreck, the wood pale and peeling, jellylike streams of ectoplasm dripping from the cracks and puddling on the floor. The couch and chairs had been reduced to blackened frames, the windows were gone, scorch marks around the doorway to the kitchen. Everything but graffiti. As he watched, a section of wallpaper unrolled itself with a plop, slime oozing out from behind it.

"You know, I really think you should pick up a little when company's coming," he ventured. She ignored him and walked to the window. "Hey, Dana…"

She raised her arms against the darkness and was rewarded with a shower of ball lightning over the West Side. Venkman shivered. Nice trick. Then she turned back to him, her body silhouetted in the flimsy gown against the fall of fire outside. Venkman felt a spasm of lust, and tried to force it back.

"We must prepare for the coming of Gozer."

Yeah, right. He edged around to the side. She was too close to the open window. She might want to go skydiving. Get her away from the edge. She was watching him, her tongue moving on her teeth. Humor her. No windows in the bedroom.

"Okay, I'll help. Should we make a dip or something?"

"He is the Destructor," she whispered, moving closer.

"Really, I can't wait to meet him." He took her hand. She felt normal except for the discharge of static electricity when their fingers met. "Hey, as long as we're waiting to meet him, I'd really like to try something with you—in the bedroom."

The bedroom was relatively undamaged. She moved immediately to the bed and stretched luxuriously on the coverlet. "Do you want this body?"

"Is that a trick question?"

She purred seductively and ground her hips into the bed. I sure can pick them, Venkman thought. Them? "Look, I'll tell you what. I'll just borrow your body for a while and get it right back to you."

"Take me now."

He groped for his penlight and flashed the beam into one eye, then the other. Hoo-boy, nobody home.

"Well, I make it a rule never to sleep with possessed people," he said, taking a step away, but she caught him by the lapels and pulled him down on top of her. The kiss almost tore his lips off. Good Lord, he thought. If she's anywhere near this good on her own, I'll marry her. After what seemed like swimming the English Channel underwater, he fought his way up for air. "Actually it's more of a policy than a rule."

"I want you," she said.

"I don't know," he said, staggering to his feet and holding her wrists at arm's length. "You've got two people in there already. It could get a little crowded. Now then, I want you to lay back and relax."

She did, her hands crossing over her breasts like an Egyptian sarcophagus. Venkman caught his breath.

"Now, I'm going to speak to Dana, and I want Dana to answer."

"I am Zuul. I am..."

"Right... You're the Gatekeeper. But I want Dana," he said commandingly. "Dana, speak to me...

Her lids rolled back, and for an instant the eyes inside were glowing red. When she spoke it was the voice of earthquakes, tidal waves, of avalanches and the grating, rumbling fall of ancient cities. It was the sound of pure chaos.

"There is no Dana. I am Zuul."

Venkman jumped back. "Whoa! Nice voice." She started to sit up again, but he restrained her with a touch on the shoulder. She smiled maniacally and did things with her tongue that made him extremely uneasy.

"All right, Zuul. Listen carefully, Zully baby. I don't know where you came from, or why, but I want you to get out of here and leave Dana alone. I'm going to count to ten, and when I'm finished you'd better be gone. Okay? Here goes. One... two..."

A shudder ran through Dana Barrett's body and she laughed soundlessly. Then, slowly, she began to rise in the air. Venkman stared in disbelief as she came to rest, floating a good three feet above the bed, the flimsy dress hanging free.

I'm not really seeing this, he thought. It's all a trick of the mind, like Mandrake the Magician. Or wires. Maybe with wires. He ran his hands over, under, and around the body, but felt nothing except the crackling of tiny electrical charges. Boy, this would have been great back in the carnival, but, as far as I'm concerned, it makes for a lousy date. He sat down on the bed, wondering how to get her down.

On the Henry Hudson Parkway, Winston Zeddemore and Ray Stantz were heading for the third call of the night. They had only a single trap left. It was just as well, as they were both completely wasted.

Winston drove, his mind on the night, as Stantz sipped from a can of beer and pored over a set of blueprints. Winston was thinking about God. That didn't surprise him. Ever since he'd started collecting the spirits of the dead he'd been wondering about his own religious upbringing. The Zeddemores were a strict Baptist family, and neither the Air Force nor the street had been able to knock that out of him. Sure, I don't go to church much anymore, but that doesn't mean I don't believe. Lately though. I'm not sure just what I do believe.

"Hey, man. What's that you're so involved with there?"

Stantz smiled. He'd liked Zeddemore from the first, and since Venkman had gotten involved with this Barrett woman and Egon and Janine had become an item, Ray Stantz tended to spend a lot of time with Zeddemore. A voracious learner, he was happily absorbing Zeddemore's experiences, idioms, folk tales, and street stories. Earlier that week Winston had taken him home for dinner, and Lucille Zeddemore had fawned all over him. Her younger children—Winston's brothers and sisters—had pressed him for stories, and he'd thoroughly enjoyed himself. The nicest thing about being out in the real world was that you got to deal more often with people. I was too insulated in the university.

"Oh, these are the blueprints of the structural ironwork in Dana Barrett's apartment building… and they're most unusual."

Winston nodded. "Are you a Christian, Ray."

"Uh-huh."

"Me too," Winston said. It made him feel better, seeing as how he was driving an ambulance full of little metal coffins—coffins full of spooks, specters, wraiths, geists, and ghosts.

Stantz rattled the blueprints and brought a section close to his eye. "Boy! Solid cores of shielded selenium three twenty-five."

"Do you believe in God?" Winston asked, continuing to disjoint the conversation.

"No. But I liked Jesus' style."

"Me too. Parts of the Bible are great."

"The whole roofcap was fabricated with a magnesium-tungsten alloy."

A car full of waving teenagers pulled around them. Neither noticed.

"Ray, do you remember something in the Bible about a day when the dead would rise up from their graves?"

"And the seas would boil…"

"Right," Winston said excitedly. "And the sky would fall…"

"Judgment Day."

"Yeah, Judgment Day."

They sat quietly for a moment, each alone with his thoughts. Stantz took a long pull on his beer, then passed it to Zeddemore.

"Every ancient religion had its own myth about the end of the world," he said softly.

"Well, has it occurred to you that the reason that we've been so busy lately is that the dead have been rising from their graves?"

"There's a thought."

* * *

Dana Barrett still floated above the bed while Peter Venkman rummaged through the drawers of her dresser. She's an artist, he thought. She's got to have some Valium somewhere.

Egon Spengler checked the needle on the big PKE gauge, the one connected to the fixed plasmatometer on top of their roof antennae. It had pegged again. He switched it to a higher scale, watched the needle drop back, and noted the new reading on his clipboard. Up 4.7 percent in the last hour alone. Something had to break soon.

Ecto-One pulled up to the great timber and stone gatehouse of Fort Detmerring. A single light burned over a placard announcing the times of tours, and opening and closing hours. Silently, Stantz and Zeddemore helped each other into their proton packs. As they finished, two figures loomed up out of the darkness, wearing dark jackets and Stetsons. Stantz nodded pleasantly.

"Evening."

"Evening," the park ranger replied, taking the clipboard and initialing the forms. He affixed a GSA purchase order and passed it back. "We've had quite a problem here for some time. I called your outfit a couple of weeks ago."

"Busy time of year," Winston said. He tested the charge on the accelerator. It looked good for one more job.

"Nobody likes to talk about this sort of thing."

"You don't have to worry about that with us, sir," Ray Stantz assured him.

"Yeah," Zeddemore added. "We'll believe anything."

* * *

"Egon, the police are here."

"Picking up or dropping off?"

"Dropping off."

Spengler wiped his hands on a rag and went upstairs, grateful for any distraction. There were times when he could swear he heard moaning from the containment, which troubled him more than he liked to admit. Janine smiled warmly as he passed by and he favored her with a wink. Venkman had told him that girls liked that. Girls were a new experience to Egon Spengler, something to be studied. And enjoyed, he decided, pleased at himself over this revelation. Janine followed him out to where a police van was idling before the building. A sergeant was waiting at the rear. He offered Spengler his hand.

"Rosenberg, Twenty-fourth Precinct. We picked this guy up and now we don't know what to do with him. Bellevue doesn't want him and I'm afraid to put him in the lockup. There's something too weird about him. He'd cause a riot or they'd kill him. Anyway, I know you guys are into this stuff, so I thought I'd check with you."

The man in the back—straitjacketed and tied to the bench with leather restraints—still retained a weird dignity, the like of which Egon Spengler had never seen. The little man looked up and asked seriously, "Are you the Gatekeeper?"

Ah, Spengler thought, perhaps the pieces are falling into place. I've been waiting for this one.

"Bring him inside, Officer."

Stantz and Zeddemore had split up at the entrance to the armory and Ray was now prowling along the parapet, swinging his detectors from side to side. Nothing. He detoured around a stack of cannonballs and made for a lighted entrance. The plaque said that this was a fully restored replica of an officer's room, complete with uniforms, furniture, and accoutrements. Fascinated, Stantz walked in.

The little man had been divested of his restraints and given a Rubik's Cube to occupy his attention. He was sniffing the various colors, trying to decide which one to eat as Spengler readied the visual imaging tracker. An aluminum collander had been strapped to the man's head, and thousands of wires connected it through the archetype transliterator to a 19-inch color TV. Janine was watching, fascinated, as the image appeared there in flickering colors. It was not the head of a man, but that of a large, doglike creature. Jeez, what a creep, Janine decided.

"Who are you?" Spengler asked.

"I am Vinz Clortho—Keymaster of Gozer," the man replied. Spengler sat bolt upright in his seat. Yes, this was the missing piece.

"And I am Egon Spengler, creature of Earth, doctor of physics, graduate of M.I.T."

Janine was going through the little man's wallet. "According to this his name is Louis Tully. And his address, it looks real familiar."

"Oh, no," Vinz said firmly. "Tully is the fleshbag I'm using. I must wait inside for the sign."

"Do you want some coffee while you're waiting?"

"Do I?"

"Yes, have some."

"Yes," Tully replied. "Have some." Janine hurried to put some water on to boil. Louis Tully was making her extremely nervous. Spengler, satisfied that his recorders and monitors were working correctly, smiled at Tully. Tully returned the smile, and took a large bite out of the Rubik's Cube, scattering the colored pieces. Spengler gently removed the remains from his hand and gave him a bowl of popcorn.

"Vinz, what sign are you waiting for?"

"Gozer the Traveler will come in one of the prechosen forms," he replied excitedly. "During the Rectification of the Vuldronaii, the Traveler came as a very large and moving Torb. Then, of course, in the Third Reconciliation of the Last of the Meketrex Supplicants, they chose a new form for him, that of a Sloar. Many Shubbs and Zulls knew what it was to be roasted in the depths of the Sloar that day, I can tell you."

Spengler stared at Tully, then looked at Janine, who made the traditional finger-circle motion for loony. The phone rang suddenly, startling them all. Spengler and Janine each made a dive for it, bumping heads. He let her take it but she handed it to him and smiled nervously. Tully gave off a raucous cackle, then went back to figuring out how to remove the popcorn from the bowl by passing the pieces directly through the glass, as Spengler raised the phone to his ear.

"Hello?"

"It's Peter, Egon. I've got a problem."

He's got a problem. "What is it?"

"I'm with Dana Barrett and she's floating three feet off the bed."

"Does she want to be?"

"I don't think so," Venkman replied haltingly. He sounded tired. "It's more of the Gozer thing. She says she's the Gatekeeper. Does that make any sense to you?"

"Some," Spengler said slowly, preoccupied with Louis Tully. The little man had given up on the bowl and was trying to scratch his ear with one foot. "I just met the Keymaster, Peter. He's here with me now."

There was a long silence. "Peter, are you there?"

"Yeah, yeah. I was just thinking. It probably wouldn't be a good idea for them to get together at this point."

"I agree."

"You have to keep him there, Egon. Do whatever you have to do, but don't let him leave. He could be very dangerous."

Spengler looked nervously at Tully. He had discovered the coffee. He poured a handful of coffee crystals into his mouth and chewed them up, then picked the pot of boiling water from the Bunsen burner. He sniffed it and took a long drink. It didn't seem to bother him.

"Egon?"

"All right, I'll try."

"I'll spend the night here and get back first thing in the morning."

"All right, Peter. Good night."

He hung up the phone and glanced at Tully, who had fallen asleep on the couch with his arms and legs in the air. Janine moved over and huddled protectively against Spengler.

"Egon, there's something very strange about that man. I'm very psychic usually, and right now I have this terrible feeling that something awful is going to happen to you." She sniffed. "I'm afraid you're going to die."

Spengler blinked at her. "Die in what sense?"

"In the physical sense."

Spengler had thought a lot about death since they had started Ghostbusters, but always in abstract terms. Death was not something that would happen to him, at least not in the sense that it happened to anyone else. Other people died. Quietly or messily, they snuffed out. But he would discorporate, transmogrify directly to another plane, go on in the vast cosmic continuum as a spark of energy. The body wasn't very important when you compared it to the mind, and Egon Spengler had a very large, though somewhat disordered mind. But Venkman had been teaching him about girls and he did vaguely understand Janine's need. She was afraid. Comfort her.

"I don't care," he said at last. "I see us as tiny parts of a vast organism, like two bacteria living on a rotting speck of dust, floating in an infinite void."

Janine sighed. "That's so romantic."

She put her arms around Spengler and held him tightly, an experience with which the scientist was totally unfamiliar. A mating ritual, he realized. Respond. He put his hands awkwardly on her back. "You have nice clavicles," he stuttered.

"You're sweet, Egon."

I wonder where Stantz is, he thought. We're going to need him.

Stantz had discovered a treasure trove. Having stripped off his pack and coverall, he was trying on a Revolutionary War officer's uniform, complete with sabre and tricornered hat. He appraised himself in the full-length mirror. Not bad. Captain Stantz reporting, General Washington. The men are ready and awaiting your orders. I would have done well back then, he thought.

He removed the saber and hung it from the doorknob, then tested the bed with his hand. Amazingly soft, probably filled with down, and pillows stuffed with feathers. Not shredded foam and kapok. God, I was born in the wrong century. He stretched out on the bed and stared up at the ceiling. Those were exciting times.

He fell asleep almost immediately, dreaming of Valley Forge, of Yorktown and Bunker Hill, leaving New York and ghosts far behind. Consequently, he didn't see the light on his PKE meter come on.

A moment later the saber began to move ever so slightly in its sheath, then the sheath itself began tapping rhythmically on the wall as a glowing light slowly seeped in through the cracks in the door. It formed into a pink cloud, then rose gently toward the ceiling, seemingly fascinated with the sleeping man. Stantz tossed in his dreams and rolled over on his back. The mist began to descend.

Stantz awoke to find himself face to face with the ghostly apparition they had come to remove, his body paralyzed with fear. And yet, she was beautiful. It seemed impossible that anything so beautiful would harm him. Then why am I so terrified?

The apparition smiled and drifted slowly toward the end of the bed. If I hold still, Stantz thought, it'll go away and I can follow it. I was a fool to let down my guard. That won't happen again. He opened his eyes. The phantom woman had vanished. Well, that's the end of that, he decided, and started to rise…

His belt suddenly came undone.

The buttons on his pants began to open one by one.

He felt an electric sensation between his legs.

You know, he thought, maybe we've been going about this all wrong. Maybe some of these spirits are friendly…

Beneficial…

Fantastic…

He closed his eyes. I don't think we're going to find this one, he thought.

Winston had come up empty. If there was a ghost at Fort Detmerring, it was a real quiet one. I wonder how Ray's doing. He came around the end of a corridor and suddenly heard voices from behind a wooden door. And light inside, through the cracks. Ray?

"Hey, Stantz. You okay in there?"

"Later, man!"

Zeddemore shrugged. He's the boss. He must know what he's doing. He ambled off in search of a cigarette.

Back in the apartment, Peter Venkman had at last fallen into a troubled sleep. And by his side, drugged, possessed, and three feet in the air, Dana Barrett slumbered on.

12

I hate all bungling like sin, but most of all bungling in state affairs, which produces nothing but mischief to thousands and millions.

- GOETHE

Walter Peck was feeling the self-satisfaction of a man who was about to get revenge on an enemy, and he wasn't entirely sure that he liked it. Revenge wasn't the point, he told himself. I'm a public servant, looking out for the public good. What I do I do out of responsibility, duty, and the law. I don't do it because I like it; I do it because it has to be done. Having told himself all of these things, he at last permitted himself a thin, sneering smile.

Duty or not, I am really going to enjoy sticking it to Peter Venkman.

The little convoy turned onto Mott Street and rolled up to the firehouse with its garish neon sign. A county sheriff's car blocked the garage opening. A New York City police car and a Con Edison van pulled up in the alley alongside. And Peck, in a burst of missionary zeal, parked his lime green United States government interagency motor pool sedan in front of a fire plug and stepped out. The others were waiting for him.

"Don't take any guff off these people, gentlemen," Peck announced. "They're a bunch of con men, so be on your toes."

"Can we get on with this?" Bennett, the NYPD captain, asked impatiently. He'd worked with Peck before and didn't like him.

"Certainly."

Peck stepped through into the garage bay, followed by NYPD, Con Edison, and two New York county sheriff's deputies. He decided to ignore the receptionist and head directly for the basement, but she jumped up and blocked his path.

"I beg your pardon! Just where do you think you're going?"

Peck was not to be trifled with. "Step aside, Miss, or I'll have you arrested for interfering with a police officer."

Janine looked to the bored captain, who nodded sourly, but held her ground. "Who do you think you're talking to, Mister? Do I look like a child? You can't come in here without some kind of warrant or writ or something."

Peck held up a sheaf of papers and ticked them off with one finger. "Cease and Desist All Commerce Order. Seizure of Premises and Chattels. Ban on the Use of Public Utilities for Non-Licensed Waste Handlers. Federal Entry and Inspection Order. Satisfied?"

He led the little troop down into the basement, Janine falling doggedly in behind. This is worse than Poland, she thought.

"Egon, I tried to stop them," she called, but Spengler and Peck were already at it.

"You are dealing with something you don't understand."

"Then I'll learn all about it as we dismantle your operation."

"No, the damage that could be caused..."

"I knew you were using harmful chemicals!"

"It's not chemicals. What's wrong with you? Don't you realize what we're doing? Don't you watch television?"

Peck sneered. "Not if I can help it."

Throughout it all, Peck's entourage had stood gaping at the workbenches, the reinforced containment wall with its warning stripes, the trap locks and recharge bins, the control panels and warning lights. Louis Tully, the Keymaster, stood in one corner, mumbling secret promises to Gozer between bites of a Twinkie. "This is impossible," Spengler shouted.

"Now, look, you fraud—" Peck began, but Captain Bennett laid a restraining hand on his shoulder.

"Watch it..."

Peck nodded. "Now, look, *Dr.* Spengler. You've seen the court orders. You are no longer in charge here. I am. Now, I want to see what's in there. Either you shut off those beams or we'll shut them off for you."

Spengler tried a reasoned approach. "You can see what's inside through the monitor if you wish. Here..."He reached up and turned it on. Peck shook his head.

"I told you, I'm not interested in television," he scoffed.

Peter Venkman appeared on the stairs, disheveled and red-eyed. "At ease, Officers. I'm Peter Venkman. I think there's been some kind of misunderstanding here, and I want to cooperate in any way that I can."

Peck rounded on him. "Forget it, Venkman. You had your chance to cooperate, but you thought it was more fun to insult me. Now it's my turn, smart guy."

"He wants to shut down the storage grid," Spengler cried. Janine ran to him and threw her arms around him protectively, and Tully, sensing what he assumed was a cue for action, huddled in to Spengler's other side. They looked like some sort of very strange war memorial. Well, Venkman thought, it has been a very strange war.

He turned to the police captain, who appeared to be the sanest of the lot.

"If you turn that thing off, we won't be responsible for the consequences."

"On the contrary," Peck snapped. "You will be held completely responsible. Turn it off."

But the Con Ed man had been looking through the monitor screen. He turned back, his face pale, and made no move to do anything. Venkman placed a hand on the man's arm.

"Don't do it! I'm warning you."

The technician looked nervously around the room, then appealed to the police captain. "Maybe he's right. I've never seen anything like this. I don't know..."

"Just do it!" Peck shrilled. "Nobody asked for your opinion."

The technician nodded, licked his lips nervously, then reached for the switch, but Venkman threw both arms around his waist. "Don't be a jerk!"

The two deputy sheriffs moved in to break up the scuffle. Venkman glared at Peck. "You dumb jerk."

"If he tries that again," Peck replied. "Shoot him."

"You do your own job, Pencilneck. Don't tell me how to do mine."

"Thank you, Officer," Venkman said.

"You shut up too. You, Con Ed. Turn it off." The technician stepped up to the switch, took hold, and looked back nervously. Venkman, Spengler, Janine, and Tully had backed away toward the stairs. The two county cops were already gone. Spengler looked at the man, and mimed a huge explosion.

"Do it, now!"

Con Ed snapped down the huge knife switch, then jumped away as if he had been stung. There was the sudden sound of dying dynamos, a falling electrical hum, and the lights went out. Red warning bulbs began to flash, a siren started to scream, and a horrible tremor ran through the floor. The monitor screen exploded. The bricks in the containment wall began to loosen, emitting streams of blinding light and the hideous drip of ectoplasm. And under it all, one deep, terrifying sigh. A sigh of relief. A sigh of satisfaction. The sound of a monstrous creature that had just become uncaged.

That was enough. They fought their way up the stairs and out onto the street, pursued by coruscations of colored light, unearthly sounds, tremors in the very fabric of reality. The old firehouse shuddered, all of the windows blew out, light bulbs exploded, and the heavy floorboards danced like piano keys. With a crack the radio and monitoring tower on the roof gave a jerk and disappeared downward, sliding into the roof, and a second later a titanic geyser of glowing energy shot skyward, a hundred feet in the air. It hung there a second before bits and trails of light began to disperse to all points of the compass. "There they go," Spengler said in awe. "I never thought I'd see it. A full four-dimensional crossrip."

"It's time. It's coming. This is the sign," whispered Louis the Keymaster, beside himself with joy.

"It's a sign all right," Janine moaned. "Going out of business."

Peter Venkman had nothing to say. He simply turned and knocked Walter Peck on his ass.

13

We learn geology the morning after the earthquake.

- EMERSON

Dozens of emergency vehicles converged on the old Mott Street firehouse, and soon the intersection was jammed with squad cars, fire engines, Con Ed trucks, ambulances, and civil defense vans. After Captain Bennett had separated Venkman and Peck and told them both to shut up, tactical command passed to Spengler. He was desperately trying to deal with dozens of "experts," while enduring the quizzing of a bomb squad man in a bulky decontamination suit.

"Does it contain TCE, PCB, or tailings from styrene esters, or any poly fluoric groupings...?"

"What's this slimy stuff all over everything?" a paramedic asked.

"... sulphur dioxide, lead alkyls, mercaptans..."

"That's ectoplasm. It's not dangerous."

"Stinks though."

"... radioisotopes, asbestos, mercuric compounds, industrial acids..."

"No, no, no. It's..." Spengler started, then realized that he wasn't sure how to explain psychic effluent to people who were used to dealing only with physical pollution. "You could call it a form of ectophenomenological fallout..."

"Fallout!?"

"No, psychic, not mineral. Like bad vibes."

"... carcinogens, mutagens, teratogens, or synergistic poisons..."

"What are the pink particles?" a fire captain asked. "What will happen if we use water?"

Spengler shook his head. They were worse than graduate students. "No. No water. There's nothing you can do."

"... solanine, oxalic acid, cyanide, myristicin, pressor amines, copper sulphate, dihydrochalcones..."

Spengler took the man's clipboard and pen and wrote the word *none* in large letters across the form. Then his ears caught a familiar, warbling moan and he looked up hopefully. Somehow the Ectomobile had found a path through the chaos and was pulling to a halt behind Peck's car. Spengler elbowed his way to the door as Stantz stepped out, gaping at the geyser of ghostly energy soaring into the Manhattan sky.

"What happened?"

"The storage facility blew up," Venkman replied. "That weasel Peck shut off the protection grid." Then he stopped, suddenly aware of the number of things out of his control. Where's the Keymaster?"

"Oh, no," Spengler gasped. "Janine, where's Tully?" Janine, trying to fend off a group of reporters, shrugged helplessly. Stantz was thoroughly confused.

"Who's the Keymaster?"

But Spengler and Venkman were already fighting their way through toward the street. Peck and Bennett were waiting at the police barrier.

"Stop them!" Peck ordered. "Captain, I want them arrested. These men have been acting in criminal violation of the Environmental Protection Act, and this explosion is a direct result."

"*You* turned off the power!" Venkman cried, again hinging for Peck's throat, but the captain hauled him back.

"You can't do that," he said. "If you hit Mr. Peck again, I'll have to charge you with assault."

Venkman looked up at the towering ghostly gusher, spewing spirits all over Manhattan and spattering the neighborhood with slime. It didn't frighten him half as much as the possibility that Tully and Dana might get together. Who knew what horror could be unleashed then? It had Egon scared white, and that really scared Peter Venkman. He made an effort to get himself coherently under control.

"Look, Captain, there was another man here… You've got to find him and bring him back. A short determined guy with the eyes of a happy zombie."

"See!" Peck cried. "They are using drugs."

"If you don't shut up, I'm going to rip out your septum!" Egon Spengler screamed with uncharacteristic fury, causing everyone for a thirty-foot radius to fall silent and stare. Peck backed away. Bennett raised both hands.

"I don't know what's going on here, but I'm going to have to arrest you all. You can discuss it with the judge. I'm going to read you your rights now, so please listen carefully…"

No one noticed Vinz Clortho as he wandered uptown. He was just one more person gaping at the spectacular display of lights in the daytime sky, but probably the only one north of the Criminal Courts Building who guessed their true significance. At least initially. As the released ghosts made their way back to their haunting grounds, a lot of people were in for some rude shocks.

As the Keymaster passed the subway entrance at Broadway and Canal Street, he failed to notice an insidious vapor swirl into the ventilation grate that served the platform for the uptown line. No one did, which was not surprising, for insidious vapors were common enough in a city with New York's air quality. But this was not air. A few minutes later the stampede started as people trampled over one another in an attempt to reach the street, their clothes blown by a raging whirlwind and splattered by ectoplasm. A uniformed patrolman responded, hurrying to see what sort of commotion was going on, and grabbed a running youth by one arm. The boy wore a red beret and a Guardian Angels T-shirt.

"What's going on, man?" the cop asked. "I thought you Angels were pretty tough."

"Not against *that* I ain't," the boy cried, shaking off the man's hand and sprinting up the street. The cop drew his gun and turned, to find a hideous green demon rising from the stairwell. It opened its mouth, exposing foot-long teeth, and let loose an ungodly scream. The cop caught up with and passed the Guardian Angel a block and a half to the north.

J. M. Shupp was standing in front of the Hotel Sedgewick, enjoying the late October sunshine. Things had beeri quiet since the night those men had removed the ghost. Of course the owners had had a fit over the damage and the publicity, but somehow Shupp had kept his job. And things had turned around. When the word got out that the Sedgewick had been the site of the Ghostbusters' first case, their bookings had filled to capacity. The owners were pleased, Shupp was pleased, and the hotel was now a tourist attraction. There was even a brass plaque in the refurbished ballroom with details of the battle.

He watched as the Sabrett man arrived with his hot dog cart and set up for the lunch rush. As usual, the man had parked within the area serving the Sedgewick's loading zone, but Shupp felt charitable today. I won't ask him to move. Instead, I'll buy one of his weiners and chat about the weather. Or perhaps baseball. A perfectly New York experience.

"What'll it be today?" the vendor asked warily, expecting Shupp to roust him, but the manager smiled.

"A hot dog, with mustard."

"Comin' up." He reached into the cart. "Anything to drink?"

"I don't think so. Uh, what's wrong?" The hot dog man was feeling about inside the cart. He withdrew his hand and came up with two inches of weiner, the end badly chewed.

"I know I had more dogs in there. I just put 'em in."

"Oh, my."

The cart began to rock back and forth, and hot water sloshed out. The two men jumped back.

"Oh, no, not again," Shupp gasped as the Hotel Sedgewick's resident free-roaming vapor, newly sprung from captivity, appeared with a mouthful of footlongs and spicy Polish. It belched loudly, spit up half a bun, and streaked for the front door of its old home, the pushcart turning and following in its wake. The vapor passed straight through the glass door, leaving only a blob of ectoplasm and several hot dog fragments, but the pushcart was not so agile. It crashed into the door and overturned in a shower of glass and hot water, leaving its blue and orange umbrella spinning on the pavement. The vendor's jaw dropped.

"Didja ever see anything like that?"

But J. M. Shupp was unable to answer. He had passed out.

* * *

A class-four free-repeating geist was streaking up the Avenue of the Americas, bursting street lights, when it spotted the marquee of the Radio City Music Hall. It did an ecstatic whirl in the air, enthralled at the number of light bulbs that the thing must contain. Now *this* was the big time.

Roger Hubbard was late for his business meeting. His secretary called ahead to make amends while he raced for the lobby and a cab. As luck would have it, there was only one, and an elderly lady was about to grab it, but he elbowed her out of the way and jumped in. "Gulf and Western Building!" he snapped. "And I'm in a hurry, so step on it."

The cabbie, a palpable reconstructor-type three, had been dead for over fifteen years, but it still remembered how to drive, and it had nothing to lose. A skeletal hand flipped up the flag on the meter and put the engine in gear.

Roger Hubbard was already buried in his *Wall Street Journal* as the taxi leaped forward, scattering trashcans, executed a diagonal high-speed drift through the center of traffic, and sped off the wrong way down a one-way alley.

"What do you make of that, Harlan?"

"Well, I'll be... It looks like the late Mayor Walker, tap-dancing on top of a municipal bus."

In the customer payroll department of Security Atlantic Bank and Trust, most of the employees had their eyes on the clock. Just fifteen minutes to lunch. From her office the department manager noticed the situation and determined once and for all to put a stop to it. We'll see how they like staying late. She rose, walked to the doorway of the section, and cleared her throat loudly. A few of the employees looked up, guilt written on their faces.

"I have something to say to you all," she began, "and this applies to more than one of you… " She stopped, puzzled. Something was tickling her legs. She looked down as surreptitiously as she could, but there was nothing there. She determined to ignore it.

"As I was saying…" My God, there's a hand tickling my legs. She gave a yelp of surprise, and slapped at the front of her dress. Someone giggled. What's happening? It feels so… She struggled to turn and headed for the rest room. She barely made the door.

The typists and clerks looked at each other and laughed. But the phantasm was not alone. They were all late for lunch.

Louis Tully, Keymaster of Gozer, was approaching his goal: the meeting with the Gatekeeper, the preparations to receive the expected one, Gozer the Destroyer. His mind was filled with the glory of the Shagganah and all the Myriad Sacred Forms of the Torb as he entered the long pedestrian tunnel in Central Park. Several forms were clustered in the darkness ahead of him. Ah, he sighed. Fellow supplicants, witnesses to the Rectification. They spread out as he approached.

"Hey, man. We're friends. Let us go through your pockets."

The Keymaster was nonplussed. This was not how it had been foretold. "Are you the Gatekeeper?" he asked.

"Come on. You want me to stick you? Come across, man."

"I am Vinz Clortho," Tully said impatiently. "I am the Keymaster."

"And I'm Mister Dave, baddest dude on this block."

Tully considered. Gozer had never before come in the form of a dude. It smacked of treachery. "Do you bar my way?"

"Are you crazy, man? You don't give, Mister Dave's gonna rip you, man. Nobody gets by Mister Dave."

Tully's eyes began to swirl. "Do you bar my way?"

"Yeah, sucker. We bar you way."

Vinz was filled with the strength of the Vuldronaii. He opened his mouth and let out a terrifying roar that snapped the blade of Mister Dave's knife and tore bricks from the inside of the tunnel. Streams of iridescent light sparked out, discharging bolts of static electricity into the muggers. They fled screaming out the north end of the tunnel.

"I thought you said we could take him, man."

"What you think I am, Ghostbusters?"

The McLean 301, a theater just off of Forty-second Street, had seen better days. Having begun life as a variety house, it had gone through a succession of remodelings and downgradings as the neighborhood around it changed. Seven years ago it had shown its last first-run film, and was now hovering on the borderline between being an emporium for bad science fiction and a porno house. Today it was science fiction. The marquee proclaimed ALL DAY ALL NIGHT 3-D SCI-FI THRILLER, and the house was packed.

At one time the McLean might have filled to capacity with sweating burlesque fans, with top music and comedy acts, or a neighborhood sprinkling of families for a night of Disney cartoons. Now it was the downtown gross-out crowd, the beer-drinking, pot-smoking, cheering locals in their cardboard 3-D glasses, who got as much loud pleasure out of *Z—the Undying Fungoid* as their more sophisticated cousins did from *The Rocky Horror Picture*

Show. The screen was old and speckled with the refuse of thrown food, the johns didn't work, and the print of the 1957 British SF flic was probably an original. No one seemed to care. For the audience, the movie was less an art form than an excuse for a social gathering one step below a riot, and they were having a great time, shouting insults, pouring beer on one another, and razzing the terrible film as it creaked and crackled through the sprockets. The undying fungoid was in the process of devouring a toy army truck when the ancient film gave a tortured gasp and parted. The screen went white, then black.

"You jerkbag, fix the demn theng," an angry voice screamed, and a chorus of supporting jeers rose, full of comments about the movie, the theater, and the projectionist's ancestry. The screen stayed dark. The chorus turned to a rhythmic stamping. Several patrons began to dismantle their seats and hurl the pieces at the projection booth.

The low whine underneath the crowd began to rise in volume until one by one the patrons quieted down to hear what it was. Like a dynamo, someone said. You never heard a dynamo in yer life, his friend replied, likening it to a distant police siren. No, a jet engine. Or a pipe organ. Suddenly the dim house and exit lights went out.

A few of the audience settled back, thinking that the show might be starting again, but most of them knew better. There was an electricity in the air, as if the entire building had been put through a giant electromagnet. The curtains crackled with it, and a pattern of soft, vague, blue static discharges crawled over the screen, flowing, concentrating. The people watched in awe as they swirled into the center, forming an intense spot of light, while behind them the theater began to vibrate with a low, moaning sound. Like voices, thought one man. No, like music, like old songs.

Suddenly the point of light leapt in a straight line to the projection booth, as if the camera had started, a beam of wavering light stretching across the audience. The moaning resolved into ghostly music, an olio of dance-hall tunes, as the first glowing phantom appeared on the lighted line. It was a strutting comedian in straw boater and checked suit, a cane in one hand. Next came a black-faced minstrel with a banjo. A fan dancer followed, then a floppy-pants comic with suspenders and a spade beard. A stripper in a feather boa. A singer in a slick gown. A juggler. A chorine.

The audience hung there spellbound as the ghosts of a century of New York theater paraded down that spectral runway and vanished into the projection booth, every sort of act that the McLean had witnessed from minstrels to matinee idols. And when the last one was gone, and the magic had gone out of the old theater, there was a long moment of silence from the stunned crowd, followed by the loudest and longest applause that McLean 301 had ever heard.

Some distance away, Winston Zeddemore was feeling far from entertained. How could he explain this to his mother? The first Zeddemore boy to ever wind up in the clink. He turned and looked at a huge biker who was watching him curiously.

"We're gonna get five years for this. Plus, they're gonna make us retrap all those spooks. I *knew* I shouldn't have taken that job."

The biker spit lazily and scratched his jaw. "Tough luck, man."

Most of the rest of the tank's occupants were gathered around Venkman, Stantz, and Spengler, who were trying to ignore them. Stantz had his blueprints spread out on the floor.

"Look at the structure of the roofcap. It looks exactly like the kind of telemetry tracker that NASA uses to identify dead pulsars in space."

Spengler nodded excitedly and nudged Venkman.

"And look at this, Peter. Cold-riveted girders with selenium cores."

But Peter Venkman was accutely conscious of their audience. He turned to the group of hoods who were trying to figure out Stantz's coverall. "Everybody with us so far?"

Stantz grabbed his arm. "The ironwork extends down through fifty feet of bedrock and touches the water table."

Venkman still didn't get it. "I guess they don't build them like they used to, huh?"

"No," Stantz cried. "Nobody *ever* built them like this. The architect was either an authentic genius or a certified wacko. The whole building is like a huge antenna for pulling in and concentrating psychic energy."

"Who was the architect?"

"He's listed on the blueprints as I. Shandor."

"Of course," Spengler yelped, startling everyone in the room. "Ivo Shandor. I saw his name in *Tobin's Spirit Guide*. He started a secret society in 1920."

Venkman rubbed his forehead painfully. "Let me guess... Gozer worshipers."

"Yes. After the First World War, Shandor decided that society was too sick to survive. And he wasn't alone. He had close to a thousand followers when he died. They conducted bizarre rituals, intended to bring about the end of the world."

Venkman nodded. "She said he was the Destructor."

"Who?"

"Gozer."

"You talked to Gozer?" Spengler asked, confused.

"Get a grip on yourself, Egon. I talked to Dana Barrett and she referred to Gozer as the Destructor."

"See?" Ray Stantz exclaimed proudly. "I told you that something big was about to happen."

Zeddemore had heard enough. "This is insane! You actually believe that some moldy Babylonian god is going to drop in at Seventy-eighth and Central Park West and start tearing up the city?"

"Not Babylonian, Sumerian," Spengler said breathlessly. "And he won't have to. Ray, do you remember what we discussed about ERMs?"

"Yes," Stantz replied. "All the psychic potential of the city released. The Big Twinkie! We've got to get out of here."

"What's he talking about?" Zeddemore whispered.

"I'm not sure," Venkman replied, "but it sounds bad."

"Hey!"

They all turned. A high-ranking police officer was standing in the corridor outside the holding cell, flanked by two jailers. He pointed at Venkman.

"Are you the Ghostbusters?"

"What about it?"

"The mayor wants to see you right away. The whole island is going crazy. Let's go."

14

That government is not best which best secures mere life and property—there is a more valuable thing—manhood.

- MARK TWAIN

Hizzoner had had an extremely successful term as mayor, and he was determined not to let it be spoiled by a few ghosts. Ghosts, fer crissake! I get along with Italians and blacks, with Poles and Irish, with Puerto Ricans and Chinese. My credibility is solid with big business and environmentalists, with Jews, Catholics, and Muslims, with liberals and conservatives. My visibility extends with impeccable clarity to the Carson show, the Letterman show, to Donahue and Griffin and *Good Morning America*. I've published a book, done cameos on *Kate and Ali* and *Ryan's Hope*. They're doing a play about my life. I've done a good job. So, what do I get? Ghosts.

Hizzoner looked up, watching his aides as they tried to keep traffic moving in and out of the big office. The police commissioner, the fire commissioner, the city and state police commandants, the archbishop of the diocese of New York, Rabbi Komgeld, the regional director of the EPA, General Petersen of the National Guard, the city comptroller, the corporation counsel, three city bureaucrats whose names and positions he'd forgotten, several state officials, officers of the Coast Guard and Navy, and the chief agent of the FBI's New York office—all of them talking at once, most of them trying to talk to him. I have such a headache, he thought. Just once a crisis shouldn't give me a headache.

Mackay, his point man, stepped into the office. "The Ghostbusters are here, Mr. Mayor."

The room fell instantly silent as Mackay ushered the four men into the room. Well, they don't look like monsters, Hizzoner decided. Just average New York crazies. The simple solution would be to dismiss them as frauds, toss them into Riker's Island, and feed the key to a seagull. Of course, that wouldn't explain the thing that came through the wall of my shower this morning. He stood up and placed his palms on the desk.

"Okay, the Ghostbusters." They nodded respectfully. "And who's Peck?"

A thin, angry-looking man in a tight suit pushed his way forward. Hizzoner disliked him on sight. He looked like the mayor's high school biology teacher, and Hizzoner had flunked frog dissecting four times.

"I'm Walter Peck, sir. And I'm prepared to make a full report." He withdrew a fat sheaf of papers from his briefcase and dropped them on the desk. Typical, Hizzoner thought. The city's falling apart and this ringding brings me a term paper.

"These men are complete snowball artists. They use nerve and sense gases to induce hallucinations. The people think they're seeing ghosts and call these bozos, who conveniently show up and get rid of the problem with a fake electronic light show."

The mayor looked sharply at Venkman. "You using nerve gas?"

Venkman shook his head emphatically. "The man is a psychopath, Your Honor."

"Probably a mixture of gases, no doubt stolen from the army..."

"Baloney!" Stantz cried, then favored the archbishop with an embarrassed smile. Peck charged on.

"... improperly stored and touched off with those high-voltage laser beams they use in their light show. They caused an explosion."

Venkman looked ready to start talking again, but Hizzoner raised his hands for silence. He looked imploringly at his staff.

"All I know is, that wasn't a light show we saw this morning," the fire commissioner said. "I've seen every form of combustion known to man, but this beats me."

The police commissioner's argument was more telling. "And nobody's using nerve gas on all the people that have seen those... things all over the city. The walls are bleeding in the Fifty-third Precinct. How do you explain that?"

The mayor couldn't, but had no intention of asking either Peck or the Ghostbusters, at least not yet. He turned to the archbishop. "Your Eminence?"

The prelate and the mayor were old friends from the days when they'd been priest and ward captain, Tim and Ed, but the formalities still had to be observed. He kissed the preferred ring. The archbishop smiled, that enigmatic smile they teach in seminary, Hizzoner thought. Too bad they don't make one for politicians.

"Officially the church will not take a position on the religious implications of these... phenomena. However, since they started, people have been lining up at every church in the city to confess and take communion. We've had to put on extra priests. Personally, I think it's a sign from God, but don't quote me on that."

"I can't call a press conference and tell everyone to start praying. Rabbi, any thoughts on this?"

Korngeld shrugged. "It's quite a deal. What can I tell you?"

A tall black man stepped forward. "I'm Winston Zeddemore, Your Honor. I've been with the company for only a short time, but I gotta tell you… these things are real. Since I joined these men I have seen jazz that would boggle your mind!"

The mayor rubbed his eyes wearily. "You, Venkman, how did this happen?"

"Everything was working fine, sir," Venkman said earnestly. "We ran a safe operation."

"Ha!"

Stantz rounded on Peck. "It was fine, just fine, until this jerk here shut down our power."

"Is this true?" the mayor asked. Venkman stepped forward.

"Yes, Your Honor. This man is a jerk."

Peck launched himself at Venkman, but two of the mayor's aides pulled him back. Hizzoner stifled a laugh and glared at Peck. "That'll be enough of that. So, wise guy, what do we do now?"

Venkman grinned. He liked the mayor. He would have done well back on the carny. "It's this way, sir. You can believe this guy here…"

"That's Peck!"

"… or you can accept the fact that this city is headed for a disaster of really biblical proportions."

"What do you mean by biblical?"

"Old Testament, Mr. Mayor. Wrath-of-God type stuff. The seas boil, fire and brimstone falling from the sky…"

"… forty years of darkness," Stantz chimed in. "Earthquakes, mass hysteria, human sacrifice…"

"… dogs and cats living together in sin…"

"Enough! I get the point." The mayor looked at the assembled multitude waiting for his word. Aides, employees, supporters, the secular arm of the office, waiting for him to pull off the big save so they would all look good, or to fall on his face. To blow it. To create a power vacuum for one of them to step into. I hate these times, he thought. He glanced at the archbishop, who winked.

"And if you're wrong?"

"If I'm wrong, then *nothing* happens and you toss us back in the can. But if I'm right, and we can stop this thing... Well, let's say that you could save the lives of millions of registered voters."

Venkman smiled.

The mayor smiled. If this guy ever goes into politics, he could be very, very dangerous. I wonder if he's a Democrat.

Peck pushed his way forward. "I don't believe you're seriously considering listening to these men."

The mayor took a long look at Peck, then motioned to his aides. "Get rid of him." Then, turning to Venkman, he said, "We've got work to do. What do you need from me?"

The mess at Dana Barrett's building hadn't gotten any better. In fact, things were considerably worse. Louis Tully wandered through a stream of tenants carrying precious possessions through the lobby as lightning roared and snapped around the building, cutting power lines, shattering windows, and blowing pieces of masonry into the streets. Policemen herded the frightened people into cabs and tried to keep the curious motorists moving on Central Park West, making sure there was room for emergency vehicles. In the confusion, no one noticed that Louis Tully was swimming upstream.

His floor was almost deserted. The lights were out, but a continual crackle of lightning was spilling from the opened apartment doors. A figure shuffled toward Tully, Mrs. Blum, a neighbor.

"Louis! What are you doing, standing there? Get out of the building... Don't you know it's an earthquake or something?"

Louis looked at her, amazed at the fleshbag's petty concerns. The woman was carrying a bowl of fish, a symbol that did not register in the pantheon of the Destructor. A Shubb, he thought. Be charitable, enlighten her. "The Traveler is coming," he said, his voice thick with reverent secrecy. But the creature would not comprehend.

"Don't be crazy. Nobody is going to come and visit you with all this commotion going on." She hurried off. Another lost soul. So be it. His duty was to Gozer.

He approached the sacred joining and knocked three times, the thunder answering in concerto as the door opened. It was Zuul, the Expected One.

"Are you the Gatekeeper?" he asked.

"I am Zuul," she said.

It was the moment. Vinz Clortho, Key master of Gozer, rushed to the joining as he and Zuul merged. She *was* the Gatekeeper and his key was ready. They sank down in the embrace that had been foretold and blew the roof off the building.

The mayor followed Venkman and Stantz through the corridors of City Hall, puffing to keep up and straining to understand. And, he was having second thoughts. By God, he thought, if these clowns screw up, I'll make sure they never again see the light of day.

The Ghostbusters had begun their preparations and the City Hall area was swarming with vehicles and support people, not to mention reporters, tourists, groupies, and a large crowd of peddlers selling Ghostbuster T-shirts and dolls. A circus, Hizzoner thought. I hate trusting someone else when I don't know what's going on.

"I don't understand it. Why here? Why now?"

Venkman shrugged. "What goes around, comes around, Mr. Mayor. The big lazy Susan of karma just keeps turning, and sometimes we get the short end of the stick."

"What's he talking about?"

Stantz clapped him on the shoulder. "This may be nature's way of telling us to slow down. You have to admit, it's kind of humbling, isn't it?"

"We're humble already," Hizzoner shouted. "Hasn't this city suffered enough?"

The Ectomobile was backed up to the loading dock, and Spengler and Zeddemore were charging the proton packs off a coaxial connected to the building current. A maintenance man was looking fearfully at the rumbling nuclear accelerators and trying not to get too close. He tapped Venkman on the shoulder.

"You're sure this is all right?"

"It's all right," the mayor grumbled. The maintenance man glared at him.

"And who the devil are you?"

"I'm the mayor, you meathead."

"Big deal."

Hizzoner himself was about to ask if it was all right when Captain Bennett appeared. He had changed into field coveralls.

"We've cleared the whole building and cordoned off the street. I'm massing our special tactics squad and the National Guard is on standby."

"Forget the tac squad," Venkman said. "There's nothing for them to shoot. But the National Guard is fine. People like soldiers. They give great crowd control."

"What's wrong with him?" the mayor whispered to Spengler.

"He's in charge," Egon replied bluntly. The mayor blanched. This is definitely going to give me an ulcer, he decided.

Spengler crossed to where Janine was standing anxiously by the Ectomobile. She smiled bravely. A romantic moment, Egon decided, and took her hand.

"Hi," he said, making a mental note to ask Peter how to talk to girls. They were far more complicated than fungus, or ghosts for that matter. He wondered abstractly whether anyone had ever done a study…

"I want you to have this," Janine said, handing him a coin.

"What is it?"

"It's a souvenir from the 1964 World's Fair at Flushing Meadow. It's my lucky coin."

"I don't believe in luck," Spengler said firmly.

"Keep it anyway. I have another one at home."

"Thank you," Egon said, deeply aware of the gravity of the situation. So, this was what history was like.

Peter Venkman was not so sure. He looked at the long convoy lined up behind the Ectomobile; a police cruiser, three National Guard trucks, three fire engines, a Con Ed van, a wrecker, and—ominously—a dozen ambulances. Okay, this is war. So be it. I'd just feel a lot better if Dana weren't involved. On the other hand, if she weren't, I wouldn't be able to ride out and rescue her.

"Hey, Peter," Stantz called from the Ectomobile. "You ready?"

Ready as I'll ever be, he thought. They were all looking at him—Stantz, Spengler, Zeddemore, Janine, even the mayor. He took a deep breath and forced a smile.

"Okay, just remember, whatever happens out there, we are the professionals. Not only are we the best Ghostbusters around, we are the *only* Ghostbusters around. It's up to us."

He gave a thumbs-up and they each returned it. Then, raising his arm in the old cavalry signal, he cried, "Move 'em out!"

15

Have the courage to face a difficulty lest it kick you harder than you bargained for.

- STANISLAUS I OF POLAND

Harlan Bojay and Robert Learned Coombs sat atop a stone wall in the park and watched the mayhem swirling about the front of the old apartment building. The NYPD barricades were keeping people out of the street, but they had lined up ten deep behind the sawhorses and, like typical New Yorkers, were beginning to divide up into religious factions, ethnic groups, and political-interest units. A chanting crowd of Hare Krishnas danced by, whirling and banging drums, followed by a contingent of punkers looking for trouble, until a mounted policeman trotted between them. The punks dispersed and melted into the crowd. Satisfied, the policeman galloped off to chase out of the street a covy of priests who were beginning an exorcism.

"What do you think, lad?"

Coombs shrugged. "Something to do with all this ghost business, I guess. Ooo-whee, look at that!"

A ring of lightning bolts enveloped the tower, shaking the old building to the bedrock. Chunks of stone and concrete rained down, bouncing on the pavement and scattering the cops and firemen. One boulder went through the top of the squad car, smashing the light bar on the roof and setting the siren going, which warbled eerily until a trooper darted out to switch it off. The crowd applauded his bravery but showed no further inclination to cross the barricades themselves.

"Rough night," Coombs grunted.

"'Twas such a night as this that Macbeth met three witches on the moors," Bojay intoned solemnly. Coombs shook his head in admiration.

"For a guy who was gonna be a jockey, you sure have a lot of culture."

"Yes," Bojay cried, "and let that be a lesson to you!"

A minyan of Hassidic rabbis went by, bobbing and chanting prayers. "It is a wondrous fact," Bojay proclaimed, "how a little bit of disaster seems to bring out the godliness in man."

"And the ambulances."

A hush fell over the crowd as attention shifted to follow this new attraction, a convoy of emergency vehicles, their lights rotating, as they drew slowly up to the building. "It's the Ghostbusters," someone cried, and others took up the cheer. It was obvious that the trouble had something to do with the ghosts that were rampaging over the city. The Ghostbusters were here. That was enough for the cheering multitude. The danger forgotten, they poured over the barricades and surrounded the Ectomobile.

"What do you think of that?" Venkman asked with a grin.

"I think they think we know what we're doing," Stantz said uneasily. "Do we?"

"Of course we do."

Stantz was taken aback by his partner's sudden confidence. "Really? What do we do then?"

"We do what we've always done," Venkman replied. "We play it by ear."

Oh boy, Stantz thought. Insight. The crowd began to press in closely, tapping on the windows and waving. Janine, who was jammed into the back with Spengler and Zeddemore, started to panic.

"They'll turn us over. Do something."

"Okay," Venkman replied, pushing the door open and stepping out. He raised his hands and smiled broadly.

The multitude stopped, caught its breath, and waited. Venkman felt his smile beginning to slip. I can con a crowd, he realized, but this bunch is almost a mob, and a mob is nothing but trouble. Spengler leaned through the window and tugged on his sleeve. "Say something," he hissed.

"What?"

"Anything!"

Venkman fumbled the PA microphone from its hook and switched on the loudspeaker. "Hello."

"HELLO!" the crowd roared.

"How are you all?" he asked. The reply was unintelligible but friendly.

"Get them out of here," Stantz whispered.

"Hey, we're the Ghostbusters—" Venkman started, but the mob went wild. The priests began praying, the rabbis started to wail, and a group of breakdancers broke into a pop-and-shuffle routine. From somewhere a gospel choir began to sing. It was like Lindbergh at Orly.

"This is nuts," Venkman called to Stantz. "Let's suit up." He tried once again.

"People, the street is dangerous! Please move back." A priest threw holy water on him and the choir slid into "Sing Low, Sweet Chariot." The storm continued to rage around the building's upper-works.

"We'll never get rid of these clowns," Stantz cried, helping Venkman on with his pack. How wrong he was.

A seismic shock wave tore through the street, tossing several of the dancers on their butts. An earthquake? In New York City? The crowd hesitated, then stampeded for the park as the street began to open up, jets of steam and water breaking through the pavement. More chunks of building roof rained down into the mob.

"Hey, an earthquake," Zeddemore cried. "What could happen next?"

The Ectomobile bounced on its tires, Janine hanging on grimly, then screaming as she saw the pavement gape wide in a huge crevasse. A squad car tilted forward and slid into the pit as the continuing force of the shocks caused the earth to liquify.

"Ray, I..."

"... never been in..."

"... earthquake before..."

"Whoa!"

And they were gone. There was nothing but the tail end of the squad car, pointing skyward like the *Titanic*'s last moment, and a cloud of settling dust. Janine detached herself from the Ectomobile and tiptoed forward to peer into the opening.

"Egon? Guys?"

Hesitantly, a hand groped above the asphalt rim, and, one by one, the four men appeared, dragging themselves up and out of the sinkhole. Venkman looked back at the police car, its rear wheels still turning.

"I've heard of underground parking but *that's* ridiculous."

"Peter, hurry, before the crowd comes back."

Venkman made his way to the back of the old Cadillac, where the team was picking up the rest of their gear. "Everybody okay?"

They nodded.

"Are we all together on this?"

He thrust his hands forward. The others did the same and they locked up like a basketball team. The men looked at one another. It was now or never.

"Let's do it!"

At that very moment, high above them, two other beings were in motion. Vinz Clortho and Zuul—in the bodies of Louis Tully and Dana Barrett—had accomplished the joining. All of the sacred conjunctions had arrived, the energy was focused, the preparations for the Traveler's return were complete. It only remained for the two guardians to return to their posts and await Gozer's entrance.

They walked slowly, formally, through the remains of Dana Barrett's apartment and into the stairwell leading to the roof, while all about them the lightning writhed, growing in intensity.

The power to the elevators was out, and by the time they reached Dana's floor, the four men were gasping and spitting. Venkman leaned against a wall to catch his breath, trying to keep his mind off the series of lurid and grisly possibilities of what they might find when they reached the roof. "I'm glad we took the stairs," he wheezed. "Good workout… makes me feel so much better."

"Ahhck," Egon Spengler replied, trying to get his head between his knees.

"Just wish I hadn't gotten Dana involved in this."

Stantz shook his head. "You didn't, remember? She came to us."

"Oh, yeah, right."

"So where's she live?" Zeddemore asked.

"This way. C'mon, Egon. You can throw up later."

Venkman stood before the door to Dana's apartment. It looked okay. What the heck? He rang the bell.

"Dana?"

"Maybe we should go downstairs and call first," Zeddemore suggested.

"Funny. Go on, Peter. Knock."

But when he did, the door came apart under his hand, pieces and fragments showering down at his feet, the wood suddenly old, rotten, and crumbling. "Hmm," Venkman muttered.

The apartment looked as if it had been cleaned out with a fragmentation bomb. The walls were gone, providing a spectacular view of Jersey and the Hudson River through the darting lightning, and wind swirled the decayed remains of Dana Barrett's furnishings about the floor. There was a smell of rot, and the telltale tracks of ectoplasm everywhere. Egon, now recovered, picked up the leg of a chair and twisted it gently. It shattered like badly made papier mâché.

"Ray. Instantaneous life-force drain. Like in the Potsdam Case of 1912..."

"Egon," Venkman said quietly. "Don't quote me cases. Not now."

Zeddemore was looking cautiously about. "Well, she's not home. Let's go."

"No. The kitchen. It'll be in there."

The others followed Venkman to the doorway, where he stood, gaping. The refrigerator was gone, totally blown away. Probably straight into an alternate universe, Venkman thought, junk food and all. The wall behind it had burned out, to reveal a long-concealed stone stairway, leading up to the roof. A secret stairway. This apartment must have been Shandor's before he died. Later, when the building was remodeled, they must have walled it over as being either useless or dangerous. But now it stood open, a formidable curving ascent, lit only by the rapid flashes of the lightning outside.

"That's it?" Ray Stantz whispered.

"That's it." Venkman slapped his shoulder. "Go!"

"Me?"

The others nodded. Stantz shrugged, switched on his accelerator, and charged up the stairs.

It took a moment for his eyes to adjust to the light, but Ray Stantz was amazed at what he saw. I expected something like this from reading the blueprints, he thought, but to think that he actually built it.

The central feature of the site was a huge stairway of carved stone steps, leading up to the temple on the east. East. Sumeria. And the weight. Those steps must weigh tons, which explained the incredible construction procedures, the reinforced steel beams sunk deep into the bedrock. They had to hold this temple above the skyline, *and* take up the shock of Gozer's return. Ivo Shandor was truly a mad genius.

The immense temple doors, cast in some iridescent metal—probably selenium—were at least twenty feet in height. Gozer must be one big mother, Stantz thought. But the temple itself could hardly be more than a facade. It was almost at the front of the building. Go through those doors and you'd drop right onto Central Park West. Or would you? He peered closely at the lightning playing around the doors, at the strange quality of depth it seemed to lend them, as if it were an optical illusion. As if the doors extended on... Of course! They did, into another dimension, another time perhaps. Where did I think Gozer was coming from,

Connecticut? Those doors are an interdimensional gate, Stantz realized, and suddenly he was deeply frightened. These accelerators may be tough but they're not that tough. Are we actually going to go up against a god?

"Dana!"

Stantz turned. The others were clustered behind him, holding on to Peter Venkman, who was trying to break free. Dana Barrett and Louis Tully were standing atop twin stone pedestals, their bodies twisting violently in the wind, their arms thrown back.

"Dana."

"No, Peter," Egon cried. "Don't do it."

He was right. Twin streams of living energy, like the beams of their accelerators but infinitely stronger, leapt out from the temple doors, striking the two tiny figures, enveloping them in a wash of light. For a brief instant Stantz swore that he could see their bones glowing beneath the skin, and then they bent forward, down on all fours, and were transformed into two hideous doglike things. Guardians. Egon was breathing hoarsely. Zeddemore whistled softly under his breath. Stantz and Venkman looked at each other. Venkman shrugged.

"So, she's a dog..."

Peter Venkman, either you are the coolest character I've ever met, or you are around-the-bend crazy, Stantz thought. He turned back to look at the temple.

"Guys..."

The doors had begun to swing back, emitting a blinding white light. The two terror-dogs jumped down and scampered up the stairs to new positions flanking the doors. Each raised a paw in salute. This is it, Stantz thought. He could hear Zeddemore mumbling a prayer. Good idea, but the only one I can remember is the one that goes "If I should die before I wake."

"Look, the light," Egon said, shielding his eyes with his hand. Yes. The light was not coming from the temple. It was a being, a single glowing figure like the filament of a bulb, moving slowly down the stairs, the brilliance fading as it distanced itself from the doors. And behind it, Ray Stantz had the satisfaction of seeing, was a strange interior, a geometric cage of glowing lines stretching away into another place entirely. I was right.

The figure stopped beside one of the hideous guardians and stroked it negligently, as if it were some sort of nightmarish house pet. The dog-thing flapped out a foot-long tongue and panted happily, as the last of the supernatural illumination drained away from its master.

"It's a girl!" Zeddemore blurted out.

"What's going on, Ray?"

"No, it's Gozer," Spengler said. "He's playing with us. He can take any form."

"Only one way to find out."

Stantz took a few steps forward, the induction rifle held loosely across his chest, and planted both feet firmly. Like a Revolutionary War minuteman, Venkman decided.

The creature turned curiously, regarding Stantz as something it had never seen before, though without any apparent hostility. It had the form of a thin, very strange young girl, apparently swathed in a clinging mist from the ankle to the neck. The hair swept up and back, not precisely cut short, but seeming to disappear, as if it linked the being to its home dimension; and its eyes were of the deepest blood red, and liquid, like two beating hearts swimming in their own juices. Happy Halloween, Venkman thought. Do your stuff, Ray.

Stantz cleared his throat. "As a duly-constituted representative of the City of New York, and on behalf of the County and State of New York, the United States of

America, the planet Earth and all its inhabitants, I hereby order you to cease and desist any and all supernatural activity and return at once to your place of origin or next parallel dimension."

"Nice going, Ray," Venkman called.

Gozer looked curiously at Stantz.

"Are you a god?" it asked.

"Uh… no."

"Then die!"

Bolts of energy shot from Gozer's outstretched arms, catching the men and throwing them backward toward the precipice. Venkman felt himself rolling end over end. I'm falling, he thought. No, he realized as he came to a stop against a stone plinth, his legs hanging free in the air. Somehow these proton packs absorbed the shock, like going over Niagara Falls in a rubber barrel. He shook his head and checked the charge indicators. They were almost on Overload. If the Goze pulls that again, we could get fried by our own equipment. Zeddemore was pulling Stantz to his feet.

"Ray, if someone asks you if you're a god, you say yes!"

Gozer stood quietly on the same spot, watching them, a mocking smile on its lips. Venkman had had the course. His patience was gone. You terrorize my city, ruin my business, turn my girl into a dog, and try to fricassee my buddies. Enough is enough.

He scrambled to his feet, snapped in the induction rifle, and took aim. "This chick is toast!" he cried, and fired, but when the beam crossed the spot where Gozer had stood, the god was not there.

"Wow!" Stantz muttered, watching Gozer leap through the air, execute a double flip with a halftwist round-off at the end, and land on both feet behind them on the parapet. It favored them with a mocking laugh.

"Agile little minx, isn't she?"

"Forget trapping," Stantz cried. "Just blast it."

All four of them opened up at once. Gozer seemed to calmly absorb the streams and then, with a brilliant pink flash, disappeared, leaving only a burnt smell in the air. Zeddemore gaped at the spot, looked around suspiciously, then let out his breath.

"We did it. Thank God!"

But Spengler was not so sure. It just seemed like it had been too easy. He pulled out his PKE meter and began tracking up and down the stairs, as Stantz bounded jubilantly up to the site and pointed at the smoke still rising from the stone. "We neutronized it. The guy's a molecular nonentity."

Suddenly the lights on Spengler's detector came on, popped, and the little meter burned itself out. "Not necessarily," he said dryly.

All of the violence up until that point had merely been a prelude for the storm that now erupted around them. The skies opened and rained fire, the winds rose, the earth shook, and the Ghostbusters crawled into the smallest nooks and crannies they could find to escape the hail of masonry and debris coming down around them. Sirens seemed to be going off all over town. Venkman wondered how the mayor was taking it. Probably signing our execution orders right now. Or calling in an airstrike on this building.

"I thought you said we got him, Ray," he bellowed.

"So, I was premature."

A huge stone gargoyle slammed down alongside Spengler, seemed to glare reproachfully at him, and then teetered over the edge. Egon checked his meters. They were all dead, overloaded. He heard Zeddemore scream.

"Winston, you okay?"

"I am *not* okay. The world is ending and I am *not* ready to go."

"Just hang on."

The rumbling lessened, then stopped so suddenly that Venkman was certain that he'd gone deaf. He crawled out of his hole and looked around. The roof was a shambles; only the stairs, the temple, and the terror-dogs seemed to be undamaged. "Hey, everybody okay?"

There were a few mumbles of assent as they regrouped. "Is it over?" Stantz asked.

The sky roiled, cracked, and opened up, revealing a brilliant spot of light.

"I don't think so," Venkman muttered.

"SUBCREATURES! GOZER THE GOZERIAN, GOZER THE DESTRUCTOR, VOLGUUS ZILDROHAR, THE TRAVELER, HAS COME. CHOOSE AND PERISH!"

"Is he talking to us?"

"You see anyone else here?" Winston asked. "What's he talking about? Choose what?"

"What do you mean choose?" Stantz cried. "We don't understand."

"CHOOSE!!" Gozer bellowed again.

Spengler placed a hand on Ray's shoulder. "I think he's saying that since we're about to be sacrificed anyway, we get to choose the form we want him to take."

Stantz was intrigued. Sort of like a last request. "You mean if I stand here and concentrate on the image of Roberto Clemente, Gozer will appear as Roberto Clemente and wipe us out?"

"That appears to be the case."

"Wait, wait," Venkman said quickly. "Don't think of anything. Clear your minds. Blank 'em out. We get only one crack at this."

They looked at one another, nodded, and tried to stand as still as possible, but the thunder rolled again.

My mind is blank, Venkman thought. *I may wet my pants, but I'm not going to think of anything.*

(. . . . .)
(. . . . .)
(. . . . .)
(. . . . X)

"THE CHOICE IS MADE. THE TRAVELER HAS COME!"

"We didn't choose anything," Venkman cried, but the swirling storm was already disappearing. "I didn't think of an image." He grabbed Spengler by the arm. "Did you?"

"No! Winston?"

"Man, my mind is a total void. Ray?"

Stantz was standing silently, his mouth open, shaking his head in terror.

"Ray!"

"I couldn't help it! It just popped in there!"

"What?" Venkman screamed, grabbing him by the collar. "What popped in there?"

Stantz pointed off toward the south, the color draining out of his face. "Look!"

They turned and strained to see what might be coming from that direction, their minds now free to supply all manner of doom, but at first there was nothing but a deep, hollow, thudding sound, like a man walking on a giant base drum. Suddenly, beyond Columbus Circle, they caught a glimpse of white moving between the buildings.

Venkman's mouth was dry. His hands shook and he wanted to run, but there was nowhere to run to. Even if he hadn't been on top of a building, they were dealing with a god, a god who had conjured up the ultimate horror—and conjured it up out of Ray Stantz's mind. "What is it, Ray? What did you think of?"

Stantz was leaning toward the edge, babbling incoherently as the white shape loomed closer, still tenuously out of reach behind the intervening buildings.

"What is it?" Zeddemore screamed.

"Ray, talk to me!"

"It can't be, it can't be!" Stantz repeated over and over again as the thing emerged from Broadway and thundered slowly across Columbus Circle, snapping light poles and trees. Venkman strained to make it out. It appeared to be wearing something—a hat and a sailor suit?

"Ray, what is it? Ray!"

Stantz's head dropped forward, like a poleaxed steer's, and he sighed. He looked up and shrugged. "It is," he said. "It's the Stay-Puft Marshmallow Man."

The marshmallow monster, a hundred feet tall and grinning insanely like its namesake, trudged slowly up the edge of the park, passing the Tavern-on-the-Green and heading unerringly for them. "I tried to think of the most harmless thing... something that could never destroy us... something I loved from my childhood."

"AND YOU CAME UP WITH THAT?" Venkman screamed.

"The Stay-Puft Marshmallow Man. He was on all the packages we used to buy as a kid. We used to roast Stay-Puft marshmallows at Camp Waconda."

"Great! The marshmallows are about to get their revenge. Still..." Venkman considered, his sense of proportion returning, "we aren't down yet." He fingered his induction gun. "We may get to roast a few tonight."

"That's a big marshmallow," Zeddemore said skeptically as the creature lumbered past the Dakota, leaving huge gooey footprints. "I wonder how they're taking this down on the street."

•

Walter Peck was not taking it well at all. Having just seen his car go under the foot of a giant marshmallow, he was having a hard time convincing himself that what he was seeing was a matter of nerve gas. I don't know how you did this, Peter Venkman, but I'll get you if it takes a hundred years.

He ducked out of the screaming, running crowd and fought his way to a policeman, who seemed to be in the process of abandoning his squad car before the approaching monster. Peck seized him by an arm. "Are the Ghostbusters up there?"

"Yeah!"

"I want you to go up on the roof and arrest them. This time they've gone too far."

The cop looked at Peck sharply, then handed him his nightstick. "You arrest them, jerkbag. I'm getting out of here."

"No, you can't… I—" Peck began, but the man was gone. Peck turned and faced the oncoming marshmallow. He shook the nightstick angrily.

"I'll get you for this, Venkman!"

The four Ghostbusters had lined up on the parapet and were watching Stay-Puft draw abreast of their perch. The fear was gone, replaced by resignation. Zeddemore was certain that he would go to heaven. Spengler looked forward to merging with the cosmic energy continuum. Stantz was hoping that his conjuring of the marshmallow man wouldn't hurt his chance for a lucky draw from the reincarnation pool. And Peter Venkman had fallen back on his sense of humor. When in doubt, cause as much confusion as you can and, with luck, there'll always be a loophole. The marshmallow man looked up at them, smiling button eyes and neat little vest, a hundred feet of rampaging cuteness.

"Hey," Venkman said. "He's just a sailor in town for a good time. We get him laid and what's the problem?"

Zeddemore peered down. "He's big all right, but he's still too short to reach us. How's he gonna get up here?"

They got their answer almost immediately as Stay-Puft began to use a nearby church as a footstool. "That does it," Venkman cried. "Nobody steps on a church in my town. Hit him!"

The streams converged on the thing's chest and exploded with a rush of blue flames as the marshmallow caught fire. The Stay-Puft Man bellowed with pain and rage, flailing the air, sending burning marshmallow in all directions and continuing to climb toward them. He no longer looked cute.

"Good," Zeddemore said. "Now we made him mad."

"Let's get out of here," Stantz screamed. They scrambled back as a flaming sucrose fist slammed down the parapet, splattering them with burning goo. The puffy white hand slipped down, then caught and held as the monster began to lever itself up.

"Regroup."

"We're going to be killed by a hundred-foot marshmallow," Venkman said, watching the immense white face appear above the skyline. The flames had eaten away at it, but there was still plenty of it left. Enough to do them in and then some.

"On the count of three. One… two…"

"No," Spengler cried. He pointed to the two terror-dogs waiting by the great temple doors. "Them. Shoot them!"

"No. You'll kill Dana…"

"AND," Spengler added, "*cross the streams*…"

"You said that crossing the streams would be *bad*!"

"Yeah," Stantz said. "It'll kill us."

"Life is just a state of mind," Spengler replied calmly.

"But it's my favorite state."

"Either way we're history. Look."

The Stay-Puft Marshmallow Man was rising above the edge of the building, blotting out the sky. It reached for them with a burning, dripping fist. Venkman grinned.

"Egon, I *like* this plan! So be it. Now."

The streams of charged particles ripped out, streaking toward the temple, blowing away the two surprised guardians. "Okay," Spengler cried as he saw the shadow of Gozer fall across him, as he felt the breath of hot marshmallow on his neck. "Cross the streams."

Venkman smiled wistfully. "See ya on the other side."

The streams touched, tangled, and broke into a billion intersecting fragments. Time stopped. The temple doors melted. The interdimensional gate closed. And Gozer, the Stay-Puft Marshmallow Man, its link to its own time gone, was consumed in a roaring firestorm. As the air rushed out, Venkman felt himself thrown forward by a great tongue of heat, rolling, bouncing, passing out…

"Everybody okay?"

Who said that? Venkman wondered. I'm supposed to be dead. He looked down and saw that his legs were gone. No pain, and they don't feel any different, he thought. Strange. His toes still wiggled. He looked up as a huge white figure came around the corner.

"Aaaaaah!"

The figure wiped a hand across its face, exposing a familiar pair of eyes. It was Stantz. "Hey, Peter. You okay?"

Venkman shrugged. "I guess so. My legs though…"

"What's wrong with your legs? Besides the marshmallow, I mean."

Marshmallow? He raised his knees up out of the white goop. Well, what do you know? "No, I guess I'm fine. What happened to Gozer?"

"He's spread all over the West Side," Stantz said, helping Venkman to his feet. "The sun is out. We won."

Venkman stumbled out of the cubby and looked about. He had tumbled into a spaced formed by two collapsing stone slabs that had caught against each other and held. Either could have crushed him but they hadn't. Well, the old man always said I was lucky. And then he saw the charred forms lying at the foot of the collapsed temple. Dana…

Stantz stepped up behind him, wiping toasted marshmallow off his clothing. He sniffed curiously. "Something smells like burnt dog…"

Venkman looked at him.

"Oh, Peter. Oh, I'm sorry, really…"

Venkman waved him off and sat down beside the roasted terror-dog. Zeddemore and Spengler were picking goop off each other but seemed otherwise unhurt. Well, we did it, Venkman thought. We won. And I feel terrible.

"Peter."

"What?"

"Look." Stantz was pointing at the terror-dog. Venkman looked closely and saw that a section of the carbonous coating on the beast's flank was pulsing. He jumped back. Ray raised his induction rifle, but Venkman held up his hand.

"Wait a minute."

The flank cracked and a section fell away. A hand poked out. "Help…" a voice called weakly. "Anyone…"

"Dana!" Venkman cried, tearing open the shell and pulling her out. Spengler and Stantz ran to break open the other dog and found Louis Tully inside. He looked around, blinking at the ruined high rise, the weary Ghostbusters, and the coating of marshmallow and exclaimed, "Jeez. Somebody must have spiked the egg salad."

"Dana, are you all right?"

She looked at Peter Venkman and nodded her head.

"Oh, sure. I'm getting used to this."

Louis Tully hurried over. "I'm innocent. Honest, Dana. I never touched you. Not that I remember anyway."

"Cool it, Louis," she said quickly, turning back to Venkman. "What happened to me?"

"Nothing. We just got rid of that thing in your kitchen."

"Really? Is it gone?"

Venkman nodded. "Along with most of your furniture and personal possessions. This one took some work."

She tried not to smile, but couldn't help it. "Thank you. Next time I want to break a lease I'll know who to call." She laughed and hugged him. "Thank you!"

"Who are you guys?" Tully asked Spengler as they headed for the stairs.

"We're the Ghostbusters."

"Really? Who does your taxes?"

On the street Walter Peck had just finished digging himself out from under a lump of melted sucrose the size of a Volkswagen. He looked around in confusion, trying to get his bearings. The street was a shambles; wrecked and flattened patrol cars littering the tom-up pavement, huge chunks of stone embedded in it like raisins in a cake. A National Guard truck lay on its side. Sirens were going off again. And there, in the center of the devastation, sitting untouched before the building, was the Ghostbusters' Ectomobile. Peck stared at it. The red-haired receptionist was standing by the fender. She waved gaily at him. Peck stumbled off, mumbling to himself.

From the safety of a tree in the park, Harlan Bojay and Robert Learned Coombs watched Walter Peck go by.

"He appears to be heading for the lake," Coombs declared.

"Probably going to wash himself off. That definitely looked like marshmallow to me."

Coombs nodded. "Sure a lot of it though."

"You would have to wonder why anyone would dump a marshmallow of that size right in the middle of the street."

Robert Learned Coombs scratched his chin shrewdly. "I wonder if there might not be a very large cup of hot chocolate somewhere in the area."

Harlan Bojay looked at his friend in admiration. "Robert, that's very good. That would definitely explain it."

As the Ghostbusters emerged on the sidewalk, Janine ran into Spengler's arms. "Oh, Egon. I was so worried about you."

"Me too. I mean, I'm glad you're okay."

"Oh, Egon, you have such nice clavicles."

Stantz and Zeddemore stowed their accelerators in the back. "Now, aren't you glad you signed on with us, Winston?"

"I don't know. We aren't going to do gods often, are we?"

Peter Venkman and Dana Barrett stepped out into the sunshine, their arms about each other. "A lot of steps," she said.

"Hey, you didn't have to walk up." He looked at her, definitely liking what he saw. "This is going to cost you, you know. Our fees are ridiculously high."

"Talk to my accountant. Louis?"

Tully rubbed his hands together. "Great! I bet we could write off all the damage as an act of God."

"Speaking of gods," Dana said. "What's going to happen to all those ghosts?"

"Well, with the Goze gone, I suppose they'll settle down a bit."

"And if they don't?"

Peter Venkman grinned. "Call Ghostbusters, of course. Suppose we discuss it over dinner."

She laughed and kissed him. "Okay, you win. I don't guess I'll be using my kitchen for a while anyway… "

"Not for about six months. That's a lot of dinners."

She kissed him again. "If you say so."

Stantz leaned out of the driver's seat. "Hey, you two lovebirds. Let's get out of here before the crowd comes back."

Peter Venkman looked at the ruined street full of potholes and marshmallow, overturned cars and confused people. At Stantz, Spengler, Zeddemore, Tully, Janine, and the Ectomobile. And at Dana Barrett. She reached out and picked a chunk of marshmallow off his cheek, popped it into her mouth, and grinned.

"Well, hotshot? What do you think?"

Peter Venkman threw his arms in the air. "I love this town!"

GHOSTBUSTERS II

A NOVEL BY **ED NAHA**

BASED ON A MOTION PICTURE WRITTEN BY
HAROLD RAMIS & DAN AYKROYD

BASED ON THE CHARACTERS CREATED BY
DAN AYKROYD & HAROLD RAMIS

AN IVAN REITMAN FILM STARRING
BILL MURRAY, DAN AYKROYD,
SIGOURNEY WEAVER, HAROLD RAMIS,
RICK MORANIS

For Suzanne,
Happy 1st

I

"The universe is full of magical things patiently waiting for our wits to grow sharper."

- EDEN PHILLPOTTS

"Spengler, are you serious about actually catching a ghost?"

- DR. PETER VENKMAN

1

A bright winter sun blazed down onto the streets of Manhattan as Dana Barrett struggled with two sagging bags of groceries while at the same time pushing a baby carriage.

Long-armed and lithe in figure, Dana was able to balance the bags in her arms while still maneuvering the carriage in a straight line.

Pausing for a moment, she took a deep breath of crisp air. She loved New York. It was the city's air of excitement, of *life* that appealed to her. As she continued walking, she thought about how her life had changed in the last four years. How many women could say that they'd been a struggling cellist, been attacked by a devilishly possessed chair, been transformed into an ancient demon, and, finally, become a mother of a bright-eyed baby named Oscar—all in the few years since she'd moved to the Big Apple?

Not many, she figured. At least not many who were allowed to roam the streets without a straitjacket.

Dana wheeled her baby up to the front of her building on East Seventy-seventh Street. At curbside, a car was being hoisted up by a city tow truck while the driver screamed, red-faced, at the parking-enforcement officer.

The man was threatening to do something to the cop that dogs usually reserved for hydrants.

Dana clutched the grocery bags, trying desperately to dig her keys out of her purse.

Glancing over her shoulder, she noticed that Frank, her building's superintendent, was leaning against a wall, pretending not to notice Dana's dilemma. Typical, she thought. Frank was the sort of fellow who lived in the future. If something needed repairing, he'd put it off until tomorrow, or next week, or, if it was really important, next month.

Dana turned and smiled sweetly at Frank. "Frank, do you think you could give me a hand with these bags?"

The unshaven, middle-aged man shrugged. "I'm not a doorman, Miss Barrett. I'm a building superintendent."

Dana resisted the temptation to hurl a few choice canned goods at Frank's head. "You're also a human being, Frank."

Frank considered this point. Yup, he was. Reluctantly he walked toward Dana. "Okay. Okay. It's not my job, but what the heck. I'll do you a big favor." With a grunt he took the sagging grocery bags out of Dana's arms.

"Thank you, Frank, you're a prince."

"Better." Frank grinned. "I'm a *super.*"

Dana set the wheel brakes on the baby carriage and rummaged through her purse. "I'll get the hang of all this eventually," she muttered.

Frank leaned over the baby buggy and began making funny faces at little Oscar. "Hiya, Oscar. What do you say, slugger?"

Oscar regarded the crazy person above him with a great deal of disinterest. The baby couldn't figure out why most adults acted goofy when they were around him. Little Oscar sighed and concentrated on his pacifier.

Frank didn't notice. "That's a good-looking kid you got there, Ms. Barrett."

Dana found her keys at the very bottom of her purse. Typical. "Thank you, Frank."

Dana turned to her superintendent. "Oh, and are you ever going to fix the radiator in my bedroom? I asked you last week."

Frank blinked in astonishment. "Didn't I do it?"

Dana flashed him a patented grin. "No, you didn't."

"Okay," Frank said, still holding the soggy bags. "That's no problem."

"That's exactly what you said last week."

Frank thought hard about this. "Phew! Déjà vu."

While Dana and Frank stared at each other, little Oscar's baby carriage began to shake and rock, as if being cradled by unseen hands.

The wheel brakes unlocked themselves.

Dana, still smiling stoically at Frank, reached for Oscar's carriage. "You wouldn't mind carrying those bags upstairs, would you, Frank?"

"Well… actually…" Frank began.

As Dana extended her hand for the carriage, the carriage moved forward, just out of her reach. Dana glanced at the carriage suspiciously, as it came to a stop two feet before her.

She walked over to the buggy and tried to grab it again. The buggy shook and shot out of Dana's reach. This time it didn't rumble to a halt. It rolled merrily down the block, little Oscar inside, clapping and chirping with glee. This was *fast*. This was *fun*.

Dana fought back the urge to emit a shriek. She continued to plunge forward through the crowds of pedestrians, shambling about the streets of Manhattan.

Behind her, a befuddled Frank still stood, holding the

leaking grocery bags. "Uh..." he considered. "Ms. Barrett? What should I do with these bags?"

Dana decided not to tell him what to do with the bags. She sprinted after the runaway carriage.

Little Oscar raised a tiny fist as his baby buggy zoomed down the Manhattan street.

The baby giggled happily, watching the Upper East Side zip by.

Dana jogged, awestruck, after the baby carriage.

She shouted to everybody, anybody, for help. "Please," she screamed. "Please help my baby! Please help him!"

Several passersby tried to reach out and stop the runaway buggy. Every time they did so, the carriage deftly swerved out of the way, leaving the would-be rescuers stunned in its wake.

Little Oscar continued to giggle as the baby carriage picked up speed and zigzagged like an Indy 500 race car.

Dana continued to gallop forward. The baby buggy seemed to have a life of its own. Dana yelled for help. One burly man tried to tackle the baby carriage and found himself being lifted and thrown *over* it by some unseen force.

In the speeding baby buggy, baby Oscar clapped his hands with glee. *Zoooooom,* he managed to gurgle. *Zoooooom.*

The buggy tilted and whirled past everyone on the street.

The buggy headed for a crosswalk.

Cars, trucks, and buses zipped through the congested intersection ahead.

Dana watched in horror as a city bus glided across Seventy-seventh Street. Effortlessly the baby buggy sailed over the curb and into the intersection.

The carriage was speeding toward the front of the bus.

Dana took a deep breath and, tilting her head down, sent her long legs pumping toward the intersection like an Olympic sprinter.

Inside, baby Oscar watched in fascination as the large vehicle zeroed in on the buggy.

The bus driver, spotting the runaway carriage, twisted the steering wheel before him frantically.

The baby carriage came to a dead stop in the middle of the street.

The bus driver, still pawing the wheel, managed to send the vehicle swerving around little Oscar, missing him by inches.

Car horns blared and brakes screeched as Dana leapt into the busy intersection, quickly snatching Oscar out of the buggy.

She held the baby tightly in her arms and stared at the baby carriage.

The carriage seemed normal—now.

It stood in the center of the intersection, immobile.

To the casual passerby it appeared to be just another carriage.

Dana backed away from the buggy, Oscar in her arms.

She knew *better.*

2

A slim, elegant 1959 ambulance tooled up Broadway on the Upper West Side of Manhattan. On the side of the vehicle was painted a portrait of a ghost, surrounded by a red circle with a crimson slash drawn through it. "No Ghosts."

The vehicle bore the license plate ECTO-1 and was, in fact, the Ghostbusters' emergency vehicle.

Inside Ecto-1, a very tired Ray Stantz helmed the steering wheel while a very bored Winston Zeddemore rode shotgun. Both wore their official Ghostbusters jumpsuits, and both were ready for trouble.

Stantz guided the vehicle around potholes. A tall, baby-faced man with a haircut that could only be described as New Wave groundhog, Stantz rubbed his eyes occasionally, trying to get the red out.

As a light turned green ahead, he gave Ecto-1 the gas. The car produced a sound that sounded like a yak in a blender.

Big, burly, and black, Winston Zeddemore slid deeper into his seat. He was beginning to hate this work. A lot.

"How many did she say there were?" Winston asked.

Stantz peered into the bus-fume-laced street before him. "Fourteen of them," he said in a monotone. "About three and a half to four feet high."

Winston heaved a sigh. "I don't think I can take this anymore, man. All the crying and the biting! The screaming and the fighting! It's starting to get to me, Ray."

Stantz nodded grimly. "I know it's rough, Winston, but somebody's got to do it. People are counting on us. Who else are they going to call… *Bozo the clown?*"

A thin smile played across Stantz's lips. "I… don't… think… so."

Stantz guided the car into a parking space before a carefully restored old brownstone. Gritting his teeth, he marched out of Ecto-1 and, strode to the back of the refurbished ambulance. He popped open the back hatch and produced two large, bulky proton packs attached to neutrona wands—ghostbusting guns hooked up to power-generating backpacks.

Winston and Stantz, grim-faced, shouldered their weapons in place and marched up to the building, their eyes darting this way and that.

They stopped before the front door. Stantz pressed a buzzer. "Who is it?" a female voice squawked over the intercom. "Ghostbusters," Stantz said coolly. "We have a job to do here."

The woman sighed over the intercom. In the background could be heard wailing and screeching voices.

"I'll say," the woman said. "Come on in. It's Apartment 1-B."

Stantz and Winston exchanged determined looks as they entered the building and walked down a dimly lit, cavernous hallway, proton packs strapped firmly in place.

"This could be a rough one," Stantz stated.

"I know it," Winston agreed. "I heard."

They paused before the door.

"This is it," Stantz declared.

Winston nodded. "This is it."

Stantz made a move to reach for the knocker on the door. Before he had a chance to grasp it, the door was flung open. A birdlike woman with blue-gray hair and what appeared to be makeup left over from an Earl Scheib paint job greeted them nervously.

"They're in the back!" she gasped. "I hope you can handle them. It's been like a nightmare!"

Stantz and Winston exchanged knowing glances. Winston nodded and his jaw tightened. "We'll do our best, ma'am."

"Oh, thank you," the woman gushed. "They're right in here."

The tiny woman led the two Ghostbusters through an expensively furnished home. She stopped in front of a pair of opened French doors, leading into a vast living room.

Ray Stantz and Winston paused before the door. They carefully adjusted their equipment.

"Ready?" Stantz asked, sweat trickling down his forehead.

"I'm ready," Winston declared, straightening himself up to his full six-feet-plus height.

"Let's *do* it!" Stantz whispered.

The two men strode past the French doors and marched into the living room.

"Oh, my God!" Winston said.

"It's worse than I thought!" Stantz gulped.

Over a dozen children—short, birthday-cake-stained, and all between the ages of seven and ten—descended upon the two helpless men.

"Ghostbusters!" they screeched.

"Yeah!" others shouted.

Stantz glanced around the room. Tables were set with party favors, dripping with left-over ice cream and birthday cake. The place was scattered with discarded toys and games. Several exhausted parents were strewn across sofas. They glanced at Stantz and Winston as they entered the room. They made eye contact. Their eyes said, "Thank you, thank you, thank you."

Winston winked at the parents and faced the horde of ice-cream- and cake-stained short people before him. "How you doin', kids?" he asked.

A freckle-faced kid with a big belly glared at Winston. "I thought we were having He-Man."

To stress the point, the mean little kid brought his right leg way back and kicked Stantz in the shin. Stantz smiled and, after making sure no parents were watching, reached down and grabbed the kid by the front of his shirt. He smiled at the little boy. "I'll be watching you," he growled. "Remember that."

He dropped the kid back onto the floor and turned to Winston with a wink. "Song?"

Winston reached into his utility belt and switched on a tiny tape recorder, which began belting out the Ghostbusters' theme song. Stantz and Winston began gyrating, singing, and bopping to the music.

Who you gonna call?" they crooned.

"He-Man," the kids replied.

Stantz and Winston glanced at each other, not breaking stride.

"It's gonna be one of those gigs," Winston hissed.

"Keep singing, we need the money," Stantz said, breaking out into the Twist.

A small eternity later, Stantz found himself surrounded by drippy-nosed children. He was trying to keep them amused by recounting the Ghostbusters' finest hour. "So," he continued, "we get up to the very top of the building, and yep, sure enough, there was a huge staircase with those two nasty terror dogs I told you about. And guess what?"

"They were guarding the entrance," the wise-guy kid said with a sigh.

Stantz tried not to strangle the little beastie. "Exactly." He smiled. "They were guarding the entrance. Well, at this point I had to take command, so I turned to the boys and I said, 'Okay, 'Busters, this is it. Fire up your throwers and let's toast that sucker!'"

The mean little kid wasn't impressed. "My dad says you're full of crap."

Stantz's eyes almost left his head. "Well, a lot of people have trouble believing in the paranormal," he offered.

"Naah," the kid continued, "that's not it. He says you're full of crap and that's why you went out of business."

Stantz flashed a smile of the sort usually used by bodybuilders hiding a groin injury. "He does, eh? I see."

Stantz snapped his fingers, getting up from the crowd of children. "Hey! How about some science? Did you ever see a hard-boiled egg get sucked through the mouth of a Coke bottle?"

The kids nodded in unison. "Yeah," they said.

"A lot," the mean little kid added.

Winston sat in a corner and shook his head. "Oh, man," he said, then sighed.

After Stantz had pummeled every Mr. Wizard trick into the carpet, the weary Ghostbusters packed up their gear and trudged out of the building.

Stantz popped open Ecto-l's back hatch and tossed his equipment inside. Winston neatly knuckle-balled his into the auto.

"That's it, Ray," he swore. "I've had it. No more parties. I'm tired of taking abuse from overprivileged nine-year-olds."

"Come on, Winston," Stantz wheedled, trying to look on the bright side of things. "We can't quit now. The holidays are coming up! It's our best season!"

The two men got into the car. Stantz attempted to get

Ecto-1 moving. He cranked the ignition key. The car made a sound that resembled an elephant in heat. The engine refused to turn over. Winston gazed out of the windshield at nothing in particular.

"Give it up, Ray. You're living in the past. Ghostbusters doesn't exist anymore. In a year these kids won't even remember who we are."

Stantz plowed a hand through his groundhog hairdo before cranking the engine again. *Snork!* the engine declared before dying. "Ungrateful little yuppie larvae," Stantz muttered. "After all we did for this city!"

Winston offered a dry cackle. "Yeah, what did we do, Ray? The last real job we had, we bubbled up a hundred-foot marshmallow man and blew the top three floors off an uptown high rise."

A dreamy smile played across Stantz's face. "Yeah, but what a *ride.* You can't make a hamburger without chopping up a cow."

Stantz turned the ignition key again. Ecto-l's engine roared to life. Then it began to grind its gears. Then, apparently, it began playing a game of last tag with itself. Stantz couldn't believe his ears as, *clunkity-clunk-clunk*, the engine began tossing off twisted little bits of itself onto the street beneath it. A massive cloud of black smoke mushroomed from the back of the car. Stantz gaped at the dashboard as every "danger" indicator lit up and Ecto-1 sputtered, shuddered, spat, and died.

Winston gave him an I-told-you-so look.

Ray Stantz considered the situation and reacted in an adult manner. He began to bang his forehead onto the steering wheel.

"You're going to hurt yourself, Ray," Winston offered.

"I know," Stantz said, slamming his forehead, again and again, onto the wheel.

"Want me to call Triple A?" Winston asked.

"Either that or a brain surgeon," Stantz replied.

Winston eased himself out of Ecto-1. "I'll see who answers first."

3

Legend has it that even as a child, Peter Venkman was incapable of a sincere smile. The farthest he could go was a heartfelt smirk. In high school he was voted Most Likely to Become a Used-car Salesman or a Game-show Host. Venkman never cared. He knew he had it within himself to achieve *greatness*. And if he didn't find it within himself, he knew he could probably pick it up somewhere at a discount.

He'd been great once. A bona fide Ghostbuster.

Now, the fellow with the twenty-four-hour smirk, the cocky attitude, and hair that looked like it had been dried by a Mixmaster sat in the tiny TV studio given to him by WKRR, Channel 10, in New York.

He sat passively in his host's seat, gazing out on an audience filled with polyester leisure suits and dresses that resembled designs lifted from Omar the tent maker.

Synthesized Muzak began to play in the background.

He glanced at the TV monitor to the right of the camera as the title *World of the Psychic with Dr. Peter Venkman* materialized against a background that looked like swirling phlegm.

Venkman screwed on his best grin (which operated at a forty-five-degree angle) and pushed his voice up to gracious-huckster volume. He was suave. He was engaging. He was the people's friend. He would do anything to pay the rent.

"Hi," he said breathlessly to both the camera and the adoring audience. "We're back to the *World of the Psychic* I'm Peter Venkman."

He glanced at his two guests: a frail man who resembled Boris Karloff after a bad day in the lab and a rotund woman who bore more than a passing resemblance to Lou Costello in drag.

"I'm chatting with my guest—author, lecturer, and of course, psychic, Milton Anglund."

He faced the dour man and cocked his head to one side in a Cary Grant kind of way. "Milt, your new book is called *The End of the World*. Isn't that kind of like writing about gum disease? Yes, it could happen, but do you think anybody wants to read a book about it?"

The dour man shrugged. "Well, I think it's important for people to know that the world is in danger."

Venkman nodded. "Okay, so you can tell us when it's going to happen or do we have to buy the book?"

Milton puffed up his sparrowlike chest. "I predict that the world will end at the stroke of midnight on New Year's Eve."

Venkman rolled his eyes. "This year? That's cutting it a little close, isn't it? I mean, from a sales point of view, the book just came out, right? So you're not even looking at the paperback release for maybe a year. And it's going to be at least another year after that if the thing has movie-of-the-week or miniseries potential. You would have been better off predicting 1992 or even '94 just to play it safe."

Milton was not amused. "This is not just some money-making scheme! I didn't just make up the date. I have a strong psychic belief that the world will end on New Year's Eve!"

Venkman raised his palms. "Whoa. Okay. For your sake, I hope you're right. But I think my other guest may disagree with you. Elaine, you had another date in mind, right?"

The heavily made-up woman from New Jersey nodded her head. "According to my sources, the world will end on February fourteenth, in the year 2016."

Venkman winked at her. "Valentine's Day? That's got to be a bummer. Where did you get that date, Elaine?"

Elaine pursed her lips dramatically. "I received this information from an alien. I was at the Paramus Holiday Inn. I was having a drink in the bar when he approached me and started talking. Then he must have used some sort of ray or a mind-control device, because he made me follow him to his room and that's where he told me about the end of the world."

Venkman grinned as he felt a good number of his brain cells check out. "Your alien had a room at the Holiday Inn?"

Elaine pondered this. "It may have been a room on the spacecraft made up to *look* like a room in the Holiday Inn."

Venkman gazed at the woman. He was losing feeling in his feet. "No, you can't be *sure*," he said with a nod. "And I think that's the whole problem with aliens. You just can't trust them. Oh, sure, you may get some nice ones occasionally, like Starman or E.T., but most of them turn out to be some kind of lizard. Anyway, we're just about out of time."

Venkman faced the camera, mentally nodding out. "Next week on *World of the Psychic*... Bigfoot: is he real or just a lumberjack from a broken home?"

He smiled at the camera. "Until then, this is Peter Venkman... good night."

After the show he cornered his producer, Norman, in the hall. Norman looked a little like Timmy from the old *Lassie* show but was slightly better dressed.

"Where do you find these people, *Normie*?" Venkman asked. "I thought we were having the telekinetic guy who bends the spoons?"

Norman was embarrassed. "A lot of the better psychics won't come onto your show, Dr. Venkman. They think you're too skeptical."

"Me?" Venkman said, astonished. "Skeptical? Norman, I'm a pushover. I think professional wrestling is real!"

Venkman looked up. There was a commotion brewing from the studio next door. Several plainclothes policemen strode out of two swinging doors, followed by a small army of men in suits, with serious expressions.

"What's all this?" Venkman asked Norman.

"They just interviewed the mayor on *Cityline*," Norman replied.

"The Mayor of New York City!" Venkman exclaimed. "Why, he's an old friend of mine."

Venkman ran down the corridor as the mayor and his top aide—a mousse-laden, no-nonsense, three-piece suit named Jack Hardemeyer—emerged from the studio next door.

"Lenny!" Venkman called, waving at the mayor. Mayor Leonard Clotch wheeled around and, spotting Venkman, wiped a trickle of sweat from his upper lip and almost ran down the hall in the opposite direction.

"Hey, Lenny!" Venkman called. "It's me! Peter Venkman."

Two plainclothes cops stopped Venkman in his tracks. Hardemeyer marched up to Venkman and, after adjusting his hair, placed a heavy hand on Venkman's chest.

"Can I help you?" He sneered.

Venkman, while appreciating the sneer, didn't like the man's attitude. "Yeah," he said, "you can get your hand off my chest."

Hardemeyer offered a serpent's smile and dropped his

hand. "I'm Jack Hardemeyer. I'm the mayor's assistant. What can I do for you?"

Venkman straightened his tie. "I'm an old friend of the mayor's. I just wanted to say hello."

Hardemeyer emitted a harsh laugh. "I know who you are, Dr. Venkman. Busted any ghosts lately?"

"No," Venkman admitted. "That's what I want to talk to the mayor about. We did a little job for the city a while back and we ended up getting sued, screwed, and tattooed by desk worms like you."

Hardemeyer offered Venkman an angry stare. "Look," he replied, bristling. "You stay away from the mayor. Next fall, barring a disaster, he's going to be elected governor of this state, and the last thing we need is for him to be associated with two-bit frauds and publicity hounds like you and your friends. You read me?"

Yeah, Venkman thought to himself, and it's strictly big print.

The two plainclothes cops flanked Venkman, helping him get the point. "Okay," Venkman said smoothly. "I get it. But I want you to tell Lenny that because of *you*, I'm not voting for him."

Hardemeyer smiled smugly and, spinning on his heels, marched off with the two plainclothes cops. Venkman watched them move out of the hallway.

Heaving a sigh, he trudged through the reception area, where a small group of his fans and possible guests were gathered.

The fans applauded him.

"No, really, you're too kind." Venkman was nearly grimacing.

One man was holding a crystal the size of a Toyota.

Another man had a small TV antenna glued to the hat he was wearing.

A fellow in full voodoo uniform sat next to the candy machine, burning incense.

A fat woman petting a hairless cat smiled up at Venkman.

Venkman smiled at them all, but at a strange angle. He was losing it. He was definitely losing it. He winked at the woman. "Nice cat. Very unusual. I had a bald collie once myself."

Venkman eased himself out the exit door and walked toward the elevator.

After thinking about it a second, he *ran*.

4

Dana Barrett walked up the stairs of the Manhattan Museum of Art, her portfolio and artist's box in her hand. She weaved her way through the crowds of tourists and visitors milling toward the museum's entrance.

Little Oscar would be safe today, she knew. She gave strict instructions to the baby-sitter not to take the boy out of the apartment.

Dana flashed her ID card at the guard at the main entrance and, ignoring his smile, walked into the back of the museum, where the large restoration studio was housed.

Since leaving her dreams of cello playing behind, Dana had earned a living restoring some of the oldest long-lost paintings of the Western world; chipping, cleaning, and urging them back into full bloom.

She stepped into the restoration studio and glanced upward with a slight shudder.

A titantic portrait of Vigo the Carpathian stared down at her. The seventeenth-century despot bore a striking resemblance to the Incredible Hulk dressed for an evening in Camelot. Vigo's dark, evil eyes seemed to leap out of the painting toward Dana.

Actually it was the artistry of a young, wiry, and decidedly quirky artist, Janosz Poha, that was bringing Vigo "to life."

Janosz was the head of the department and incredibly talented. He was also incredibly creepy to Dana's way of thinking. What he saw in the ugly painting of Vigo was beyond her.

Dana walked over to a nineteenth-century painting, this one a landscape, her mind still on little Oscar, and began to clean the years of soot and dust off its surface.

Janosz stopped working on Vigo for a moment, and staring longingly at Dana, softly padded up behind her. He looked over her shoulder and smiled. He opened his mouth and spoke, his words emerging in a thick Eastern European accent.

"Still working on the Turner?" he said casually, sounding a tad like a talking Veg-O-Matic.

"Oh?" Dana said, startled. "Oh, yes. I got in a little late this morning, Janosz. I'm sorry. I'll have it finished by the end of the day."

Janosz twisted his scarecrow face into a grin. "Take your time. The painting's been around for a hundred and fifty years. A few more hours won't matter."

Dana forced herself to emit a polite laugh. She began to work again, hoping her young boss would just go away. "You know," Janosz continued, "you are really doing very good work here. I think soon you may be ready to assist me in some of the more important restorations."

"Thank you, Janosz," Dana said, still not facing the man. "I've learned a lot here, but now that my baby's a little older, I was hoping to rejoin the orchestra."

At the mention of Dana's baby, the figure of Vigo in the painting seemed to glow slightly, its dark eyes gleaming. Slowly, deliberately, the painting turned its mighty head and gazed down at Dana.

Dana, her back toward the mural, did not notice. Neither did Janosz, who was deeply involved in gazing at Dana himself. "Oh, I'm sorry to hear that," he said. "We'll be very sorry to lose you."

Dana continued to clean her landscape. "I didn't really want to quit the orchestra in the first place," she explained. "But it's a little hard to play a cello when you're pregnant."

Janosz emitted a braying, nasal laugh. "Of course. Perhaps I could take you to lunch to celebrate your return to the Philharmonic?"

"Actually I'm not eating lunch today," Dana said, putting down her cleaning tools. "I have an appointment."

She gazed at her wristwatch. "In fact, I'd better go."

Dana replaced her tools. Janosz was clearly disturbed. "Every day I ask you to lunch, and every day you've got something else to do. Do I have bad breath or something?"

Dana smiled at him. "Something. Perhaps some other time."

Janosz brightened. "Okay. I'll take a rain check on that."

Dana walked out of the room, leaving a smiling Janosz to return to his easel. "I think she likes me." He winked at the towering painting above him.

Reaching for his small tape-player, Janosz flipped on a tape and began practicing his English phraseology as he once again resumed work on Vigo.

High above the unsuspecting Janosz, the portrait of the all-evil Vigo rolled its eyes heavenward.

Silly mortals.

5

A gaggle of Manhattan University graduate students carefully examined a small, rectangular bit of nouveau scientific gadgetry in a lab at the university's Institute for Advanced Theoretical Research while Egon Spengler, the last of the original Ghostbusters, sat at his desk listening to a thoroughly distraught Dana Barrett recount her tale of the baby buggy with a mind of its own.

Egon's face was a portrait of intense concentration, which wasn't surprising, considering that Egon had two expressions. Intense concentration and *more* intense concentration. Egon had been born to wear a lab coat. He felt out of place when not involved in some sort of experiment involving techno-wizardry.

Egon had a hawklike face and a neatly kept hairdo, separated by a pair of horn-rimmed glasses that, while out-of-date, fit his concerned face perfectly. Nothing seemed to faze earnest Egon. He had grown up idolizing two men: Albert Einstein and *Star Trek's* Mr. Spock. Neither were known as party animals.

Dana finished her tale of roller-coaster carriage goings-on "... and then the buggy just suddenly stopped dead in the middle of the street."

Egon nodded sagely. "Did anyone else see this happen?"

"Hundreds of people," Dana replied. "Believe me, I didn't imagine this."

Egon's brain was already in high gear. "I'm not saying you did. In science, we always look for the simplest explanation."

A graduate student ran up to Egon. "We're ready, Dr. Spengler."

Spengler didn't take his eyes off Dana. "We'll start with the negative calibration."

The student handed Egon the small black box. Spengler glanced at it, adjusting its controls.

"What are you working on, Egon?" Dana asked.

Egon got to his feet. "You might find this amusing," he said, attempting to smile. It hurt his face. "I'm trying to determine whether human emotional states have a measurable effect on the psychomagnetheric energy field. It's a theory Ray and I were working on when we had to dissolve Ghostbusters."

Dana didn't understand a word he was saying. "Oh, I see."

Egon led Dana to a large curtain. One of his students pulled back the drapes to reveal a large picture window. It was actually a two-way mirror looking into a small waiting room. Inside the waiting room, Dana saw a young couple apparently in the midst of a heated argument.

Egon pointed to the couple. "They think they're in here for marriage counseling. We've kept them waiting for two hours and we've been gradually increasing the temperature in the room."

He checked a heat sensor located next to the two-way glass. "It's up to ninety-five degrees at the moment. Now, one of my assistants is going to enter the room and ask them if they'd mind waiting another half hour."

He turned to Dana confidentially. "This should be good."

As Spengler, Dana, and the research team watched, one of Spengler's assistants entered the waiting room and, gesturing wildly, told the young couple about the delay. The two people leapt to their feet and began screeching at both the assistant and each other.

Spengler calmly raised the small black box and took the readings from the room.

Dana stood there, baffled.

"We'll do the happiness index next," Spengler explained.

"I-I'm sure you will," Dana said.

"As for your problem," Spengler went on, "I'd like to bring Ray in on your case, if it's all right with you."

"Okay, whatever you think," Dana answered. "But please, not Venkman!"

Spengler almost laughed out loud but caught himself in time. "Oh, no. Don't worry about *that*."

Dana attempted to look casual. "Do you, um, ever see him anymore?"

"Occasionally," Egon said.

"How is he these days?" Dana asked.

Spengler cast her a wise look. "Venkman? I think he was borderline for a while there. Then he crossed the border."

"Does he ever mention me?" Dana queried.

Spengler turned to a second pair of curtains. "No," he said with a shrug. "Not that I can recall."

He drew the drapes and peered down on a tiny little girl playing with a wonderful array of colorful toys.

Dana tried to hide her disappointment about Venkman's lack of interest in her. "Well," she said, sighing. "We didn't part on very good terms, and we sort of lost track of each other when I got married—"

One of Spengler's aides interrupted. "We're ready for the affection test."

"Good." Egon nodded. "Send in the puppy."

"I thought of calling him after my marriage ended," Dana babbled on, "but… anyway, I appreciate your doing this, Egon."

Egon watched as another assistant entered the playroom with an adorable cocker spaniel puppy. He gave it to the little girl. Spengler monitored her as she jumped for joy and embraced the tiny puppy affectionately.

Dana thrust a card in front of the busy Spengler's nose. "This is my address and telephone number. Will you call me?"

Spengler studied the little girl and the puppy. "Huh? Oh, certainly. Yes."

"And, Egon," Dana continued, "I'd rather you didn't mention any of this to Peter if you don't mind."

"I won't," Spengler said absentmindedly.

"Thank you," Dana said, shaking the preoccupied Spengler's hand before leaving.

Spengler watched the little girl oooh and aahh over the puppy dog.

Spengler nodded knowingly to his study team. "Now… let's see how she reacts when we take the puppy away."

6

Ray Stantz's Occult Bookstore sat on a small, quaint block in Greenwich Village. The window was crowded with occult artifacts and ancient books filled with arcane metaphysical lore that appealed only to the very rich, the very bored, or the very addled.

Stantz sat inside the shop on a bar stool behind the main counter while Egon Spengler waddled up and down the aisles of the tiny place, occasionally stopping to peruse a volume.

Stantz, reading glasses on, prepared a cup of herb tea for his old Ghostbuster crony while chewing on a pipe that emitted an odor reminiscent of week-old sweat socks.

The phone rang.

Stantz was amazed. A customer! Summoning up his most pleasant voice, he picked up the phone. "Ray's Occult," he said sweetly. "Yes. Uh-hmmmm. What do you need?… What have I got?"

Stantz took a deep breath. "I've got alchemy, astrology, apparitions, Bundu magic men, demon intercessions, UFO abductions, psychic surgery, stigmata, modern miracles, pixie sightings, golden geese, geists, ghosts. I've got it all. What is it you're looking for? Don't have any. Try the stockyards."

Stantz slammed the phone down.

"Who was that?" Egon asked.

"Some crank"—Stantz sighed—"looking for goat hooves. Come up with anything?"

Spengler cradled a book in his hands. "This one is interesting. Berlin, 1939. A flower cart took off by itself and rolled approximately half a kilometer over level ground. Three hundred eyewitnesses."

Ray Stantz took a toxic puff of his pipe. "Hmmmm. You might want to check the *A.S.P.R.*, volume six, number three, 1968–1969, Renzacker and Buell, Duke University, mean averaging study on controlled psychokinetics."

Spengler nodded enthusiastically. He had missed working with Ray. "Oh, *yes*. That's a good one."

The front door suddenly flew open, sending the tiny bone chimes above it clanking. Peter Venkman strode in, wiggling his eyebrows at Ray. "Oh, hello, perhaps you could help me. I'm looking for an aerosol love potion I could spray on a certain *Penthouse* Pet that would make her unconditionally submit to an *unusual* personal request."

Stantz continued to brew his tea. "Oh, hiya, Pete."

Venkman walked up to the counter. "So, no goat hooves, huh?"

Stantz was stunned. "I *knew* that voice sounded familiar. What's up? How's it going?"

"Nowhere... fast," Venkman replied, staring at the piles of old books around him. "Why don't you lock up and buy me a sub?"

Ray was bad at being evasive, but he gave it his best shot. "Uh, I can't. I'm kind of working on something."

Spengler chose that moment to step out from behind the stacks of books on the paranormal.

Venkman extended his arms in a mock embrace. "Egon!"

"Hello, Venkman." Spengler frowned.

Venkman trotted over to Egon and put an arm around the man's shoulders. "How've you been? What are you up to? You never call, Egon. Shame on you."

"You don't have a phone," Spengler replied logically.

"Oh, yeah, right." Venkman nodded. "Well, I'm negotiating with AT&T right now. So how's teaching? I bet those science chicks really dig that big cranium of yours, huh? Ooooh."

"I think they're more interested in my epididymis," Spengler answered.

Venkman flinched. "I don't even want to know what that is."

Venkman strolled behind Ray's counter and, reaching into a mini-fridge, removed and popped open a beer. He began guzzling it.

Stantz was clearly nervous having Venkman in the store. "Oh, uh, your book came in, Venkman." He reached behind the counter and produced a large paperback. "*Magical Paths to Fortune and Power.*"

Venkman took the book and began rifling through the table of contents. "Hmm. Interesting material here. Money. More money. Even more money. See: Donald Trump."

He glanced at Stantz. "So what are you guys working on?"

Stantz swallowed hard, flashing a nervous look at Egon Spengler. "Umm, just checking something out for an old friend."

Venkman leaned over the counter. "Who?"

Stantz began to sweat. "Who? It's... just someone we know."

Stantz slumped down on the stool as Venkman stood above him, a twisted smile on his face. "Oh, Ray. I am heartbroken."

"Y-you are?" Stantz gulped.

Venkman shook his head from side to side. "Truly. I have this horrible, awful, *terrible* feeling that you, one of my oldest and closest friends, are hiding something from me."

Egon rolled his eyes. "Oh, brother."

Venkman, still smiling, reached down and grabbed Ray by the ears. He pulled Ray up off his perch by his earlobes. "Who is it, Ray? Who? Who? Who?"

"Aaaah!" Ray yelled, his ears now extended enough to qualify him for a free pass to Disneyland. "Nobody! I mean, somebody! I mean, *I can't tell you*!?"

"Who, Ray?" Venkman cooed, his hands still firmly attached to Ray's ears.

"Dana!" Ray blurted. *"Dana Barrett!"*

Venkman let go of Ray's ears and smiled. Spengler stared at Stantz with disgust.

"Thank you, Ray." Venkman smiled. 'You are one heck of a good friend... and I mean that from the heart."

7

Dana stood in the bedroom door and watched Maria, the young Hispanic woman who provided day-care service for her, feed little Oscar in the kitchen. Everything had seemed to go all right since Oscar's buggy decided to go rock and rolling across town, but still, Dana was worried.

When her front doorbell chimed, she instinctively knew that help was on the way.

"I'll get it, Maria," she said, rushing toward the door and flinging it open. Outside, in the hallway, were Ray and Egon.

"Ray," she said, hugging the tall Ghostbuster. "It's good to see you. Thanks for coming."

Stantz was slightly embarrassed. "No problem. Always glad to help… and hug."

"Hi, Egon," she said, shaking the bespectacled scientist's hand. She let them into her tastefully furnished apartment and was about to close the door when she heard a familiar voice.

"Hi, Dana."

Dana gulped, suddenly feeling as if she had a few hamsters doing treadmill tricks in her stomach.

Peter Venkman stepped into her doorway, wagging a

"naughty, naughty" finger in the air. "I *knew* you'd come crawling back to me."

Dana found herself smiling, in spite of her shock. She was always both amazed and amused at how quickly Venkman's mouth formed words. She often wondered if his brain ever had the time to catch up. "Hello, Peter," she said with a sigh.

Venkman stepped inside the apartment. "You know, Dana. I'm very, very hurt that you didn't call me first. I'm still into all this stuff, you know. In fact, I'm considered an expert. Haven't you ever seen my TV show?"

"I have." Dana nodded coolly. "That's why I didn't call you first."

Venkman clutched his heart, as if mortally wounded by an arrow. He gazed at the ceiling. "I can see that you're still very bitter about us," he said.

Then he added with a shrug, "But in the interests of science I'm going to give it my best shot. Let's go to work, boys."

Stantz and Spengler rolled their eyes. It seemed just like old times... unfortunately. The two former Ghostbusters produced their small PKE measuring devices, hand-held creations that looked a tad like electric razors with wings. They carefully passed the monitors over and around little Oscar before checking out the rest of the apartment for any residual psychokinetic energy.

Venkman, leaving the others to handle the hardcore science, thrust his hands in his pockets and decided to give himself a tour of Dana's apartment.

He nodded as he checked out the furniture. Pretty nice. It sure beat the raunchy stuff he was using right now. He gazed meaningfully at Dana's plush couch. Up until last week he had been using a series of packing crates to sit on. It must be nice not to get splinters sitting on a couch.

"So," he said casually, "what happened to Mr. Right? I hear he ditched you and the kid and moved to Europe."

"He didn't 'ditch' me," Dana said, bristling. "We had some... problems. He got a good offer from a company in England and he took it."

Venkman held his smile. "He ditched you. You should've married me, you know."

"You never asked me," Dana shot back. "And every time I brought it up, you'd get drowsy and fall asleep."

Venkman seemed shocked. "Hey, men are *very* sensitive, you know. We need to feel loved and desired too."

"Well"—Dana smiled thinly—"when you started introducing me as 'the old ball and chain,' that's when I left."

Venkman saw the logic in this. "I may have a few personal problems," he admitted, "but one thing I am is a total professional."

He marched meaningfully across the room to Spengler. Egon had little Oscar sprawled on the couch and was in the middle of taking a complete set of body and head measurements of the lad, using a tape measure and calipers. Venkman was intrigued.

"What are you going to do, Egon? Knit him a snowsuit?"

Spengler ignored the remark and handed Venkman a small jar. "I'd like to have a stool specimen," he muttered.

"Yeah, you would," Venkman agreed. "Is that for personal or professional reasons?"

Spengler shot Venkman a look that equaled the phrase *zip it*. Venkman withered into silence. He gazed down at little Oscar. He had never seen a baby so close-up before. He tilted his head down at the boy. Was the kid smiling at him?

He picked up the baby in his hands. "Okay, kid. Up you go."

He held the giggling baby over his head and pressed his nose into the baby's belly, making the baby laugh even more.

"He's attacking!" Venkman cried. "Help! Please, somebody help me! Get him off! Quickly! He's gone completely berserk."

Ray and Egon sighed and smiled, continuing their readings of the house. Dana was mildly surprised at Venkman's latent daddy prowess.

"What do you think?" she asked him as Venkman continued to clown with the baby.

"There's no doubt about it," Venkman said, staring into the boy's cherubic face. "He's got his father's looks. The kid is ugly... extremely ugly. And smelly."

Venkman grinned at the baby and jiggled him. The baby whooped with glee. "You stink, baby. It's just horrible. You are the stinkiest baby I ever smelled."

He turned to Dana. "What's his name?"

"His name is Oscar."

Venkman flashed a sad smirk at Oscar. "You poor kid."

Dana finally lost her patience with Venkman's kidding. "Peter, this is serious. I need to know if you think there's anything unusual about him."

Venkman held Oscar directly in front of him. "Hmm. Unusual? I don't know. I haven't had a lot of experience with babies."

"Sample?" Spengler reminded him from across the room.

"Right." Venkman nodded.

Venkman laid the baby down on the couch and attempted to remove its little sleeper. He wasn't sure whether to pull it down over the child's feet or up over its head. Oh, well, he figured. He had a fifty-fifty chance of getting it right.

Dana snatched the jar away from him. "I'll do it," she snapped.

"I'll supervise." He smiled.

"You'll do no such thing," she said.

"Right." Venkman nodded, seeing Oscar's diaper. "I'll do no such thing."

Venkman strolled into Oscar's nursery, where Ray Stantz was carefully monitoring every piece of furniture and every toy for traces of psychokinetic energy. Venkman sidled up to Ray. Ray rubbed his groundhog hair, puzzled.

"Well, Holmes," Venkman asked. "What do you think?"

"It's an interesting one, Pete. If anything was going on, it's totally subdued now."

Egon Spengler entered the room, similarly confused.

Venkman recognized the look. Intense concentration. "What now, brainiac?"

"I think we should see if we can find anything abnormal on the street," he said.

Venkman nodded. "Finding something abnormal on a New York street shouldn't be too hard."

Moments later Dana Barrett was leading Stantz, Spengler, and Venkman down East Seventy-seventh Street, carefully retracing the route Oscar's baby buggy had taken after it developed a mind of its own. Stantz and Spengler worked in silence, monitoring the PKE valences from the pavement and the buildings.

Venkman ignored them, chatting up Dana as he gazed up and down the street. "Brings back a lot of sweet memories, doesn't it?" he said, waxing nostalgic.

He pointed to several points of interest. "There's our old cash machine. And the dry cleaners we used to go to. And the old video store."

Venkman heaved a phony sob and wiped a nonexistent tear from his eye. "We really had some good times, didn't we?"

"We definitely had a moment or two," Dana said. She suddenly stopped at the intersection and pointed to the middle of the street. "That's where the buggy stopped."

Venkman stared at the street. "Okay. Let's take a look."

Venkman stepped out into moving traffic, ignoring the don't walk sign and the cars whizzing around him. He held up his arms and began rerouting traffic like a cop would.

"Okay, buddy," he said sternly. "Slow it down. And you? Back it up. Aha! Caught you. Simon didn't say 'Back it up.'"

He motioned for Dana, Stantz, and Spengler to join him in the middle of the street. "Okay, kids. It's safe to cross now."

Stantz was the first to arrive. "Is this the spot?"

Dana extended a finger. "A little to the left."

Stantz moved his PKE monitor slightly.

"Right there!" Dana exclaimed. "That's where it stopped."

Stantz read the meter. "Nothing," he said, puzzled. "Not a trace."

Spengler lapsed into his *more* intense concentration mode. "Why don't we try the Giga meter?"

"What's that?" Venkman blinked.

Traffic was at a standstill for blocks now. Venkman ignored the honking cars and screaming drivers.

"Egon and I have been working on a gauge to measure psychomagnetheric energy in GEVs," Stantz explained. "Giga electron volts."

"That's a thousand million electron volts," Spengler clarified.

Venkman nodded sagely. "I knew that."

Spengler reached into his small carrying bag and removed the small machine he had demonstrated for Dana earlier in his lab. He passed the small device over the spot in the street where little Oscar's buggy had come to a sudden stop. Egon's eyes grew wide as the machine began to click wildly, and the GEV indicator shot into the red zone and stuck there.

Stantz gazed over Egon's shoulder, gaping. "I think we hit the honey pot, folks. There's something brewing under the street."

Dana gulped, glancing at Venkman. "Peter," she said, her voice trembling. "Do you think maybe I have some genetic problems or something that makes me vulnerable to these supernatural things?"

Venkman put a reassuring arm around her shoulders. "You mean like the time you got possessed and turned into a monster terror dog? Naaaah. Not a chance. Total coincidence."

He smiled at Stantz and Spengler. "Am I right?"

Stantz and Spengler looked first at each other, and then at Venkman. They were clearly not buying the coincidence theory.

"I said," Venkman repeated, "'Am I right?'"

"Oh, yeah," Stantz nodded.

"Sure," Spengler agreed.

Venkman led Dana, Spengler, and Stantz back to the curb. He faced the frozen traffic behind him. "Gentlemen!" he called. "Start your engines."

Within seconds, traffic on East Seventy-seventh Street was as frantic as usual. The New York street once again looked perfectly normal... for now.

8

The late-afternoon sun shed an orange glow on the Manhattan Museum of Art as dusk began to fall. Cheerful security guards ushered the last guests out of the vast museum complex while other workers shut the museum's huge glass doors for the day.

In the back of the museum, in the restoration studio, wiry Janosz Poha didn't notice the time.

He continued to work on the gigantic painting of Vigo, one of the crudest dictators in the history of the Western world. He was disturbed momentarily by Rudy, one of the museum's security guards. Rudy was a third-generation New Yorker, an Irishman whose father and grandfather had been cops. He'd always loved art, so he managed to combine his two callings by becoming an "art cop."

Rudy, making his early-evening rounds, looked up as Janosz worked carefully on restoring the ugly painting. Rudy didn't exactly know art, but he knew what gave him the willies. That painting gave him the willies.

"Oh, hello, Mr. Poha." Rudy smiled. "You working late today?"

Poha attempted a carefree grin. It looked as if he had

just backed into a live wire. “Huh? Oh, yes, Rudy. I’m working on a very important painting.”

Rudy looked at the canvas. Spook-house stuff, if you asked him. Still, Poha was supposed to be a pretty bright young guy. “Just be sure to sign out when you leave,” he said, turning his back on the portrait of the mighty warrior.

Janosz went back to his restoration work. High above him, the eyes of Vigo of Carpathia slowly flickered to life. Vigo stared down at the tiny mortal working far below his eyes. An evil grin twisted across his lips.

Janosz, unaware that he was being watched, once more raised his brush to the canvas. He screamed in terror as a powerful bolt of blood-red, crackling energy hit the brush full blast. The bolt of power shot through the brush and wormed its way through Janosz’s body, forcing the confused artist to his knees.

Groggy from the sudden charge, Janosz gazed up at the visage of Vigo.

He rubbed his eyes in disbelief.

The entire painting seemed to come alive.

Vigo slowly lowered his massive head and sneered at the cowering collection of flesh and blood trembling before him. “I am Vigo,” he announced in a voice that resonated like thunder, “the Scourge of Carpathia, the Sorrow of Moldavia. I, Vigo, command you.”

Janosz was mesmerized. “Command me, Lord,” he whispered.

Vigo smiled at his newfound servant. “On a mountain of skulls in a castle of pain, I sat on a throne of blood. Twenty thousand corpses swung from my walls and parapets, and the rivers ran with tears.”

Janosz nodded dumbly. Yes, that sounded like Vigo’s hometown, all right.

"By the power of the Book of Gombots," Vigo thundered, "what *was* will *be,* what *is* will be *no more*! Past and future, now and ever, my time is near. Now is the season of *evil.* Find me a *child* that I may *live* again!"

Two jagged streams of crimson energy emerged from Vigo's baleful eyes and swirled down toward hapless Janosz. Janosz tried to scream but could not. He tried to move but could not. The bolts of energy smashed into Janosz's eyes, sending the cowering man sinking farther down onto the floor.

His consciousness swam.

He found himself getting to his feet.

He stared at the painting of Vigo. It was quiet now. Janosz clenched his teeth. He felt new confidence. New power. He had been given a command.

He knew what to do.

He knew how to make Vigo happy.

He knew how to make Vigo powerful.

And if he was a very good servant, perhaps he, too, would share in Vigo's glory.

Janosz marched out of the restoration studio and through the darkened corridors of the museum.

He strode toward the rear exit of the building, past the security-guard station, and out the door, leaving a bewildered Rudy sitting at his security desk, pen in hand.

"Hey! Mr. Poha!"

Rudy watched the wiry artist disappear into the night.

Rudy shook his head sadly. Eggheads. "I knew he'd forget to sign out." He sighed.

In the darkness of Manhattan, Janosz walked calmly, his eyes ablaze with Vigo's power.

They shone a bright, bloody red.

9

Venkman and Stantz emerged from an all-night coffee shop on East Seventy-seventh Street as a cold wind howled through the dark canyons of Manhattan. Carrying a small armful of pastries, sandwiches, and coffee, Venkman was the picture of enthusiasm... a concept that made Ray Stantz nervous. He had seen Venkman like this before. When Venkman was happy, trouble was on the way.

"I love this," Venkman said, gushing. "We're on to something really big, Ray. I can smell it. We're going to make some headlines with this one."

Ray Stantz frowned. "Hey, hey, hey, stresshound! Are you nuts?"

Venkman pondered the query but didn't reply.

"Have you forgotten we're under a judicial restraining order?" Stantz pointed out. "The judge couldn't have been clearer—no, I repeat, *no* ghostbusting. If anybody found out about this, we'd be in serious trouble. If we're going to do this for Dana, we've got to keep this whole thing low-key, low-profile, nice and quiet."

"What?" Venkman replied. "I can't hear you!"

Stantz winced. Venkman *couldn't* hear him, and the reason was standing three yards away. Egon Spengler, wearing a hard hat and work clothes, stood in the middle of the intersection pounding a hole in the street with a huge jackhammer. Safety cones and reflectors had been set up, and Egon had lit the whole area with powerful work lights.

Stantz handed Venkman his half-chewed Danish and walked into the work area, tapping Spengler on the back. Spengler nodded and handed Stantz the hard hat and the jackhammer. Ray took a deep breath and proceeded to rip the street to shreds.

Egon walked wearily over to Venkman, rubbing his sore right shoulder. Venkman smiled and handed him a cup of coffee. Egon wasn't overly impressed. "You were supposed to help me with this."

"You need the exercise," Venkman replied.

The two men put down their coffees and sandwiches and stood, picks and shovels at hand, ready to clear the rubble.

Venkman glanced over his shoulder.

A police cruiser was slowly making its way up the street toward the men's impromptu construction site. Venkman heaved a sigh. There was always a cop around when you didn't need one.

Stantz, in the middle of the road jackhammering away, didn't see or hear the police car approach.

The two cops brought the car to a halt directly behind Stantz and waited.

Stantz, noticing a new source of illumination behind him, stopped the jackhammer. He heard a car idling very close behind him. He turned and, flashing a smile known only to beauty queens and politicians, froze in his tracks.

"How ya doin'!" one of the cops yelled from inside the patrol car.

Stantz began to sweat. "Fine!" he said, his mind reeling. "It's cutting fine now."

The cop inside the car considered this and frowned. "Um," he offered, "*why* are you cutting?"

Stantz glanced over at Spengler and Venkman. Venkman offered a beats-me expression.

Ray began to lose it. "Why are we cutting? That's a great question, Officer."

He turned sweetly to Venkman. "Uh, *boss*?"

Venkman tossed on a Consolidated Edison hard hat and, his lips working overtime, executed a fine imitation of a typical New York Con Ed repairman.

"What's the trouble?" he groused, ambling over toward the squad car.

"What are you doing here?" the cop asked.

"What the hell's it look like we're doing?" Venkman spat.

The cop was dumbfounded.

"I tell you what the hell we're doing," Venkman continued. "We're bustin' our butts over here 'cause some *nitwit* downtown ain't got nothin' better to do than make idiots like us work late on a Friday night. Right, Rocky?"

He faced Egon Spengler. Spengler nervously raised a fist. "Yo!" he barked, stymied.

The cops in the car nodded, accepting the explanation.

"Okay, boys." The driver of the patrol car nodded. "Take it easy."

The patrol car puttered away. Ray Stantz heaved a mighty sigh of relief, trying to get his heart to stop pounding through his work clothes. Taking a deep breath, he hunkered over the jackhammer and began pounding into the street again.

Bzzzzark.

The jackhammer stammered to a stop.

"I've hit something, guys," Stantz called. "Something metal."

Spengler and Venkman used their picks and shovels to clear away generations of paving material. There, at the bottom of the hole, was an ornate iron manhole cover. Stantz stared at the ancient slab of circular metal. On its top was engraved a strange logo, along with the letters NYPRR.

Stantz squinted at the weird manhole cover. "NYPRR? What the heck does that mean? Help me lift this."

Venkman and Spengler picked up crowbars and removed the manhole cover from the bottom strata of street. Stantz produced a flashlight and peered down into the dankness.

"Wow!" he theorized. "It's an old air shaft! It goes on forever!"

Spengler pushed his head inside the hole, along with his Giga meter. The indicator on the meter nearly flew off the machine. "Very intense," he said thoughtfully. "We need a deeper reading. *Somebody* has to go down there."

Venkman smiled at Stantz. "I nominate Ray."

"I second," Egon blurted.

"All in favor?" Venkman injected before Ray could respond.

"Aye," both Venkman and Spengler chorused.

Venkman turned to Stantz and pumped his hand. "Congratulations, Ray. *You* are nominated. You're one lucky guy."

Stantz nodded sadly. "Thanks, boys."

Standing as forlornly as a child being snapped into a bulky snowsuit, Ray Stantz allowed himself to be strapped into a harness by Venkman and Spengler. A cable attached to a huge winch was secured to his back. Ray strapped to his belt a radio, the Giga meter, and a small extension hook with a scooping device.

He sighed and climbed into the manhole, his companions slowly cranking him down into the darkness.

"Is that dedication or what?" Venkman said to Spengler.

"Keep going," Ray called from the shaft. "More. More. Easy does it."

Inside the seemingly endless air shaft, Stantz rappeled off the metallic walls, descending slowly into a land of total darkness.

Stantz, unable to yell up to the surface, grabbed his radio. "I'm okay," he reassured Venkman and Spengler. "Lower… lower."

He flicked off the radio and gazed into the murkiness around him. "Gee," he concluded sagely, "this is really deep."

Suddenly he felt himself kicking against thin air. The long shaft had ended. Stantz found himself spinning wildly at the top of some titanic tunnel. Stantz felt like a yo-yo on its last big spin.

"Hold it!" he cried into the radio. "Hold it."

The cable stopped moving.

Ray pulled out the powerful flashlight from his utility belt and, flicking it on, aimed it at the vast tunnel below.

Ray suppressed a gasp. He was dangling near the top of a beautifully preserved chamber with rounded, polished tile walls adorned with intricate, colorfully enameled Art Nouveau mosaics. Ray felt as if he had just leapt backward in time. He trained the flashlight on a finely inlaid sign that identified the location, VAN HORNE STATION.

Ray whistled through his teeth, scanning the walls with his flashlight.

The place looked like a subway passenger's vision of heaven.

Smiling to himself, he raised his radio. "This is it, boys," he whispered reverently. "The end of the line. Van Home Station. The old New York Pneumatic. It's still here."

Aboveground, Venkman shot a puzzled glance at Egon. "The New York Pneumatic Railway," Spengler explained.

"It was an experimental subway system, composed of fan-forced air trains. It was built around 1870."

Ray's voice crackled over the radio. "This is about as deep as you can go under Manhattan without digging your own hole."

Spengler cradled the walkie-talkie in his hands. "What's the reading, Ray?"

Belowground, Stantz shone his flashlight onto the Giga meter. The meter was going crazy. He whistled into his radio. "Off the top of the scale, Egon. This place is really *hot*. Lower me to the floor, will ya?"

Stantz felt the cable quiver.

Soon he was being lowered closer to the old tunnel's floor. He slowly scanned the area with his flashlight, eventually spotlighting the floor.

Stantz's eyes grew wide in terror. "Hold it!" he yelled into the radio. "Stop! Whoa!"

In the beam of his flashlight, Stantz saw not a solid floor below him, but rather a river of bubbling, pulsating, glowing slime. A torrent of disgusting ooze.

The cable jerked to a halt.

Stantz found himself dangling above the torrent of psychokinetic mucus.

He lifted his feet as high into the air as he could, to avoid the splats of slime emitted by the constantly churning river.

Sweat began to form on his forehead. Gradually he became aware of the sounds of the city echoing around him: engines throbbing and pulsing in the bowels of the city; water rushing through pipes; steam hissing through air ducts; the muffled rumble of the ever-grinding subways; and the roar of traffic high above.

What Ray noticed most, however, were the echoes of people in conflict and pain. Voices of citizens shouting in anger, screaming in fear, groaning in agony. Ray sagged under the weight of the sad and eerie chorus.

Suddenly Ray's walkie-talkie barked to life. "What is it?" asked Spengler from above.

Ray grimaced into the ooze. "It's a seething, bubbling psychic cesspool," he blurted. "Interlocked tubes of plasm, crackling with negative GEVs. It's glowing and moving! It's... it's a river of slime!"

"Yccch," he heard Venkman comment from above.

Stantz gritted his teeth. He had a job to do down here. He unhooked a long, slender device from his utility belt and pulled a trigger on it. The device shot out a long, telescoping fishing pole with a plastic scoop on the end. Reaching down tentatively, Stantz scooped up a sample of the slime and carefully started reeling it in.

The ooze beneath his feet began to churn and turn.

Without warning, a grotesque arm of slime reached up toward Ray, extending its glistening, skeletal fingers in the direction of Stantz's dangling feet. Ray screeched and jerked his legs up high into the air as other hands of ooze bubbled upward, reaching for him, clawing at him. Ray found himself squirming at the end of the cable in a near fetal position. He felt like a piñata from another dimension.

"Haul me up, Venkman!" he bellowed into the radio. "Now!"

On Seventy-seventh Street, Venkman and Spengler ran to the winch and started to crank the cable upward. Just as they began their rescue attempt, a Con Ed supervisor's car pulled up. Behind it was the same police car that had patrolled the area earlier. Venkman and Spengler exchanged nervous glances.

"What now?" Spengler asked.

"Act like nothing is wrong," Venkman advised.

The burly Con Ed supervisor rumbled up to the two men, followed by the pair of cops.

"Okay," the man demanded, "what's going on here?"

Venkman and Spengler stopped pulling up the cable. Venkman quickly doffed his Con Ed hard hat and put on a phone-company helmet. He stared angrily at the Con Ed man.

"What, I got time for this?" he blustered. "We got three thousand phones out in the Village and about eight million miles of cable to check."

The Con Ed man smiled thinly. "The phone lines are over there," he said, pointing toward the curb.

Venkman turned to Spengler and, forming a fist, hit him over the head. "I told ya!"

Stantz's voice suddenly emerged from the walkie-talkie. "Help! Help! Pull me up! It's alive! It's eating my boots."

Venkman offered the cops a quick grin and switched off the radio. "You ain't with Con Ed," the first cop concluded, "or the phone company. We checked. Tell me another one."

Venkman scanned his brain for a comeback. He faced the cop. "How does a gas leak sound?"

Down below the street, caught halfway up the air shaft, Stantz gazed at the scene unfolding beneath his feet. The slime was now bubbling up the air shaft after him. The ooze seemed angry. Determined. Hungry.

Stantz panicked. Nobody was receiving him over the radio. He gazed upward at the tiny manhole opening, far, far above him. "Get me out of here!" he screamed.

No response.

Desperation and fear getting the best of him, Stantz began kicking wildly at the air shaft. The old metal began to creak and groan under the assault by Stantz's boots.

A section of an old conduit came loose and began to topple over.

Stantz watched its journey, befuddled. “Uh-oh,” he whispered.

The conduit fell on a heavy electrical transmission line. It ripped through the cable neatly. A shower of sparks lit up the air vent.

“Definitely uh-oh,” Stantz theorized as the sparks seemed to illuminate every underground passageway extending outward from the air shaft.

Venkman was in the midst of attempting to sell the police another story when there was a sudden buzzing sound from deep within the open manhole.

Venkman and Spengler exchanged worried looks as Stantz’s shouts emerged from deep beneath the city streets.

“Whooaaaah!” Stantz exclaimed.

“What the—” the Con Ed man had time to offer before, one by one, all the lights on the street flickered and then went out.

Then all the lights in the neighborhood followed suit.

The cops, the Con Ed man, and the two Ghostbusters watched in awe as, neighborhood by neighborhood, all of New York was plunged into total darkness.

From deep within the earth came a feeble voice, the voice of Ray Stantz.

“Sorry,” he said.

10

As the lights flickered out all over New York City, Dana Barrett suddenly found herself engulfed in darkness. Always prepared, she felt her way around the living room, lighting various candles she had left out for just such an occasion.

Locating a small transistor radio, she turned it on and tried to find a special news report.

She had tuned in too quickly.

Most of the radio stations in New York were still scrambling to turn on their emergency generators.

Dana suddenly felt the overwhelming compulsion to check on little Oscar.

Grabbing a candle, she began to tiptoe toward the nursery when she was interrupted by a pounding on her front door.

Candle still in hand, she walked cautiously to the door and, leaving the guard chain on, opened it a crack. Outside, the hallway, eerily lit by a dim red emergency spotlight at the far end of the corridor, offered a visitor.

A hyper, wiry man.

"Janosz?" she asked.

Janosz smiled at her. "Hello, Dana. I happened to be in the neighborhood and I thought I'd stop by to see if everything was all right with you. You know, with the blackout and everything? Are you okay? Is… *the baby*… all right?"

Dana felt a chill insinuate itself down her spine. She put up a nonchalant front. "We're fine, Janosz."

The minion of Vigo tried to stick his head farther inside the chained door, hoping to scan the apartment. "Do you need anything?" he said, still grinning. "Would you like me to come in?"

"No," Dana replied a little too quickly. "Everything is fine. Honestly. Thanks, anyway."

Janosz took the refusal in stride. "Okay. Just thought I'd check. Good night, Dana. Sleep well, don't let the bedbugs *bite* you."

"Good night, Janosz," Dana breathed, easing the door closed. She stood there, panting. There was something about Janosz. He had always been weird, but now he struck her as being *weirder.* She quickly double-locked the door.

She stood in the middle of her candlelit apartment. Very alone.

Very afraid.

Outside Dana's door, Janosz smiled evilly at the closed portal.

Closed doors didn't bother him.

Locks meant nothing to him.

He had a job to do, and in time he would do it. Janosz turned and gazed down the darkened corridor. Blackouts. Hah! He reached deep down into himself and touched the power within. Slowly his eyes began to flicker… then to shine brightly.

Small beams of crimson-red energy lit up the hall enough for Janosz to walk down it without stumbling.

It was good to have a friend.

And Vigo was his best friend, *ever.*

11

By morning, New York City had its power restored, and Spengler, Stantz, and Venkman had their hands full.

They sat in a courtroom, sharing the defense table with Louis Tully, C.P.A., perpetual target of a bad haircut, former demonic possession victim, and now lawyer extraordinaire, thanks to a quick course in the Famous Lawyer's School and Dry Cleaning Emporium.

Louis Tully pushed his glasses higher on his nose, which in turn made his nose run. He pulled out a hankie from his badly cut suit, which caused the plastic pen holder to tumble out of his pocket onto the floor.

"S'cuse me." he muttered to the three Ghostbusters as he stooped to pick up his pens, nearly knocking over a pitcher of water on the defense table.

Across from him, the prosecuting attorney, an attractive young woman who seemed to want to see Spengler, Stantz, and Venkman hanged, glared at Louis.

Louis quickly straightened himself and began poring through an avalanche of law books he had gathered for the occasion.

"All rise," the bailiff said.

Everyone in the courtroom stood as Judge Roy Beane

strode into the room. A compact, balding man with the deep eyes of a ferret and a small, neatly trimmed mustache, the judge gaveled the court into session.

The three Ghostbusters slid into their seats as the judge began. "I want to make one thing very clear before we go any further," he said severely.

"The law does not recognize the existence of ghosts, and I don't believe in them, either. So… I don't want to hear a lot of malarkey about goblins and spooks and demons. We're going to stick to the facts in this case and save the ghost stories for the kiddies. Understood?"

"Understood, Your Honor," the prosecutor said with a grin.

"Uh-huh," Louis muttered.

Stantz leaned over toward Spengler. "Seems like a pretty open-minded guy, huh?"

Egon nodded, the hair on the back of his neck bristling. "His nickname is the Hammer."

Venkman spotted Dana in the visitors' gallery and slowly backed toward her, leaving Spengler and Stantz trapped with Louis. Louis nervously glanced up at Spengler. His voice was in high-whine mode. "I think you're making a big mistake here, fellas. I do mostly tax law, and some probate stuff occasionally. I got my law degree at night school."

"That's all right," Egon reassured him. "We got arrested at night."

Venkman and Dana exchanged looks. "I wish I could stay," Dana whispered. "I feel personally responsible for you being here."

"You *are* personally responsible. If I can get conjugal rights, will you visit me at Sing Sing?"

"Please don't say that!" Dana blurted. "You won't go to prison."

Venkman puffed out his chest. "Don't worry about me. I'm like a cat."

"You mean you cough up hairballs all over the rug?"

Venkman shot her a look. "I'm El Gato. I always land on my feet."

"Good luck," Dana said, giving Venkman a quick, unexpected kiss before dashing out of the courtroom.

"Thanks," Venkman said, savoring the kiss for a long moment. He walked back to the defense table. Across the aisle, the mayor's top aide, Jack Hardemeyer, was goading the pretty prosecutor on for the kill.

Venkman strained his ears to listen.

"How are you doing, hon?" Hardemeyer asked. "Just put these guys away fast and make sure they go away for a long, long time."

Venkman wasn't pleased.

"It shouldn't be hard with this list of charges," the prosecutor replied.

Venkman sighed. He should have finished that Danish last night. It might be a long time before he experienced another one.

"Good." Hardemeyer smiled. "Very good. The mayor and future governor won't forget this."

Venkman scurried to his seat at the defense table. Hardemeyer made a major production of removing his well-groomed presence from the D.A.'s team and walking slowly past the defense table on his way out of the courtroom.

He looked down at Spengler, Stantz, and Venkman. "Nice going, Venkman," he cooed. "Violating a judicial restraining order, willful destruction of public property, fraud, malicious mischief... smooth move. See you in a couple of years—at your first parole hearing."

Hardemeyer turned and marched out of the room. Louis watched the retreating figure, his face turning the color of damp chalk. "Gee, the whole city is against us. I think I'm going to be sick."

Spengler offered Louis a wastebasket as the prosecutor called her first witness.

The Con Ed supervisor took the stand.

Venkman sat at the table and began to doodle. He knew what was coming. He'd been railroaded before.

Venkman battled to keep from dozing off as the supervisor rattled off a list of crimes that he, Stantz, and Spengler had inflicted on the poor streets of New York.

He snapped to when he noticed a court employee carry some very familiar equipment into the room and place it on a nearby table.

The prosecutor was still hammering away at the Con Ed man. "Mr. Fianella," she said, "please look at Exhibits A through F on the table over there. Do you recognize that equipment?"

Spengler, Stantz, and Venkman exchanged uh-oh glances as the Con Ed man surveyed the table. There, spread out on its top, were the basic tools of the Ghostbusting trade. Three proton packs and particle throwers. A few unsprung ghost traps. The Giga and PKE meters.

The Con Ed man nodded vigorously. "That's the stuff the cops found in their rented van."

"Do you know what this equipment is for?" the prosecutor asked.

"I don't know." The burly man shrugged. "Catching ghosts, I guess."

The prosecutor whirled toward the judge. "May I remind the court that the defendants are under a judicial restraining order that *specifically* forbids them from performing services as paranormal investigators and eliminators?"

The judge with the ice-blue ferretlike eyes nodded. "Duly noted."

"Now," the prosecutor continued, "can you identify the substance in the jar on the table marked Exhibit F?"

She walked over to the exhibit table and picked up a large specimen jar. In it was housed the slime sample Stantz had removed from the swirling, churning tunnel floor.

The Con Ed man screwed up his face in confusion. "Lady," he said, "I been working underground for Con Ed for twenty-seven years and I never saw anything like that in my life. We checked out that tunnel real early this morning and we didn't find nothing. If it was down there, *they* must have put it down there."

Venkman and Spengler shot a suspicious look at Stantz. Ray withered under their gaze. "Hey," he said defensively, "I didn't imagine it. There must have been ten thousand gallons of it down there."

Egon Spengler stroked his square jaw. "It may be ebbing and flowing from some tidal source," he concluded.

Louis leaned toward the two men, nearly knocking over his books. "Should I say that?"

Spengler patted Louis's hand. "I doubt that they'd believe us."

Louis uttered a plaintive moan and slithered farther down in his chair. Why couldn't he have taken the dry-cleaning course instead of law? By now, he would have known what one-hour Martinizing really meant.

The Con Ed man was dismissed, and within minutes Peter Venkman found himself on the stand, facing his own lawyer, the rattled, diminutive Louis. Louis had been babbling for about a minute, Venkman encouraging him with a helpful nod, a wink, or a hearty "Hear, hear." That gave Venkman the chance to think of what he would do when he was finally paroled. Not much, he concluded.

"S-so," Louis said, stammering. "Like you were just trying to help out your old friend because she was scared and you didn't really mean to do anything bad, and you really love the city and won't ever do anything like this again, right?"

Before a smiling, modest Venkman could reply, the prosecutor was on her feet. "Objection, Your Honor! He's leading the witness."

The judge glared at Venkman. "The witness is leading *him*. Sustained."

Louis blinked. "Ummm, okay. Let me rephrase that question."

Venkman smiled sweetly at Louis as the little man chirped, "Mr. Venkman, didn't you once coach a basketball team for underprivileged children?"

"Yes, I did," Venkman said proudly. "We were city champs."

"Objection!" the prosecutor spat. "Irrelevant and immaterial."

The judge sighed. "Sustained." He focused on Louis. "Mr. Hilly, do you have anything to ask this witness that actually may have some *bearing* on this case?"

Louis turned to Venkman. "Do I?" he asked.

Venkman flashed Louis a reassuring smirk. "No, I think you've helped them enough already."

Louis shrugged at the judge. "No, I guess not. Your witness, Mrs. Prosecutress."

The prosecutor slowly rose out of her seat and approached the witness stand. She was practically salivating over the prospect of destroying Venkman's credibility. Venkman was prepared. He had seen this kind of woman before. Actually he'd dated many of them in college.

"So," the prosecutor began. "*Doctor* Venkman, would you please explain to the court why it is that you and your codefendants took it upon yourselves to dig a big hole in the middle of the street?"

Venkman considered this. "Seventy-seventh and First

Avenue has so many holes already, we didn't think anyone would notice."

The citizens gathered in the visitor's gallery laughed. The judge raised his gavel and hammered for order. He glowered at Venkman. "Keep that up, mister, and I'll find you in contempt!"

Venkman offered a shy grin. "Sorry, Your Honor, but when somebody sets me up like that, I just can't resist."

"I'll ask you again, Dr. Venkman," the prosecutor said, going in for the kill. "Why were you digging the hole? And please remember that you're under oath."

Venkman tried (unsuccessfully) to emulate Egon's very concerned mode. "I had my fingers crossed when they swore me in, but I'm going to tell you the truth. There are things in this world that go way beyond human understanding, things that can't be explained and that most people don't want to know about, anyway. That's where *we* come in."

Venkman nodded toward Spengler and Stantz.

"So what are you saying," the prosecutor asked, grinning like a barracuda. "That the world of the supernatural is your special province?"

"No," Venkman explained. "I guess I'm just saying that weird shit happens and *somebody* has got to deal with it."

The gallery began to cheer. Venkman took a bow. The judge gaveled for order.

Two hours later a frowning Venkman sat at the defense table. Stantz and Spengler had been similarly browbeaten on the witness stand, although, in Venkman's humble opinion, they didn't please the crowd *nearly* as much as he had.

The trial was now nearing its end. The judge nodded toward a trembling Louis to make his final summation.

"Does the counsel for the defense wish to make any final arguments?" he growled.

Louis slowly got to his feet, his knees knocking so hard that they sounded like Morse code. "Your Honor?" Louis squeaked, "may I approach the bench?"

"Yes, yes," the judge said impatiently.

Louis waddled over to the bench and gazed upward.

"What is it?" the judge demanded.

Louis gulped. "Can I have some of your water?"

"Get on with it, Counselor!"

Louis backed away from the bench and wasn't quite sure who to speak to. "Your Honor, ladies and gentlemen of the jury..."

"There's no jury here." The judge sighed.

"... of the audience," Louis corrected himself, staring at the gallery. "I don't think it's fair to call my clients frauds. Okay. The blackout was a big problem for everybody. I was stuck in an elevator for about three hours and I had to go to the bathroom the whole time, but I don't blame them, because once I turned into a big dog and they helped me. Thank you."

Louis rushed back to the defense table and scrambled into his seat. Stantz and Spengler, dazed, stared at their knees in disbelief. Venkman leaned over the table and patted Louis on the back. "Way to go. Concise and to the point."

Obviously the judge was still in shock. He gazed at Louis. "That's *it*? That's *all* you have to say?"

Louis was confused. "Did I forget something?"

Louis began to plow through the hastily taken notes he had scrawled during the trial. The judge bared his teeth at the diminutive man. "That was unquestionably the worst presentation of a case I've ever heard in a court of law! I ought to cite you for contempt and have you disbarred. And as for your clients, Peter Venkman, Raymond Stantz, and Egon Spengler, on the charges of conspiracy, fraud, and the willful destruction of public property, I find you guilty on all counts. I order you to pay fines in the amount of $25,000 *each,* and I sentence you to eighteen months in the city correctional facility at Rikers Island!"

Stantz lifted his eyes. He caught a glimpse of the specimen jar, still perched on the exhibit table. The goop inside the jar began to glow and churn. He leaned toward Spengler. "Uh-oh. She's twitchin'."

The judge grew angrier and angrier with each word. The slime grew more and more animated as the judge's voice rose. "And on a more personal note," the judge intoned, "let me go on record as saying that there is no place in decent society for fakes, charlatans, and tricksters like you who prey on the gullibility of innocent people. You're beneath the contempt of this court!

"And believe me, if my hands were not tied by the unalterable fetters of the law, a law that has become, in my view, far too permissive and inadequate in its standards of punishment..."

The entire jar of slime seemed to change its shape, growing into something resembling an oval.

"... I would invoke the tradition of our illustrious forebears, reach back to a sterner, purer justice, and have you *all* burned at the stake!"

He slammed his gavel down on the bench. The gallery erupted into a chorus of boos and jeers. The judge was about to slam down his gavel again when he felt the floor beneath his massive desk begin to tremble.

The gallery lapsed into silence.

A low, rumbling noise grew in volume, echoing through the room.

The prosecutor glanced at the exhibit table. "What the..."

The slime began to pulse and swell in earnest, gradually forcing up the lid of the jar.

Stantz gaped at the jar.

The slime was moving quickly now, expanding at an incredible rate.

"Under the table, boys!" he yelled.

The three Ghostbusters dove under the table, yanking Louis under after them.

The rumbling increased to a deafening roar.

And that roar evolved into the psychic equivalent of a volcanic eruption of pure paranormal power.

"Wow," Stantz said, wide-eyed, as a hurricane-force wind from another dimension slammed into his face. "Isn't this *something*?"

12

A fierce, ethereal whirlwind whipped above the heads of Louis, Spengler, Stantz, and Venkman as the slime jar began to spout glowing, sparkling wads of goop up into the air.

A sizzling, undulating cloud of gooey vapor formed near the courthouse ceiling.

Aghast, the judge sat behind his desk, as two figures—one rotund, the other, emaciated—began to materialize high above. The judge recognized them immediately.

"Oh, my God," he whispered. "The Scoleri brothers!"

The ghostly Scoleri brothers, their fingers crackling electrical sparks, their hair sparking as well, glared down at the timid judge and emitted a loud eerie laugh. The two floating apparitions positioned themselves high above either side of the judge's massive desk and then, without warning, shrieked down into the desk, sending the large wooden frame sailing across the room in pieces.

The judge found himself sitting behind the smoldering ruins of his desk. The Scoleri brothers had dematerialized for the time being.

As the prosecutor stood stunned at her table, the spectators in court scrambled from their seats and ran for the back exit of the courtroom.

The judge, getting down on all fours, crawled toward the defense table and quickly rolled underneath it. Sweating and shaking, he faced Spengler, Stantz, and Venkman. "You've got to do something!" he cried.

"Who are they?" Venkman asked.

"They're the Scoleri brothers. I tried them for murder. They were electrocuted up at Ossining in '48. Now... they want to *kill* me!"

"Maybe they just want to appeal." Venkman shrugged.

"I don't think so." Louis moaned, watching the table slowly rise into the air above them.

From out of nowhere the Scoleri brothers materialized and, hair and fingertips crackling, the long dead criminals lifted the defense table high into the air!

"This way," Spengler yelled, pointing to the rail of the jury box. The three Ghostbusters, the judge, and Louis darted across the room and dove behind the heavy oak wall of the jury box.

The Scoleri brothers roared and sent the defense table smashing into the wall above their heads.

"These boys aren't playing around," Venkman noted.

The Scoleri brothers, still hovering near the ceiling, noticed the prosecutor for the first time. Exchanging ghostly glances, they began to hover closer to her. The woman let out a bloodcurdling scream. The Scoleris emitted a howling laugh and promptly disappeared.

The prosecutor exhaled and slowly began to back toward the courtroom's exit doors, twisting and turning nervously, scanning the air above her for any sign of the angry apparitions.

She reached the door intact and, breathing a sigh of relief, reached for the door's handle.

She heard a crackling sound.

She smelled the aroma of ozone.

The woman's hair nearly straightened as suddenly the ghost of the skinny Scoleri brother sparked to life before her. The ghost emitted an unworldly screech as it blocked the door with its transparent body.

The prosecutor turned and ran toward the front of the courtroom, the skinny apparition following her. Before she could reach the jury box, she heard a strange rumbling noise. Pop! Blocking her path was the plumper ghost brother.

The big ghost glided forward.

The prosecutor froze in her tracks.

Hidden behind the jury box's railing, the judge pleaded with Stantz, Spengler, and Venkman. "You've got to stop them, please!"

Wide-eyed, Stantz blinked innocently at the judge. "I'm sorry, we can't. You issued a judicial restraining order that prohibits us from ghostbusting. Violating such an order could expose us to serious criminal penalties."

The judge blinked at honest, heartfelt Ray. A woman's scream cut through the air.

The judge slowly peeked over the jury-box railing. All color drained from his face. The titanic ghost of the obese Scoleri thug was calmly dragging the screeching prosecutor by her feet toward the rear of the courtroom, laughing and drooling devilishly.

The upside-down woman squirmed in the grip of the spirit, trying desperately to keep her dress from sliding up over her head.

The exit doors to the courtroom mysteriously burst open. The fat ghost carried the screaming prosecutor out of the room, and as the doors swung closed, it vanished into thin air.

Behind the jury-box railing, the judge slowly sank into a sitting pose. He was defeated. "All right. All right. I'm rescinding the order. Case dismissed."

He noticed that he was still holding his gavel in his right hand. He pounded the floor judicially.

"Satisfied?"

"I guess so," Louis offered.

"Now," the judge said, fuming. *"Do something!"*

With that the three Ghostbusters leapt over the rail of the jury box and dashed across the room to the exhibit table. Their proton packs were lying there, tossed aside as useless evidence.

The three Ghostbusters strapped on their packs hastily, glancing above their heads for any signs of the Scoleri brothers.

Venkman felt like the Hunchback of Notre Dame as he affixed the pack to his back. "Geez, I forgot how heavy these things are."

Stantz cradled his particle thrower in his hand. "Okay"—he grinned at his long-lost high-tech friends—"let's heat 'em up."

The three Ghostbusters flipped on their proton-pack power switches in unison, then raised their particle throwers toward the ceiling.

"All right, throwers," Stantz barked, authority surging through his body. "Set for lull neutronas on stream."

Stantz, Spengler, and Venkman switched on their throwers and raised them upward.

The throwers remained on standby. There was no sign of anything paranormal in the room.

All seemed quiet.

All seemed *normal*.

Suddenly, from the back of the courtroom came a ruckus. Chairs began to fly up into the air and then drop harmlessly to the floor. It seemed as if something were burrowing deep down underneath them, toward the front of the courtroom. Toward the Ghostbusters.

Stantz, Spengler, and Venkman stared at the courtroom before them.

There was nothing to be seen.

Stantz smiled thinly. Ghosts were goofy, perhaps, but pretty crafty. He stared at the empty ceiling above him.

"On my signal, gentlemen." He grinned.

He *felt* the Scoleri brothers nearby.

He was right.

A bolt of electrical energy shot across the ceiling above them and from out of the yellow mist appeared the gaunt and obese floating forms of the executed killers.

"Open 'em up!" Stantz yelled. *"Now!"*

The three Ghostbusters shut their eyes as their wands emitted squiggling, undulating, powerful streams of energy.

Not having used the weapons in four years, Spengler, Stantz, and Venkman fired wildly, allowing the harpy-like Scoleri ghosts to dodge the fluttering beams easily.

The ghosts emitted a ghastly cackle and then promptly dematerialized.

The Ghostbusters were too shaken to notice. They continued to fill the air with orange-hot rays. Venkman took out an overhead lamp. Spengler blew up the courtroom railing. Stantz managed to obliterate half of one of the courtroom's towering pillars.

The three Ghostbusters opened their eyes as one. "That ought to do it," Venkman said with a smirk. "Spengs, take the door. Ray, let's try to work them down and into a corner."

Working as a team, they fanned the area.

Spengler carefully backed up toward the exit doors.

Venkman cautiously circled the exhibit table, his weapon trained toward the ceiling.

Stantz walked to and fro before the jury box. The judge and Louis stayed well down behind the protective gate.

A howl shook the air.

The emaciated Scoleri ghost materialized from behind Stantz and lunged downward.

"Get down, Ray!" Venkman shouted as the ghost swooped down on his buddy.

Stantz leapt onto the ground and rolled out of the line of fire as Venkman let go with an undulating stream of rays that effectively trapped the screaming apparition within its force field.

"That's it, Venky!" Spengler yelled from the rear of the room. "Watch your streams. Hold him there."

Spengler moved toward the exhibit table, where two rectangular ghost trappers were set up, connected to five-foot-long cables attached to foot releases.

Spengler carefully moved the traps to the center of the courtroom.

"Easy, Venky," he cautioned.

"I got him." Venkman nodded nervously.

"Just keep the beam on him and ease him over there. Pull him down this way. That's it. That's it."

A shriek cut through the air. Spengler spun around and saw the ghost of the fat Scoleri bearing down upon him, fast. He couldn't reach his weapon in time to save himself.

Stantz leapt to his feet and opened fire. The fat ghost chortled with glee as he easily dodged the blast.

He headed down for Spengler once again.

Stantz gritted his teeth and let go with a second stream. This time the spiraling rays smashed into the fat ghost, effectively trapping him in a pulsating, levitating cage.

Spengler made sure there were *two* rectangular traps placed on the floor in front of what had once been the judge's bench.

He pulled the foot springs back some five feet.

Stantz and Venkman held the screaming ghosts trapped in their steady stream of rays.

"Okay," Spengler said, coaching them. "You're doing fine. Watch your streams. Easy, now. Venky, bring him left. Stantz, pull them down."

The two Ghostbusters nodded and slowly maneuvered their captive, screeching spirits down toward the rectangular traps.

Spengler watched their progress, sweating. "Okay. Trapping… trapping… *now!*"

Spengler stomped down hard on two foot-control pedals at the end of the pair of cables. The rectangular traps' top doors opened and a bright light streamed up from within.

Stantz and Venkman guided the two ghosts into the white-hot light.

"Cease fire!" Spengler yelped. "Now!"

An exhausted Stantz and Venkman lowered their weapons.

The two traps surged into full-tilt power, emitting an inverted triangle of ethereal light up toward the floating spirits. Gradually the ghosts dissipated, and then suddenly zipped into the two traps.

The traps snapped shut and an LED light on the outside of each trap flashed brilliantly.

Venkman staggered up to his trap. He smiled at Spengler. *"Ocupado."*

The three Ghostbusters faced each other, exhausted. They exchanged smiles. They hadn't felt this good in years.

The judge slowly stuck his head up from behind the jury box. Louis peeked up as well. The judge looked around in total shock.

Louis and the exhausted Ghostbusters walked to the back of the courtroom and flung open the door.

Outside, dozens of reporters and spectators waited to greet them with a rousing cheer.

Spengler glanced to his left. The prosecutor was hiding beneath a plastic chair, shivering her well-educated butt off. "Brilliant summation." He smiled.

Flashbulbs went off in the three men's faces.

Reporters surged forward.

Venkman faced his two comrades and uttered, loud enough for everyone to hear, "Case closed, boys. We're back in business."

The halls of the courthouse echoed with the cheers and applause of a devoted crowd.

II

"True heroes are those who die for causes they cannot quite take seriously."

- MURRAY KEMPTON

"This is going to cost you, you know. Our fees are ridiculously high."

- DR. PETER VENKMAN

13

The refurbished firehouse that once housed the original Ghostbusters business was under siege by a small army of workmen. The old "No Ghosts" logo, now dilapidated by years of disuse, came crashing to the ground with a resounding thud.

The workmen fought back sneezes as a cloud of dust wafted into the air.

A group of men struggled with a pulley as a new logo was hoisted into place over the main entrance of the building. It looked exactly like the old logo, but now the trapped ghost in the red circle held up two fingers.

Venkman strolled up to the firehouse and gazed at the Ghostbusters' shiny new symbol. Nice, he thought. Very, very nice.

Inside the firehouse's reception area, Janine Melnitz, a veteran New Yorker and the Ghostbusters' first (and only) receptionist/aide, hastily set up her desk. She spread out family photos. A Garfield doll. Bound editions of *Cosmopolitan*. She hardly noticed Louis as he waddled out with a handful of forms. Louis certainly noticed Janine. Why was it he had never seen how pretty she was? Oh, yeah, now he remembered. The last time he had been in the firehouse, he had been possessed by a demon.

Louis tiptoed up to Janine's desk, clearing his throat. He sounded like Shirley Temple with a hairball. "Uh, Janine? I'm filling out W-2 forms for the payroll and I need your Social Security number."

Janine carefully positioned her Garfield doll. "It's 129-45-8986."

Louis produced a small pad from his shirt pocket and jotted down the number. "Oh," he said, wheezing. "That's a good one. Mine is 322-36-7366."

Janine gazed up at Louis. You know, she thought, Louis was kind of cute in a *Wild Kingdom* sort of way. "Wow!" she exclaimed. "Three threes and three sixes."

"Uh-huh," Louis acknowledged.

"That's very strong in numerology," she continued, running a hand through her mousy brown hair. "It means you're a person with a great appetite for life and a *deeply passionate* nature."

Louis blinked, embarrassed. He almost fogged his glasses. "You can tell all that from my Social Security number?"

The sparrowlike Janine leaned forward and smiled. "Oh, yes. Numbers are very revealing. If I knew your phone number, I could tell you a lot more."

Louis swallowed hard. "My phone number?"

Venkman chose that moment to march into the room. Both Louis and Janine snapped to immediately.

"Louis, how are we doing on that bank loan?" Venkman asked.

Louis cleared his throat. "Oh, I called the bank this morning... but they hung up on me."

"Try another bank." Venkman shrugged. "Do I have to do *everything* around here?"

Venkman looked up as Stantz, Spengler, and Winston

walked sheepishly downstairs wearing the Ghostbusters' uniforms Venkman had commissioned for their new incarnation. The uniforms were designed in a weirded-out, military style in Day-Glo colors, dripping with medals, and topped by ridiculous berets. Venkman took note of the trio's embarrassed faces and tried to bluff his way through it.

"Incredible!" he oozed. "*This* is a *very* good look!"

Winston heaved a heavy sigh. "We look like the Bronxville High School Marching Band."

Venkman sidled up to the trio. "Will you just *trust* me on this? It's all part of the new plan—higher visibility, lower overhead, deeper market penetration, *bigger profits* Just wait until we open the boutique."

Stantz blinked. "What boutique?"

Venkman took him by the arm and pointed to the sky outside the firehouse. "The Ghostbusters Gift Boutique," he said enthusiastically. "It's a natural. I've been working on it all day."

He whipped a small piece of paper from his pants pocket and began reading. "You'll *love* it. Ghostbuster T-shirts, sweatshirts, caps, visors, beach towels, mugs, calendars, stationery, balloons, stickers, Frisbees, paperweights, souvenirs, tote bags, party supplies, motor oil, toys, video games."

Spengler frowned. "Our primary concern should be the continued integrity of the biosphere. It's a responsibility shared by all conscious beings."

Venkman stared at Spengler. "Isn't that what I just said?"

Stantz turned to Venkman. "Look, Venkman, we don't have time for this. We've got customers waiting—*paying* customers. You can wear pink diapers and go-go boots if you want. *We're* sticking with the *old* coveralls." The three Ghostbusters marched back up the stairs. Venkman trotted up behind them.

"Coveralls," he shouted. "Great! Very imaginative, Ray. They make us look like we should be walking around the airport sprinkling sawdust on puke!"

Stantz shouted down from above. "We're wearing them. And that's final!"

Venkman took this in and shouted up, with a smile, "Okay, we'll wear coveralls—but think *boutique*!"

14

The TV screen flickered to life displaying a very awkward married couple, played by Louis Tully and Janine, in bed, reading.

Suddenly a "ghost," actually a puppet that seemed to have been created in an out-therapy class in a laughing academy, bounced above the bed on a badly concealed wire.

Janine looked up and emitted a terribly acted scream.

"What is it, honey?" Louis blinked.

Janine crossed her arms and watched the puppet bounce off the plasterboard walls. "It's that darn ghost again," she said stiffly. "I don't know what to do anymore. He just won't leave us alone. I guess we'll just have to move."

Louis offered a wise smile, which resembled the one worn by Alfred E. Newman. "Don't worry, honey. *We're* not moving. *He* is."

Louis reached for the prop telephone.

"Who are you going to call?" Janine asked.

Louis winked at the screen. *"Ghostbusters."*

As Louis dialed, Spengler, Stantz, and Venkman marched into their room, clad in their old Ghostbusters jumpsuits. They walked as stiffly as wooden soldiers and weren't any better actors than Louis and Janine.

The threesome faced the screen.

"I'm Ray."

"I'm Peter."

"I'm Egon."

Stantz took a deep breath. "And we're the..."

"Ghostbusters!" the three men announced in unison, while in the background Winston appeared, traipsing after the phony ghost with what looked like a massive butterfly net in hand.

"That's right," Stantz said, sweating into the TV screen. "Ghostbusters! We're back and we're better than ever, with twice the know-how and twice the particle power to deal with all your supernatural elimination needs."

He glanced over his shoulder, where Winston was still trying to catch the "ghost" without messing up the puppet's wires. "Careful, Winston," Stantz called. "He's a mean one."

Stantz faced the screen again. Sweat trickled down his nose. "And to celebrate our grand reopening, we're giving you twice the value with our special half-price 'Welcome Back' service plan."

Venkman expressed exaggerated shock. "Hold on, Ray!" he exclaimed theatrically. "Half price! Have you gone crazy?"

"I guess so, Pete," Stantz replied, wearing a Cheshire cat smile. "Because *that's not all!* Tell them what else we've got, Egon."

Egon's mind apparently went blank for a moment. Rolling his eyes and frowning, attempting to remember the script, he suddenly recalled his line. "You mean the Ghostbusters hot-beverage thermal mugs and free balloons for the kids?"

Egon held up a mug bearing the Ghostbusters logo and a limp, uninflated balloon. He glanced at the balloon. Darn. He knew he had forgotten something.

Stantz didn't miss a beat. "You bet, Egon. That's *exactly* what I mean."

Stantz walked toward the screen as bold, flashing letters appeared below him. fully bonded—fully licensed—se habla espanol.

"So," Stantz announced, "don't you wait another minute. Make *your* supernatural problem *our* supernatural problem. Call now, because we're still…"

He glanced over his shoulder. All the Ghostbusters faced the screen and pointed to their unseen viewers. "… ready to believe *you*."

An unseen hand clicked off the TV as Regis Philbin appeared, chatting up a thirteen-year-old pop starlet plugging a TV film about Wisenheimer's disease… a sickness that afflicts elderly stand-up comedians.

Rudy, the Manhattan Museum of Art's chief security guard, watched the TV set go blank before he returned to his treasured edition of the *New York Post*. On the front page the headline screamed: ghostbusters save judge!

His reading was interrupted by the presence of a guest. Peter Venkman faced Rudy. "Excuse me. I'm looking for Dana Barrett."

Rudy glanced at the visitor. "Room 104. The restoration studio."

Rudy's eyes grew wide. "Hey! Dr. Venkman—*World of the Psychic*. I'm a big, big fan. That used to be one of my *two* favorite shows."

Venkman was obviously flattered. "Thanks," he said suavely. "What's the other one?"

"Bass Masters," Rudy replied. "It's a fishing show. Ever see it?"

Venkman backed away from the security desk. "Yeah, it's really great. Caught it when Meryl Streep was a guest. Take it easy."

Venkman stalked off down the hall, coming to a halt in front of the studio. He eased the door open and entered the large room.

At one end of the studio Dana was hard at work, cleaning a valuable Dutch still life. At the other end Janosz still toiled over the terrible painting of Vigo the rotten.

Dana smiled at Venkman. "Oh, hello, Peter. What are you doing here?"

Venkman shrugged. "I thought you might want to knock off early and let me chase you around the park for a while."

Dana laughed softly. "Thanks, sounds delightful, but I'm working."

Venkman studied the painting she was working on. "So this is what you do, huh? You're really good. Is that a paint-by-numbers job?"

"I didn't paint it," Dana said with a laugh. "I'm just cleaning it. It's an original Vermeer. It's worth about ten million dollars."

Venkman squinted at the painting, holding up his thumb in a classical artist's pose. "What a rip-off! "You can go to Art World and get these huge sofa-size paintings for about forty-five bucks. And those black-velvet jobs? Can't top them."

He glanced around the studio, taking in the various pieces of artwork assembled.

"I'm sure they're lovely." Dana sighed. "So are you here just to look at art?"

"As a matter of fact," Venkman replied, "I stopped by to talk to you about your case. We think we know what was pulling the buggy. We found tons of this ecto glop under the street. It's pretty potent stuff."

Dana was confused. "But nothing on the street was moving. Why would the buggy move? Why do these things happen to me?"

Venkman was about to answer when Janosz stuck his head between them. "Dana," he said. "Aren't you going to introduce me to your friend?"

Dana blushed slightly. "Oh, I'm sorry. This is Peter Venkman. Peter, Janosz Poha."

Venkman warily shook Janosz's hand. It felt like grabbing a dead trout. Venkman tried to size Janosz up. Bela Lugosi material in a size petite, he concluded. Janosz avoided Venkman's gaze.

"Pleasure to meet you," he said, staring at his shoes. "I've seen you on television. Not here on business, I hope."

Venkman disengaged his hand. "Naaah. I'm trying to unload all my Picassos, but Dana's not buying."

Venkman looked up and spotted the portrait of Vigo. "What's that you're working on, Johnny?"

Janosz winced at the nickname but let it go. Venkman strolled toward the towering portrait of Vigo, Dana in tow. Janosz sprinted to his post in front of the painting and stood before it, as if on guard duty.

"It's a painting I'm restoring for the new Byzantine exhibition," he blurted. "It's a self-portrait by Prince Vigo the Carpathian. He ruled most of Carpathia and Moldavia in the seventeenth century."

"Too bad for the Moldavians," Venkman concluded, sizing up the painting. Vigo looked like one of the bad guys on a Saturday night wrestling special but with better tights.

"He was a very powerful magician," Janosz said, coming to Vigo's defense. "A genius in many ways and quite a skilled painter."

Venkman made an O shape with his mouth.

"He was also a lunatic and a genocidal madman," Dana pointed out. "I hate this painting. I've felt very uncomfortable since they brought it up from storage."

Venkman understood, "Yeah, It's not exactly the kind of thing you'd want to hang up in the rec room. You know what it needs?"

Venkman grinned and picked up one of Janosz's brushes. "A fluffly little white kitten in the corner."

Venkman made a move for the Vigo portrait. Janosz quickly lunged and snatched the brush away from Venkman, smiling nervously. "We don't go around altering valuable paintings, Dr. Venkman."

"Well, I'd make an exception in this case if I were you." He turned to Dana for support. She frowned at him. Venkman was defeated. He patted Janosz on the back. "I'll let you get back to it. Nice meeting you."

"My pleasure," the thin artist replied.

Venkman walked Dana back to her work space. "Interesting guy," he muttered. "Must be a lot of fun to work with."

"He's very good at what he does," she said.

"I may be wrong, but I think you've got a little crush on that guy."

Dana shook her head. "You're a very sick man."

"That's a given," Venkman said, arching an eyebrow. A beeper attached to his belt started wailing. "Uh-oh," Venkman said. "Gotta go to work. I'll call you."

Venkman headed for the door, calling over his shoulder. "Catch you later, Johnny."

Paintbrush in hand, Vigo towering above him, Janosz winced at the thought of his European name being so crassly Americanized.

Soon the world would know him *and* his name.

15

The garage door to the Ghostbusters' firehouse headquarters rumbled upward, and the team's newly purchased and refurbished ambulance, the EctolA, zoomed onto the street. Its ghostly siren moaned and wailed as Winston, in the front seat, went over a laundry list of the day's assignments.

He smiled to himself.

A full day's work.

And not one of the assignments involved kids covered with birthday cake or ice cream.

Diminutive Louis, left out of the action, stood sadly in the garage bay, watching the ambulance disappear. He allowed the garage door to close and was about to return to his office when he began sniffing the air.

There was an odor present. The type of odor he hadn't encountered since some kid passed off a bar of Ex-Lax as Hershey's chocolate to Louis in grade school.

"Oh, jeez," Louis sniffed. "Smells like somebody took a really big—"

Louis froze. Hovering before him was a spud-shaped green ghost, its pipestick arms flailing away, gleefully chomping down the bag of lunch Louis had brought with him that day. Louis recognized the creature as one of the first trapped by the Ghostbusters years earlier... the Slimer.

Slimer, unaware of Louis's presence, glanced downward as Louis glanced upward.

Both Slimer and Louis let out bloodcurdling yells and ran in opposite directions. Slimer was the better for it. He disappeared through a wall. Louis collided with the firehouse's brick wall and knocked himself more senseless than usual. "Help!" he screamed to no one in particular. "There's a *thing*!"

Louis ran out of the room, knowing full well that Slimer would be back for more food and that Louis had just lost at least three perfectly good Twinkies to an apparition.

New Yorkers have a habit of running. They run for subways. They run for cabs. They run from muggers. At the Reservoir in Central Park, however, they run to stay in shape... even if it kills them.

On this bright winter's day a gaggle of joggers, of both sexes and all ages, trotted dutifully around the track encircling the Reservoir. They huffed and they puffed, determined to take off the poundage put on during the recent Thanksgiving holiday and to prepare themselves for the edible tonnage they'd consume during the impending Christmas season.

Eventually, it seemed, they all got into step, so that their feet pounded the track in a synchronized manner.

Thump. Thump. Thump.

From behind them, however, came a new sound. Someone was running twice as fast as any jogger present. Someone was going to pass them, and soon.

The last jogger in the pack glanced over her shoulder and let out a bloodcurdling scream.

Gaining on the pack was a strange, skeletal runner, obviously long dead.

The determined spirit sprinted onward, his body encased by a strange, shimmering aura of ethereal light.

Hearing the commotion, the other joggers in the pack turned their heads as the ghostly runner jogged into their midst. The joggers screamed and panicked. Some stumbled and fell onto the track as the spirited spirit strode ever onward.

Other joggers leapt off the track and ran deep into the park at a speed rivaling that of the Concorde, screeching their heads off.

The ghostly jogger didn't seem to notice.

Still running at a steady speed, he raised two bony fingers to his skeletal neck and glanced at his cobweb-encased watch, cautiously checking his long-gone pulse.

A half mile in front of the striding spirit, Venkman and Stantz sat calmly on two benches situated across from one another. The jogging track was sprawled directly in front of them both. Venkman read a particularly scintillating edition of the *New York Post* while dunking a greasy doughnut into a Styrofoam cup filled with coffee.

Across the track, Stantz affected the attitude of Mr. Casual, calmly surveying the jogging track.

Within seconds he saw a lone jogger approaching.

Just your typical, dead-as-a-doornail New York runner surrounded by an unearthly glow.

Stantz cleared his throat.

Across the track, Venkman nodded and continued analyzing the latest installment of *Hagar, the Horrible.*

The ghostly jogger picked up speed.

He barreled down the stretch of track that ran directly between Stantz and Venkman.

As the spirit sprinter passed their benches, Stantz and Venkman simultaneously smashed their feet down on concealed foot switches.

A ghost trap they had previously buried a quarter inch below the dirt jogging track sprang open. The ghost jogger emitted a tiny whimper as the trap caught him full blast, catching him in a shimmering, inverted triangle of light and energy.

The ghostly jogger froze in mid-step, glancing around him. He felt the power of the ghost trap slowly draw him farther and farther down toward the earth.

Within seconds the ghostly jogger was gone.

Trapped.

Stantz slowly got to his feet. Venkman, still pondering the joke in today's *Hagar,* swallowed his doughnut and joined Stantz in closing the rectangular ghost trap.

Stantz held up the glowing trap. Venkman checked his watch. "Do you know that he ran that last lap in under six minutes?" he said.

"Yeah," Stantz agreed. "If he wasn't dead, he'd be an Olympic prospect."

Stantz guided the screaming Ecto1A up in front of the towering World Trade Center, near Manhattan's Wall Street. Venkman, riding shotgun, gazed up at the buildings looming above him and smiled. Big money, he thought.

Winston and Spengler climbed out of the back of the ambulance, carrying their basic monitoring devices.

Stantz made a move for one of the proton packs. Venkman waved him off. He didn't think they'd need any heavy combat equipment.

The four jumpsuited men entered the building.

Moments later they were ushered into the ornate office

of Ed Petrosius, a short, sweating super-successful and very tightly wound bond salesman.

Petrosius gaped at the Ghostbusters as they marched into his office. He was in the middle of a phone conversation but he clearly wasn't pleased at seeing the quartet in full ghostbusting regalia. He placed a hand over the mouthpiece of the phone.

"What is this?" he hissed. "I'm trying to keep this quiet. Couldn't you put on a coat and tie? You look like janitors."

Venkman glanced at Stantz. They both nodded. Pinhead, they concluded. Rich, spoiled pinhead.

Petrosius barked into the phone, "I'll call you back, Ned. Watch Southern Gulf. If it goes past eight, start buying. Later."

He slammed down the phone and swiveled his chair to face the four Ghostbusters.

"All right," he said impatiently. "How long is this going to take, and what's it going to cost me?"

Venkman offered him a sincere insincere smile. "Well, it depends. Generally we charge an arm and a leg."

Petrosius punched a button on his desktop with a closed fist. His office door automatically slammed shut.

"Look, I got a lot to do and I can't afford to waste a lot of time on this, so don't jerk me around."

Stantz tried the reassuring tack. "Why don't you just tell us what the problem is."

Petrosius stared at his hands.

"Puh-leeeze?" Venkman said, wheedling.

"All right," Petrosius muttered. "Sometimes, every once in a while, things just sort of—well, they just... they just kind of *burst into flames*."

He looked up at the Ghostbusters. "You know what I mean?"

Venkman nodded scientifically. "Sure. Things just kind of burst into flames."

"Yeah, you know," Petrosius continued. "Like, I'll be working or talking on the phone and the top of my desk will just catch on fire. You've heard of that, haven't you?"

Venkman rubbed his chin. "Oh, yeah, happens all the time."

"You have a lot of paper around," Stantz offered. "It could be simple spontaneous combustion."

Spengler furrowed his thick brows. "Or it may be *pyrogenesis*."

Petrosius was baffled. "Pyrowhatsis?"

Spengler adjusted his glasses. "Pyrogenesis is the ability some people have to generate great amounts of heat."

Before Petrosius could take that in, the phone on his desk buzzed. "Damn," he muttered, yanking the phone up to his ear. "Yeah? What?"

His eyes grew large. "What are you talking about? I worked the whole thing out with Bill! Forget that crap! Tell Donald to talk to Mike. He okayed the whole thing. And now, one word from Donald and he wants out? No way. We have a deal! Oh, really? My lawyer is an ex-Green Beret!"

He picked up a contract from his desk and began waving it in the air.

Spengler slowly lifted the small, ebony Giga meter and scanned Petrosius while he screamed into the phone.

"No, Bob," Petrosius said, boiling. "*You* eat it! You want to come over here and make me? Anytime, you lying sack of—"

To the right of Petrosius's desk, a wastepaper basket suddenly exploded into flame.

The Ghostbusters exchanged startled looks.

Petrosius glanced at the smoking wastebasket. "Damn it!"

The contract in his hand began to smolder and smoke.

He dropped it onto the desktop. It, too, burst into spirals of orange and yellow. Tongues of flame shot forth from the in and out boxes on his desk. And the desk calendar. And the blotter.

Venkman watched more and more of Petrosius's world explode. "Whew! Somebody get the burgers and weenies. This guy is incredible."

Venkman reached over the desk and grabbed a pitcher of water. He tossed it into Petrosius's steaming face. Winston ran to the corner and yanked the inverted plastic bottle from the watercooler. He rushed back to the desk and doused the fire in the wastebasket.

Petrosius watched the water drip from his face and cascade down onto his clothing. He glared at Venkman. "This is a twelve-hundred-dollar suit!" he bellowed.

At that point the curtains behind him caught fire.

Stantz marched bravely up to Petrosius. "I hate to do this, sir," he announced, "but you are a public fire hazard."

Ray Stantz cocked his left arm back and threw a haymaker that caught Petrosius squarely on the jaw. The yammering businessman pitched back into his swivel chair. His chin dropped to his chest.

"Out cold," Winston noted.

"Good policy, Ray," Venkman said, staring at the unconscious man. "From now on let's beat up *all* our customers."

The curtains behind the desk continued to burn, the tongues of flame licking upward. High above the room, the automatic sprinkler system suddenly kicked into action.

The entire office was caught in a machine-made downpour.

Undeterred, a cogitating Spengler walked over to the watercooler. He stuck his hand into the open top and found that the interior sides of the cooler were coated with psycho-reactive slime.

"Interesting," he said.

He glanced at his three companions. They were lilting Petrosius out of his chair.

They carried the unconscious man out of his office and into the reception area like a sack of wet laundry.

Venkman paused momentarily before Petrosius's shocked secretary. "I think Ed's going to be taking some time off."

The Ecto1A pulled up in front of the high-priced store on New York's Fifth Avenue.

A crowd of people was gathered in front of the store's window gazing inside, dumbfounded.

The Ghostbusters jogged up to the locked front door. "Ghostbusters," Winston announced.

The small, frightened manager of the store let them in immediately.

The four Ghostbusters gazed at the strange sight before them.

The high-priced shop sold mostly precious glass. At this moment all the expensive pieces of crystal were floating in the air, several feet above the glass shelves and display tables that had once supported their weight. Stantz and Venkman walked up to the worried, mousy manager while Winston and Spengler set up their small battery of electronic devices in each corner of the room.

Stantz, after studying the phenomenon, turned to the manager. "It's just a straight polarity reversal."

"It is?" The manager blinked.

"Some kind of major PKE storm must have blown through here and affected the silicon molecules in the glass," Stantz continued. He offered the manager a smile and a friendly nod of his groundhog hairdoed head. "We'll have it fixed in a jiff."

"Ready, boys?" he called.

"Ready," Spengler and Winston replied.

"Okay," Stantz commanded. *"Activate!"*

Spengler and Winston simultaneously threw the switches that operated the electronic reversal machines located around the store. A myriad of laserlike beams emerged from the gizmos and engulfed the perimeters of the room, crackling, snapping, and buzzing.

The floating crystal began to shimmy and shake.

The manager of the store watched, horrified, as all the glassware suddenly dropped out of the air. The valuable crystal pieces smashed through the glass shelves and splintered all the display tables. In a moment there was nothing to be seen in the store but tiny shards of sparkling glass.

Spengler and Winston switched off their machines.

Stantz faced the manager with a smile. "See?"

The manager emitted a low moan.

Stantz put a bearlike arm around the tiny man. "So, will that be cash or check?"

The four Ghostbusters emerged from the store to the sound of cheering from the assembled crowd.

From inside the store came an anguished howl.

The crowd froze and turned.

Was it a spirit? A strange and dangerous apparition?

They peered through the window.

No, it was just the weeping manager armed with a straw broom and a dustpan.

Back at Ghostbusting headquarters, would-be spook-chaser Louis lurked surreptitiously behind a pillar leading to the office area, a ghost-trapping pedal near his feet.

Hanging suspended from a string above his desk were several pieces of Kentucky Fried Chicken.

Louis would rid the Ghostbusters of the apparition. He knew he could do it. He had the stamina, the gusto, the intellect. Well, at least the stamina and the gusto.

Louis held his breath as the green Slimer emerged from behind a wall, furtively sniffing the air. Slimer spotted the chicken, cackled, and flew directly toward it.

"Gotcha!" Louis squeaked, slamming his foot down on the foot pedal.

The ghost-trapper popped open and shot a powerful cone of light up toward the ceding. Slimer munched the chicken calmly as the ghost-trapping rays shot harmlessly by him. What the rays did ensnare was a big chunk of the ceiling, which promptly came crashing down at Louis's feet.

"Uh-oh," Louis moaned.

"Burp," Slimer commented.

Louis slunk out of the room, dejected. On his salary he could never afford the repairs.

He'd do the right thing when the Ghostbusters returned. He'd explain how the ceiling caved in.

He'd lie.

16

Peter Venkman and Winston Zeddemore entered the firehouse's living quarters, exhausted after a tough job. They'd had to trap the spirit of a long-dead game-show host who was inhabiting the set of a TV soap opera. It was a fairly frightening experience for the actors involved. Every time they opened a door on any of their sets, a new prize materialized. The young male lead had nearly ruptured himself when he'd darted out a living-room door and crashed into a brand-new Amana freezer—"with an automatic ice maker," a ghostly voice had intoned as paramedics arrived on the scene.

Venkman fell over onto a sofa. "This pace is too much," he said, moaning. "I'm just going to take a little nap. Wake me on Wednesday."

"Today's Monday," Winston said with a sigh.

"I know that," Venkman replied, his eyes fluttering.

Stantz walked over to the horizontal forms of Winston and Venkman, beaming proudly. "Before you guys pass out, come over here. Spengler and I have something *really* amazing to show you."

"It's not that thing you do with your nostrils, is it?" Venkman said.

Stantz scurried off to the refrigerator. He opened up the freezer and, pushing aside an avalanche of TV dinners and frozen pizza, pulled out a specimen of slime housed in a Tupperware container.

Stantz trotted over to a barely conscious Venkman. "We've been studying the stuff that we took from the subway tunnel."

He ran over to the fire station's microwave oven and popped the container inside. He allowed it to thaw for a moment.

"What are you going to do, eat it?" Venkman groused.

"No," Stantz said. "I'm just restoring it to its normal state."

Winston and Venkman slowly sat up in their chairs. Stantz took the specimen out of the microwave and moved over to a table. He carefully poured a few drops of the ooze into a large petri dish.

Stantz winked at Venkman and Winston. "Now watch *this*."

He leaned over the dish of slime and began to shout at it. "You worthless piece of *slime*!" he bellowed in mock anger.

Venkman watched in awe as the slime in the dish began to twitch and glow.

Stantz took another deep breath and screamed, "You *ignorant, disgusting blob*!"

The small specimen of ooze began to bubble and swell. Every time Stantz yelled at it, the mess changed its color and slowly began to grow in size.

"I've seen some real *crud* in my life," Stantz continued screaming, "but you're a *chemical disgrace*!"

The specimen suddenly doubled its size and started to spill over the rim of the petri dish. Egon Spengler smiled thinly in a corner of the room. Stantz turned to him. "Okay, Egon, I think that's enough for the day. Let's calm it down."

Spengler picked up an acoustic guitar, slung it over his shoulder, and padded softly up to the petri dish. He nodded at Stantz. Stantz nodded in return. Spengler strummed an opening chord, and then the two Ghostbusters began to serenade the slime.

"Kumbaya, my Lord," they warbled. "Kumbaya."

Venkman and Winston watched the impromptu hootenanny wide-eyed.

As Spengler and Stantz continued to play and sing, the slime stopped bubbling. Slowly but noticeably, the ooze began to calm down and actually shrink.

Stantz and Spengler ended their tune with a flourish. Stantz turned to Venkman. Venkman screwed up his face into the fleshy equivalent of a question mark.

"*This* is what you do with your spare time?"

Stantz excitedly pointed to the ooze. "This is an incredible breakthrough, Venkman. Don't you see? We have here a psycho-reactive substance! Whatever that stuff is, it clearly responds to *human* emotional states!"

Spengler nodded. "And we've found it at every event site we've been to lately."

Venkman leapt to his feet. "Mood slime. Now *there* is a major Christmas-gift item."

Stantz motioned for Venkman to be seated. "No way. That would be like giving someone a live hand grenade. This stuff is dangerous. I'm telling you, Pete, based on what we've already seen, we could be facing a major paranormal upheaval."

Winston stared at the slime. "You mean, this stuff actually feeds on *bad vibes*?"

"Like a goat on garbage," Stantz said.

"I love it when you talk science terms," Venkman said, sacking out on the couch.

17

A baleful moon peeked through the starlit skylight above the restoration studio in the near-deserted museum as Dana Barrett cleaned off the last of her brushes and began to put away her supplies. She was bone-tired. It had been a busy day. On the plus side, she had managed to clean a small Renaissance painting. That wasn't bad for a day's work.

Across the studio, the mighty head of Vigo of Carpathia shimmered to life. His eyes lit up as he watched Dana walk past his oil-colored feet.

Dana stopped in her tracks. Someone was watching her. She *felt* it. Yet there was no one else in the studio. She glanced up curiously at the titanic portrait of Vigo. A chill crept through her. She was just being silly, she concluded, and continued to walk toward the exit.

Vigo's thick neck pulsed to life, allowing his head to follow her toward the door.

Dana spun around and caught the movement of the one-dimensional piece of art.

Teasing, she edged back toward the exit door and scrambled through it, slamming it securely behind her.

She nearly ran out of the museum. It would be good to be home with little Oscar, safe and secure in her apartment.

* * *

Within two hours Dana had chalked up the entire incident to her nerves. She had been on edge since the baby buggy had gotten away from her. Long hours. Seeing Venkman again. The last two weeks had been a whirlpool of conflicting feelings.

She cradled a cooing Oscar in her arms and carried him into the bathroom. She lowered her child into his bassinet, and wrapping her bathrobe around her nightgown, she bent over the old claw-foot bathtub and turned on the tap.

"Bath time," she called over her shoulder to Oscar.

The water gushed out of the faucet and into the tub. Dana carefully stuck her wrist under the stream of water, checking its temperature. She then turned to Oscar and, bending over the bassinet, began to undress her child.

"Look at you." She smiled adoringly. "I think we got more food on your shirt than we got in your mouth."

The baby clapped appreciatively at his mother's wit.

Behind Dana, the water gushing from the faucet slowly changed into shining, shimmering slime. The slime hit the gathered water in the tub with a resounding plop and settled itself at the very bottom of the tub. Both of the spigots on the tub began to spin wildly as more and more slime burrowed beneath the surface of the water.

Dana, unaware of the change in the tub's attitude, routinely reached over to a shelf and squirted a stream of bubble bath into the water.

She returned her attention to Oscar. The rim of the tub puckered up like a clamshell and its sides convulsed as the newly animated piece of porcelain sucked up the bubble bath.

Belch.

Dana proudly picked up her beautiful baby boy out of his bassinet and held him above the tub.

"Bathies," she cooed.

She lowered Oscar toward the waiting tub. Without warning the tub began to shimmy and shake before her, its sides rising up like a gigantic, snapping clamshell, poised to snap up the boy and drag it down to the awaiting layer of glop.

Dana screamed and raised her baby.

The bathtub snapped at her.

Dana clutched Oscar to her chest and slowly backed away from the convulsing tub. Creak. Creak. Creak. The tub's stumpy legs slowly began to creep across the tile floor toward Dana.

Dana turned and ran out of the bathroom.

The tub made an attempt to dash after her but found the doorway too narrow a passageway to clear.

The tub growled in anger, vomiting up buckets of creeping, crawling slime.

Dana dashed through her apartment. She grabbed her keys and headed for the front door. She had to find a safe place to hide. A place no spirit would *dare* invade.

Peter Venkman lay sprawled upon the floor of his apartment, sound asleep. He was still fully clothed and had not quite made it into his bedroom, nodding out some three feet away from its entranceway.

Venkman's loft apartment resembled the site of a recent spate of tornadoes. Tattered, mismatched pieces of furniture were covered with old magazines, books, newspapers, videotapes, and a few very ripe pieces of half-eaten pizza.

Venkman's eyes fluttered as his front doorbell chimed.

He slowly got to his feet, and trying carefully not to step on any debris that would either break under his weight or stick to his shoes, he zigzagged sleepily to the door.

He eased the door open.

Outside stood Dana, wearing her short nightgown under an overcoat. Baby Oscar was in her arms, naked but for a baby blanket hastily wrapped around him.

"I'm s-sorry," Dana stammered. "Were you on your way out?"

Venkman looked down and saw that he still had on his coat, scarf, and hat. "No. I just got in… a couple of hours ago. Come on in."

Dana entered the messy apartment. Venkman gazed at her nightgown. "Are we having a pajama party?"

"Peter," Dana blurted, "my bathtub tried to eat Oscar!"

Venkman stared at Dana. So young. So beautiful. Possibly so nuts. He thought a moment. "You know, if anyone else told me that, I'd have serious doubts. But coming from you, I can't honestly say I'm surprised."

"I must be losing my mind," Dana said, near tears. "At the museum today I could have sworn that terrible painting of Vigo *moved* and looked right at me!"

"Who could blame him?" Venkman shrugged. "Were you wearing this nightgown?"

"I don't know what to do anymore," she said with a moan.

"I'll get Ray and Egon to check out the bathtub. You better stay here."

Venkman trotted off to his bedroom. Dana glanced around the loft. She was amazed at the disorder. It looked like Hiroshima after the A-bomb blast. Venkman jogged back into the room, carrying an old football sweatshirt. He gently lifted Oscar from Dana's arms. The baby's blanket fell away.

"Now this kid has a *serious* nudity problem," he surmised.

He spread the sweatshirt out on the sofa, placed Oscar on it, and began tying it around the child like a diaper.

"This is Joe Namath's old number, you know," he informed the baby, "You could get a lot of chicks with this. Just don't pee in it."

Dana stood, trembling. "Peter, what about the *bath-tub*?"

"We'll take care of that," he said, reaching for a phone and dialing. "Ray? Pete. Listen. Get over to Dana's right away. Her bathtub pulled a fast one. Tried to eat her kid."

"It was full of this awful pink ooze," Dana offered.

Venkman nodded, still cradling the phone. "Sounds like another slime job, Ray. No, they're both all right. They're here now. Right. Let me know."

Venkman hung up the phone. "They're going over there right now. You might as well make yourself at home. Let me show you around."

He carefully walked into the kitchen area. "This is the *cuisine de maison*," he announced.

The kitchen looked worse than the living room. The sink boasted a mountain range of dirty dishes, and the counters were stacked with all sorts of rotted food and crunched TV-dinner boxes. Venkman smiled suavely and pulled a colossal trash bag from a drawer. He tossed it onto the floor and started stiff-arming trash off the counter into it.

He glanced at the junk-coated dishes in the sink. "Umm. We may have to wash some of these if you get hungry."

He stumbled toward the refrigerator and eased open the door. A horrible stench emerged. He slammed the door shut. "But... there's no real food, anyway, so forget about it. I have all kinds of carryout menus if you feel like ordering."

He yanked open a cabinet drawer. Inside were at least a hundred dog-eared menus. There was everything from Chinese and Mexican cuisine to a flyer from Mr. Nut's International House of Peanut Butter and Jelly.

He strode across the loft to a door. "And the bathroom's right here," he said with a flourish. "Uh, let me just tidy up a few things."

Dana smiled. "Peter, this is very nice, but you don't have to do any of this, you know."

Venkman grinned gallantly and, slinging another trash bag over his shoulder, dashed inside. A toilet flushed. The shower ran. The sound of glass, tin, and wood could be heard tumbling into the trash bag.

Within a minute Venkman emerged, carrying a full trash bag over his shoulder. "The shower works but it's a little tricky," he advised. "Both spigots are marked 'hot.' It takes a little practice, but at least this one won't try to eat you."

Dana began to ease herself onto Venkman's ratty sofa. Venkman walked by her, the trash slung over his shoulder. "Be careful on that sofa, though. It's a butt biter."

Dana nearly leapt to her feet.

"But the bed's good." Venkman smiled. "And I just changed the sheets, so if you get tired, feel free. In fact, I think you should *definitely* plan on spending the night here."

Dana offered him a crooked grin. "Really? And how would we handle the sleeping arrangements?"

Venkman dropped the second trash bag in the kitchen and pondered the problem. "Hmm. For me, it's best if I sleep on my side and you spoon up right behind me with your arms around me. If we go the other way, I'm afraid your hair will be getting in my face all night." Dana stared at Venkman. "How about you on the sofa and me in bed with the baby?"

Venkman nodded. "Or we could do that."

"Thank you," Dana said, picking up Oscar. She cradled the baby in her arms. "Poor baby. I think I should put him down now."

Venkman walked up to them both. "I'll put him down for you."

He stared at the child. "You are way too short! And your belly button sticks out! And you're nothing but a burden to your poor mother!"

He picked up the giggling baby and carried Oscar into the bedroom.

Dana watched Venkman play daddy, and smiled.

For the first time in ages she felt relaxed.

And safe.

Very, very safe.

She savored the feeling, sensing that it wouldn't last for very long.

18

Peter Venkman paced back and forth in front of the Manhattan Museum of Art, watching the building's first horde of art lovers make their way up the front stairs toward the entrance.

He checked his watch.

The Ecto1A screeched to a halt in front of the curb. Stantz, Spengler, and Winston scrambled out, Winston muttering under his breath about crosstown traffic.

Venkman, clearly concerned, cornered Stantz. "Did you find anything at Dana's apartment?"

Stantz shrugged. "Nothing. Just some mood-slime residue in and around the bathtub."

"But we did pay an interesting visit to Ray's bookstore this morning," Winston said, grinning.

Venkman rolled his eyes. There was *nothing* interesting in Ray's bookstore if you didn't count the cockroaches.

Stantz smiled and whipped a small, dog-eared volume out of Ecto1A. "We turned up some intriguing stuff on this Vigo character you mentioned."

He held up the book. It was nearly falling apart. "I found the name Vigo the Carpathian in Leon Zundinger's *Magicians, Martyrs, and Madmen*. Listen to this! Egon?"

Spengler held up a photocopy or two taken from the crumbling book. "'Vigo the Carpathian, born 1505, died 1610—'"

Venkman blinked. "A hundred and five years old? He really hung on, didn't he?"

Stantz smiled knowingly. "And he didn't die of old age, either. He was poisoned, stabbed, shot, hung, stretched, disemboweled, and drawn and quartered."

"I guess he wasn't too popular at the end there," Winston theorized.

"No," Spengler agreed. "He wasn't exactly a man of the people."

He began reading again. "'Also known as Vigo the Cruel, Vigo the Torturer, Vigo the Despised, and Vigo the Unholy.'"

"This guy was a bad monkey," Stantz explained. "He dabbled in all the black arts. And listen to this prophecy: Just before his head died, his last words were: 'Death is but a door, time is but a window. *I'll be back!*'"

Venkman wasn't impressed. "That's *it?* That's all he said? 'I'll be back'?"

Spengler shrugged. "Uh, it's a rough translation from the Moldavian."

Venkman sighed. "Okay. Let's visit Viggy."

The Ghostbusters picked up their paranormal monitoring equipment and walked up the front steps toward the museum.

Dressed in full gear, they marched through the lobby. Rudy, the security guard, stared at them in disbelief. Venkman was in the lead.

"Hey, Dr. Venkman," Rudy asked with a smile, "what's going on?"

"We're just going back to the restoration studio for a minute," Venkman replied.

Rudy frowned. "Oh, I can't let you do that. Mr. Poha left strict orders. He told me not to let you back there anymore."

Venkman stiffened. His eyebrows knitted together. He glared at Rudy in ultra mock seriousness. "Okay," he said confidentially. "We were trying to keep this quiet, but I think *you* can be trusted. Tell him, Ray."

Stantz walked up to Rudy and in a clipped tone announced, "Mister, you have an ecto-paritic, subfusionary flux in this building."

Rudy was aghast, although he wasn't quite sure why. "We got a *flux*?"

Winston strode forward. "Man, you got a flux and a *half*."

Rudy looked to Venkman. Venkman glanced at Stantz. Rudy shifted his gaze to Stantz. Stantz nodded grimly, raising his left hand. He began counting fingers. "Now, if you don't want to be the—one two three four—*fifth* person ever to die in meta-shock from a planar rift, I suggest you get down from behind that desk and don't move until we give you the signal, 'Stabilized—all clear.'"

Rudy nodded and swallowed hard. He slowly slithered out of his chair and crouched down behind his desk, and the Ghostbusters marched back toward the restoration studio.

Inside the studio, Janosz was patiently working on the horrible portrait of Vigo the Lowlife when the Ghostbusters barged through the door. Janosz hastily tossed down his paints and brushes and rushed over to the door in an attempt to bar their entry.

"Dr. Venkman?" he blurted. "Uhh, Dana is not here."

Venkman flashed him a cool smile. "I know."

Janosz was sweating now. "Then why have you come?"

Venkman pushed the agitated artist aside. "We've got a major creep alert, and we're just going down the list. Your name was first."

Janosz stood, quivering in terror. Stantz turned to Winston and Spengler. "Let's sweep the area, boys."

The three Ghostbusters pulled out their hand-held monitoring devices and began to stroll through the studio area. Janosz was growing more and more nervous. Venkman sidled up to him.

"You know," he said, "I never got to ask you: Where are you from, Johnny?"

Janosz mind reeled. "Uh, the Upper West Side."

Spengler glanced at his PKE meter. "This entire room is extremely hot, Peter."

Janosz turned to Venkman. "What exactly are you looking for?"

Venkman offered him a totally insincere, reassuring smile. "We'll know it when we find it. You just sit tight, Johnny. This won't take long."

Stantz pulled out the shoebox-shaped Giga meter. It began to click in his hand. The needle began to quiver and quake, eventually sliding to the extreme right-hand side of the small screen. Stantz looked up. Inadvertently he had aimed the Giga meter directly at the Brobdingnagian-sized portrait of Vigo the louse. Venkman joined Stantz.

He looked up at the painting of the fierce warrior. "This is the one that made ga-ga eyes at Dana."

Venkman walked up to the portrait. He stared up into Vigo's dull eyes. "Hey, *you*!" he called. "Viggy! Look at me! Down here! I'm talking to you, stud! Hey! Look at me when I'm talking to you!"

Stantz and Venkman watched the painting for any sign of movement.

On the canvas Vigo's eyes remained motionless, focused lifelessly on something far off in the distance.

Stantz sighed. Venkman's tactics weren't working. Venkman, however, refused to give up. He whipped out a small camera and began darting to and fro at die base of the painting, snapping away.

"Beautiful, beautiful, Viggy. That's it. Work with me, baby. Just have fun with it."

Venkman snapped away. After a full roll was used, he stopped his photography riff and turned to Stantz. "Okay, so he's playing it cool." Venkman shrugged. "Let's finish up and get the heck out of here."

Stantz nodded. "I'll get one more reading."

Venkman walked off, disgusted. Stantz, left alone in front of the towering painting, scanned the canvas one last time with his Giga meter. He started with the feet and worked his way up the legs to the torso, then aimed the meter at the neck. Finally Stantz found himself gazing at the face of Vigo.

Vigo's eyes slowly flickered to life.

Stantz felt his body stiffen.

A fierce red light welled up Vigo's evil eyes.

Stantz felt the power of Vigo enter his eyes and burn itself right down to the depths of his very soul.

Stantz stood before the painting, transfixed. Deep down within him he knew what was happening to him. He knew he should turn away, but the conscious being known as Ray Stantz was gradually fading away, enslaved by a new evil being. Stantz's childlike eyes narrowed to reptilian slits. His open, optimistic face began to grow taut. His lips, capable of a smile at the most dire of occasions, slowly twisted themselves into a terrifying sneer.

Stantz felt an arm on his shoulder.

He blinked.

His body regained fluidity.

"Now that's one *ugly* dude," Winston said to Stantz.

Stantz shook his head. "Huh? What?"

Stantz made a concerted effort to figure out what had happened to him during the last minute or so. Everything was a blank.

"You finished here?" Winston asked.

"What? Huh? Oh, yeah. Sure. Sure," Stantz said, his legs still feeling wobbly.

"Are you all right?" Winston queried. "You coming down with something?"

Stantz managed a feeble smile for his good and loyal friend, Winston. "No, I'm fine. I just got lightheaded for a second there. Let's go."

Winston aimed Stantz toward the exit door. "Okay, buddy, but if you feel like calling it an early day, it's okay. I'll pick up the slack."

Stantz nodded woozily. "I appreciate that, Winston. I really do."

The Ghostbusters left the portrait of Vigo and the figure of Janosz Poha behind them.

Janosz turned to the painting of Vigo and smiled.

Soon, he realized, the Ghostbusters would stand in their way no more.

19

The Ghostbusters walked down the museum's front steps toward Ecto1A.

"There's definitely something going on in that studio," Spengler surmised. "The PKE levels were max-plus, and the Giga meter was showing all red."

Winston agreed. "I'd put my money on that Vigo character."

Venkman smirked. 'Yeah, *that's* a safe bet."

Venkman and Spengler climbed into the rear of the Ecto1A. Venkman glanced at Stantz before shutting the rear hatch. "You and Spengler see what else you can dig up on Vigo and this little weasel, Poha. Those two were made for each other."

Stantz said nothing. He nodded. He was getting a headache. A bad one.

"Want me to drive?" Winston asked.

"No," Stantz said. "I'm fine."

Stantz slid in behind the wheel. Winston eased himself into the passenger's seat.

A strange smile played across Ray Stantz's face as he turned the ignition key and slammed his right foot down on the gas, sending the Ecto1A screeching away from the curb.

Winston gave him a nervous look.

Stantz sent the ambulance skidding and swerving around the streets of Manhattan as he ostensibly headed back for the firehouse. His eyes seemed vacant. His face was devoid of any awareness of the commotion he was causing all around him. Stantz swerved suddenly. He slammed his hand down on the car's horn.

"Idiot!" he shrieked to a passing motorist.

He cut off another car. "Move it, you jerk!" he roared.

Winston glanced into the rear of the Ecto1A, where Venkman and Spengler were being tossed around like rag dolls, along with their ghostbusting equipment.

Stantz began to pick up speed. Thirty-five. Forty. Fifty miles an hour. He roared through red lights, narrowly avoiding pedestrians.

Winston looked at Ray, beads of perspiration dribbling down his forehead. "Going a little fast, aren't we, Ray?"

Stantz glared at Winston. His eyes were deranged, unfeeling. "Are you telling me how to drive?" he asked, sneering.

"No, I just thought—

"Well, don't think!" Ray bellowed.

He stood on the accelerator, fishtailing in front of a bus and two cars.

In the back of Ecto1A, Venkman and Spengler continued to bounce around.

"I want to talk to our mechanic about these shocks," Venkman muttered, his head slamming into the roof of the auto.

Venkman and Spengler clung to the safety straps above their heads, twirling like aerial stars in a circus.

In the front seat, Winston moved from panic level to out-and-out we're-gonna-die mode. He turned to Stantz. "Are you crazy, man? You're going to kill somebody!"

Stantz emitted a devilish cackle. He turned to Winston

and smiled demonically. "Wrong," he announced. "I'm going to kill *everybody*!"

Stantz sent the Ecto1A sailing off the street and headed for a small public park.

He carefully aimed the vehicle for a large tree.

Winston's eyes widened in disbelief as he watched the tree loom larger and larger.

At the last possible moment he reached over and coldcocked Stantz with a strong right hook. Stantz's body went limp. Winston reached over and, yanking the wheel, slid his left foot across the front of the seat and slammed on the brakes.

The car lurched to a halt. It barely grazed the tree.

The four Ghostbusters tumbled out of the car, dazed and shaken but unhurt.

Stantz dropped to all fours, shaking his head. It was as if he were awakening from a deep, long sleep. He staggered to his feet, his senses still swimming. He glanced confusedly at Venkman.

"What happened?"

"You just picked up three penalty points on your driver's license," Venkman informed him.

Stantz gaped at the Ecto1A and the tree. Within seconds Winston was at his side. "Are you all right?"

Stantz nodded, the first flickerings of understanding playing across his face. "Yeah, I guess so. It was the strangest thing. I knew what I was doing but I couldn't stop. This really *terrible feeling* came over me and—I don't know—I just felt like driving into that tree and ending it all. Whew! Sorry, boys."

Venkman turned to Spengler. "Watch him, Egon," he whispered. "Don't even let him shave."

Winston inspected the damage to the car. "No big deal," he said with a sigh. "Just another fender bender in the Big Apple."

Venkman rolled his eyes. Yeah. Right.

20

Venkman and Winston walked into the firehouse, bone-tired after spending most of the morning haggling with an auto mechanic about getting the repairs done on Ecto1A as quickly and as cheaply as possible. The mechanic wasn't too responsive until Venkman threatened to summon up the spirit of the guy's long-dead mother-in-law. Within ninety minutes the Ecto1A looked fine. The mechanic even threw in a tune-up for free.

In the firehouse lab area, Stantz and Spengler were hard at work. Stantz took a small sample of the psycho-reactive slime out of a small container. He had painted a smiley face on the lid to keep the ooze calm.

"What's up?" Winston asked.

"We now know the *negative* potential of this stuff," Stantz announced. "We've isolated this specimen and we're running tests on it to see if we can get an equally strong *positive* reaction."

Venkman was intrigued. "What kind of tests?"

Stantz shuffled about before the container, embarrassed. "Well, we sing to it. We talk to it. We say supportive, nurturing things…"

"You're not *sleeping* with this stuff, are you?" Venkman asked in mock horror.

Spengler coughed, reacting as if he *might* be. Venkman and Winston watched intently as Stantz spooned some of the psycho-reactive slime into an old toaster.

"We've mostly been going with the music angle," he said.

"We've identified several songs that seem to have a calming or a mediating effect on the slime," Spengler added.

"We tried all the sappy stuff," Stantz continued. "'Kumbaya,' 'Everything Is Beautiful,' and 'It's a Small World' all scored high."

Spengler offered a thin smile. "But the song that really goosed its molecules is the 1967 Jackie Wilson hit, 'Higher and Higher.'"

Venkman didn't believe it.

"Watch this." Stantz grinned. He walked over to a boom box and flicked on a tape. The sweet, silky voice of the late, great Jackie Wilson blasted through the room.

The slime-encased toaster began to shake and spin. Winston's jaw dropped open as the toaster actually started to swivel back and forth—in time with the pulsating music. Venkman gaped in astonishment at the bopping toaster as it actually shot two pieces of darkened bread into the air and, swerving on the tabletop, caught them back in its slots without missing a beat.

"I don't care what you say," Venkman said, beaming. "We're going to bottle this stuff and sell it. We'll make a fortune."

Winston was a tad more skeptical. "Right, and the first time someone gets mad, their toaster will eat their hand."

Venkman wasn't daunted. "Okay. Okay. So we'll put a warning on the label."

Stantz switched off the Jackie Wilson tape and the toaster sputtered to a complete standstill.

"We're investigating the practical applications," Spengler said. "But stocking stuffers isn't one of them. We think it could be a useful tool against certain types of spiritual manifestations."

Venkman didn't get it.

"We have a prototype designed for a pressure-forced, neutronically metered, fully portable delivery system," Stantz announced.

Venkman still didn't get it.

Stantz sighed. "Basically it's a *slime-blower*."

He held up a bazookalike tube attached to a set of compressed air tanks.

Venkman wasn't overly awed. "Yeah, well keep up the good work. See if you can keep it under a hundred and fifty pounds."

Venkman walked over to the toaster and stuck his fingers in one of the slots.

Venkman sneered at the slime within. "Go ahead, I dare you."

Venkman suddenly screamed, as if the toaster were gnawing the flesh off his fingers. He couldn't remove his hand from the goop-empowered mechanism. The other three Ghostbusters leapt forward to his aid.

Venkman faced them with a smile. "Just kidding," he said, easily removing his hand from the toaster.

With that he left the room, leaving the other three Ghostbusters relieved, but more than slightly p.o.'d, behind him.

After making a quick stop at Dana's deserted apartment, Venkman made his way downtown to his loft. He walked up to the front door, tentatively holding a small bouquet of flowers, as well as one of Dana's small suitcases.

He produced his keys, unlocked the door, and swung it open.

"Honeeeeey," he called. "I'm home!"

He eased the door shut behind him. He gazed in terror at the sight before him. Never in all his years as a Ghostbuster had he witnessed such an appalling sight.

"I knew it!" he muttered. "She *cleaned!*"

The loft was spotless.

The withering leftovers had been removed.

The old newspapers and magazines had been banished.

Books were now neatly stacked on shelves.

The thirteen layers of dust in the kitchen had been washed away.

The hairballs—and Venkman didn't even have *pets*—had been vacuumed from the furniture.

Venkman heard the shower running in the bathroom. Placing the suitcase and the flowers down, he slowly tiptoed to the bathroom. The door was half open. He peeked inside. He could barely make out the form of Dana, clad only in layers of soap, behind the shower curtain.

Sighing, he eased the door closed and moved to the bedroom, where little Oscar lay asleep. Dana had surrounded the tyke with large pillows to prevent him from taking an impromptu swan dive off the bed.

Venkman smiled.

Maybe *this* was what he needed in his life. He slammed the flat of his hand into his forehead. Naaah. This kind of life was for normal people, not Ghostbusting kind of guys.

He spun around and collided with Dana as she exited the bathroom wrapped only in a towel. She quickly darted back inside.

Venkman made a concerted effort not to drool. He had just gotten his shirt cleaned.

Dana reemerged from the bathroom wearing a long terry-cloth robe. Venkman leered at her. "Now, don't tell me you didn't do that on purpose. You're trying to torture me, aren't you?"

Dana regarded him impassively.

"Are you all squeaky clean now?" Venkman asked.

Dana shot him a withering smile. "Yes, I'm very clean. Did they find anything in my apartment?"

Before Venkman could answer, Dana marched past him and entered the bedroom, closing the door in his face.

"Nothing," Venkman shouted through the door. "They stayed there all night, went through your personal stuff, made a bunch of long-distance calls, and cleaned out your refrigerator. That's about it."

Dana opened the door, still wearing the heavy robe. "So what do I do now?"

Venkman grinned. "You get dressed and we go out. I've got a baby-sitter and everything. Trust me, you need it."

Dana was tempted. "You don't have to entertain me, you know."

"I know," Venkman said, trotting into the living room and returning with her suitcase. "I brought some of your clothes."

Dana smiled, took the small suitcase, and eased the bedroom door shut. "Wear something intriguing," Venkman said to the closed door.

He walked down a small corridor and opened his closet, looking for his good suit. "Did you happen to see some shirts on the floor in here?" he called.

"I put them in your hamper," Dana said from the bedroom. "I thought they were dirty."

Venkman shook his head mournfully. "Next time ask me first, okay? I have more than two grades of laundry. There are lots of subtle levels between *clean* and *dirty*."

He walked into the misty bathroom and attacked the hamper, yanking out pieces of clothing. Shirts. Slacks. Socks.

"Hmm," he muttered, "these aren't so bad yet. You just hang them up for a while and they're fine." He smelled the armpit of one shirt, frowned, and, reaching into the medicine cabinet, sprayed it for a full minute with deodorant. He sniffed it a second time. Better. Definitely better.

Pouring a healthy splash of after-shave into each sock, Venkman smiled.

He was all set for a night on the town.

21

Janine sat in the reception area of the Ghostbusters' firehouse, working late. Above her, she heard noises coming from the lab area that she knew should have been deserted.

She wasn't alarmed. She realized it would be Louis. Poor Louis, she thought with a sigh. The closest he would ever come to a brainstorm was a slight drizzle. Still, there was something about him that appealed to her.

He *meant* well. Janine supposed what appealed to her about Louis was that he exuded the same type of personality as the pets she'd chosen as a child. While all the other kids picked pedigreed dogs, she'd always gone for the stray mutts. Dogs who were so goofy and out of whack that you didn't expect anything from them. If they gnawed the newspaper instead of carrying it into the house, who could blame them?

She covered her computer and made her way up toward the lab, a warm smile on her elfin face.

Inside the lab, Louis was dressed in a Ghostbusters jumpsuit. It fit him like oversize feety pajamas. He had a proton pack strapped onto his back, but the straps were so loose that the pack banged into his rear end whenever he moved.

"Okay, Stinky," he muttered. "This is it. Showdown time. You and me, pal. You think you're smarter than I am? We'll see about that!"

He faced the ceiling and squeaked. "Oh, hello, Pizza Man! Oh, two larges! I ordered only one. Pepperoni and pineapple, my absolute favorite. I guess *I'll have to eat these both by myself*!"

The green ghost Slimer poked his head down through the ceiling and scanned the room for the grub.

"Okay, let's boogie," Louis whispered.

Louis whirled around and fired a proton stream at Slimer just as Janine entered the room. Slimer retreated easily. Janine gulped and ducked as a ragged bolt of energy streaked across the lab and seared the wall behind her.

Louis stood there, trembling. "Ohmigod!" he shouted. "I'm sorry. I didn't mean to do that. It was an accident."

He flip-flopped across the lab to Janine. The receptionist slowly straightened up. "What are you doing up here?" she asked him.

Louis began to sweat. "I was trying to get that smelly green ghost. The guys asked me to help out. I'm like the fifth Ghostbuster."

Janine smiled at him sweetly. "Why would you want to be a Ghostbuster if you're already an accountant?"

Louis thought hard. "Oh, no. It's not like that. It's just if one of the guys calls in sick or gets hurt."

Louis quickly slipped off the proton pack. The pack slid to the floor, nearly toppling Louis onto his back.

"So," Janine said, "have you made any plans for New 'fear's Eve?"

Louis shrugged. "No. I celebrate at the beginning of my corporate tax year, which is March first. That way I beat the crowds."

Janine was impressed. "That's very practical. I hate going out on New Year's Eve too."

Louis and Janine exchanged smiles. Suddenly Louis felt awkward. There was a warmth welling up within him. He was either very attracted to Janine, or else he was experiencing the aftershocks of a Thai food lunch Venkman had talked him into.

"Well," Janine said, turning, "good night, Louis."

Louis stumbled forward, his mouth getting the best of his brain. "Janine, do you feel like maybe getting something to eat on the way home? Have you ever been to Tad's? It's a pretty good deal. You get a steak, baked potato, a roll, and a salad with your choice of dressing for $5.29. You can't beat that!"

Janine faced Louis, bestowing upon him a wide, adoring smile. "I'd like to, Louis, but I told Dr. Venkman I'd baby-sit for his friend."

Louis's face fell instantly. "Oh," he murmured. "Maybe some other time, then."

"Do you want to baby-sit with me?" Janine offered.

Louis brightened. "Oh, *sure*!" he exclaimed. "That sounds *great*!"

Louis trotted up to Janine, and the twosome left the firehouse together.

Downtown, Venkman sat waiting for the baby-sitter in the center of his living room. His recently sprayed suit and socks ensemble looked mighty fine, even if he did have to say so himself.

His front doorbell rang.

He leapt out of the couch and trotted to the door, expecting to welcome Janine.

Instead he gazed upon Stantz, Spengler, and Winston. They stood in the hallway wearing over-the-hip rubberized wading boots, firemen's slickers, and miners' helmets. They each carried several sensing devices, meters, collection jars, and photographic equipment. If Venkman didn't know better, he would have sworn they were heading out on a major *National Geographic* spelunkers' expedition.

Venkman motioned them in. "Don't tell me, let me guess. All-you-can-eat barbecued rib night at the Sizzler?"

"Better!" Stantz beamed. "We're going down into the sewer system to see if we can trace the source of that psycho-reactive slime flow. We thought you might want to come along!"

Venkman snapped his fingers theatrically. "Darn it! I wish I'd have known you were going. I'm stuck with these silly dinner reservations."

Spengler ignored him. "You know, animals and lower life forms often anticipate major disasters. Given the new magnetheric readings, we could see a tremendous breeding surge in the cockroach population."

"Roach breeding?" Venkman replied. "Gosh! This is sounding better and better!"

Venkman called through the closed bedroom door. "Dana? The boys are going down under the sewers tonight to look for slime. Egon thinks there might even be some kind of big roach-breeding surge. Should we forget about dinner and go with them instead?"

Dana emerged from the bedroom looking gorgeous in a long, slinky evening gown, her auburn hair cascading down onto her shoulders.

"Wow!" Stantz concluded.

Dana surveyed the Ghostbusters' grab-bag outfits. "Hi!" she offered meekly.

The Ghostbusters, slightly flustered, nodded and waved back.

Venkman faced Stantz and Spengler. "Ray? Egon? I

think we're going to have to pass on the sewer trip. Let me know what you find out."

He led the Ghostbusters to the door. Stantz heaved a sigh. "Okay, but you're missing out on all the fun."

Venkman eased the door shut behind them.

In the hall, Stantz, Spengler, and Winston passed Janine and Louis in the hall. They smiled at each other.

Louis was awestruck by the professional-looking trio. "Hey!" he exclaimed. "Where are you going?"

The Ghostbusters walked into the elevator without saying a word.

"Okay," Louis said. "Talk to you later."

Janine knocked on Venkman's front door. Louis was impressed with Janine's importance. He had never visited Venkman at home before. In fact, up until now, he hadn't realized Venkman *had* a home.

Venkman swung the door open, clad in his dapper suit and looking very suave.

Louis sniffed the air. It reeked of drugstore cologne, spray-on deodorant, and talcum powder.

"Come in." Venkman smiled.

"I just saw the guys in some nifty outfits," Louis said enthusiastically.

"They were helping change a diaper," Venkman said, leading them into the apartment. "It was a pretty messy one."

Janine looked around the loft, frowning. Even when tidied up, the place resembled nothing more than a clubhouse from the old *Our Gang* comedies. "You actually live here?"

"Yes, Janine, I do," Venkman confessed.

"I think it's *neat,*" Louis offered.

Venkman smiled at Janine. "But I'm thinking of moving out soon."

Janine shrugged and, grabbing the TV listings, sat before the battered television to see if it worked. Louis chatted up Venkman. "I hope you don't mind me being here. I just thought I could keep Janine company."

"It's fine," Venkman said, putting a fatherly arm around the diminutive nerd. "Knock yourself out. But I don't want to come home and find you two making out on the couch!"

"Oh, no." Louis blushed. "We're just good friends."

"Okay, let's keep it that way." Venkman winked, leading Dana out the door.

Hailing a cab, he escorted Dana to one of the swankiest new restaurants in Manhattan: Armand's. It was the kind of restaurant that catered to the very rich and the very blow-dried. Raw fish was served alongside Southwestern cuisine. The wine tasted like Ripple but cost fifty times as much, and the piped-in Muzak sounded like vintage elevator music but was called new age subliminal. Venkman would have preferred a pool hall or an Irish pub, but he figured this was more Dana's style.

The cab pulled to a stop in front of Armand's. Venkman frowned. When he had moved to New York, the place had been a Laundromat. He sighed. He could use a Laundromat right about now.

He guided Dana through the front entrance and slipped the maître d' a five-dollar bill.

"Your best table, Armand," Venkman cooed, feeling like Douglas Fairbanks.

The maître d' peeked at the bill and grimaced. Venkman made sure that Dana missed that, and frowning, whipped out a twenty. He stuffed it into the maître d's hand. The man smiled.

"This better be good," Venkman said to the man.

The maître d' escorted them to a wonderful table. Venkman glanced over his shoulder. The couple next to them had ordered a fish that still had the head attached. A cold eye stared blankly at Venkman.

Jeez, he thought, sitting down. At least they could have put a *smile* on the thing.

He glanced at the menu. His heart sank.

No burgers.

Venkman sighed and made the best of it, ordering caviar and champagne. A slavish waiter brought their appetizer and spirits immediately.

Venkman raised a glass to Dana. "To a wonderful lady. A ninja warrior. A woman who stands tall," he toasted. "It's *your* night."

Dana smiled sadly and raised her glass. "To the most charming, nicest, kindest…"

"Why, you're talking about me!" Venkman grinned.

"… most unusual man I've ever broken up with." They both sipped their champagne.

"Speaking of breaking up with really neat guys," Venkman said casually. "So, tell me why you *dumped* me."

Dana slid back into her chair. "Oh, Peter. I didn't dump you. I just had to protect myself. You really weren't very good for me, you know."

"Hey," Venkman replied, "*I'm* not even good for me."

"Why do you say things like that?" Dana said. "You're so much better than you know."

"Thank you." Venkman grinned. "If I had that kind of support on a daily basis, I could definitely shape up by the turn of the century."

Dana smiled, her forehead feeling the first buzz of the champagne. "So why don't you call me in the year 2000?"

Venkman leaned over to kiss her. "Let me jingle you right now."

Dana pulled back. "Maybe I should call Janine."

Venkman continued to lean and pucker. "Don't worry.

Janine has a very special way with children. I know. I've seen her."

Venkman's lips touched Dana's. For a split second all the worries and all the pressures of the day faded. For a split second they were together. In love.

Things were not quite as lovely at Venkman's apartment. Janine sat transfixed before the television, watching a particularly engrossing episode of *Jake and the Fatman*.

Louis, meanwhile, paced around the living room with a screeching Oscar cradled in his arms. He was trying to feed the tyke a bottle of milk. The baby was having no part of it.

"Maybe a bedtime story would help," Louis muttered. "You want a bedtime story, baby?"

The baby belched.

Louis took that as a definite yes.

"Okay," he began. "Once there were these seven dwarfs and they had a limited partnership in a small mining operation, and one day this beautiful princess came to stay with them and they bartered room and board in exchange for housekeeping services, which was a very good deal for all of them because back then they didn't have to withhold tax and Social Security, and I guess she didn't have to file state and federal income-tax returns, either, which I'm not saying is *right*, you understand, because they could've got in a lot of trouble doing that, but it's just a story, so I guess it's okay."

Louis gazed down at Oscar.

The little boy had nodded out.

Louis heaved a sigh. "I can finish this later if you're tired," he advised the child.

Janine munched popcorn before the TV.

On the screen a blurb for the evening news appeared. A man with a toupee that looked like a muskrat faced the camera. "Ghosts. Are they worse than street gangs? Film and Ouija board at eleven."

22

Deep within the bowels of New York City, Stantz, Spengler, and Winston stood on an ancient train platform, their powerful flashlights blazing. They quickly unhooked themselves from the cables that had lowered them down to the ooze-laden substrata of Van Horne Station, and gazed down into the churning, glowing, whirling river of slime beneath them.

It was an awesome sight. The slime belched and bubbled, swished and swirled.

Stantz stared grimly into the "live" river. "Let's get a sounding on the depth of that flow."

Stantz grabbed a long coiled cord with a bobbing flotation device on die end. It was attached firmly to his utility belt. "Stand back," he ordered his companions.

He took the cord in his hand and, swinging the flotation device over his head, cast the line into the water like a master fisherman. The bob at the end of the line sank beneath the depths of the slime.

Spengler watched the line sink farther and farther down, calculating the depths on a small hand-held device. "Six feet. Seven feet. *Eight* feet."

The line stopped moving.

"That's it," Stantz announced. "It's on the bottom."

Suddenly the line began to wriggle again. Spengler continued to calculate. "Nine feet. Ten feet."

Winston was confused. "Is the line *still* sinking?"

Spengler gaped at the river. "No! The slime is rising."

Stantz glanced down and saw the slime climbing up over the edge of the train station platform and oozing around his boots.

"Let's get out of here, boys!" he yelled.

He made an attempt to pull the cord out of the water. The cord seemed stuck. Worse yet, the line seemed to be tugging back!

"Help me!" Stantz yelled. "It's stuck!"

Winston leapt in front of his good friend Ray and began to pull the cord as well. Winston and Stantz couldn't budge the cord from the river of slime, and slowly the slime began to pull the two men toward the edge of the platform… closer and closer to the bubbling, churning, *living* depths below.

Spengler tossed down his monitoring device and joined the tug of war. The three men grunted, sweated, and strained, but whatever was pulling on the cord from below was clearly stronger… in a superhuman way.

Stantz worked a free hand furiously, trying to cut the cord from his utility belt.

If he didn't sever the tie, he was a dead man. Or at least a very slimed man.

The cord held fast to his belt.

Stantz grimaced and attacked his belt buckle. Quickly, frantically, he worked at the belt. Finally he yanked the entire belt from his waist.

The belt and cord were yanked toward the river of slime.

Spengler and Stantz broke free from the cord in time. Winston, however, unaware of Stantz's lifesaving move, held fast to the cord.

The startled Ghostbuster found himself yanked off his feet and high into the air.

Still clutching the cord, Winston was pulled deep down into the slime river.

"Ray!" he yelled, gurgling. "Egon!"

Stantz and Spengler glanced at each other.

"Bummer," Spengler muttered.

The two remaining Ghostbusters, summoning up every ounce of courage, dove headfirst into the swirling slime after their comrade.

Stantz and Spengler were unable to swim through the percolating muck. As helpless as flies trapped in molasses, they floated out of the station and into a swirling tide of ooze.

The slime twisted and turned, Stantz and Spengler bobbing like corks in its wake. They tried their best to surface every so often to fill their lungs with air.

Stantz squinted into the swirling stream of slime. Bobbing before him was the flailing form of Winston.

Stantz and Spengler felt the pull on their bodies lessen. The flow of ooze was slowing down. Breaking up to the surface of the slime swirl, they found themselves in a massive chamber. The end of the old New York Pneumatic Railroad line. The slime seemed to calm down, grow dormant.

Sputtering, coughing, and gagging, the three Ghostbusters floated atop the gunk at the edge of the last platform of the long-deserted transportation line.

Winston pulled himself out of the slime first. Lying on his stomach, he reached down and yanked out Stantz. The two of them then dangled over the platform and ensnared Spengler, dragging him up out of the ocean of ooze in one violent motion.

The three lay sprawled on the platform, gagging.

"Let's retreat," Stantz whispered.

"Retreat?" Spengler coughed. "I don't know the meaning of the word...."

"It means," Winston clarified, "let's get the hell out of here."

Spengler pondered this. "Oh. Okay."

Moments later the three slime-encased Ghostbusters eased their way up through a dislodged manhole cover in the center of the Upper East Side of Manhattan.

For a moment the three men sat, exhausted. The slime covering their rubber suits began to percolate.

Winston suddenly leapt to his feet, thoroughly angry. "Nice going, Ray!" he roared. "What were you trying to do, drown me?"

Stantz's body tensed. He scrambled up to face Winston. "Look, Zeddemore," he replied menacingly, "it wasn't my fault that you were too stupid to drop that line!"

Winston's blood bubbled. He shoved Ray away from him. "You better watch your mouth, man, or I'll put your lights out... maybe for good."

Stantz's face formed an evil sneer. "Oh, yeah? Anytime, man, anytime. Just go ahead and try it."

Egon Spengler snarled and jumped between the two of them. He raised his fists in a classic boxer's pose. "If you two are looking for a fight, you got one! Who wants to try it first? Come on, Ray. Try me, sucker."

Stantz wheeled on Spengler. "Butt out, you pencilnecked geek. I've had it with you."

Ignoring the still frothing Spengler, Stantz and Winston grabbed each other by the shoulders and began to wrestle and tussle, their movements resembling a slam-dance polka.

Spengler shook his head clear.

He knew what was happening.

Dashing between the two adversaries, he pulled them apart. "Break it up!" he commanded. "Break it up!"

His voice was so authoritative, the two fighters backed off, blinking. They were confused, addled.

"Strip!" Spengler yelled. "Right now! Get out of these clothes."

Spengler began yanking off his slicker and wading boots. Bewildered, Stantz and Winston also started to disrobe in the middle of Manhattan. Spengler stripped himself to his long johns first. When he was done, he helped the other two Ghostbusters wriggle free of their slime-encased outfits.

Spengler gathered up the discarded clothes and tossed them down the open manhole cover.

The three men, now clad only in their long underwear, stood in the middle of the street.

They found that they weren't angry anymore.

They weren't hateful, only bewildered.

Well, also cold.

Winston rubbed his head. "What were we doing?"

He faced Stantz. "Ray, I was ready to kill you!"

Stantz's face reflected his state of mind. He was totally animated. "Don't you see? It's the *slime*. That stuff is like pure, concentrated *evil*!"

Stantz cased the street and discovered that the three Ghostbusters were standing directly in front of the Manhattan Museum of Art.

Spengler caught Stantz's eye. "And the slime," he intoned, "is all flowing right to this spot."

"What are we going to do?" Winston asked.

"We have to get Venkman involved," Stantz stated. "And *now*!"

They began to trot at a hectic pace through Central Park and toward the Upper West Side.

Twenty minutes later, at Armand's Restaurant, the maître d' felt his heart skip a beat. He was too young for a heart attack, he assured himself.

Three sweating men in long johns skidded to a halt before him. He tried to act suave. "May I help you?"

Stantz glanced into the dining room and spotted Venkman. "No," he told the maître d'. "It's all right. I see him."

The three Ghostbusters, ignoring their attire, jogged past the startled maître d' and into the restaurant.

Venkman was in the midst of pouring another toast of champagne for the now decidedly tipsy Dana when he noticed Ray, Egon, and Winston jogging forward. He shook his head from side to side. He never realized that champagne could pack that powerful a wallop.

"You should have been there, Venkman," Stantz shouted, reaching the table. "Absolutely incredible!"

Venkman snapped to. "Yeah, sorry I missed it."

He gazed at his friends in their skivvies. "I guess you guys don't know about the dress code here. It's really kind of a coat-and-tie place."

Stantz didn't hear him. "It's all over the city, Pete... well, actually, it's all *under* the city."

Dana stared at the trio, her jaw agape.

"There's *rivers* of the stuff down there!" Winston yelled.

"And it's all flowing toward the museum," Spengler noted.

Spengler made a sudden move, pointing in the direction of the museum. A big glob of slime, still affixed to his hand, flew across the restaurant. It smacked a well-dressed diner directly on the schnozz.

"Sorry!" Spengler called out.

Dana came to. "Maybe we should discuss this somewhere else?"

Venkman noted the look of embarrassment on Dana's face and got up from the table. He pulled his colleagues to the side of the restaurant and whispered, "Boys, listen. You're scaring the straight crowd here. Let's save this until tomorrow, okay?"

Spengler furrowed his bushy eyebrows. "This won't wait until tomorrow, Venkman. It's hot and it's ready to pop."

Venkman glanced over Spengler's shoulder. The maître d' was leading two New York cops toward the Ghostbusters. Venkman rolled his eyes. One hell of a date.

"Arrest these men!" the maître d' commanded.

One of the cops recognized Spengler, Stantz, Winston, and Venkman. "Hey! *It's the Ghostbusters!*"

He gazed at the three men in their underwear. "Umm, but you're out of uniform, gentlemen."

Stantz, for the first time, gazed down at what he was wearing. What a disgrace! "Uh, well, we had a little accident and we... *but forget that!* We have to see the mayor as quickly as possible!"

The first cop withered under Stantz's determined stare. "Oh, gee, Doc. They got a big official dinner going on up there at Gracie Mansion. Maybe you should go home, get a good night's sleep, and then give the mayor a call in the morning. Whaddaya say?"

Spengler glared at the two policemen, using his "more concerned" look. "Look, we're not drunk and we're not crazy. We were almost *killed* tonight. This is a matter of vital importance!"

The two cops exchanged puzzled glances. Venkman heaved a colossal sigh. So much for romantic evenings. He marched toward the law officers, the very portrait of perfect authority. "Maybe I can straighten this out, Officers."

The two cops sighed. "Peter Venkman!" the second cop cried. "*World of the Psychic!* That's one of my two favorite shows!"

Venkman nodded. "Please! Don't tell me the other one. Just do me a favor? Get on the phone, call the mayor. Tell him the city's in danger and that if he won't see us right now, we're going to *The New York Times.*"

The first cop gasped. "What's up?"

Venkman leaned forward and collared the cop. Glancing to his left and to his right, he whispered confidentially into the policeman's ear. "Bad caviar. Tons of it. Iranian terrorists. One in every five eggs is poisoned, and we know which ones. We've got to get there before they serve the canapés."

The policeman shot Venkman a skeptical look.

Venkman didn't back down.

"Just call the mayor!"

III

"There is no great genius without a mixture of madness."

- ARISTOTLE

"My mind is a total void."

- WINSTON ZEDDEMORE

23

Carl Schurz Park, on the Upper East Side of Manhattan, glistened under a sparkling winter sky. The twinkling of the stars was rivaled by the flashing, blinking lights of a police cruiser as it made its way through the park on the East River at Eighty-eighth Street, the Ecto1A in close pursuit.

The two vehicles screamed into an underground parking garage leading to the mayor of New York's residence, Gracie Mansion.

The two cars sputtered to a stop in the parking area. Peter Venkman, still feeling like Douglas Fairbanks, emerged, well dressed if overly cologned, from the vehicle. His three long-johnned companions, now wearing police raincoats, were ushered into the house by a startled butler.

They were led up several flights of twisting stairs and down a hallway to a massive set of double oak doors. The butler knocked lightly and then opened the door.

Inside the antique-littered den, in front of a roaring fireplace, sat the mayor of New York. Well coiffed, well dressed, Jack Hardemeyer stood at his side, a Doberman in *GQ* mode. Both men were wearing tuxedos, although Hardemeyer's was clearly more expensive than the mayor's.

The Ghostbusters strode into the room.

The mayor was clearly fighting back an outburst of sudden, albeit sincere, anger. He wasn't happy about being dragged out of a formal reception. He was even less happy about seeing the smirking face of Peter Venkman again.

His doctor had warned him about his blood pressure.

Right now he felt about as stable as a Pop-Tart in a microwave.

"All right," the mayor hissed. "*Ghosssstbusters.* I'll tell you right now... I've got two hundred of the heaviest campaign contributors in the city out there eating bad roast chicken just waiting for me to give the speech of my life. You've got two minutes. You'd better make it *good.*"

Stantz clumped forward. "Mr. Mayor, there is a psychomagnetheric slime flow of immense proportions building up under this city!"

The mayor gaped at Stantz. "Psycho *what?*"

Spengler waddled toward the mayor. "We believe that negative human emotions are materializing in the form of a viscous, semiliquid living psycho-reactive plasm with explosive supranormal potential."

The mayor heaved a heavy sigh. "Doesn't anyone speak *English* anymore?"

Winston braced himself and walked up to the mayor. "Yeah, man. What we're trying to tell you is that all the bad feelings, all the hate and anger and violence of this city, are turning into this *strange* sludge. I didn't believe it at first, either, but we just took a bath in it and we ended up almost *killing* each other."

Hardemeyer clenched his carefully shaved jaw and leapt forward. "This is *insane,*" he intoned in a voice used only by Ivy League grads.

He turned to the mayor. "Do we *really* have to listen to this?"

Venkman marched into the fray. "Hey, hairball, butt out!" he said.

He stood before the mayor. "Look, Lenny, you have to admit there's no shortage of bad vibes in this town. There must be at least a couple of million miserable assholes in the tristate area."

He pointed to Hardemeyer. "And here's a good example."

Stantz joined in. "You get enough negative energy flowing in a dense environment like Manhattan and it starts to build up. If we don't do something fast, this whole place will blow up like a frog on a hot plate!"

Winston nodded. "Tell him about the toaster."

Venkman shrugged. "I don't think Lenny is ready for the toaster."

The mayor shook his head from side to side. "Being miserable and treating other people like dirt is every New Yorker's *God-given right* I'm sorry, none of this makes any sense to me. If anything *does* happen, we've got plenty of paid professionals to deal with it. Your two minutes are up. Good night, gentlemen."

The mayor leapt out of his chair and rushed out of his den. The Ghostbusters stared at Hardemeyer. Hardemeyer ran a comb through his neatly groomed hair, offering the quartet a well-rehearsed smirk. "That's quite a story."

Venkman retorted, 'Yeah, I think *The New York Times* would be interested, don't you? I know, sure as heck, that the *New York Post* would have a lot of fun with it."

Hardemeyer's eyes flipped to their "cold and calculating" stare. "Before you go running to the newspapers with your story, would you consider telling this slime epic to some people *downtown*?"

Venkman smiled. "*Now* you're talking."

Hardemeyer allowed the Ghostbusters to leave Gracie Mansion. He picked up the phone, grinning.

"I hope you geeks like straitjackets," he said with a sneer.

God, politics was a *great* life.

24

Parkview Hospital was a great place if you happened to be one card short of a full deck. Most patients either talked to themselves, took orders from extraterrestrial beings, or were sure that they were the second coming of the deity of their choice.

Since Venkman, Stantz, Spengler, and Winston didn't claim *any* of those things, they weren't too excited about being locked up in a padded cell. The four stood handcuffed in the rubber room, their cuffs firmly attached to the thick leather belts strapped tightly around their waists.

The psychiatrist in the room, a squinty-eyed man who looked like he ate flies for a living, tried to pry the truth out of Stantz, Spengler, and Winston. Venkman, having posed as a shrink once or twice in the past, knew what they were up against. He passed his time by slamming his forehead into one of the padded walls.

Stantz tried to be truthful with the psychiatrist. "We think the spirit of Vigo the Carpathian is alive in a painting at the Manhattan Museum of Art."

"I see." The psychiatrist nodded. "And are there any other paintings in the museum with bad spirits in them?"

Spengler was losing his patience with the squinty-eyed mole man. "You're wasting valuable time!" he declared. "We have reason to believe that Vigo is drawing strength from a psychomagnetheric slime flow that's been collecting under the city!"

The shrink smiled. "Yes, tell me about die slime."

"It's potent stuff," Winston said. "We made a toaster dance with it, then a bathtub tried to eat Peter's friend's baby!"

Winston pointed at Venkman. The shrink glanced in Venkman's direction. Peter stopped pounding his head for a moment. "Don't look at me. *I* think they're nuts."

The psychiatrist got up and left the cell in silence.

The four Ghostbusters stood forlornly in their cell. They had blown it and blown it in a big way. There was nothing, no one, who could save them, now.

As dawn approached, Dana Barrett tossed in her sleep at Venkman's place. Louis and Janine had remained at the apartment, not wanting to leave Dana alone and unguarded. She had spent half the night worrying about Venkman and the boys. Within the last five hours it seemed as if they had disappeared off the face of the earth.

It would be morning soon. It wasn't like Venkman not to call, especially when the stakes were so high.

Huddled in front of the TV, Louis and Janine watched a rerun of *Family Feud*.

Dana's work area in the museum stood deserted. Across the restoration studio, an impatient Janosz Poha stood before the mighty painting of Vigo. Vigo's eyes shimmered, and the portrait gradually came to life.

As usual, the first thing the thundering voice of Vigo did was to recite the litany of his power. Janosz sighed. He'd heard this all before, many times. Frankly it was beginning to appeal to him as much as a broken record.

"I, Vigo, the scourge of Carpathia, the sorrow of Moldavia, command you…."

Janosz nodded. Yeah, yeah, yeah. "Command me, Lord."

"On a mountain of skulls in a castle of pain, I sat upon a throne of blood…"

Janosz rolled his eyes. "The skulls again."

"Twenty thousand corpses swung from my walls and parapets, and the rivers ran with tears."

The wiry artist nodded. "… the parapets. Yes, I know."

"By the power of the Book of Gombots, what was will be, what is will be no more. Then, now and always, the kingdom of the damned."

Janosz checked his wristwatch. "I await the word of Vigo," he muttered.

Vigo's glowing mouth began to twitch. "I have watched the centuries wither before me and waited for the time when the tide of men's sins would swell to bring me forth again. *Now* is that time and *here* the place. Beneath this realm there flows a foaming, unholy pile *born* from the *evil* in men."

Janosz's attention perked up. *This* was new.

"Upon this unholy matter," Vigo continued, "will I float the vessel of my freedom. The season of evil begins with the birth of the New Year. Bring me the child that I might live again."

Janosz found himself transfixed with awe. "Lord Vigo, this woman, Dana, is fine and strong. I was wondering—well, would it be possible?—could I have her?"

Vigo emitted a thunderous laugh. "So be it!" the spirit vowed. "On this day of darkness she will be ours! *Wife* to you. *Mother* to me!"

Vigo's laughter echoed through the restoration studio. It grew stronger and stronger, more and more Olympian.

So strong, in fact, that it reached forward into the heavens and split the sky.

Janosz looked up through the room's skylight as a strange and terrifying sight unfolded over New York.

Darkness caressed the city as the sun above it was sent, magically, into an eclipse.

At the Parkview psychiatric ward dayroom, Peter Venkman sat among a small gaggle of patients who had trouble breathing and blinking at the same time. He carefully worked at his occupational therapy, weaving on a hand loom.

Suddenly the room was plunged into darkness. Venkman wasn't pleased. "Hit the light there, Winston. I'm trying to finish my pot holder before lunch."

Winston didn't respond. He, Spengler, and Stantz stood in the center of the room, gazing through the mesh-covered windows into the newly darkened sky.

Stantz's mouth dropped open. "Total, spontaneous solar eclipse!" He gasped.

He faced his two companions. "This is it, boys. It's starting. Shit storm two thousand."

The three men faced each other, not knowing whether to feel relieved or terrified. On the down side, it was the end of the world as they knew it.

On the plus side, they'd be a lot safer in Parkview right now than anyplace on the streets of Manhattan.

25

While meteorologists, astronomers, and city officials tried to explain to a startled public exactly *why* New York had been embraced by the shadows caused by a total eclipse, the effect of Vigo's power began to make itself felt.

At a Hudson River pier, a leaky drainpipe suddenly began dripping shimmering, pulsating slime into the river near the Cunard Line docks.

Shortly thereafter, at the refurbished Central Park Zoo, the polar bears, lounging in their outdoor cage, lazily allowed a zookeeper to hose down their mountainous terrain. The zookeeper put down the hose and started to sweep around the top of their cage. Unbeknownst to him, the water the hose was gushing grew thicker and stranger, sparkling and undulating. Slime. Lots of it.

By the time the zookeeper finished sweeping the upper reaches of the outside enclosure, he was vaguely aware that something was wrong. He turned to pick up his hose. There was no water running out of it.

It was bone-dry.

He heard a screech coming from nearby.

He spun around and jumped back in surprise.

A full-sized pterodactyl screamed at him and then launched itself up into the dark, cloud-laden sky.

The zookeeper made a beeline for the exit door.

The polar bears exchanged startled glances. New York sure wasn't like the Arctic!

At Fifty-ninth and Fifth, the massive fountain located across from the swank Plaza Hotel suddenly began to change color. Instead of water zooming up out of its spout, torrents of psycho-reactive slime emerged, splashing, cascading, and oozing all over the surrounding sidewalk.

At the Plaza Hotel, a well-heeled man and woman emerged from a limousine. As they walked up the front steps leading to the hotel, a wad of slime landed on the woman's luxurious full-length mink coat.

As the doorman eased the front door open with a bow, the woman yelped in pain.

"Something *bit* me!" she said, glaring at the startled doorman.

The doorman looked curiously at her. He yelled in terror and leapt backward as the woman's slimed coat quivered to life. Small, ferocious mink heads popped out of the thick fur, snarling, barking, and yapping. Their sharp little teeth nipped at the air.

Reacting quickly, the doorman yanked the coat off the woman's back and threw it onto the sidewalk. He tried to stomp the coat to death, but the beady-eyed varmints in the coat were too quick for him.

As the doorman, the woman, and her husband looked on, flummoxed, the mink coat, its hydra-head of critters snapping and snarling, skittered off, trotting down Fifth Avenue with a vengeance.

The woman glared at her husband. "I told you we should have stayed in Palm Beach," she said, her face ashen.

At the Midtown North Police Precinct, a squad room filled with busy detectives noticed a change in the flood of calls they were receiving.

Initially they were trying to explain just what a total eclipse *was* and *wasn't*.

For the past hour, however, the calls had gotten a tad more, er, squirrelly.

"Look, lady," said one cop into the phone. "Of course there are dead people there. It's a cemetery.... What?... They were asking you for *directions*?"

"Was this a big dinosaur or a little dinosaur?" another cop asked. "Oh, just a skeleton, huh? Heading toward Central Park?"

Another detective sighed and shook his head. "Wait a second. You say the park bench was chasing you? You mean someone was chasing you in the park, don't you?... No, the bench itself was galloping after you. I see...."

He raised his eyes to heaven and pushed the hold button on his phone. He called to his lieutenant, "Sir? I think you better talk to this guy."

The lieutenant faced the cop. "I have problems of my own."

"What's up?"

"It's some dock supervisor down at Pier 34 on the Hudson. The guy's going nuts!"

"What's the problem?"

"He says the *Titanic* just arrived!"

"Car 54 is in the area, isn't it, Lieutenant? Can't you just have him check it out?"

"Good idea."

Moments later two uniformed patrolmen and a very stunned dock supervisor stared out at the Hudson River. There, moored to a dock, was an ocean liner bearing the name R.M.S. *Titanic*. The gangplank was lowered and hundreds of long-drowned passengers disembarked. They were sopping wet and drenched with seaweed. Behind them, cadaverous porters off-loaded waterlogged baggage.

"I don't believe this," one cop said to another.

"And look at the water," the dock supervisor said. "It almost looks solid. It's spooky, Officers. Damned spooky!"

"Who're we gonna call?" the second replied.

"The lieutenant!" the first cop declared.

He ran to his squad car and began dialing the precinct. Beyond him, all hell was breaking loose in New York City.

... and that was just for starters.

26

Dana sat, curled in the couch before Venkman's battered TV set, watching a *Star Trek* rerun. Janine and Louis continued to munch popcorn. Every so often the network would interrupt with a local bulletin announcing that nobody in New York—or America, for that matter—knew what the heck was going on in the streets outside Dana's window.

"Mass hysteria" was how one wild-eyed reporter phrased it.

Dana grew uneasy as she watched the television. She should have heard from Venkman by now. The sky outside the window was dark and foreboding.

Without warning, a howling gust of wind blew open the French windows in Venkman's living room.

"What the...?" Louis yelped.

Dana heard the baby cry out. A sense of alarm welled up within her. Oscar!

She hurried to the bedroom to check on her son, a frantic Louis and Janine trailing behind her.

The bed was empty.

Oscar was nowhere in sight.

The windows to the bedroom, however, were open.

Dana, Louis, and Janine ran to the window and peered outside.

"Oh, my God," Janine said, pointing.

Dana glanced to her left. On the ledge, towering above the busy streets of lower Manhattan, crawled little Oscar.

He knelt on the very edge of the ledge at the corner of the building, some fifty feet above the ground. The baby seemed calm, almost expectant.

Dana took a deep breath and climbed out onto the ledge, bracing her back against the strong support of the building. She daren't look down. She was afraid of losing her nerve. Slowly, cautiously, she inched her way along the eight-inch-wide ledge.

A bubbling light flared up in the sky above her, causing her to stop in her tracks.

An apparition was forming.

Something straight out of a fairy tale.

A sweet, kindly-looking English nanny formed in the sky, pushing an old-fashioned, albeit transparent baby carriage. The woman was strolling on thin air toward the ledge, dozens of feet above any solid matter.

The woman was smiling.

Dana gaped, recognizing the smile and trying to place the face.

The airborne nanny marched through the sky directly toward little Oscar. She extended a strong hand and deftly snatched up Dana's baby.

The nanny drew a delighted little Oscar into the transparent carriage, turning and smiling at a startled Dana.

"No!" Dana screamed.

She watched in helpless horror as the nanny soared off into the darkened skies, little Oscar huddled securely in the ethereal baby buggy.

The nanny chuckled.

Dana snapped to. She recognized the smile. She recognized the chuckle. She recognized the face!!!

"Janosz!" she breathed.

Louis and Janine helped Dana back inside the apartment. She headed straight for the door. "Louis, you have to find Peter and tell him what happened!"

"Where are you going?"

"To get my baby back," Dana said, slamming the door behind her.

Meanwhile, seated silently around a table in Parkview's woo-woo ward dayroom, Venkman, Winston, Stantz, and Spengler carefully listened to the conversations offered by the newest members of the laughing academy.

The squinty-eyed shrink had his hands full. A well-heeled woman who claimed she was a guest at the Plaza Hotel was screaming at him.

"I'm telling you, Doctor, my mink coat bit me and ran off down the street!"

The doctor was clearly out of his league. He turned to a nearby nurse. "Where did you put the zookeeper who saw the pterodactyl?"

The nurse sighed. "He's in Room 5, and I have the three men who saw the *Titanic* in Rooms 10, 11, and 12."

She consulted her list. "The walking-dead witness is in 13, the strolling dinosaur skeleton is in 4. I seem to have misplaced the Elvis Presley spotter, though."

The doctor sighed. "I hate working on New Year's Eve. It really brings them out of the woodwork, doesn't it?"

"I think that eclipse thing has everybody spooked," the nurse replied.

"What about my coat?" the Plaza woman yelled. "Do you have any idea how much that coat cost?"

The Ghostbusters sat at the table, listening intently.

Venkman turned to Stantz. "You were right. The whole city is going nuts. If we don't do something fast, it's all going to go downhill from here."

Winston nodded. "Do you think all those predictions about the world coming to an end in the 1990s are true?"

A Parkview patient with a face resembling a jack-o'-lantern waddled up to them. "The year will be 1997. My *dog* told me."

"What kind of dog?" Venkman asked.

"Labrador."

Venkman shook his head sadly. "Habitual liars. They can't help it. It's in the breed."

The man nodded sadly and stumbled off. Spengler faced his colleagues. "Objectively speaking, all these apocalyptic predictions about the millennium make no sense at all. The year 2000 is a fiction based on a completely arbitrary calendar. The only thing that gives these predictions power is people's willingness to believe in them!"

Stantz agreed. "Sure. If everyone believes that things are going to start falling apart in the year 2000, they'll probably start falling apart."

Winston rubbed his chin. "Yeah, well, there are an awful lot of people out there who *don't* believe in the future anymore—their own or anybody else's."

"And that's where Vigo gets his power," Stantz deduced. "He's just been laying back, hiding in that jerky painting until enough bad vibes built up to spring him."

"I don't think there's any shortage of bad vibes in *this* town," Venkman replied. "This is one of the few towns where killing your landlord is considered a misdemeanor."

Spengler stared at his knuckles thoughtfully. "All Vigo needs now is a living human being to inhabit. He's had his eye on Dana, literally. So it's obvious that he's chosen

Dana's child to make his reentry into our world. We all know that she has a psychic vulnerability to hostile entities. She's probably passed that onto her baby. Janosz Poha may be the human link between Vigo and Dana."

Venkman sneered. "I *knew* that guy was a wiggler the second I laid my eyes on him."

A thin Parkview patient leaned over the Ghostbusters' table. "Forget Vigo," he whispered confidentially. "It's *Hitler* you should go after. I saw him hanging around the Port Authority."

"Where was he heading?" Venkman asked.

"New Jersey," the man said. "I think it was the 134 local bus."

"Thanks for the info," Venkman said, offering a crooked smile.

Downstairs in a Parkview examining room, Louis Tully was arguing with his cousin Sherman, a badly dressed and coiffed gnat of a man who defined the word "nebbish" almost as well as Louis did.

"Come on, Sherm," Louis whined. "You're my cousin. Do this for me. I'm begging you."

Sherman shook his head, flashing a superior smile. "I can't do it, Louis. It isn't ethical. I could lose my license."

"Why can't you just have them released? You're a doctor."

"I'm a dermatologist. I can't write orders for the psych ward."

"Sherman, I've done lots of favors for you, haven't I?" Louis wheedled.

"Like what?"

"I got you out of those bad tax shelters."

"*You* were the one who got me in."

"I fixed you up with Diane Troxler, and she put out, didn't she?"

Sherman thought hard about this. “Yeah, I had to give her free dermabrasion for a year too. Forget it, Louis. I could get in a lot of trouble.”

“I’m telling you, Sherm, we’re all going to be in big trouble if we don’t do something fast. This ghost guy came and took my friend’s baby and we’ve got to get it back. It’s just a scared little baby, Sherm.”

“Then you should go to the police,” Sherman pointed out. “I don’t believe in any of that ghost stuff.”

Outside the window, shrieks and howls echoed through the darkened sky. The city seemed to grow darker and darker and darker.

Sherman faced the window. He could have sworn he saw a pterodactyl fly by.

“Do you believe now, Sherm?”

A half hour later the four Ghostbusters, in lull uniform, stood next to Ecto1A, together with the Tilly cousins. “Good work, Louis. How did you get us out?”

“Oh, I pulled a few strings. I wouldn’t want to say more than that.”

Louis winked at Sherman. “This is my cousin Sherman. Sherm, say hello to the Ghostbusters.”

Louis leaned toward Stantz. “I promised him a ride in the car if he got you out.”

“How bad are things getting?” Venkman asked.

“Real bad, Peter. You’d better get to the museum right away!”

“Why? What happened?” Venkman asked.

“A ghost took Dana’s baby. She’s gone to the museum to get it back.”

Louis pointed to the Ecto1A. “I brought everything you asked for, and I gassed up the car with super unleaded. It cost twenty cents more than regular unleaded, but you get much better performance and in an old car like this, that’ll end up saving you money in the long run. I put it on my credit card, so you can either reimburse me or I can take it out of petty cash."

The four stone-faced Ghostbusters, fully suited and well armed, dove into the Ecto1A and sped off, leaving Louis in mid-sentence.

Louis watched the car speed away. "Hey!" he shouted. "Wait for me."

The auto zoomed out of sight.

Louis sighed. "Okay, I'll meet you there."

Sherman stared at his cousin skeptically. "I thought you were like the fifth Ghostbuster."

Louis smiled smugly. "I let them handle all the little stuff. I just come in on the big cases."

27

Dana Barrett jumped out of her cab and rushed up the front stairs to the Manhattan Museum of Art. She flung open two large doors and dashed inside. The doors closed behind her with a resounding *ka-thud*. As the doors locked themselves shut, a deafening roar of thunder shook the sky. The ground seemed to tremble.

From deep within the earth beneath the museum, small, slender hands of glowing, shimmering slime reached up toward the building's walls.

The slime burst forth from the bowels of the city and crept and crawled up and over the building.

Within seconds the slime had completely engulfed the museum, effectively sealing Dana inside.

Two passersby stopped before the museum, a pair of old men out for an early-evening stroll.

"Now that's something you don't see every day, Mike," one said to the other.

"What's that, Al?"

"An ocean of goop scooping up and over a museum."

"Hmm." The second man nodded. "And it seems to be hardening too."

"Think we should call the cops?"

"I dunno. What time is *Moonlighting* on?"

"We got time. Come on, there's a phone booth over there. I used to walk my poodle there, until she got mugged by squirrels."

"I hate rodents."

"Me too. I never even liked Mickey Mouse."

"Me neither. Although I always liked Mighty Mouse. He has a great voice."

The two old men strolled to the phone booth.

By the time the Ecto1A screeched up to the curb across from the beleaguered museum, hundreds of spectators had gathered. They stood in awe, gawking at the slime-encased building. The four Ghostbusters leapt out of their vehicle and jogged across the street.

They stood spellbound at the sight before them.

The museum was now totally covered in a shell of psycho-reactive slime. City workmen and firemen were trying to cut their way through the hardened gunk with a series of blowtorches, jackhammers, and assorted power tools. Paramedics were on the scene, attempting to munch through the solid slime using the "jaws of life."

They couldn't even make a dent.

The Ghostbusters retreated to the Ecto1A and donned their proton packs.

"It looks like a giant Jell-O mold," Stantz breathed.

"I hate Jell-O," Venkman replied.

"I'm not even crazy about Bill Cosby," Winston said, grimacing.

The quartet strode across the street and approached the main entrance to the building.

Stantz walked up to a bewildered fire captain. "Okay, give it a rest, sir. We'll take it from here."

The fire captain was clearly skeptical. "Be my guest, gents," he said with a smirk. "We've been cutting here for almost an hour. What the hell is going on around this town? Did you know that the *Titanic* arrived this morning?"

Venkman shrugged. "Better late than never."

The workmen and firemen assembled before the slime-encrusted museum backed away as the Ghostbusters aimed their powerful particle throwers.

Spengler whipped out his Giga meter. He nodded grimly to his three comrades. "Full neutronas, maser assist!"

The four men adjusted the settings on their wands and prepared to fire.

Stantz gritted his teeth. "Throw 'em!"

The four men triggered their particle throwers and sprayed the front doors of the building with powerful, undulating bolts of proton energy. The energy beams bounced harmlessly off the hardened slime.

Venkman sighed and turned to a fireman. "Okay, who knows 'Kumbaya'?"

A few of the firemen and workmen tentatively raised their hands. Venkman grabbed them and lined them up at the entrance to the museum, assuming a drill sergeant's voice. "All right, men. Nice and easy. 'Kumbaya, my Lord, Kumbaya…"

Stantz, Spengler, Winston, and the firemen and workmen began to sing along.

Venkman forced them all to join hands and to sway back and forth while lifting their voices to the night sky. Stantz ran forward during the folkfest and inspected the hardened wall of slime that entombed the museum. Using his infra-goggles, he found that the singing had managed to produce a hole in the gunk barely the size of a dime.

Stantz sighed and turned to the assembled. "Forget it. The Vienna Boys Choir couldn't get through this stuff."

"Good effort," Venkman called to the hastily assembled ensemble. He turned to his buddies. "Now what? Should we say supportive, nurturing things to it, Ray?"

Spengler, deep in thought, missed the sarcasm. "It won't work," he muttered. "There's no way we could generate enough positive energy to crack that shell."

Stantz wasn't convinced. Ever the optimist, he cried, "I can't believe things have gotten *so* bad in this city that there's no way back. Sure, it's crowded, it's dirty, it's noisy. And there are too many people who'd just as soon step on your face as look at you. But there's got to be a few sparks of sweet humanity left in this burned-out burg. We just have to *mobilize* them!"

Spengler nodded in agreement. "We need something that everyone can get behind. You know, a *symbol...*"

Spengler's eyes accidentally fell on Ecto1A's New York State license plates. On the front plate was a line drawing of the historic Statue of Liberty.

He nudged Stantz. Stantz gaped at the plate. "Something that appeals to the best in each and every one of us," he babbled.

"Something good," Spengler continued.

"And pure," Venkman added.

"And decent," Winston concluded.

The four men were awakened from their reverie by a murmur in the vast crowd behind them. A limo screamed up to the site. The mayor of New York arrived with a police escort. His limo pulled into a no-parking zone. The mayor and Jack Hardemeyer stepped out of the limo and marched up to the museum entrance.

Hardemeyer motioned the mayor back.

The top aide, with a small army of police bodyguards, ambled up to the Ghostbusters, confrontation clearly the goal.

"Look," the well-tailored Hardemeyer spat, "I've had it with you *Ghostbusters*. Get your stuff together, get back in your clown car, and get out of here. This is a city matter, and everything's under control."

Venkman felt his blood start to boil. He stared down the yuppie-pup. "Oh," he said with a sneer, "you *think* so? Well, I've got news for you. You've got Dracula's brother-in-law in there, and he's got my girlfriend and her kid. Around about midnight tonight, while you guys are partying hearty uptown, *this* guy's going to come to life and start doing amateur head transplants. And *that's* just round one."

The mayor traipsed forward. "Are you telling me there are people *trapped* in that building?"

Hardemeyer ignored the mayor. He turned to one of his flunkies. "This is dynamite," he said enthusiastically. "I want you to call AP, UPI, and the CNN network. I want them down here right away. When the police bring this kid and his mama out, I want to be able to hand the baby right over to the mayor, and I want it all on camera."

Stantz wasn't impressed with Hardemeyer's approach. He turned to the mayor. "Mr. Mayor, if we don't do something by midnight tonight, you're going to go down in history as the man who let New York get sucked down into the tenth level of *hell*!"

The mayor considered this. He turned to the fire captain. "Can you get into that museum?"

The fire captain offered a sad smile. "If I had a nuclear warhead... *maybe*."

The mayor turned to Venkman.

"You know why all these things are happening?"

Venkman was angry now. "We tried to tell you *last* night, but Mr. Hard-on over here had us packed off to a loony bin."

Hardemeyer felt himself losing it. He didn't care. The Ghostbusters were his enemies. "This is preposterous!" he whined. "You can't seriously believe all this mumbo jumbo, Mr. Mayor. It's the twentieth century, for crying out loud!"

He bared his teeth to Venkman. "Look, *mister,* I don't know what this stuff is or how you got it all over the museum, but you'd better get it off *now,* and I mean *right now*!"

Hardemeyer ran up to the museum's entrance like a madman possessed. He began to pound at the wall of slime with his fists.

Both the mayor and the Ghostbusters watched in amazement as the wall of slime seemed to give in for a fleeting instant. Hardemeyer's fist plunged through the wall. He flashed a defiant sneer at Venkman. His sneer, however, soon turned to something more closely resembling the letter O.

Within seconds the wall promptly sucked Hardemeyer inside the slime curtain, emitting a gushy, *slooooosbing* sound.

Before anyone had the time to react, Hardemeyer was gone.

Only his three-hundred-dollar shoes remained… hanging from the re-hardened wall of slime.

The mayor of New York emitted a heavy sigh. He turned to the Ghostbusters. "Okay," he whispered, "just tell me what you need."

28

The quartet of Ghostbusters sat stonefaced in the tiny diner with the mayor of New York City.

The mayor was sweating.

The Ghostbusters regarded him coolly.

Outside the small burger joint, a dozen security men patrolled silently.

The mayor was nearly in a state of panic. "Did you know the *Titanic* arrived this morning?"

Venkman nodded. "So I've heard, and I bet all the hotels have weird bookings... this being New Year's Eve and all."

"Don't get cute with me." The mayor barked. "Just tell me why all these things are happening!"

Venkman sipped his coffee. "We *tried* to, Yer Honor. But you wouldn't believe us. I don't wanna get too technical here, but basically, things are going to hell because people in New York act like *jerks*."

The mayor nearly swallowed his catsup-covered weenie. "What?"

Stantz smiled sweetly at the paranoid politician. "Imagine an ocean's worth of bad vibes being poured into a small glass, the glass being this city. That's the situation we're up against. We have about four hours before that glass, under pressure from the flow, *shatters*."

Winston took the opportunity to thrust a mighty forefinger into the mayor's chest. "Plus, you've got one mean lean Carpathian mother in that museum who is just *ready* and *willing* to pick up the pieces and go *gung ho*."

The mayor emitted a small moan. "And it had to happen in an election year. Well, who is this guy and what does he want?"

Stantz stared at the mayor. "He wants it *all*. In every great social breakdown there has been some evil, power-mad nutball ready to capitalize on it. This one just happens to have been dead for at least three hundred years."

"It's happened before," Spengler informed the mayor. "Nero and Caligula in Rome. Hitler in Nazi Germany..."

Stantz jumped in. "Stalin in Russia. The French Reign of Terror!"

Winston decided to put his two cents in: "Pol Pot? Idi Amin?"

Venkman turned toward the fidgeting mayor. "Cardinal Richelieu, George Steinbrenner, Donald Trump!" The mayor caved in, his face resembling a three-day-old Mr. Potato Head. "But being miserable and stomping on people's dreams is every New Yorker's *right*... isn't it? What do you expect me to do? Go on the TV and tell eight million people that all of a sudden they have to be *nice* to each other?"

Venkman grinned, crocodile-style. "Naaaah. We'll handle that part. We only need *one* thing from you."

The mayor nodded up and down, like a Slinky toy.

He felt a sudden surge of relief. Dr. Venkman only needed *one* thing from him. Maybe the mayor would come out of this looking okay. Maybe next year's election wouldn't be affected.

Then Venkman explained what the Ghostbusters needed.

At that point the mayor fainted.

29

Behind the Ghostbusters, the skyline of Manhattan sparkled radiantly, ready to embrace the New "Year. They stood at the feet of the Statue of Liberty on Liberty Island, donning their new equipment. They strapped compression tanks to their backs and hooked up nozzles from their backpacks to the bazookalike weapons Stantz and Spengler had created. They adjusted the gauges, valves, and regulators on the prototypes of the latest ghostbusting weapons.

Weapons that were untested.

Weapons they had never used before.

Slime blowers.

Venkman tightened the shoulder straps on the slime blower, gazing up at the Statue of Liberty. "Kind of makes you wonder, doesn't it?"

"Wonder what?" Winston asked.

"If she's naked under that toga," Venkman replied. "She's French, you know."

Spengler missed the humor. "There's nothing under that toga but three hundred tons of iron and steel."

Venkman's face fell. Another dream dashed.

Stantz was clearly worried about their hastily conceived plan of attack. "I hope we have enough stuff to do the job."

"Only one way to find out," Venkman said, facing Stantz. "Ready, Teddy?"

Venkman and Stantz entered the base of the statue and began the long, torturous climb up the spiraling iron staircase within Lady Liberty. The staircase corkscrewed some one hundred feet inside the hollow superstructure.

Down below, at the base of the statue, Spengler and Winston assembled hundreds of wires connected to dozens of relays. They carefully mounted the relays to the interior of the gigantic structure.

At the top of the stairs, Venkman and Stantz installed large auditorium-sized loudspeakers on a section of the statue near Lady Liberty's head.

That done, Stantz raised his slime blower and gazed at the interior of the Statue of Liberty. "Okay, boys," he commanded. "Let's frost it."

Venkman and Stantz let loose with wave after wave of psycho-reactive slime. Venkman watched the slime ooze down the interior of the statue, hoping that the plan worked.

Hoping that he and his ghostbusting buddies had the wherewithal to save Dana and her child.

Across the river, in the slime-encrusted museum, Janosz smiled in front of the massive portrait of his master, Vigo. Dana sat helplessly in a corner, watching her baby float, suspended in midair, below the horrible face of Vigo.

Janosz, brush in hand, walked merrily up to the baby and carefully began painting mystical symbols on its little arms and legs.

Dana felt faint.

The symbols were identical to the ones Janosz had uncovered on the ancient portrait.

Unable to take it any longer, she made a mad dash for her child, arms outstretched.

Before she could make it to little Oscar, she was hit

full force by some sort of invisible energy. She was thrown across the room, back into her chair.

She collapsed in a heap. What had happened to the Ghostbusters? Why hadn't she heard from Louis?

Louis Tully stood proudly in the Ghostbusters' firehouse. With Janine watching adoringly, he slipped into a Ghostbusters uniform and slung a heavy proton pack onto his back, nearly knocking off his glasses. Louis tested out his mobility, waddling around the lab area on a slight angle. Janine was now worried. There was too much power pack and not enough Louis.

"I'm not sure this is such a good idea," she told him. "Do the others know that you're doing this?"

Louis nodded. "Oh, yeah, sure... well, *no*. But there's really not much to do here, and they might need some backup at the museum."

He adjusted his glasses, pulled up his socks, and headed for the front door.

Janine ran up to him. "You're very brave, Louis. Good luck."

Janine kissed Louis tenderly.

His glasses fogged. "Uh, well, I, uh, better hurry."

Louis dashed out of the firehouse fully armed and marched manfully into the night.... Where, fifteen minutes later, he caught a bus to take him to the museum.

"I'm not sure I have the right change here, but believe me this is important and—"

He sniffed the air.

Behind the steering wheel of the bus was Slimer.

Slimer sent the bus roaring down the street.

"You're going in the wrong direction!" Louis whined. "I bet you never even got a real driver's license!!"

30

Venkman, Stantz, Spengler, and Winston stood apprehensively in the observation windows of the Statue of Liberty. Perched in the crown of Lady Liberty, they gazed down at Liberty Island, far below them.

"It's now or never," Stantz whispered. He plugged in a huge cable that fed into a portable transformer. He checked his watch. "It's all yours, Pete. There's not much time left."

Venkman nodded and attached a speaker cable into his tiny tape recorder. He snapped his fingers and tapped his left foot. "Okay, a one, and a two, and a three, and a *four*!"

He pushed the play button on his Walkman, and instantly the interior of the statue was filled with the soulful strains of Jackie Wilson.

As the sweet soul music echoed through the statue's hollow interior, the slime dripping from its sides began to vibrate.

Slowly, magically, the head of the Statue of Liberty turned this way and that. The Ghostbusters held on to the railing of the observation deck for dear life.

"She's moving!" Stantz exclaimed.

Winston was awestruck. "I've lived in New York all my life and I never visited the Statue of Liberty. Now I finally get here and we're taking her out for a *walk*!"

Spengler clutched his Giga meter. "We've got full power."

Stantz picked up the control paddle from a home video game and started pushing buttons. Venkman picked up a hand-held microphone. "Okay, Libby," he commanded, "let's get in *gear*."

The statue quivered in response. Lady Liberty raised a titanic left foot and brought it splashing down into the Hudson River. Her right foot followed suit.

Soon Liberty Island was deserted.

New Year's Eve celebrants on the shore of New York City, waiting for the traditional fireworks display, were astounded. The Statue of Liberty was *swimming* toward New York!

Lady Liberty walked calmly across the bottom of the Hudson, almost completely submerged. Only her head, from the nose up, was visible, the four Ghostbusters navigating her movements from the observation deck.

The water seemed to be rising rapidly toward them.

"How deep does it get?" Winston asked. "That water's cold and I can't swim."

"It's okay. I have my senior lifesaving card," Venkman said reassuringly.

Spengler couldn't help himself. He started calculating. "Let's see, with a water temperature of forty degrees, we'd survive approximately fifteen minutes."

Stantz had a maritime navigational chart spread out before him. "I'll keep to the middle of the channel. We're okay to Fifty-ninth Street. Then we'll go ashore and crosstown and take First Avenue to Seventy-ninth."

"Are you kidding?" Venkman replied. "We'll hit all that bridge traffic at Fifty-ninth. Take Seventy-second straight across to Fifth. Trust me, I used to drive a cab."

Stantz continued to maneuver the statue. Jackie Wilson's voice boomed within Lady Liberty's hollow shell. The mood slime continued bopping.

In Times Square, thousands of people stood shoulder to shoulder, noisemakers and confetti in hand. All eyes were glued to the gigantic clock high above their heads. In ten minutes the crowd would begin the countdown for New Year's.

Suddenly one spectator pointed.

Then another, and another.

From downtown, heading north, marched the most magnificent of sights. The Statue of Liberty was walking up Broadway, striding in step to the superamplified song "Higher and Higher."

A great cheer arose from the crowd. Party hats and confetti were tossed into the air as the crowd began to dance and sing along with Jackie Wilson.

Inside the observation deck, Spengler grinned, checking his Giga meter. "Listen to that crowd! The positive GEVs are climbing."

Venkman patted the statue. "They love you, Lib. Keep it up."

The colossal statue headed up Broadway toward Central Park. From there Lady Liberty would be a hop, skip, and a jump away from the Manhattan Museum of Art.

Much to Venkman's amazement, half of the New Year's Eve celebrants from Times Square decided to follow Lady Liberty. He couldn't blame them. They probably didn't get a chance to see something like this too often.

Lady Liberty and the throngs proceeded toward the museum.

Farther uptown, the museum, still slime-encrusted, stood, guarded by police.

Inside the darkened building, Dana watched her child dangle in midair before Vigo. Janosz walked up to her, smiling. "No harm will come to the child," he assured her. "You might even say it's a privilege for him to be the vessel for the spirit of Vigo. And you… well, you will be the mother of the ruler of the world. Doesn't that sound nice?"

"If this is what the world will be like, I don't want to live in it," Dana vowed.

Janosz glanced over his shoulder at Vigo. "I don't believe we have the luxury of choice."

"*Everybody* has a choice," Dana said, simmering.

"Not in this case, my dear," Janosz pointed out. "Take a look at that portrait. That's not Gainsborough's *Blue Boy* up there. That's *Vigo*."

"I don't care who he is. I may not be able to stop you, but someone will!"

Janosz smirked. "Who? The Ghostbusters? They are powerless. Soon it will be midnight and the city will be mine… and Vigo's. Well, mainly *Vigo's*… but we have a spectacular opportunity to make the best of our relationship."

Dana looked the wiry artist in the eye. "We don't have a relationship."

"I know," Janosz agreed. "Marry me, Dana, and together we will raise Vigo as our son. There are many perks that come with being the mother of a living god. I'm sure he will supply for us a magnificent apartment. And perhaps a car and free parking."

Dana pushed the man away. "I hate and despise you and everything you stand for with all my heart and soul. I could never forgive what you've done to me and my child."

Janosz thought about that. "Many marriages begin with a certain amount of distance, but after a while I believe we could learn to love each other. Think about it."

"I'd rather not."

Janosz didn't mind Dana's aloofness. She'd come around once Vigo was reborn. There was nothing that could spoil Vigo's plan for conquest.

Janosz didn't notice the slight vibration in the floor beneath his feet.

The source of the vibration strode up Fifth Avenue, led by a squadron of screaming police motorcycles, with tens of thousands of cheering people marching in her wake.

Lady Liberty, still walking in step to Jackie Wilson's percussive beat.

From the observation deck the Ghostbusters could spot the museum.

"So far, so good," Venkman said.

"I'm worried," Spengler muttered. "The vibrations could shake her to pieces. We should have padded her feet."

"I don't think they make Reeboks in her size," Stantz replied.

Venkman patted the statue. "We're almost there, Lib."

He turned to Stantz. "Step on it."

Stantz diddled with his controls. Lady Liberty's foot came crashing down on a police car. Stantz grimaced. He called down to the startled police in the street "My fault!"

"She's new in town," Venkman added.

He glanced at his watch. The Ghostbusters had less than one minute left to save Dana, her child, and the world in general.

31

The crowd at Times Square began counting down the final seconds left in the old year. Ten, nine, eight, seven…

In the Restoration Studio of the museum, Janosz also watched the large wall clock while painting the last of the mystical symbols on the levitated baby's chest.

Soon the world would be *his*… well, *partly* his.

He glanced at the portrait of Vigo. A strange aura began to spread over the painting. Vigo's eyes glowed. His entire body seemed to radiate energy. The figure in the painting began to spread its arms wide. Slowly but powerfully, Vigo's mighty torso began to assume three dimensions. Vigo was *pulling* himself out of the painting.

His long-dead lungs emitted a mighty, stagnant breath of long-rotting air. "Soon," Vigo intoned, "my life *begins*! Then, woe to the *weak*! All power to me. The world is *mine*."

Vigo extended a bloodstained hand toward baby Oscar. The baby's body began to glow eerily as Vigo's hand approached it. Dana let out a sob. She had lost. She had lost everything that had ever mattered to her.

Janosz emitted a wheezing laugh.

He was caught in mid-wheeze as a large shadow fell over the room. He gaped up through the skylight.

The Statue of Liberty stood towering above the museum, a look of righteous anger on her freedom-loving face.

The statue knelt down next to the museum and, drawing back its titanic right arm, smashed into the ceiling with its torch of freedom.

Janosz let out a feral screech and skittered away, hiding his head from the shower of broken glass and debris. From out of the sky, the four Ghostbusters swung into the room on ropes attached to Lady Liberty's crown.

Stantz, Venkman, Spengler, and Winston trained their slime blowers on Janosz.

The wiry artist tried to retreat.

Dana leapt into action, running across the studio and diving at her child, effectively snatching floating Oscar from Vigo's outstretched, murderous hand.

Dana and her child tumbled onto the floor safely.

Venkman sneered at Janosz. "Happy New Year."

Janosz trotted in front of Vigo's animated portrait. His master would save him. Vigo bellowed in rage.

Spengler found himself grinning at both the ghoul and his human henchman. "Feel free to try something stupid."

With Vigo to back him up, Janosz now felt powerful. "You pitiful miserable creatures! "You dare to challenge the power of Darkness?"

Janosz emitted a harsh cackle. "Don't you realize what you are dealing with? He's *Vigo*! You are like the buzzing of flies to him!"

Venkman shook his head sadly. "Oh, Johnny, did *you* back the wrong horse."

With that the four Ghostbusters let loose with their slime blowers, hosing down Janosz from head to toe. The force of the flying mood slime knocked Janosz across the room.

The four men then turned to the twitching, roaring portrait of Vigo. Vigo was now almost completely solid, almost free of his prison. He was now held in the portrait only from his knees down. He spat and bellowed at the Ghostbusters, trying to unleash his black-magical powers full tilt.

The Ghostbusters stood firm, secure in the knowledge that the source of Vigo's power had been neutralized by the love and goodwill of the people of New York.

"You will be destroyed!" Vigo roared.

Stantz walked forward. "Viggy, Viggy, Viggy, you have been a *bad* little monkey."

Venkman smiled at the sputtering painting. "The whole city's together on this one, Your Rottenness. We took a vote. Everybody's down on you. The people have spoken."

"So"—Winston smiled, raising his slime blower—"say good night now."

Vigo roared and, focusing his magic directly down on Stantz, transformed the stunned Ray into a sputtering, wild-eyed demon. Demon Ray leapt in front of the painting. "The power of Vigo is *greater* than anything you *wield,"* demon Ray howled. *"We will destroy you!"*

"Don't shoot!" Spengler yelled. "You'll hit *Ray*!"

Winston, the nearest to the portrait, inhaled and, gritting his teeth, fired the slime blower. Both Ray and Vigo were coated with a thick layer of ooze.

Vigo bellowed and howled at the sky. His body began to quiver and shake. He felt his strength ebbing. His hands went numb. Ray Stantz was sent tumbling onto the floor. Vigo emitted one last primal howl and then fell back onto the canvas, solidly one-dimensional and harmless.

The paint on the canvas began to bubble and melt. It dribbled slowly down the portrait and onto the floor. Parts of another painting, one done years earlier on the same canvas, began to reveal itself.

Venkman, Spengler, and Winston rushed over to Ray and knelt beside him. Stantz was completely inundated with slime.

"He's breathing," Spengler said.

Winston wiped the mood slime off Ray's face. Stantz blinked and stared at his three friends.

"Ray," Winston whispered. "Ray! How do you feel?"

Stantz smiled beatifically. "Groovy. I've never felt better in my life, man."

Venkman rolled his eyes skyward. "Oh, no. We've got to *live* with *this*?"

The Ghostbusters helped Ray to his feet. Stantz beamed at them all. "I love you guys. You're the best friends I've ever had."

Stantz hugged each one of his buddies, leaving a residue of slime on them all. Venkman pushed him away. "Hey, I just had this suit cleaned!"

From across the room Janosz emitted a low moan. Venkman turned to Winston and Spengler. "Take care of the wiggler, will you?"

Venkman walked over to Dana. She cradled Oscar in her arms and gave Venkman a big hug. "What is this?" he asked. "A love-in?"

Venkman smiled down at little Oscar, noting the symbols painted on the child's body. "Hey, sailor, I think that tattoos are a little much, don't you?"

He picked up the child and hugged him.

Dana smiled at them both. "I think he likes you. I think I do too."

Venkman winked at her. "Finally came to your senses, huh?"

Across the room, Spengler, Winston, and Stantz helped the slimed Janosz to his feet. The wiry artist shook his head. "What happened?"

"Sir," Stantz intoned, "you've had a violent, prolonged, transformative psychic episode. But it's over now. Want a coffee?"

Janosz shook Ray's hand sincerely. "That's very kind of you."

Spengler examined the artist quickly. "He's fine, Ray. Physically intact, psychomagnetherically neutral."

Janosz blinked. "Is that good?"

"It's where you want to be." Winston smiled.

Janosz, the Ghostbusters, and Dana, with Oscar, walked out of the studio, passing by what had been the portrait of Vigo. The original scene, painted on the old canvas, now shone through clearly. It was a beautiful painting in the high Renaissance style depicting four archangels hovering protectively over a cherubic baby. One held a harp. One held an olive branch. The third, a book. The last, a sword.

"Late Renaissance, I think," Spengler noted. "Caravaggio or Brunelleschi."

Winston stared at the painting. "There's something very familiar about that."

He shrugged and left the room with his comrades.

A full moon shone down on the painting.

The faces of the four angels bore an uncanny resemblance to those of Venkman, Stantz, Spengler, and Winston.

The Ghostbusters exited the de-slimed museum and were greeted with cheers from the massive crowd. Venkman pointed to Dana and her baby. The crowd spontaneously broke out into "Auld Lang Syne."

Someone handed Stantz a bottle of champagne. He held it up for the crowd's approval.

At that point a city bus pulled up in front of the museum. Louis skittered out, in full uniform lugging the oversize proton pack. He turned back to the smiling Slimer in the driver's seat.

"Okay, so Monday night we'll get something to eat and maybe go bowling? Can you bowl with those little arms?"

Slimer grunted and slobbered a reply, flexing his rubber-band biceps.

"Okay." Louis nodded. "I have to go save Dana. I'll see you later."

Slimer howled and sent the bus zigzagging off. Louis struggled through the celebrating crowd and stumbled up to the Ghostbusters.

"Am I too late?" he whined.

Stantz smiled at the diminutive fellow. "No, Louis. You're right on time."

Stantz popped the cork on the champagne bottle and handed it to Louis as the crowd continued to sing.